30p

John Masters was born in Calcutta in 1914.
After being educated in England, he returned
to India in 1934 and joined the Fourth Prince
of Wales's Own Gurkha Rifles, then serving
on the North-West Frontier. He saw active
service in Waziristan in 1937 and, after the
outbreak of war, in Iraq, Syria and Persia.
In 1944 he joined General Wingate's
Chindits in Burma. He fought at the Singu
Bridgehead, the capture of Mandalay, at
Toungoo and on the Mawchi Road. John
Masters retired from the Army in 1948 as
Lieutenant-Colonel with the D.S.O. and
O.B.E. Shortly afterwards he went to the
USA where he turned to writing and soon
had articles and short stories published in
many well-known American magazines.

The first of his novels, *Nightrunners of
Bengal,* was published in 1951. It was followed
by *The Deceivers, Bhowani Junction, To
the Coral Strand, The Ravi Lancers* and
The Field-Marshal's Memoirs, among
others.

Also by John Masters in Sphere Books:

FANDANGO ROCK
NIGHTRUNNERS OF BENGAL

C. Barne
1978.

The Field-Marshal's Memoirs

JOHN MASTERS

SPHERE BOOKS LIMITED
30/32 Gray's Inn Road, London WC1X 8JL

First published in Great Britain by Michael Joseph Ltd 1975
Copyright © Bengal Rockland
First Sphere Books edition 1976
Reprinted 1977

TRADE
MARK

This book is sold subject to the condition that
it shall not, by way of trade or otherwise, be lent,
re-sold, hired out or otherwise circulated without
the publisher's prior consent in any form of
binding or cover other than that in which it is
published and without a similar condition
including this condition being imposed on the
subsequent purchaser.

Set in Intertype Plantin

Printed in Great Britain by
Hazell Watson & Viney Ltd
Aylesbury, Bucks

For

TOM HAMILL

Artist, Big Chief Tamale;

companion of the long trails, the high hard days;

friend.

This book is entirely a work of fiction and no reference is intended in it to any person living or dead, except that a few historical characters are mentioned. My Balkan Campaign is, of course, imaginary. There was an Italian Campaign in reality, but it was not the imaginary one which forms a small part of the background of *The Field-Marshal's Memoirs*.

J.M.

Man with his burning soul
Has but an hour of breath
To build a ship of Truth
In which his soul may sail,
Sail on the sea of death,
For death takes toll
Of beauty, courage, youth,
Of all but Truth.

John Masefield

CHAPTER ONE

The limousine purred down the by-pass under the lights, the uniformed chauffeur a silhouette beyond the glass dividing screen. The spaced lamps regularly threw an orange light on the white hair, gaunt cheekbones and five bright rows of medal ribbons of the old man leaning back in the left corner seat, his head nodding. Martin Ruttledge, in the other corner, did not hear the hiss of the tyres or the hum of the engine, for the thunder of applause still rang in his head ... seven thousand people, all on their feet, filling the vast hall, drowning even the massed bands. Those who had fought in the great battle were old now, so that from the back of the dais he had looked out over a sea of white and pink. The walls were hung with flags, and in the audience waved a thousand hand-made banners of Armies and Corps and Divisions, of Groups and Wings and Squadrons, a myriad strange devices, once known from Norway to the Nile, now half forgotten, to be brought out this one night of each year, the anniversary of the Battle of Vojja Lovac.

This year, the twenty-eighth anniversary, the Prince of Wales had come, and the Chief of the General Staff, and of course Henry Bartlett, and Lloyd Irby the American general, and even their opponent of that long ago, the German Field-Marshal Ritter von Heldenmark. The speeches had been short and good – moving, to the point, evocative, but not flag wagging. They had all in effect said the same thing: thus many years ago, we who are here now took part in a great event; we are met to recall our hour of purpose, and our comrades who died then and have departed since; and to honour the architect of that day – Field-Marshal Sir John Durham. It had all ended with everyone on his feet, yelling, cheering, the massed bands blaring out *Land of Hope and Glory*, the great hall dark, shaking with the stamping of feet, a spotlight shining on the eagle head of the one tall old man standing on the dais, facing them, his right hand raised, just touching a jutting white eyebrow.

He seemed to be dozing now, Martin thought, though with him you could never be sure. His blue dress uniform hung loose round his neck, for it was four years since he had had it taken in and at seventy-nine the flesh wilts rapidly off the bone. His

9

field-marshal's baton was clutched in his hand and his red-banded gold-braided cap lay on the seat between them. It had been a long day, and it was always particularly exhausting for the Old Man, for every year there were more gaps in the ranks, more condolences to be shared with widows and sons.

The Old Man spoke suddenly out of the darkness. 'That's the last one I shall go to.'

Martin said nothing for a while; then, 'They're very tiring.'

'That's not it,' the Field-Marshal said, a touch of irritation in his voice, 'It's all nonsense. It's false.'

Martin did not understand and the Old Man seemed to be in no very good mood; certainly he was very far from sleepy, whatever impression he might have given.

'Do you have that flask on you? I'll have a nip.'

Martin found the whisky flask he usually carried when accompanying the Old Man on occasions like this. On doctor's advice, he sometimes took a nip when he was feeling tired or strained, to help his heart.

He took one now, wiped his lips with the back of his long thin hand and gave the flask back to Martin.

'All nonsense,' he repeated, with even more energy. He was sitting up straight now, the baton across his lap, the brass buttons winking down the front of his tunic, the broad red stripe glowing on the outside of his leg.

'I don't quite understand, sir,' Martin said.

The Field-Marshal said, 'The atmosphere inside that hall was like the atmosphere in the whole country – the world, as far as I can tell . . . foggy with sentiment, thick with half truths and half untruths, damp with unreasonable and unreasoned emotion . . . emotionalism. Who the hell in all that crowd knows what really happened in the war, more than what he personally saw, or felt? And most of them have deliberately buried half of that, or transformed it into something more graceful . . . gracious . . . more fit to be remembered . . . I am hailed as a great general, a great hero, but not one soul in that hall, or in the country, knows what I really did, or how, or why . . . I feel like a bloody monument, that appears to be made of marble, but is in fact made partly of steel, partly of clay, partly of sand, but it's all been painted over – to look like marble.'

Martin said hesitantly, 'I think most people realise that everything was not quite what it was supposed to be. After all, everyone knows from his own observation, that what he himself saw was not exactly or precisely what was reported . . . but the overall thing, that's not false, surely, sir? We did fight the campaign in the Balkans, we did win Vojja Lovac, on St George's Day, 1945, we did take a hundred and twenty-five thousand prisoners, we . . .'

'Immaterial – fodder for encyclopaedias!' the Field-Marshal said, thrusting his baton like a pointer staff. 'The real truth is not out. But it's going to come out. I shall write my Memoirs. I shall tell everything. The inside as well as the outside. The private as well as the public. What we did that was shameful as well as what was noble. What reflects discredit on me, the army, the country, as well as what was creditable. I owe it to the public . . . they can't be truly informed unless the only ones who can tell them the whole truth, do so.'

What made you decide on this now, after so many years? Martin wanted to ask; but the Field-Marshal answered his question before he had opened his mouth.

'I don't have long to live. I've decided I don't want to go to my grave unpurged, so to speak, of my responsibility to the truth. There is such a thing, you know. . . . You shall help me.'

'Yes, sir,' Martin said, feeling dazed. The Field-Marshal had congratulated him briefly on his own foray into literature – *The Balkan Campaign of 1945* – but had never seemed to believe that he possessed great writing talent. He said, 'I'll do my best to . . .'

'Your best isn't what I want,' the Old Man growled. 'I want the truth, all of it, all the time.'

'Yes, sir.'

The long head turned suddenly toward him, 'You'll be involved, you know.'

Martin nodded. Yes, he would; he'd been close to the Old Man, militarily at least, since March 1944; and after the war he'd married Lois, his daughter; Clive and Caroline were the Old Man's only grandchildren. They would all be involved.

My dear Stefanie,
... the spring is late this year and I don't expect to be able to start hybridising for another month or more, but when I do, I have high hopes that some of the Night hybrids (they were formerly called Lady Sackville) will sport very dark, as they did last year, and then we shall be a step closer to the Black Durham ... perhaps!

I have decided to write my Memoirs and have asked my son-in-law, Martin, to help. He has his security job with the government still, of course, but can do something in his spare time ...

as always,
John.

CHAPTER TWO

Martin twirled the stem of the sherry glass gently between finger and thumb and moved so that the light fell more obliquely on the painting he was looking at. 'I like that very much, Charles,' he said, 'I've never met the man, but I feel you've got him to a T.'

The painter laughed briefly. 'It's good, for what it is – the way I pay my bills. That fellow's made millions in soap and wants himself immortalised. I do it in four or five days . . . for ten thousand. Oh, I have sittings spread over a longer time, or people like that won't think they're getting their money's worth. Behind the easel, where they can't see, I'm usually working on something like that . . .' He jerked his head at a group of oils stacked against the studio wall.

Martin shook his head. 'I wish I could appreciate those, but it's no use. I can't.'

'That's real art,' the painter said. 'This . . . Sargent with a touch of vitriol. And, as I say, it comes too easy to me. With realistic painting you've either got what you were aiming at, or you haven't. With abstractions like those, the first question is – what are you aiming at? What is that image inside your head which you're trying to bring out?'

He jerked his head and his long hair, obviously dyed to achieve its strong shade of auburn, cascaded back over his neck. Charles Gibson had an amazing animation, Martin thought, which made one forget his affectations. Women fell for him in windrows, which was easy to understand, but the Old Man liked him too, and that was another matter altogether.

'What are we talking shop for?' the artist exclaimed with a sweeping gesture of his free hand. 'I invited you here to have a drink on your way back to the bosom of Stockbrokers' England. How's the Old Man?'

'Great. He never seems to change. His hair's a little whiter, but no thinner. But didn't you see him a couple of weeks ago?'

'Yes. He had a brandy and told me about his Memoirs. He said he had made up his mind to write an honest chronicle of what it was like, for the public good. Really bare his mind and soul, not just record what orders he gave. Even that's been enough to frighten the wits out of some of the politicians.

They're afraid old skeletons might fall out of the cupboard . . . but I told him it wasn't enough. I told him he'd left it a little late. The war's been over twenty-eight years – his name's no longer so well-known as it used to be. I told him he'd have to think of a gimmick.'

'What do you mean?'

'Oh, fill it with scandal and gossip . . . invented, if necessary. Introduce all kinds of quite imaginary happenings. There'd be such an uproar, so many furious denials, accusations and counter-accusations, that he'd be famous again overnight. And rich!'

Martin laughed at the other's contagious eagerness. Charles Gibson was actually only two years younger than himself, but usually made him feel that the difference in age was at least twenty years.

'I'm afraid it's not very likely that the Old Man will write that sort of book,' he said.

'I know,' the other answered. 'Discipline! Facts! An overpowering sense of responsibility! But what fun it would be if he broke loose!'

'I'm helping him with the Memoirs as a matter of fact, acting as a sort of part-time secretary.'

'Should be interesting. . . . How's the family?'

'Oh, chugging along. . . . Lois spends most of her time on her catering business. It keeps her busy. Clive's got a company, temporarily, and his battalion arrived back from Northern Ireland last week. They'll be on public duties for the next six months.'

'What does Clive think of the situation over there?'

'He doesn't. He just does what he's told, like the rest of them. He says all the Irish are the same – barbarians. Caroline's at university. She had a boy friend, long-haired shaggy type . . .'

'Like me?'

'Hair about the same, but he didn't wash. Anyway, we haven't seen him for a month or so. She's home now, as a matter of fact, recovering from flu. . . . Well, if I'm going to get to Waterloo in time to catch the five-thirty-eight, I'd better be going.'

They were standing in the window looking out on the Thames from three stories up in the big house on the Embankment. The May evening was bright and opalescent. 'A Whistler nocturne on its way,' Charles murmured. A tug crawling up

14

river with a string of barges against the falling tide hooted imperiously.

'Thanks for the sherry.'

'Not a bit. Give my regards to the Old Man. . . . Does Lois do any painting?'

Martin shook his head. 'No. Just the catering.'

'She has talent, you know. She was painting a lot when I first met her. Very young and imitating Picasso as all of them do at that stage – but good.'

'She's given it up. I've never seen her paint and we've been married twenty-seven years.'

'Pity. Well, take care. I'll be seeing you on the third.'

'Eh! Oh yes, the Old Man's birthday. Good.' He waved his hand as he went out and down the long flights of stairs.

He was smiling to himself as he walked fast along the Embankment, past the heraldic gryphons marking the boundary of the City, past H.M.S. *Discovery* and *Wellington*, and on to Waterloo Bridge. Trust Charles to come up with an idea like that about the Memoirs.

At the station he bought a paper and after a short wait, got into his usual 1st class compartment when the 5.38 came in. He folded the paper and began to read. Cricket results. Unrest in the Middle East. Bombs in Londonderry. . . . People would say Clive was lucky to get out of there without a scratch and of course, in a way it was true, but it could hardly compare with El Alamein, or Tobruk, or Cassino, or Vojja Lovac. God, what a week of slogging that had been before the Germans broke . . . the battlefield looking like a catastrophe, casualties heavy, our tanks and vehicles going up in flames by the hundred, corps commanders, divisional commanders, politicians, even the Army Group commander, all begging him to disengage, break off the battle . . . only the Old Man holding the 16th Army to the job, and at last the greatest single disaster to German arms of the whole war, after Stalingrad . . .

A foreign name caught his eye – *Zvornos*. He remembered it. A village dominated by a big castle, on the far side of the Magitor Range. It had been on the dividing line between the 16th British and the 20th U.S. Armies. He read the piece. . . . The date line was Belgrade. A museum in New York had acquired a Rembrandt from a private collection for three-quarters of a million dollars. The Yugoslav government believed that the painting was originally from the Zvornos Col-

15

lection. This had been amassed by the Counts of Zvornos over centuries and held in their various castles and palaces, including Zvornos Castle itself, all over what had been Serbia and Montenegro. Many of the paintings had disappeared during the war. The Counts had never treated their art treasures as a public trust, and had never allowed any cataloguing to be done, so it was not known for certain what they had owned, or where. But the Yugoslav government had evidence that this Rembrandt had definitely been seen at Zvornos Castle in 1938; and they knew of other works that had been in the collection. The report made it clear that the Committee of Three, which ruled Yugoslavia, expected the American Government to institute inquiries and find out who was holding what they regarded as State property – for, of course, all such treasures had been nationalised when Yugoslavia became Communist.

Martin rested the paper on his lap. The train slowed through Clapham Junction and regathered speed. Zvornos . . . there had been some message about state property from Army Group and a Civil Affairs truck. The village, which was on one side of a stream, had been in the American area but the castle, on the other side, in the British area. It was a long time ago and he couldn't remember any details. He'd had a lot on his mind then, as Brigadier, General Staff at the Old Man's headquarters. More than he could cope with and keep his sanity, he'd sometimes felt. Quite a change from now, when he knew that half the time he was making work and the other half the work wasn't worth the effort. Well, someone had to oversee the security of the government's offices and procedures, and some people would find it fascinating, or would make it so – but not he. The planning for Vojja Lovac, now, that had been . . .

'Have I offended you in any way, Brigadier Ruttledge . . . or have I become invisible?'

He had been looking through the man opposite. Now he was speaking, smiling slightly. Round, moon-face, ruddy, blue suit, horn-rimmed glasses, slight Yorkshire accent . . . Crookenden, a publisher. Martin knew him quite well, met on this train often enough, usually in the morning . . . lived in Cowcross, the next station beyond Ashwood.

'Sorry,' he said, 'I was miles away.'

'In the Balkans, perhaps?'

Martin nodded. The man was shrewd, but was it so obvious in his face that he had been daydreaming of past glories?

He said, 'This article about the Rembrandt made me think back a bit . . . quite a bit.'

'Quite. . . . How's the security of H.M.G.?' the other said, folding his paper away.

'Chugging along. I always keep hoping to uncover a master spy.'

'A lady in a slinky black dress, naturally.'

'But all I turn up are Defence Department clerks who've lost a copy of the Manual of Office Procedures on the Bakerloo somewhere between Charing Cross and St John's Wood.'

'Ha ha! Family all well? I saw the Scots Guards were back from Northern Ireland.'

'Yes. They're all fine . . . we don't see much of the young, of course.'

'Lois still running that catering business?'

'Yes. It gives her something to do.'

'Quite.'

The train slowed and curved off the main line under the arches of the Hampton Court flyover. Martin gathered his bowler hat and briefcase, put away his newspaper and took down his tightly rolled umbrella.

Crookenden said, 'I hear that the Field-Marshal is preparing his Memoirs.'

Martin said, 'That's true.' People seemed to be taking quite an interest, contrary to his belief that the public had had enough of 'generals' books'.

Crookenden said, 'I'd be grateful if you would ask him to give us the chance to publish them. We have a good reputation in the publishing world, as anyone in it will confirm. Here's my card.'

'I'll tell him,' Martin said. 'He's having his eightieth birthday on the third. Well, here we are. See you tomorrow, perhaps.'

'Some day. On the line.'

Martin got down on to the platform, showed his season ticket, walked over the footbridge to the car park and climbed into his Morris 1100. Lois used to drive him to and from the station but a couple of years ago she'd decided she had to have a van for her catering and that had enabled him to take the Morris. And if that was being used for some reason, the Old Man welcomed the opportunity to come and fetch him in the Bentley. . . . *The Bentley*, it should really be thought of and so spelled – a 1929 Short Chassis Red Label 3-litre Bentley, one of the year and mark and model that took the Le Mans

17

three years running. It had a top, but the Old Man had never put it up, which made winter trips something of an ordeal.

He parked the Morris carefully in the garage recently built on the east side of Ashwood House and went in. Twelve minutes past six by the hall clock. The Old Man would be out in the garden, working on his new approach to the problem of creating the Black Durham. Lois would be in the kitchen; Caroline in Bloomsbury ... no, she was here, convalescing; Clive in his flat at Chelsea Barracks; and he was here, it was a lovely evening, and all was right with the world. Right, but boring.

He walked back to the kitchen and opened the door.

'So I says to her ...'

'Then they had to get married, though nowadays they don't seem to care, do they?'

'Pass the salt, dear.'

He closed the door silently. There were four women in there, Lois and three of her helpers. None of them had seen or heard him. He didn't know how Lois could stand it. They were nice women, kind, hard working, full of all the virtues ... but there had been a time when continuous talk of food and babies had bored her as much as it bored him. And what was *his* talk of? Security regulations. Security risks. Safer means of passing information from one government building to another. Methods to reduce the risk of hiring undesirables, without getting into trouble over discrimination or deprivations without trial.

He walked through the house and out of the open back door into the garden. It was a big four-square Georgian house, built in the days when the landed gentry of England were as prolific as Italian peasants. It had been in Lois's mother's family for a long time and now the Old Man, her father, had his own study and bed and bathroom on the east side, upstairs, while he and Lois used the rest, with room for guests and returning children. The Old Man kept saying he should live by himself somewhere; but at his age there ought to be someone close to him ... and his pay helped keep the place up. A Field-Marshal's salary was quite considerable, even in these days of inflation and soaring prices.

It was a good solid house, with a lovely lawn, elms, great copper beeches and a monkey puzzle in front; the house itself two-storey with attic dormers, white painted, bow windows on all the ground floor front rooms and large clear sash windows above. And at the back there were these five acres of vegetable and rose garden, sheltered by an old red brick wall and the trees of the converted farmhouse behind.

He walked on down to the rose garden. The Old Man liked you to take an interest in his experiments. He said he would rather be remembered as the creator of the Red and Black Durham Roses than as the victor of Vojja Lovac. The Red Durham was a beautiful rose, hybrid tea, very fragrant, double petalled, with a colour like . . . like the full dress tunic of an old soldier of the Royal Oxford Fusiliers, the Field-Marshal's old regiment; but he had not been satisfied with the Blacks he'd bred so far. Martin thought he'd read somewhere that a true black flower was an impossibility . . . something to do with the properties of light and plant growth. Anyway, the Old Man hadn't read it or didn't believe it. He kept slogging away, ready to take advantage of any opportunity to jump in with all his strength and skill the moment he saw a break . . . just like Vojja Lovac.

He opened the door of the greenhouse, which everyone called The Factory, and peered round. No one there. He went out and looked about. He wasn't in the garden at all. Odd. He'd almost always be here on an evening like this. Perhaps he wasn't feeling well, and Lois was too busy with her wedding or reception or whatever the damned thing was, to notice. He walked back up the centre path and into the house.

The Old Man was on the upper landing, leaning over the balustrade, the white hair heavy round the thin bony face, the light from the landing window gleaming on his beak nose and the big hands, bony knuckled, grasping the banister.

'Evening, Martin,' he said.

'Evening, sir. I was looking for you in The Factory.'

'I was there earlier. There's a very promising sport just blooming. Have you got half an hour?'

'Yes, sir.' He started up the stairs. It would have been easy to convert a couple of rooms on the ground floor for the Old Man, but he'd said that as long as his legs functioned he'd stay upstairs, where he could see the Surrey hills rising to the south, and when his legs gave out he'd go to a place by the sea, and lie by a front window, watching it.

In his study the Old Man said, 'Whisky?'

'I'd better have a sherry. I had a couple with Charles Gibson. He said you should fill your Memoirs with juicy scandal – made up, if necessary.'

'You know Charles. He likes to stir up ants' nests to watch them all scurrying about.'

Martin drank his sherry. He asked, 'Have you decided to take the Memoirs back as far as the Great War?'

The Field-Marshal shook his head sharply. 'No. I think about that a lot, but I don't want to write about it. . . . We should decide on a publisher.'

Martin said, 'I know a man called Crookenden slightly – he's a publisher. He told me he'd like to do your Memoirs.'

'The Mermaid Press,' the Old Man said. 'I met him last year at Sandown. Will you talk to him?'

'Certainly. We'll have lunch together as soon as I can fix it. Tomorrow perhaps. I can call him now. I know he's home.'

The Old Man said, 'And will you speak to Harry Mullins? He's Editor of the *Sunday Journal*. You remember him?'

'The tall cockney fellow who was doing publicity work for 16th Army?'

'And very good, too. A lot of people thought I was trying to get publicity for myself at home, but I wasn't. That little paper went to all the troops. *They* were the people I wanted to know me. An Army commander can't be physically visible to everyone in his command, however hard he tries. It's too big and too spread out. Mullins has asked me two or three times to let him know first if I ever think of writing a book.'

Smiling, he pushed a piece of paper across to Martin. Martin saw that it had been carefully lettered:

MEMORIES OF ITALY AND THE BALKANS
by
FIELD-MARSHAL SIR JOHN DURHAM,
G.C.B., G.B.E., D.S.O., M.C.

That night Martin went to bed at his usual time. Lois was already cleaning her teeth as he undressed.

'The Mermaid Press want to publish your father's Memoirs,' he said through the open bathroom door.

'I suppose people will still be interested,' she said. She came out and began to rub cold cream into her face. Her dark hair was streaked with grey, though her pale skin was little lined. She still had a good figure but the spark seemed to have gone from her. Her grey eyes, bare now that she had taken off her glasses, were flat and empty. Her mind was on – what? Pounds of spread for sandwiches? Number of bottles of cheap champagne for a cup? Strawberries? Cream?

When he came out of the bathroom she was propped up in the wide double bed, reading a book. Her reading light was on. He saw that it was Antonia Fraser's life of Cromwell. He took his place on his side of the bed, switched on his own reading light, picked up the thriller he had half finished the night before and began to read.

After a couple of pages, he put down the book. 'How's Caroline? I meant to see her, but forgot after talking to the Old Man.'

'Better,' his wife said, still reading. 'She's getting up tomorrow and will go back to university on Thursday.'

Martin read a couple of pages more, but found himself dozing off. He turned out his light and soon fell asleep.

Martin lifted his umbrella out of the stand and looked at the hall clock. Eight-thirty-five. He'd have to walk a little fast. He heard the crunch of a car's wheels on the gravel and frowned. Who could be visiting at this hour? Well, Lois would have to deal with them. He opened the door. Three men were getting out of a black saloon car and walking toward him. Two were burly men in early middle age with the unmistakable look of police officers; the third was tall and thin, with a prominent Adam's apple, and Martin thought he had seen him somewhere before. All three were wearing shiny blue suits.

The leading man said, 'Brigadier Ruttledge?'

'Yes.'

'I'm Superintendent Hayes, sir. I have a warrant to search this house.'

Martin stared at him, the words not yet sunk in. 'A warrant?'

'Yes, sir.' The man produced a large document from his breast pocket. 'Signed by Mr Unwin, Justice of the Peace.'

Martin suddenly remembered where he had seen the third man, the thin one. 'You're in M.I.5,' he said. 'We've met.'

The man said nothing. The Superintendent looked at Martin reprovingly. It wasn't done to mention M.I.5. You shouldn't have done that, the look said, I'll have to report this to your superiors.

'What's your authority?' Martin asked, turning back to the Superintendent.

'It's in the warrant, sir. Information laid on oath under the Official Secrets Acts 1911, 1939.'

Martin looked at his watch. Now he'd have to run to catch

the 8.47; but he couldn't leave these idiots alone to do what they wanted. He turned back into the house, throwing curtly over his shoulder, 'Come in.'

Once inside the Superintendent said, 'You or the Field-Marshal should accompany us on our search, sir. And, of course, we will give you a receipt for any material seized.'

The Field-Marshal came out of the dining room, newspaper in hand.

Martin said, 'The police, sir. With a search warrant under the Official Secrets Act. I can't imagine what they're after.'

The Old Man's face was closed and grim. 'I can,' he said.

'They want you to accompany them.'

'I'll go. You'd better get off to work.'

'I don't think I should leave you, sir. Not with this going on.'

'Please yourself. Follow me, gentlemen.'

Martin remembered where he had seen the Old Man's expression before. It was in the oil painting of him in the dining room, on the field of Vojja Lovac, a look on his face both ardent and stern, as of battle joined.

He waited in the drawing room, trying to read. The police had been in the house over two hours now.

Lois burst in. 'They've found pistols and ammunition and stolen jewels and money in Caroline's room!' she blurted out. 'In a suitcase under her bed.'

'Pistols? Stolen jewels?' Martin cried, jumping to his feet. 'That's impossible!'

'They've found them!' his wife shouted. 'I've seen them!'

The superintendent came in, carrying a suitcase. 'Do you know anything about this, sir?' he asked. In spite of his training he looked astonished, almost frightened, like a man gone fishing for mackerel who hooks a shark. He wasn't asking Martin an officious question, but genuinely seeking enlightenment.

Martin said, 'That's not Caroline's suitcase. At least, I've never seen it before.'

The superintendent opened it and Martin saw two automatic pistols of medium calibre, with several boxes of cartridges, scattered jewellery and several thick wads of ten-pound notes.

'The pistols are Czech made,' the superintendent said. 'I don't know where the other stuff comes from, but if it's stolen, we'll find out soon enough.'

Martin hurried out of the room and up the stairs, two at a time. Caroline was sitting on the edge of her bed, wrapped in a

22

dressing-gown, staring defiantly out of the window. The other policeman stood stolidly by the open door, his arms folded.

'What are these automatics doing here, Caroline?' Martin cried. 'Are they yours, who gave them to you? When did you bring them here?'

'I'm not going to tell anyone anything,' the girl said and snapped her mouth shut, but Martin saw that she was fighting to hold back tears and her lower jaw was trembling.

The superintendent was at Martin's shoulder. 'We'll have to take her along with us, sir.'

'Fascist fuzz!' Caroline cried. 'You can torture me but I won't say anything!'

'I don't expect there'll be much torture, miss,' the superintendent said. 'Now, if you'll get dressed . . .'

'Well, get out of my room,' Caroline snapped.

On the stairs the superintendent said, 'Is she at university, sir?'

Martin said, 'Yes.'

'That could explain the guns. We've seen these Czech automatics before – taken them off kids who think they're revolutionaries. Your daughter could belong to one of those groups . . . like The People March, Students for Democratic Action, half a dozen others. But the jewels and the money, that beats me . . . assuming they are stolen,' he added hastily.

They were back in the drawing room. The Field-Marshal came in, followed by the man from M.I.5, who was carrying a bulging briefcase.

Martin told the Old Man about the discoveries in Caroline's room. The superintendent said, 'We'll take her to Rackleigh police station, sir, and charge her there.'

'Telephone Forsythe, Lois,' the Old Man said. 'He's our solicitor, superintendent. He'll be with you right away. They've taken some of my papers, Martin. The ones marked "Keep out of files". My personal papers.'

He seemed extraordinarily placid about this outrage, Martin thought. But that was what the German commander had thought in the early days of Vojja Lovac, before the main counter stroke destroyed him.

The M.I.5 man said apologetically, 'They're official documents, sir. Government property.'

'We'll have a question asked in the House,' Martin said angrily.

The Field-Marshal's glance wandered momentarily across

23

him and the superintendent turned away. Was he imagining it, or had he turned to hide the hint of a burgeoning smile?

Caroline came downstairs, followed by the plain clothes man. She had obviously been crying and looked very pale; but then she'd barely recovered from flu, Martin thought. She was wearing one of those appalling granny dresses that Martin detested. This one was black with miscellaneous spots and patches on it. It swept the carpet as she moved. Under it peeped out the toes of a pair of army boots, without hobnails at least, but heavily worn and newly mended where one toe had worn through. Her hair hung in a long pigtail down her back, and she had a Red Indian sweatband of orange cloth tied round her forehead. Even this deliberate ugliness could not conceal the womanliness of her tall figure or the lithe grace of her movements.

She said curtly to the superintendent, 'I want to speak to my father, in private.'

'I'm afraid I'd have to listen in,' the other said.

Caroline sniffed and said, 'Well, I'll say it aloud, to everyone. I knew the pistols and ammunition were there, but not the other stuff. That's all.'

Martin said, 'Are you a member of some revolutionary group, Caroline?'

'She needn't answer,' the superintendent cut in quickly.

'I want to,' the girl said, 'I'm not ashamed of it. I'm a member of T.P.M., The People March.'

'Well, sir,' the superintendent said, 'we'd better be going.'

'You had,' the Field-Marshal said.

Ten minutes later Lois and Martin were standing facing the Old Man as he sat in his usual chair in the drawing room. His voice was sharp, its tone of determination unclouded by anger.

'First, what's The People March?'

Martin said, 'A sort of society. We have had a little trouble with them. They're mostly students ... believe the world will be put right if they blow it up first. They preach revolution and are often armed – to protect themselves and the poor against police brutality, they say – but they talk more than they act. The jewels and the money, I simply don't understand.'

'The police didn't expect to find anything in Caroline's room,' the Old Man said. 'They were only searching it in case I'd hidden papers there.'

'That's what I thought.'

'So I'm responsible for getting Caroline into trouble.'

'Daddy!' Lois exclaimed, 'how can you say that? It's her own fault entirely! It's absolutely disgraceful that she . . .'

'We all do disgraceful things sometimes,' the Old Man said, 'especially when we're young. . . . They took the transcript of the wire recording, as I expected.'

'What wire recording?' Martin asked.

'You never knew of it,' the Old Man said, without further elaboration. 'And the note from Henry Bartlett about Zvornos Castle . . .'

A notion suddenly came into Martin's head, with the force of a powerful flash of light. 'Were you expecting . . . ?'

'As soon as the police mentioned the Official Secrets Acts I began to think what I have which could conceivably come under that heading, or what might be pushed under that heading if it would save somebody embarrassment. Somebody important. Until yesterday I would have said there was only one such item – the transcript from the wire recording made at a conference I attended with Henry Bartlett and Matt Jordan a few days after Vojja Lovac. They've taken the transcript, but they were hoping to find the original wire. They'll take some further action against me soon. It'll probably seem quite unconnected with the wire recording, but its real purpose will be to force me to give it up to them.'

'You said "till yesterday",' Martin said.

The Field-Marshal said, 'Yesterday there was a piece in the evening paper about the Yugoslav government believing paintings had been stolen from Zvornos Castle near the end of the war. I had a note in my personal papers, dated in February 1945, from Henry Bartlett directing me to let a Civil Affairs truck in there to rescue something the Committee of Three wanted as part of their price for further co-operation with us. The M.I.5 man took that note.'

Lois said, 'So both these things affect Sir Henry?'

The Field-Marshal said, 'Yes. But that doesn't prove he was behind this search.'

Martin said slowly, 'But that's why you looked at me a little oddly when I said we'd get questions asked in the House. And the Super turned away, smiling. Sir Henry's our Member! But I can't believe . . .'

'I can't believe our daughter's a thief,' Lois said wearily, 'but she is. She must be!'

The Field-Marshal said, 'I don't think it's a matter of believing or not believing. It's a matter of facing facts. That's what we're all going to have to do, starting with me. Who would be in charge of this business, Martin?'

Martin thought and said, 'My boss, eventually, I suppose. Under the Prime Minister, of course.'

'The Secretary to the Cabinet Committee on Government Security? Victor Terrell?'

'Yes, sir.'

'Well, talk to him tomorrow, please. Tell him from me that I want all the documents that have been taken, back, as I need them for inclusion in my Memoirs. It won't work but it will show them that I don't intend to be frightened off. . . . Give me a sheet of paper, Lois. I'm going to make a copy of Henry's note about Zvornos, from memory.'

Martin sat up in bed, thinking. Lois read steadily beside him. Did it mean nothing to her that her daughter was in jail? Caroline might be bailed, she might not, for the jewels and money had been traced: they had been stolen two weeks earlier, in the armed robbery of an old widow living alone in North London. Forsythe hadn't seemed to take the matter of the pistols very seriously, when they met at Rackleigh police station: girls will be girls, his attitude implied; but the stolen goods were another matter. Caroline swore she knew nothing about them; but who would believe her unless she told everything she did know. And what was that?

The Old Man was going to let them have it. All of it. This morning's attempts to muzzle him had only ensured that no one would be spared, no smallest shame glossed over. The whole tenor of the Memoirs would change. So far, there had been little actual writing, just collecting notes, organising files, thinking what books would be needed for reference. Now, the mutter of artillery had intruded on that bookish calm.

They were going to be involved, he had thought to himself, driving back that evening in the limousine that the C.G.S. had provided for the Old Man. But he realised now that the involvement would be deeper and more personal than he had expected. He himself had drawn a curtain over some of the events and emotions of that time. We all do, for different reasons, he thought. Now the curtain was being pulled aside, and the subconscious part of his mind was dredging up names for his inspection: Cunningham . . . Armstrong . . . Jastrec . . .

He felt oddly as though he were going into battle, as so many years ago, leading the 40th Lancers, Frontier Force, in their armoured cars ahead of the attacking divisions in Africa, or scouring the roads northward from the heel of Italy. Only yesterday he'd been moaning about the boredom of his job, and – face it – his marriage, his life. Anxiety gnawed at him. He wished suddenly that the clock would wind back and all be as it had been, say, twenty-four hours earlier.

His tension relaxed, as it always had when battle was actually joined, to be replaced by suppressed excitement. For a time he would relive, if only in the telling, those days of intense purpose, of doing and being and working at the highest level.

He switched off his light, turned over and willed himself toward sleep. Lois read on, unmoving, breathing quietly and evenly.

Giovanni!

How exciting about your Memoirs! But why did you not think to do it years ago, when all the other generals were writing books to explain how they never made a mistake in the war? You really didn't. I hope you will not try to keep yourself out of it, because people are much more interesting than fact and figures, especially such a person as you. . . .

. . . I am using a new manure this year and the gardener promises it will work wonders. We shall see . . .

You are in my thoughts, as always . . .

CHAPTER THREE

Lois Ruttledge surveyed the salmon with a practised eye. Eleven people, of whom Charles would certainly have a second helping, and probably Caroline, too. Hilda Ross could be quite a trencher-woman, if she wasn't drinking – but she would be drinking. She always did in Daddy's presence. The salmon was big enough. She began to spread fresh cucumber round the fish where it lay on the big dish. Through the short pantry passage she heard Vetch whistling tunelessly through his teeth as he laid the table in the dining room. On the kitchen sideboard the birthday cake towered up three tiers high, surmounted by a field-marshal's crossed batons and laurel wreath in icing sugar, and a single candle. The window beside her gave on to the vegetable garden and there her father was stooped gathering lettuce. The bells of the village church across the common had just stopped ringing.

She thought she heard a car drive round to the front of the house, and a few moments later her son Clive came in and kissed her perfunctorily on the cheek. 'Morning, Mummy. Ah, salmon . . . had that yesterday.' He was not yet twenty-six, but his manner was one of intense boredom. His clothes and tone of voice exactly matched the way actors and cartoonists used to portray Guards officers when she had been younger. She wished she knew whether it was really just a pose with Clive. Perhaps, behind that languid ennui, he was really enthusiastic, even interested, in something. If so, she had never found out. At that age she . . . no, at that age she was already married, had had a child, given up painting . . . given up, full stop. She was in no position to tell Clive he was wasting his life. None of them could, except her father.

'Is Caroline still, ah, incarcerated?' Clive asked.

'No. They released her on bail last night. . . . Why don't you help Grandpa with the lettuce?' she said. 'His back's aching, I can see.'

'Good idea,' the young man said and wandered out.

This time she had not heard a car when hands were put round her eyes from behind and a kiss planted on the nape of her neck. 'I didn't hear you drive in,' she said softly, turning.

Charles Gibson kissed her gently on the lips. He was wearing purple bell-bottomed trousers with matching velvet jacket, and a green silk shirt with a spotted cravat.

'You're not supposed to hear Rolls-Royce motor cars at that distance,' he said. 'Who's coming to the feast to hear the Old Man pronounce sentence?'

'What do you mean?'

'The Memoirs. There was a squib in the evening paper on Thursday about it. About him going to tell it like it was, as I believe they say across the Atlantic. That caused quite a bit of excitement in certain circles, I can tell you. The Old Man must know even more than I do about some people's pasts. Who's been invited?'

'Sir Henry Bartlett . . .'

'Ah! Because he was the Old Man's Army Group Commander in the Balkans. And your M.P. And interested in the Memoirs. Very interested.'

'Daddy's never exactly liked Sir Henry but they've known each other for donkey's years. They were at Sandhurst together.'

'I bet he was just as much of a snob then. Who else?'

'The Rosses.'

'Perhaps the Old Man will tell the true story of the Sacking of Stephen, at last. *He* was at Sandhurst with Bartlett and the Old Man, too, you know, but that didn't stop the Old Man sacking him out of hand. And seeing that he never even got a K.'

'I don't believe Daddy did that. He likes General Ross more than he likes Bartlett.'

'Perhaps. But Mrs Ross doesn't like *him*, I can assure you. She is sure the Old Man is responsible for it that she is plain Mrs R and not Lady R. . . . Anyone else?'

'Mr Crookenden, of the Mermaid Press. They're going to publish the Memoirs. And his wife, of course.'

'I know him. Yorkshireman, mad on soccer, smokes a pipe the size of a loo bowl and peers at you through pebble lenses in horn rims.'

'We asked Mr Mullins, editor of the *Sunday Journal*, but he couldn't come. He wants to serialise the Memoirs. There, that's about done. Vetch!'

'Yes, mum?'

'I'm done here. Will you cover it all up? Put the salmon dish in the fridge. The Field-Marshal will be bringing in some lettuce in a minute. Please wash it carefully, put it in that bowl

30

and put the bowl on the bottom shelf of the fridge. I'm going to tidy up. The Brigadier's in his study. Will you remind him people will be arriving any minute?'

She walked slowly upstairs. Charles never changed, he was dyeing his hair, his eyes always shone with a sort of fire. Usually it looked as it did today, a sparkling enthusiasm; but sometimes, particularly in the evening, it had seemed to her that the glow was more eerie. She remembered times when she had compared it in her mind to a will o' the wisp, or the bluish sheen of marsh gas on a summer night. Then she had wondered what was the true source of his enthusiasm and had visions of him dancing like a devil over a field of beings in despair – their wailing misery brought about by him solely to provide music for his dance.

She ran a comb impatiently through her hair. Daddy's book, which wouldn't be ready for over six months yet, had already set the cats among the pigeons. Well, her own secrets were not military, and it had all been so long ago. . . . What had happened to that woman Madeleine whom Charles had been keeping before she herself met him? They'd met once, by accident, and Madeleine had been trying not to cry. Now – where was she? What? Lonely probably – like herself. In her fifties. No longer the luscious curvy sort of blonde she remembered. The sort most men seemed to like when it came to the point, however much they sneered about chocolate box prettiness or busty barmaids in the abstract. Jealousy was such a waste of time, and yet . . . if she found that Martin was having an affair, she wouldn't be jealous and the reason was obvious. She didn't care.

She went downstairs, just in time to greet Lieutenant-General and Mrs Ross at the front door. Hilda Ross opened her arms and hugged her. They felt thin and old now, but she remembered the comfort they had once given. There was a faint smell of sherry on her breath, which she had apparently been trying to drown by chewing a mint. The sharp nose and sallow cheeks were heavily powdered and she'd applied her lipstick generously but not very accurately.

The General pecked her on the cheek. 'Hullo, m'dear. You're looking well.'

She smiled absently as she led the way into the drawing room. 'Martin, give Stephen and Hilda a drink . . .' A bell trilled and she returned to the front door.

The man standing there in a light-weight grey suit was small and round of face, the features and thin hair very like the usual portrait of Napoleon, altered by the natural processes of ageing, for Sir Henry Bartlett was the same age, within a month, as her father. Yet age had dealt more leniently with him than with the Field-Marshal, for there were few wrinkles in the smooth skin, the wide brown eyes were unshadowed and clear, and the hair was barely grey.

He put out a small-manicured hand. 'Good morning, Lois. What a pleasant occasion!' He walked briskly down the hall at her side.

In the drawing room he exclaimed, 'Why Stephen . . . Hilda . . . you've come down from London for the occasion!'

Martin handed him a glass of whisky and soda. 'Ah, you always remember what I like. Good staff officers are like elephants . . .' He turned as the Field-Marshal stood in the door, his grandson Clive behind him. Bartlett went forward, hand extended. 'John . . . you look wonderful. By heaven, I wonder what odds we'd have got about July 1, 1916, if we'd bet that the three of us would be celebrating our eightieth birthdays this year.'

'What happened on that date?' Lois asked.

'The Battle of the Somme began,' her father said sombrely. 'Dick Newby was killed the next day. Six machine gun bullets. His brains were blown into my eyes so that I had to use my handkerchief before I could see again.'

There was a silence. Then General Ross said, 'Seen the letter in the *Journal* today about the Zvornos Collection, Henry?'

'No,' Bartlett said shortly, 'I don't read the *Journal*.'

General Ross's watery blue eyes turned back to the Field-Marshal. 'It was from a chap called Greville, who said that sometime in February 1945 he was commanding the troop of tanks that was manning a road block behind Zvornos. They had a platoon of infantry with them. He said a U.S. Army truck came down from Zvornos Castle, driven by a U.S. private, and there were also two men from Civil Affairs in it. They said they had rescued some art from Zvornos Castle which Civil Affairs wanted to save from being looted or destroyed if the Castle was shelled or bombed. . . .'

'It never was,' the Field-Marshal interjected. 'There was very little fighting in that area. Being so close under the Magitor Range made it a bit of a dead end.'

Stephen Ross said, 'Well, these people said Civil Affairs were going to restore the art to Yugoslavia when it had a proper government again, and . . .'

'What has all this to do with John's birthday?' Bartlett said irritably.

'Wait a minute, Henry,' General Ross said, 'Greville said he looked into the truck and saw a lot of things that could have been paintings stacked there, covered with sacking and sheets. He was a little suspicious as to why an American truck would have been involved, as Zvornos Castle was apparently in John's 16th Army area, so he radioed his division headquarters asking whether he should send the truck to them under escort or what . . .'

The Field-Marshall said, 'I happened to be at the division headquarters at that moment, and I had just received . . .'

Sir Henry Bartlett got up from his chair and walked toward the drink cabinet. 'Martin, can I have another of these, please?'

'. . . a note authorising the removal of the art,' the Field-Marshal continued. 'So I told them to let the truck go, which they did.'

'That's what Greville said in his letter,' General Ross said. 'Now the Yugoslav government seem to be saying that they never got the paintings or whatever they were.'

Henry Bartlett was standing by a window, his back to them. Hilda Ross had had two more sherries and was staring – almost glaring – at the Field-Marshal. Old General Ross droned on.

Caroline swept in and Lois winced. She was wearing the same clothes the police had taken her away in, even to the boots tied with broken leather laces.

Caroline said, 'Hi, everyone. How do you like my prison pallor?'

She stooped and kissed her grandfather the Field-Marshal on the top of his thatch of white hair. 'Many happy returns of the day, Grandpa.'

'Thank you, Caroline,' he said, looking up at her with a bony smile. 'Are you sure you wouldn't like a heavier pair of boots than those? Vetch has a pair of old shooting boots of your grandmother's that might fit you.'

The girl tossed her head. 'I have better things to spend my time on than bourgeois adornment.'

'Well, stealing certainly isn't better,' Lois heard herself snapping.

Why, oh why, did she always snap at her daughter? Too late

33

now. Caroline was looking coldly at her, and saying 'I did *not* steal! As to the pistols, everyone knows that this rotten society doesn't respond to needs, only to pressures. And only then if it can be frightened out of its self-satisfied selfishness. . . . I suppose I'm allowed a sherry?'

She helped herself. Lois sighed quietly. That boy Bernard she used to bring down had seemed a nice young man, behind the beard, though nothing like strong enough for Caroline. That was probably the trouble, for now she'd apparently dropped him. When would she ever find a husband if she went about looking like a tramp's mother . . . or a tramp in female disguise? And she was so tall. Yet she did have a sweet face and a firm high bosom. She must talk with Martin about her. Fix a time. . . . Had it come to this, then, that they had to make appointments now, to talk with each other about their children?

'Lunch is served, madam,' announced Vetch from the door.

She led the way into the dining room. A quick glance confirmed that everything was as it should be. Vetch, once a private of the Royal Oxford Fusiliers, for three years her father's batman when he commanded the 1st battalion of the regiment in Palestine, now part-time gardener and butler, knew what had to be done and always did it reliably and without fuss.

They helped themselves at the sideboard to the cold salmon and salad, and sat down. Vetch poured a Chablis. They began to eat, while conversation became general round the table. After fifteen minutes, when most plates were empty or nearly so, Sir Henry Bartlett tapped his glass and rose to his feet.

'We've all known John Durham for a long time, some of us for a very long time, indeed. I know I can speak for all of us when I say – however long it is, it isn't long enough. There's a great deal to John, and we need and would enjoy, more time with him. So here's wishing you many happy returns of the day, John . . . for our sake as well as yours.'

'Hear, hear!' murmured General Ross.

'Well said,' called Charles Gibson, banging his fist on the table. Behind him his life-size oil of General Durham as commander of the 16th Army stared proudly down from the wall, jagged mountains and a burning German tank vague behind the dominant shirt-sleeved figure with the slung binoculars and carbine. That was about the best portrait Charles had ever done, Lois thought; and early in his career, too. Perhaps the better for that, for it had been before he achieved his present extraordinary facility. All of her father was in that painting . . . and

34

more of Charles than he usually allowed to appear, in the point of view, a subtle blend of admiration and cynicism, of remote respect and secret intimacy, as though Charles were announcing, 'This is how *you* see John Durham. You and I know better, John . . . don't we?'

Her father was on his feet. 'Thank you, Henry,' he said. 'It's kind of you all to come and say nice things about me. I may be trading on your friendship in the next few months, because as you know I'm going to write my memoirs of Italy and the Balkans. And I'm going to tell it all, good or bad.' He sat down again.

'My goodness!' Charles broke in, raising his hands in mock horror. 'Are you going to tell about my affair with that lady commissar from the Partisans? The *liaison* officer.'

'What's that, what's that?' General Ross said, bending his head and cupping one ear in a palsied hand, 'Ah, I see. Jolly good!'

Martin said, 'There won't be anything scandalous or personal, I'm sure – will there, sir?'

'I'm not so sure,' the Field-Marshal said. 'I am coming to believe that all things are interlocked. What if it had been my affair, not yours, Charles, and what if, as a result of tomcatting all night instead of resting, I made a bad military decision the next day? Would not the affair then be relevant? Then there are decisions that have been influenced by factors other than purely military – an attack to capture a distillery, for instance . . . something done not for its own sake but to show up someone else's inadequacies. . . . No, one can only tell the truth, and go where it leads.'

'Be careful, John,' General Ross said. 'It sounds cowardly, but often it's best to let sleeping dogs lie. Especially at our age. We might wake up the dog but not be here to get him to go to sleep again . . . or curb him if he gets out of hand.'

The Field-Marshal said, 'I was going to call the book *Memories of Italy and the Balkans* by Field-Marshal Sir John Durham et cetera et cetera, but I've changed my mind. It will be called just *Memoirs . . . Durham.*'

'That's better,' Crookenden the publisher said. 'Plain, short . . . strong.'

'And stripped,' the Field-Marshal said. 'I value my orders and decorations and honours, but it's me, the naked me, if you like, that wants to tell what really happened, what I really felt and thought – as far as I can. War's terrible, but it's important.

35

We professionals too often haven't told the truth. Only Slim did, and he was too much of a gentleman to emphasise failures, crookedness, mental and moral cowardice. I'm not a gentleman. I'm a soldier . . . an old man, about to die. We who are about to die . . . tell the truth.'

'We at the Mermaid Press are delighted with your decision, sir. Your Memoirs would in any case have been an important document, which it would have been a privilege to publish. But what you now plan can be a great book as well as a document . . . and a very successful one.'

His little birdlike wife chirped up. 'And oh, Field-Marshal, did you know that all the Sunday papers have given quite a story to you and the Memoirs.'

Sir Henry Bartlett looked at his watch. 'Oh dear, I'm afraid I shall have to go, Lois. The P.M. wanted to see me at three.'

'I'm afraid we were a little late starting . . .' Lois began.

'Don't worry, my dear. I've had some excellent salmon and Chablis. . . . Don't bother to see me out; the chauffeur's waiting.'

He went out, waving at the Field-Marshal. The men sat down again. 'What a life a politician leads,' General Ross said. 'Can't call his soul his own, even on Sunday.'

'Nor could we, in the army,' the Field-Marshal said.

'Why doesn't he retire?' Clive asked, leaning back in his chair. 'I would think he'd done all that could be expected of any man. . . . Army Group Commander in the last war, President of the Board of Trade, Minister of Defence, now Chancellor of the Duchy of Lancaster.'

'He wants to be Prime Minister,' Charles Gibson said as Vetch refilled his glass. 'Or get a life peerage.'

'He'll never be Prime Minister now,' Martin said. 'He's too old. His moment came after Macmillan. But then a lot of people were still thinking of him as a general. The British don't like generals as Prime Ministers. All that's left for him to aim at now is the peerage.'

'He always liked peers,' Hilda Ross said.

Her voice was blurred and her face flushed, Lois saw. She ought to signal to Vetch not to give her any more wine . . . but you couldn't do that to Hilda Ross. If she wasn't given wine, she'd just ask for it.

Her father said, 'Henry could have had his peerage at the end of the war. And been promoted to Field-Marshal, too . . . but by then he'd made up his mind to go into politics and become

36

Prime Minister, so he didn't want to go to the Lords, and asked to be excused when he was offered a peerage. And he dropped using his rank.'

'A very ambitious man,' Charles Gibson said, 'and a very clever one. It's always been his head that chooses his friends, not his heart. Do you remember the Honorable Daphne Fuller?'

'Never heard of her,' Clive said, stifling a yawn.

'Only child of some peer, stinking rich, looked like a blond cart horse, not an original thought in her head, twenty years older than him . . . but Henry and his wife were thick as thieves with her before the war, and during it for that matter. Reason – she knew the right people in London society, from dukes and Prime Ministers downwards. I always wondered how the Bartletts managed to keep up with her, financially. He had money after the war when he retired, but that was later.'

'That came from his wife, I believe,' the Field-Marshal said.

'Did they find a body in the basement?' Hilda Ross said suddenly. The Field-Marshal turned to look at her. The others kept their eyes averted, for she was now obviously tipsy. 'The police, when they searched the house and found Caroline's guns . . . ?'

'What body, Hilda?' Lois said, thinking she'd better humour the old lady.

'Bodies,' she said. 'Bodies of the officers who obstructed John's rise to his baton, and subsequently disappeared without trace . . . or should it be consequently?'

'Hilda!' her husband exclaimed. 'That's not a nice thing to say, even as a joke.'

'I'm not joking,' she muttered, her head now bent.

The Field-Marshal was nodding slightly at her, as though in agreement.

General Ross said, 'The police acted pretty high-handedly, didn't they – searching the house and taking some of your papers?'

'It was typical,' Caroline said.

'You and I have done worse,' the Field-Marshal said to General Ross.

'But that was war. We had authority.'

'I bet you exceeded your authority sometimes, when you thought you had to, to do your job, meet your responsibilities, call it what you like. I know I did. Anyway, these people had their authority.'

He stood up, holding on to the edge of the table till he had regained his balance. 'I will propose a toast . . . the same that I propose every birthday.' He stood to his full six foot two and raised his glass, 'Absent friends!'

'Peter, Dick, Jim and Ted,' Charles Gibson said, swallowing his wine.

The Field-Marshal said, 'You remember. You always do.'

She stared at the page, unseeing. How could Caroline do such an awful thing? And now the university had suspended her, so she'd be at home all the time, getting in the way, sprawled on the sofa smoking endless cigarettes, looking appalling. She saw suddenly her own mother's face, materialised on to the page. The face was aggrieved, not understanding, full of angry frustration, without love. She remembered the face well, and the reason for the expression. It was because she, Lois, had tried to intrude into her mother's private world, with her own problems, her young woman's folly and – to her, at least – tragedy. That was 1944, eight years after Andrew's death. Surely eight years was long enough to neglect a husband and surviving child. But the terrible thing was that she was now looking at Caroline as her mother had looked at her.

'You haven't turned a page for half an hour,' Martin said beside her. 'What are you thinking of?'

'My mother,' she said.

'You've never talked about her.'

Lois thought, I should tell him. Tell him that I felt abandoned, unwanted, because all my mother's energy and love had been buried with the dead son. She should tell him that the happiest day of her life, to that point, was when they told her her mother had been killed.

But she couldn't speak to Martin of any of this. It was too deep inside her.

'We ought to talk about Caroline,' she said.

'And Clive,' Martin said, with an edge to his tongue. 'But you don't give a damn about either of them.'

'I do,' Lois said.

'Then why didn't you come to the police station with Forsythe and me?'

'I had an important meeting with a client,' she said.

'You always have something better to do than care for Clive or Caroline.'

She picked up her book and turned her back slightly towards

him. It was no good talking about the children, because they didn't know them. And they didn't know them because they didn't know each other; and never had.

June 4, 1973

. . . had my birthday party here yesterday. It was rather more exciting than such occasions usually are, as my Memoirs are causing quite a stir. Various people in the government are even trying to prevent me from writing them, for fear of what I might reveal that they wish kept secret. They claim their objections are based in public policy, but that is not necessarily so.

I will do my best to give something of myself in the book, as you ask, but it will have to come by inference. I can not say – 'I am such and such a sort of man.' I can only say – 'I did this, for these reasons; now you decide what sort of man I am' – and of course I shall not take off my underwear to dance in public, as some well-known figures seem to delight in doing . . .

CHAPTER FOUR

The Field-Marshal stood in the greenhouse, staring at his roses, but not seeing them. He could see Ted Crandall's body as though the veil of fifty-nine years had been snatched away, leaving the scene as clear as that August morning of 1914. German machine gun fire was sweeping the wheat stubble in front of Le Cateau, where he was lying flat, waiting for a lull so that he could run forward and take command of B Company. He was a couple of months past his twenty-first birthday, and as he lay there he'd thought of his birthday party at the Trocadero – the three friends from the regiment, 2nd lieutenants all, and Peter Curran just down from Oxford, and Dick Newby learning to be a solicitor . . . when the Germans switched their fire to the right, he had jumped up and run forward a hundred yards to throw himself into a low ditch running down the side of the next field. He found a dozen men of the battalion crouched there, under a sergeant. They were facing their front, rifles outthrust. Now and then one fired though John could see nothing at the far side of the field mid the dense growth of brambles and hazel that marked the edge of a brook.

'Thank God you've come, sir,' the sergeant cried. 'All our officers gone! The major shot between the eyes, the captain blown to bits, Mr . . .'

'That's enough,' he'd said. 'Where are the other platoons?'

Then he'd seen Ted. He was lying in the field twenty yards away, on his back, one knee up, both arms outstretched, his face turned toward them. There was no sign of a wound and no blood. He looked calm and composed, as though arranged for a tableau. It was impossible to believe he was dead.

'Through the 'eart, sir,' the sergeant said, seeing the direction of his stare.

'Are you sure he's dead?'

'Yes, sir.'

Ted lay pale, still, sculpted against the stubble, his swagger cane still in his right hand, his revolver in its holster. Even from here John could see how brilliantly his belt shone with the deep oxblood tone that was the special colour to which the Royal Oxford Fusiliers polished all their leather work. One of the five who had sat down to that celebration only three months ago,

41

gone. And he'd killed him. . . . That was ridiculous! He had not fired the shots. He had not sent Ted out. Or failed him in any way. Yet he had felt, there in the ditch, a poignant sense of guilt. However he rationalised, proving his innocence over and over again, it would not leave him, and never had.

The field of stubble faded. Ted's blood-red belt turned a paler shade. Light was falling through green glass. The red stain was draining from his hands. He was in the Factory, staring at a row of roses. The veil of years descended again, and all the past was dim and dark.

He shook his head. One of the Night x Lisboa crosses from three years back was showing a very dark bloom. He'd cross that with a 'Charlotte Armstrong', making the latter the female. He began to collect his hybridising equipment; tweezers, small plastic-bags, coloured threads, record books. . . .

A shadow fell across the roses and he looked round. 'Hello, Lois. I thought you were reconnoitring someone's house for a wedding.'

'I'm going in a minute. Mr Forsythe rang up. Caroline's trial's been fixed for the twenty-sixth, Central Criminal Court.'

'That's quick work. She should be back in London, you know. There's not much for a young girl in Ashwood. I imagine that's what got her into T.P.M. – boredom. Though she was in London then.'

'I can't understand it,' his daughter said. 'We've certainly raised her carefully enough . . . given them the best education, every opportunity. Clive would never do a thing like that.'

'I wonder,' the Field-Marshal said. He looked at his daughter dispassionately. What was she now – forty-nine, forty-eight? She was good-looking in a sturdy, commonsense way, and she didn't show her age. She had his grey eyes, even though you couldn't see them well because of the glasses. She'd been through a lot, one way and other. It was a pity that she and Martin didn't . . . well, excite or interest each other very much. He sometimes wondered whether they ever had.

She said, 'Caroline told me that when the police were questioning her they hinted that she'd get off lightly if she'd tell them all she knew about T.P.M. at the university – who's in it, when and where they hold their meetings, what their plans are.'

'Did she tell them?'

'She said she told them to go and blank themselves. Only she used the word. You know how girls are these days.'

The girl was obstinate, he thought – and loyal – and one who preferred the sense of independence even at the price of isolation. Lois used to be like that. Now, he was not so sure.

Lois said, 'She still swears she knows nothing about the stolen stuff.'

'Then she probably doesn't,' the Field-Marshal said.

'But she won't say what she *does* know!'

The Field-Marshal said, 'Well, of course, I don't know, but suppose some other member of T.P.M. told her the police suspected he had the guns and gave her the locked suitcase – it *was* locked, and she did not have the key, she's told me that, twice – telling her the guns were in there, to bring it down here, where he thought the police would never think to search. Caroline would do that, if she were a loyal member, wouldn't she?'

Lois said, 'I suppose so.'

'I'm sure of it. . . . But suppose this fellow really had stolen goods to hide. He'd know that Caroline would rebel at that, especially if they were stolen at gun point from some old woman. So the man put the loot in with the guns.'

'It could be that,' Lois said. 'But why, oh why, doesn't she say so, then?'

'She can't, without betraying the man, and T.P.M. And she feels betrayed, herself, because they've let her down, let down their own high ideals, that got her into the movement in the first place.' He bent again to his work, saying, 'She'll tell us the truth one day. Fairly soon, too. This has hit her very hard.'

After a time Lois said, 'I must go now. I'll be back for lunch, but perhaps a little late. About one. Mr Mullins is coming, isn't he?'

He nodded and turned again to his roses. While he was talking to his daughter clouds had drifted up from the south-west and now it began to rain, the drops tinkling rhythmically on the glass roof. He stared up, absently playing with the tweezers. Was the fault Lois's or Martin's? Although he had not met Martin till March 1944, in the middle of the Italian campaign, he felt that he knew him better than he would ever know his own daughter. He had been abroad so much when she was very young; and Margaret, who should have been looking after her and writing to him about her, had just said, 'Lois is all right.' But in the end it had been clear that Lois was not all right. He should feel guilty about that, too. Lois didn't seem to blame him, though, rather the reverse.

43

But Martin he knew, as a soldier and as a man. He was a man who needed not war as war, but as a struggle, a purpose visibly leading to accomplishment, achievement. That was why he had done so well in the war. But when peace came he had not been able to find anything in the army to replace what war had provided. He had obviously stifled his considerable early ambition, because he could not see any worthy object for it . . . and tried to find happiness in work where accomplishments were negative. That sort of work could not bring contentment except as a background to a happy home life. He and Lois did not quarrel, but there was certainly no achievement, no passion. And if none here, and none there, what did Martin's soul feed on?

He saw Vetch approaching down the gravelled path under an umbrella. At the door he said, 'Telephone for you, sir. In your study.'

'Who is it?'

'A gentleman from the American Embassy. I think he said he was the Minister.'

The Field-Marshal put aside his gloves and walked up to the house, while Vetch held the umbrella over both of them.

The telephone was lying on its side on his desk. He picked it up. 'Field-Marshal Durham here.'

'Field-Marshal, I'm Mike McGowan, Minister at the United States Embassy here in London. I had the honour of meeting you at a City dinner last year.'

'I remember,' the Field-Marshal said; the voice was Irish-American, the man big and shrewd under a hearty mask of blarney. He probably ran the Embassy while the millionaire business men who occupied the ambassador's chair did what he told them to.

'I'll come to the point, sir. . . . Is this phone bugged?'

'Not at this end . . . as far as I know,' the Field-Marshal said.

'Now that the news is out that you're going to write your Memoirs it seems that some people would like to know what you're going to say. We've had enquiries from Washington about a certain incident that took place in April of 1944.'

The Field-Marshal let his mind run back. February – Cassino. March – still Cassino. April – begin a hard slugging advance through the mountains on the Adriatic side.

'To do with the 2nd Battalion of our 798th Infantry regiment.'

'I remember,' the Field-Marshal said.

44

'Washington is very anxious that nothing should be published to bring that incident back into the public's mind. There were rumours at the time, of course, but we were able to suppress all mention of the facts under operational security powers.'

'And again just after the war there was some talk, I think.'

'Yes, but it all died away, and until recently had been forgotten. Several newspapers published the story about your Memoirs, and that led to some renewed mention of the incident. You know, we have influential people – and not just Irish – who are only too happy to work up bitterness against the British.'

'Who wants to keep it quiet?'

'My word is from the State Department, sir, but they assure me it comes from the highest authority.... The talk's dying down and we're pretty sure it will soon be forgotten, this time for good ... unless someone in a position to know brings it forward again, especially yourself.'

The Field-Marshal said, 'Mr McGowan, in writing these Memoirs I've undertaken to tell the whole truth about my war. I think what happened to the 798th Infantry must come out, and I think it should.'

McGowan had the sense not to argue. He said, 'I was afraid you'd say that. I'll probably ask the ambassador to try to persuade you. We really do put a lot of weight on this ... when it's so important to maintain the goodwill of our people towards Britain. Thank you for listening to me, Field-Marshal. And congratulations on your recent birthday.'

'Thank you.' He hung up, and sat looking at the telephone a long time, drumming his fingers on the desk. His skin was getting blotched and brown in patches and his knuckles stood out like bare bones. Well, what could you expect?

The telephone rang. A woman's voice said, 'The Permanent Under-Secretary of the Ministry of Defence would like to speak to Field-Marshal Durham.'

'Speaking.'

He waited. A man came on the line. 'Whitmore here, Field-Marshal. How are you this morning?'

'Very well. What can I do for you?'

'Is this telephone bugged ... or are you making a recording of any sort?'

'I'm not. I wouldn't answer for your end, after the way we were treated here on the twenty-ninth.'

'That was a Cabinet decision, Field-Marshal. . . . I want to ask you whether you intend to say anything, in your Memoirs, about the affair of the Military Governor of Caltera.'

The Field-Marshal remembered that well. He was an Italian general called Giovanni Ballino. He said, 'I hadn't thought about it, but I imagine I shall relate what happened.'

'Which was?'

'Soon after my XIV Corps crossed the Straits of Messina we were approached by agents from this General Ballino and told that he would arrange to surrender all Italian troops in his military district – Caltera – if we got him a hundred thousand pounds in gold. We got it. It was handed to his emissary. Then the Italians didn't surrender. I've always supposed that the Germans got wind of the plan and forestalled it. Ballino disappeared for a long time. He was a prominent Fascist. I heard that he had appeared again some years back.'

'And you weren't interested?'

'No. It was a long time ago, even then.'

'Field-Marshal, you realise that there's no evidence that the gold was in fact handed over.'

The Field-Marshal looked at the telephone for a few seconds. He had heard a strange tone, a cutting edge, in Lord Whitmore's voice; he was not used to it.

He said politely, 'There is. There's a receipt signed by Ballino's emissary, in my papers. It was seized by the police, with other papers, in their raid here on May 29. Have you seen it?'

'No. Who was it made out to?'

'Me. I handed over the gold personally. I went to meet Ballino's emissary myself, with my A.D.C., Eden, as escort, and another subaltern from my headquarters, I can't remember his name, to drive the vehicle – it was a fifteen hundredweight. I had hoped Ballino himself would come.'

'I see. So both the witnesses were, ah, part of your official family.'

'Yes,' the Field-Marshal said gently. It was getting easier every moment to see where this conversation was leading.

'The Minister is having a difficult time in the House over the pay of high-ranking officers. The Opposition is hammering away at the difference in living standards between the private soldier who risks his life every moment, and the general who . . .'

'Dies in bed. I know the argument. Go on.'

'You have friends in the House, but you also have enemies.

It was known at the time at Army Headquarters, and Supreme Headquarters, Mediterranean, that the money had been authorized. When there was no surrender, you will understand that it was whispered . . .'

'That someone on our side pocketed it.'

'Yes. At any moment those whispers could start again . . . and become so loud that we would be forced to make an official enquiry. It might be hard for us to prove, from unbiassed witnesses, that the receipt was not a forgery.'

'I see.'

The voice at the other end reverted to its habitual smoothness. 'There is another matter. You may not be aware of it, but we have in the M.O.D. secret files, a 1945 complaint from Tomaso Parini that you shielded Fascist criminals from justice when you were in Ancona.'

'Parini, the man who's Foreign Minister of Italy now?'

'Yes. He was very young then, but he was Ancona's leading anti-Fascist.'

'I don't remember his name,' the Field-Marshal said. 'When we were forming 16th Army in and around Ancona, preparing for *Wolfpack*, bands of ragged-arse Italian guerrillas began to lynch people they didn't like, and loot houses and stores belonging to them. We couldn't launch an invasion out of a city in a state of semi-anarchy. I ordered the guerrillas disbanded, and anyone caught lynching or looting to be shot at sight. I believe military guards were provided for a few weeks to men whom the local authorities told my staff were in special danger.'

'Those were the Fascists.'

The Field-Marshal waited a long time. Then he said, 'You've brought this up, after having the files searched, in order to hint that you can get Parini to repeat his accusation. Then you could order another inquiry into my conduct.'

He waited another minute. The man at the other end neither confirmed nor denied the accusation.

The Field-Marshal said, 'What's your price?'

The answer was immediate this time. 'Her Majesty's Government have decided that it is in the best interests of this country that no further mention should be made of the alleged theft of the Zvornos Collection of art from Zvornos Castle in Yugoslavia. Nor should any information be given out, in writing or by word of mouth, about events having any relation to the alleged theft.'

The Field-Marshal looked out of the window. Still raining,

47

a gentle lovely summer rain. Good for the roses along the borders and on the north wall.

Into the telephone he said, 'A few minutes ago McGowan called me from the American Embassy, asking me to keep another matter quiet. Are you all working in conspiracy?'

'There's no conspiracy, but there's a great deal of concern. We all have our responsibilities, and sometimes they overlap. . . . What am I to tell the Minister?'

'Is your message from him?'

'From the Cabinet, Field-Marshal.'

'Tell them to look up what another British field-marshal answered to another blackmailer. His name was Wellington.' He hung up.

He got up, stretched and stood in the window, looking out over the vegetable garden and the rose garden, his hands in his pockets. *Publish and be damned*, had been the Iron Duke's words. These bloody politicians and their Civil Service staff were like spiders, weaving a web all over Whitehall; touch one part, the whole web shook, and out they came, sliding along their threads, all apparently independent but in reality all working together with unrehearsed skill ... because they all thought the same way about any problem. Now they were saying – keep quiet about Žvornos or we'll reopen enquiries into the missing hundred thousand pounds and the protecting of Fascists. But the gold wasn't missing: Ballino had it. A dishonest man but not a fool. When he'd found himself staring down the muzzles of a German panzer division, he'd done nothing. Not brought up in the Cheltenham and Sandhurst tradition. Who expected him to be? It had been worth trying, to save hundreds, perhaps thousands of his men's lives – not to mention Italians.

He tried to think back to the guerrilla business in Ancona. It was hazy. He'd had a great deal on his mind ... planning *Wolfpack* and seeing that the plans were converted into action, to a tight timetable: contingency planning for *Bushmaster* to follow *Wolfpack*: training of the Army: signal exercises to practise the newly formed 16th Army Headquarters staff and signals, about to be thrown into that most complicated operation of war, a combined assault landing on a hostile seacoast. Many of the guerrillas were Communists, too. He disliked Communists just as much as Fascists and Nazis. He may well have saved a few men who would otherwise have been strung

48

up like pigs in a butcher's shop, the way Mussolini and his mistress were. And he'd do it again.

He'd heard it whispered that Angelo Grimani had been a Fascist. Stefanie said No, but she was a loyal woman, in her way. He'd protected Angelo, in *his* way. It hadn't saved him for long.

Ballino, Ballino. He thumbed through the weighty London telephone books, found a number and dialled.

When a girl answered he said, 'This is Field-Marshal Durham. I would like to speak to the Ambassador, please.'

'Certainly, sir.'

The ambassador came on in a few moments. The Field-Marshal said, 'I won't waste your time, Your Excellency. I'd like to know the present address of General Giovanni Ballino, retired. He was Military Governor of Caltera in 1943. I believe he is now living in Rome.'

'I know the name, Field-Marshal,' the ambassador said in accented English. 'He is an old wartime comrade of yours . . . on the other side, perhaps?' He chuckled heartily.

'In a way,' the Field-Marshal said.

'It will be no problem. If you will give me your telephone number . . .'

As soon as he had replaced the receiver he picked it up again and dialled. 'Secretary to the Chancellor of the Duchy of Lancaster,' a man's educated voice answered.

He gave his name and said, 'I would like to speak to Sir Henry, please.'

When Bartlett came on, the Field-Marshal said, 'Henry, you're in the Cabinet. I've just been told by Whitmore that it's a Cabinet decision to keep official secrecy about everything to do with the missing Zvornos Collection. Is that true?'

'Well, it's not quite as definite, as clear cut as that, John.' The voice was a little distant, and cool. 'The matter was discussed, briefly. It was certainly agreed that it would be best if Zvornos was forgotten.'

'I'm not going to forget it,' the Field-Marshal said. 'Do you remember sending me a note to let a U.S. Army truck manned by Civil Affairs people through to rescue art treasures?'

'I don't recall sending you such a note.'

'I see,' the Field-Marshal said. That meant that the government were going to keep the note they had taken from his files and not allow any copy to be made.

'You don't recall the incident at all?'

'Barely. I don't want to. John, there are reasons why it would be much better for all of us if you didn't want to either. Believe me. Now, if you'll excuse me . . .'

The Field-Marshal hung up and sat resting, immobile, in his desk chair for a time. Henry had passed out first from Sandhurst . . . brilliant, brave, intelligent, well read, unorthodox – a snob, of course – but there had always been a doubt about him in many army minds: was he quite straight, true blue to the core? It might be jealousy. There might be a reason for the doubt, there might not. In sixty years, he himself had been unable to decide.

He rummaged in a drawer, examined the contents of an envelope and then dialled the Ministry of Defence and asked to speak to General Sir Sam Herrick, Chief of the General Staff.

'Sam? John Durham here.'

'Good morning, sir.'

'When the police raided us a fortnight ago . . .'

'We had nothing to do with that here, sir. Honestly. As soon as I heard about it I protested most strongly to the Minister, but he said he was sorry, it was a political matter.'

'They'll try to drag you in. . . . One of the documents they took was the receipt for a hundred thousand pounds in gold, signed by some Italian colonel as emissary and authorized representative of General Giovanni Ballino. They – the politicians – are going to try to keep it, for purposes of blackmail, so that they can make a case that I stole the money myself.'

'I can't believe it, sir.'

'You'd better. I presume you don't want a Field-Marshal to be accused of theft?'

'Good God, no, sir. It would be terribly bad for the army in every way.'

'Get that receipt back. Or a Xerox copy of it, before they "lose" it.'

'I'll see what I can do, sir.'

'You may have to go a long way, Sam.'

He hung up. Sam had had a battalion under him in 16th Army. He was the same age as Martin, but from British infantry where Martin had been Indian cavalry. A good man, but perhaps not very strong. And lucky to have only just got command of his battalion when it ran amok at Mitrovica, and so not been held to blame for it. That would have to come out in the Memoirs. He wondered how far Sam Herrick's principles would carry him in a vicious fight that was really someone else's, especially as his inclinations might be on the other side. He was Colonel of the North Wessex and wouldn't be at all happy to have Mitrovica splashed all over the headlines.

He thought back a moment to the details of the search. The M.I.5 man had only glanced at the pile of Stefanie's letters, and put them back. They weren't remotely connected with anything military, of course, and had nothing to do with the Memoirs, but it might be wise to keep them somewhere else . . . but to hell with M.I.5, he didn't want to be without the letters. He had been telling himself for nearly thirty years that the love affair had ended when he sailed for the Balkans – because that was the only way, it had seemed, that he could survive with his sanity. But it had never been true; it had not ended. Only one thing *could* end it.

It was still raining. He put on his trench coat and cap and walked to the garage. The Bentley sat there in its coat of British racing green. Starting her would soon be beyond him, but by seeing that the plugs were spotless, the gap correct and the timing perfect she usually fired on the first swing. He leaned over the driver's narrow bucket seat and adjusted the mixture and hand throttle controls, went back to the front and swung her twice; then switched on, and again swung the brass handle. She fired with a bang and a rumble. The four big cylinders grumbled lazily and he climbed carefully into the driver's seat. After a minute he pressed gently on the accelerator, let in the clutch, put her in gear, released the outside hand brake and rolled out onto the drive.

Once through the white painted gates he turned left and headed south-east, rows of small suburban houses on his right, Ashwood Common on his left. He loved this car. They'd been together how long now? . . . forty-three years. Each cylinder seemed to fire no more than once every hundred yards, yet he was doing a comfortable forty miles an hour. The high bonnet, leather strapped, swung round the narrow corners . . . the village green of Oakdene, the church with its Victorian spire. Peter Curran had lived here. His name was on the War Memorial on the little triangle of grass outside the church wall, together with four others from the Kaiser's War; and, below, three from this last Hitler's War. On, faster now, up the straight rise to Hawkford, the road pointing for two miles at the square Norman tower of Hawkford Church . . . past, and at once the nose dipping steeply, southward, down the winding grade of

Hawkford Hill. There was the wall, on the left. The damage had long been repaired and now, with the passing of the years, you couldn't even distinguish which were the new bricks. He swung the wheel at the last moment and made the sharp corner, the thin tyres screaming. A bit closer than he had meant, that time. But what *did* he mean? This wasn't the first time he had driven down this hill since coming back after the war, nor the fiftieth.

He turned left down a narrow lane, after a mile turned left again, and so slowly home, by narrow ways and fields not yet being developed, back to Ashwood House under the rain. In the garage he spent half an hour carefully washing and drying the Bentley and rubbing the paint with a chamois leather.

Harry Mullins of the *Journal* came at half past twelve, as invited. He was taller even than the Field-Marshal, a cockney with a bony lantern face, a long jaw and a wide mouth, a man of violent gestures and sharp amused eyes, usually laughing, sometimes suffused with rage.

'Long time since Vojja Lovac, Field-Marshal.'

'Too long. Sherry? Whisky?'

'I'm a newspaper man, Field-Marshal. I'd lose my reputation if I were seen drinking sherry. . . . Thanks. You know, we're very excited about publishing the Memoirs, especially now that you've let it out that they're going to be hot stuff. They'll give us a big boost in circulation and, between you and me, we can do with it.'

'I don't know that either Brigadier Ruttledge or myself is equipped to cut the Memoirs into the proper sort of pieces for serialisation.'

'Don't worry about that. We'll do it – and of course, show you what we've done, for your approval. . . . What I'd like to know now is, what's going to come out that has so far been swept under the rug. We don't want to go off at half-cock with our publicity long before the book's ready, but on the other hand, if we can get a whispering campaign started . . . Field-Marshal's going to say this . . . accuse so-and-so . . . reveal this piece of dirty work . . . then we can keep the pot boiling and clean up when we publish.'

The Field-Marshal put his glass down. 'I don't know yet. I'm beginning to organise my notes. As far as things that have been kept secret go, I suspect that more will come out – things I've forgotten perhaps – as people get nervous and beg me to keep quiet. One or two matters have already been raised. The shelling of the 2nd Battalion of the 798th U.S. Infantry near San Prospero in April, 1944.'

'I got a telex from our correspondent in New York mentioning that one of those columnists said he'd heard that Field-Marshal Durham was going to write his Memoirs, and wondered whether the Field-Marshal would own up to shelling American boys through a blunder. Is that the case?'

'Yes. But it wasn't a mistake.'

'*What?*'

'We did it on purpose. The British. My XIV Corps Artillery.'

'How many people were killed?'

'Six. Plus some wounded, none seriously. . . . Then there'll be the bribing of General Ballino. I gave him a lot of money to surrender and he didn't. Today a senior government official as good as told me I would be accused of stealing the money, and other crimes, if I didn't keep my mouth shut about the theft of the Zvornos Collection.'

'I've been reading something about that. What really happened?'

'I don't know, but I intend to find out, if I can. I authorised a truck to go in to rescue art treasures and come out again with them, because I was told to do so in a note from the Army Group Commander. . . .'

'That was Bartlett then! A Cabinet Minister now. Phew! This is tremendous!'

'Perhaps. But that note has been taken from my private files. I can prove, I think, that I did not steal the paintings – but who did, and how, I don't know. I am not a pauper but it would cost a fortune to dig up the truth of that affair, especially after so many years. I shall probably just have to publish what I know and leave it at that.'

'Anything else?'

'I was out taking the Bentley for a spin just now, and thinking. I always think clearly in the Bentley. . . . I owe it to the truth to tell what really happened about the dismissal of General Ross and the planning of Operation *Bushmaster*.'

'Oh. I see. A bit technical for the general reader, perhaps.'

'Perhaps. Perhaps not. There are very personal matters connected with it. Stephen and Hilda Ross were close friends of ours. It would always have been extremely painful for me to relieve Stephen Ross of command. At that moment, it was . . . agony. And afterwards, why didn't I do more to get him another job? His K, at least? I could have. And this is part of war, of being an army commander, yet a human being. Often it's not possible to be both at the same time.'

Yes, he thought to himself, I shall tell the truth about Stephen, and myself; but not Stefanie.

Mullins said, 'The government's really after you over these Memoirs, then?'

The Field-Marshal said, 'It's just a defensive attack, the kind you make at the beginning of a campaign. You remember the counter stroke Ritter von Heldenmark made just before Vojja Lovac, to try to throw my offensive out of stride? This is the same. If it works, it's fine. If it doesn't, it leaves you with fewer troops, and they're worn out before you fight the main battle.'

The telephone in the next room rang. The Field-Marshal listened for a few moments and then said, 'Excuse me,' and went through to answer it.

It was Charles Gibson, saying, 'I tried your study number, but. . . .'

'I'm downstairs, with Harry Mullins.'

'Oh. I'll be brief. There's an American who wants to meet you and I said I'd give him an introduction. I've known him for a couple of years – he was asking me some questions about an artist, a painter, who's been sent to jail for some sort of extortion racket. His name's Burrisk, and I really don't know anything else about him, except that he's given me several red hot tips on the gee-gees. Must have put a couple of hundred quid in my pocket, and . . .'

'What does he want to see me about?' the Field-Marshal interrupted. Charles talked too much.

'He's an admirer . . . seems to have studied your campaigns . . . perhaps he just wants your autograph. Or to be able to say he's shaken your hand. You know what Americans are. Give him a couple of minutes, for my sake.'

'All right,' the Field-Marshal said, none too cheerfully. 'When's he coming?'

'He'll write or call. Thanks. I'll give you ten per cent of what I make on his next tip.'

The Field-Marshal hung up, half smiling. Charles was irrepressible.

He returned to the drawing room and almost at once Vetch announced that lunch was served.

... *I am longing to read your Memoirs. Then I shall be able to imagine much more clearly what you were doing, what you were thinking, after you left. Those were sad days, for I had never been so happy and then suddenly it ended. I could not, before, have imagined that such happiness existed. The memory of it was all that kept any feeling alive in me. Otherwise I would have been numb and without sensation or emotion....*

CHAPTER FIVE

The intercom on Martin's desk buzzed gently and a disembodied female voice said, 'The Secretary would like to speak with you please, Brigadier.'

Martin pressed down a button and said, 'I'm on my way.' He released the button and got up. The Secretary's office was on the top floor of the old building, four floors above Queen Anne's Gate, and there was no lift from his own small cluttered quarters on the second floor. He ran up the stairs two at a time, as he had made his practice since noticing the incipient bulge at his waistline soon after he retired from the army, and that was twenty years ago. He paused a moment on the landing to steady his breathing and then went into the outer office. The Secretary's personal secretary smiled and nodded to the inner door – 'Go straight in, Brigadier.'

He straightened his tie – Frontier Force – and opened the door. Sir Victor Terrell was standing in the window looking down into St James's Park and did not turn round as Martin entered.

He said 'Come and look here, Martin. . . . See that old boy asleep on the grass there by the round flower bed? The other old boy, the respectable looking one beside him, has just gone through his pockets and now he's emptying his wallet. . . . But I saw them arrive together an hour or so ago, just after lunch. Ah well, you never know who your friends are till you've counted the spoons. . . . Sit down. I believe your daughter's coming up for sentencing today.'

'Yes, sir. At four o'clock in the Central Criminal Court – Mr Justice Wightman.'

'Good. Before you go, Sir Henry Bartlett wants to speak to you. Don't bother to come back here afterwards, even if it's over very quickly. . . . How are our government secrets being guarded, Martin?' He looked at him quizzically over his pince-nez, a diplomat of the old school in black coat and striped trousers, stiff collar and black tie.

'All right, I think, sir. I'm still not happy about the way we screen people for sensitive jobs. In effect we have to let doubtful cases in and then wait to catch them being careless, or passing inside rumours to their wives or girl friends. It wastes a lot of manpower.'

'I know. I'm thinking about it. But at that level, as you know, we have to proceed by the book, guarding everyone's rights as laid down in Magna Carta, the Bill of Rights, and a couple of dozen statutes. At the upper levels, where people are more important and hence more vulnerable, we don't have to go through all that rigmarole. We can act as we believe the security and efficacy of the government demands. In fact, we must. And we can use our very powerful and well established machinery to see that what we do, stays done. . . .' He pulled a half-hunter gold watch out of his waistcoat pocket and peered short-sightedly at it. 'We have a few minutes. . . . Martin, we want a wire recording your father-in-law made, secretly and without authorisation, at a conference with Sir Henry Bartlett and Mr Matthew Jordan, then the chief Civil Affairs adviser to 17th Army Group, on April 26, 1945, after the Battle of Vojja Lovac.'

Martin felt dizzy. The Secretary's tone of voice had not changed, but his look and manner had. He was holding the pince-nez in his hand now, thrusting them at Martin, and his classically handsome face was set, his eyes glinting.

'You are to get it, within the next week. I don't care how you do so. You will be protected against any charges arising out of what you have to do. *Any* charges. Do you understand?'

Martin could not speak for a long time. Then he pulled himself together and said, 'I understand, sir, but . . .'

'No buts. You'd better go to see Sir Henry now. I advise you to listen very carefully to what he has to say to you. Although the Prime Minister retains ultimate responsibility for all security decisions of national importance, he has delegated the study of such cases and the duty of advising him, to the Chancellor of the Duchy of Lancaster. In that field, I am the Chancellor's executive arm.'

'Yes, sir.'

The Secretary nodded in dismissal and Martin went out, the personal secretary smiling at him again. He went slowly down to his office, picked up his umbrella, brief case and bowler hat and left the building, signing out in the entrance hall. The offices of the Duchy were some distance away and he walked briskly along, but only vaguely aware of the hurrying fleets of taxis, the shadows passing across the afternoon sun, the rumbling passage of the big red buses. . . . The Secretary had warned him, in no veiled terms, to do what Sir Henry Bartlett told him. And ordered him to steal the Old Man's wire recording. What on earth could be on it, to cause such strong reactions, so many years later? He'd ask the Old Man when he was telling him what he had been ordered to do . . . but should he tell? If he didn't obey his orders, he would be dismissed. Perhaps the Old Man was in the wrong. No one could be right all the time. The Memoirs were going to cause a lot of trouble, awkwardness, embarrassment, and worse, for a lot of people . . . including himself. No time now to decide what he ought to do. He was at the offices of the Duchy. . . .

Sir Henry Bartlett was waiting for him in almost exactly the same pose as the Secretary had been – standing in the tall window, looking down, this time into the bustle of a busy street loud below, for the windows were open. Turning now against the light the Napoleonic resemblance was obvious, heightened by the pose he had adopted.

'Sit down, Martin,' he said, staying where he was. Psychology, Martin thought. It have to peer at him against the light, my eyes screwed up, while he can see every twitch of muscle in my face.

'I've asked you to come here, Martin, to emphasise the importance of seeing to it that the Zvornos Collection affair is not brought to public notice. I've tried a couple of times to tell John this – warn him off without being too explicit, if you know what I mean . . . but John was never a man to take the oblique course, and he has not understood, or has chosen not to. You follow me?'

'Yes, sir,' Martin said. Now perhaps the information would not be quite so oblique and by innuendo.

'John has said that I wrote him a letter authorising this truck to go to Zvornos. I may indeed have – it is a long time ago and I had a major campaign, reaching a point of crisis, on my hands – but as I have said, I do not recall doing so. So who did write the note now in our possession, on which my signature may have been forged?'

Martin, taken aback, considered that for a moment. He himself had never seen the note, or been told of its contents. There were witnesses, the Old Man had said; but where were they? How on earth could they be found and made to testify? Was the Old Man, well, not lying, but imagining things? He was, after all, rather old. . . .

'Difficult, isn't it?' Bartlett said pleasantly, 'and it would get a great deal more so as you proceeded. There are two reasons why we – the government – don't want the matter raised, which could lead to demands for a full investigation. The first is to do with our present negotiations to allow British companies to share in exploiting the oil discoveries on the North Slope of Alaska. Do you know who is the controlling figure on that issue, in America? Senator Matt Jordan, chairman of the Senate Energy Committee.'

'The same man who was your Civil Affairs adviser in the Balkans, sir?'

'The same. A very capable man and one I call a friend, but sometimes thought to be somewhat less than scrupulous. A man who rose from humble beginnings, got to Yale on full scholarship, and was chosen for the Civil Affairs job before he was thirty-five. Then, after the war, the Senate, though I and others expected him to aim for the Presidency. A man who started poor ... was a millionaire by 1950 ... a multi-millionaire by 1960.'

Martin waited.

'Suppose it were to come out that Matt Jordan had asked me, verbally and in private, to see that a truck he would personally vouch for was allowed to rescue Yugoslav national treasures out of Zvornos?'

'That would be – interesting,' Martin said, feeling the inadequacy of the response even as he made it.

'Not for Jordan,' the Chancellor said. 'For him it would, or could, be highly embarrassing. He has many enemies. He would have to start explaining. He might have a good explanation, he might not.'

'Did he give you any explanation or reason, sir?'

'I didn't say he ever asked me anything, did I, Martin? I said *suppose* it were to come out that, et cetera. We must all be very careful not to jump to conclusions in this matter, and that is precisely what we fear ... that the public, British and American, will do, if John publishes what he knows, which is only a small part of the whole.'

'Does anyone know the whole truth, sir?'

Bartlett looked at him, weighing him, and then said, 'I believe not. The problem is that *trying* to find out would cause as much trouble as finding – however bad the final truth might seem to be. ... Jordan's request might have been motivated by agents of Count Zvornos – or agents of the Committee of Three.'

Panaz, Mallac and Sovik, Martin thought; the Terrible Trio of the tabloids, the Communist committee which ruled Yugoslavia. Panaz was young and dynamic and thought to be the strong man of the trio; Mallac was quiet, rumoured to be an infighter, always aware of where the strength lay; and Sovik was an old revolutionary, leader of the guerrillas during the war, member of the first Committee of Three formed in 1943.

'Sovik is still in power,' Sir Henry said, emphasising the word *still*.

'You mean . . . you suggest that Mr Jordan might have been acting for Sovik? And if that came out, Sovik would have to explain what happened to the Collection?'

'That, too, is possible. And Sovik is the best friend Great Britain and the U.S.A. possess in the Communist world . . . I want you to persuade John to think again, Martin. He is a determined man, we know, but he is not stupidly obstinate. And he is patriotic. Put it this way to him. . . . Suppose, first, that Matt Jordan indirectly stole the Zvornos Collection for his own benefit, and in consequence made, say, five million dollars. This country stands to make a thousand million, ten thousand million dollars, over the years, out of Alaskan oil . . . if we are allowed to participate. This is not to mention the employment generated, the extra power we will wield, the independence we will have from Arab oil sources, and many other less material advantages. Is it worthwhile taking the slightest risk of antagonising the man who can get that oil for us? Is it patriotic? . . . Suppose next that Sovik is the one who got the five million dollars. We are at present negotiating with Yugoslavia a trade deal which will be worth forty-seven million pounds to us in the next two years. Panaz and Mallac are thought to be against it – they want to make the deal inside the Communist bloc. Sovik is working for us, and stands a very good chance of succeeding – as long as he retains his power and reputation. And even if there were no such trade agreement in the works, the value of having a man in Sovik's position as a friend literally has no cash value . . . it's invaluable. If it were suspected, let alone proven, that Sovik was responsible, and perhaps has millions in a Swiss bank account, he would be lucky to escape with his life. . . .

'Her Majesty's Government have to deal with the present and the future, Martin, not the past. We have more important matters on our minds than punishing petty crimes committed twenty-eight years ago. I say petty because no one's life was

60

or is involved, except perhaps Sovik's. Some Yank, some Yugo-slav *may* have got away with some money that didn't belong to him. The Americans would say – so what? I believe you can persuade John. . . . See you at the Hawkford fete next Satur-day, perhaps?'

'I hope so, sir.'

His father-in-law was already in court when he arrived and sat next to him. A few reporters muttered to each other in the front of the court, a few of the men and women who spend their days in courtrooms half-filled the little room.

The Field-Marshal whispered, 'Lois couldn't come at the last minute. Some emergency that she might have been sued over if she hadn't fixed it.'

Martin grunted. Whatever the emergency she ought to have come, with her daughter facing the most terrifying moment of her life. Why couldn't she train some of those other women to deal with emergencies, instead of having to be there herself all the time?'

Two policemen brought in Caroline, and a moment later the Clerk of the Court intoned, 'Rise!'

The judge was thin and sad-looking, his scarlet robe brilliant in the lights. Old Mr Forsythe was sitting below Caroline. Caroline stood very straight, wearing blue jeans and a tie-dyed blue shirt, with a string of her favourite beads. Her hair was neatly braided.

The judge said, 'Your name is Caroline Ruttledge?'

She said 'Yes,' obviously meaning to say it boldly, her head thrown up, but her voice broke and she squeaked it; then re-peated it in a loud voice, 'Yes!'

'And you are – how old?'

'Twenty-one.'

'When was your twenty-first birthday?'

'February 28 this year.'

'I see. . . . A few days ago you pleaded guilty in this Court to a charge of possessing firearms contrary to Section (1)(a) of the Firearms Act 1968. A little later a jury found you guilty of a charge of handling stolen goods contrary to Section 22 (1) of the Theft Act 1968. I explained to you and to the members of the jury that the essence of that later crime is awareness that the goods had been stolen. You could so easily have told us how, in your opinion, the goods came to be in that suitcase, and how the suitcase came to be in your possession, but you refused, and by so doing refused to help the police solve a serious crime against a helpless old woman. The jury had no option but to convict and . . .'

'I know all that,' Caroline said and shut her mouth.

The judge said reprovingly, 'As I told you during the trial, it is customary – and no more than good manners – to address me as "my lord" in this Court.'

Caroline stayed defiantly silent. The judge said, 'Your counsel produced evidence of your good character at the trial, and made an eloquent plea in mitigation of sentence. If you had been half as eloquent in telling us what you know, I could treat you more leniently now. . . . The police report that you were not cooperative in helping them to identify the other members of this anarchistic group you belong to, or, as I said, in helping them solve the robbery which produced the stolen goods. . . . You are the grand-daughter of Field-Marshal Durham?'

'I don't see what that's got to do with it . . . my lord,' she said, but not quite so defiantly.

'I had the honour of serving under him in the Balkans,' the judge said. 'A lot of us, led by men like him, made it possible for people in this country to continue to live by their own customs and institutions. To vote people in and out of office instead of shooting them, or having them appointed by foreign dictators. I would not have liked my grandfather to feel ashamed of me, especially if he were Sir John Durham. . . . You are young and thoughtless, but I believe your heart is in the right place. You have to learn to use it in conjunction with your head and the eyes and commonsense God gave you. We have ways to change society – though everyone will not necessarily agree on what changes should be made. Those ways do not include allowing minorities to blast us into submission. Become a majority and you will not have to use violent means to achieve your aims. . . .

'You have been found guilty of committing a very serious crime and I am of the opinion that there is no other appropriate way of dealing with it than imposing a sentence of imprisonment. Accordingly, on the first charge, of possessing firearms, I sentence you to pay a fine of one hundred pounds. On the second charge, of handling stolen goods, I sentence you to two years' imprisonment, the sentence to be suspended for two years. . . . Now, listen carefully while I explain to you what this means. It means that if within this two-year period, starting from today, you commit an offence for which, on conviction, you could be punished with imprisonment, then the sentence I have just given you can be put into effect, either wholly, or in part, in addition to whatever other sentence you might be given for the new offence. . . . Is your father or mother present in court?'

'I don't know.'

Martin stood up. 'I am her father, m'lord. Brigadier Rutt-ledge.'

The judge peered down at him from the high dais under the carved coat of arms. 'Is that the Field-Marshal beside you?'

'Yes, my lord.'

'I am honoured that you should visit my court, sir. Brigadier, I am empowered to make a supervisory order, which would place your daughter under the supervision of a probation officer. But I would prefer not to issue such an order, rather to ask you to exercise the sort of supervision intended . . . which means, obviously, do your best to guide her so that she does not get herself into trouble again, nor do anything that might cause the suspended sentence to be put into effect.'

The Field-Marshal rose slowly to his feet, standing tall, the head stooped and eagle-like, the thick white hair and bushy eyebrows shining in the electric light.

'I would like to do that, my lord,' he said. 'It is sometimes better in a case like this that the supervisor – and counsellor – should not be as close as a mother or father.'

'I agree. Thank you, sir. . . . Now, Caroline, realise that a two-year sentence hangs over you. Listen to your grandfather because I have given him authority . . . because he is your grandfather . . . because he's a very wise man . . . and because he obviously loves you. . . Next case.'

The policeman standing behind Caroline in the dock stood aside, and when she did not move gave her a pat on the shoulder and a gentle shove towards Martin, who was going forward to meet her. Together the three of them left the court, after a brief bow in the doorway to the judge, now as remote from them as though they had become invisible.

A quarter of an hour later they were sitting in a 1st class compartment rocking round the Vauxhall curves. Caroline stared out of the window, saying nothing, but Martin saw that the corners of her eyes were damp. The Field-Marshal read the evening paper until, as they were leaving Surbiton, he folded it away, leaned forward and said, 'Are you going back to the university?'

63

She shook her head wordlessly, still looking out of the window.

'You don't want to?'

'No. Anyway they've kicked me out.'

The Field-Marshal said, 'Would you like to help me with my Memoirs?'

She turned then, fumbling for a handkerchief in her jeans, finding it, blowing her nose vigorously, wiping her eyes.

'What can I do?' she said at last.

'Plenty, I'm sure. There's more to this than meets the eye, you know. Your father can only help me after work, and he needs spare time to himself for his golf and fishing. I need a secretary – well, call it collaborator. Not much money in it, I'm afraid.'

'If you think I can . . .'

'Of course you can. You're hired. Fifteen pounds a week to begin with, and all found. You'll have to live at home.'

She nodded, without speaking, but her tears had dried up.

At the house Lois met them at the door. 'What happened?'

'He gave me a suspended sentence,' Caroline said briefly. 'If they can pin anything else on me in the next two years, I go to jail.'

'It was a very light sentence, considering how unco-operative you've been,' Martin said with vexation.

'And you think I'm guilty of handling stolen goods, like the jury?' Caroline said belligerently.

Martin said, 'I think you might tell *us*, at least, the truth about who gave you the suitcase, and why.'

'She will,' the Field-Marshal said. 'Leave her alone now.' He looked towards a large black American car parked on the gravel near the garage and asked, 'Who's here?'

Lois said, 'Oh, I forgot. It's a man called Burrisk. He called almost immediately after you left the house. Said Charles Gibson had spoken to you about him and could he come down. I knew you had nothing on, so I said yes. He's been here about half an hour . . . more. His chauffeur's in the kitchen with Vetch.'

The Field-Marshal said, 'I remember. Charles did speak about him. Some American who gives Charles good racing tips and wants to shake my hand. I suppose I'd better get it over with. When I say I have to change, you take over and politely get rid of him as soon as you can.'

Caroline ran upstairs, Lois turned back into the kitchen. She

64

ought to be following Caroline, Martin thought, looking angrily after her. The girl needed talking to, ticking off, encouraging ... well, something, but Lois was going back to her bloody buns. He followed the Old Man into the drawing room.

The Field-Marshal went forward briskly, 'Mr Burrisk? I'm Field-Marshal Durham.'

The man rising from the sofa was just under six feet, built like a boxer, complete with a broken nose, an appearance that didn't match the carefully manicured hands, the scent of a heavy application of eau-de-cologne, the bright blue suit and white-on-white shirt, with white patterned tie. His hair was thick and dark, his skin a smooth even brown, like a woman's face when she has applied too much powder base. Sunlamp tan, Martin thought; and he was wearing dark glasses though the sun was low and the light in the room not strong.

'Peter Burrisk,' he said, shaking hands. 'Your daughter was good enough to give me a drink, Marshal. This is a good Scotch, a straight malt, I guess.'

'It is,' the Field-Marshal said. 'Laphroaig. You are a connoisseur?'

'No. Just in the business ... among others.' He turned his head toward Martin in an oddly aggressive gesture and Martin said, 'I'm Martin Ruttledge, the Field-Marshal's son-in-law.'

'Martin!' The hand thrust into his own felt like a dead squid, boneless and cold.

The Field-Marshal said, 'Sit down ... Martin, pour me a short whisky and soda, please. Now, Mr Burrisk ...'

'I've come down here to tell you I think you're a great man, Marshal, yes, a great man. And to have the honour of shaking you by the hand.'

'That's very kind of you.'

'And to offer my help. Charlie Gibson – great painter, that guy – told me you were writing a book about the war. It's been in the papers, too. Is that right?'

'It is.'

'I'd like to help. I wasn't in the war – I was one of the guys who had to stay back home and keep the factory chimneys smoking – although, hell, I was only twenty-one when it ended, but I've read everything I could lay my hands on about it, especially the Italian campaign, and the Balkans. . . . The way you fooled the Krauts when you broke out from the beachhead, making them think you disagreed with General Ross and then doing just what he advised – that was terrific! And Vojja Lovac ...

round about the fourth, fifth day you must have been ready to climb the walls, but you stuck to your plan – and won!'

Martin listened in astonishment as the man kept on, quoting little incidents of the campaigns, mentioning battles long forgotten except by the participants, now barely even footnotes to history. And he had obviously read Martin's own book.

The Field-Marshal said, 'You have certainly studied the campaigns extensively, Mr Burrisk, but I don't see how . . .'

'Two ways,' Burrisk said decisively, 'First, investigation. You'll need to trace people, documents. I can help.' He found his wallet, opened it, riffled through a mass of plastic-covered cards, and handed the Field-Marshal one.

'I'm European manager of International Investigations and Information, Incorporated – we call it the Four Is Corp for short. Four Eyes, get it? Investigations made and information gathered, anywhere, on any subject. We have quite a staff over here and we call in local guys when we need to.'

'We will need that sort of service,' the Field-Marshal said slowly, 'But I'm sure we wouldn't be able to pay your bills.'

Burrisk waved a beringed hand. 'It'll be on the house, Marshal – a way of paying you for what you did to save democracy.'

The Field-Marshal said, 'That's very kind of you, but . . .'

Burrisk interrupted again, 'Marshal, believe me, I have fifteen guys in London alone, and right now most of them are sitting on their butts, doing nothing. I have to pay their wages anyway. Let me put 'em to work for you. Of course, if it looks like we're going to run into some real big expense, I'll get your O.K. first, but the rest – a birthday present from Four Eyes. Item two – I can find you an American agent, who'll get better terms for you for publication of your book over there than you'd get any other way.'

Ah, Martin thought, now we're coming to the milk in the coconut. The Field-Marshal threw him a questioning look.

Martin said, 'The present understanding is that the Mermaid Press will handle the American publication for us. I think we'd better leave it at that, sir. We don't want to upset Crookenden. As to the investigation . . .'

He stopped. He had been ordered to see that no investigations were made. He felt his job going, saw Sir Victor Terrell's cold gaze: he finished his sentence, 'I don't see how we can accept Mr Burrisk's offer . . .'

The Field-Marshal said briskly, 'I don't agree. It's come like manna from heaven. I accept, on the terms just described. . . . As a first objective, I want to find out what happened to the paintings taken from Zvornos Castle in Yugoslavia on February 16, 1945. They were removed by a U.S. Army truck with a driver in U.S. uniform and two men wearing Civil Affairs armbands. The original order to permit the truck to go to Zvornos and take the paintings was given to me by General Sir Henry Bartlett, then commanding 17th Group. . . .'

Martin thought recklessly, might as well be hanged for a sheep as a lamb. He'd been an idiot to imagine he could deflect the Old Man from his purpose.

He said, 'Sir, today Sir Henry said he couldn't recall writing that note to you. He hinted that it's a forgery. He also hinted that Matt Jordan asked him, verbally, to see that the truck got through.'

Burrisk whistled, 'The senator from Florida?'

The Field-Marshal said, 'Henry didn't actually say that, he just hinted it?'

'Yes, sir.'

'H'm. At all events, the truck went forward and took the paintings. On its way back it was stopped by a standing patrol commanded by Lieutenant Greville of the 28th Hussars. I ordered Greville, by radio, to let the truck pass.'

'He's a banker now,' Martin said, 'At the head office of the Westminster.' Burrisk had a diary out and was scrawling notes with almost painful slowness: a man not over-familiar with the written word, Martin thought.

Martin said, 'Sir Henry also said that the mover behind Jordan's request might have been either Count Zvornos, who would presumably know where the paintings were hidden – they must have been hidden somewhere or the Germans would have got them long since . . . or Sovik.'

Burrisk whistled again. 'The Commie boss over there? This sure as hell is *not* going to be easy. We'll have to check out the Count, of course. Wherever he is, if he's alive, I guess he won't be in Yugoslavia. Those Commies don't like counts. And we'll have to find out something about Sovik. It'll take time, but we have a lot of friends, Marshal, whose business it is to keep their ears open. Between them all, what they don't know, or can't find out, ain't hardly worth knowing. Especially if it involves money. . . . Did you tell me how much these paintings were worth, Marshal?'

The Old Man shrugged, saying, 'I have no idea. I know nothing about art.'

Martin said, 'Sir Henry mentioned five million dollars, but in an article in one of the papers I saw that the Yugoslav government claim they were worth eight million when they vanished, about double that by now.'

'Sixteen million bucks!' Burrisk said, his voice low and full of a kind of ritual force, like a man reciting a sacred prayer. The lines round his mouth hardened and the broken-nose fighter in him became visibly dominant. 'Now that's real money. We sure as hell don't need any contribution from you to help us locate that kind of lettuce, Marshal. We'd *pay* you to let us help.'

'But where would you get your recompense?' the Field-Marshal asked.

'Anyone who can locate where that sort of money is hiding, can get a piece of it,' Burrisk said. 'A big piece. It's a matter of finding the angles.'

He got up, looked again into his wallet and produced two more cards, handing one each to Martin and the Field-Marshal. Martin read his name and the address – 43 Cadwallader Street, London W.2, and a telephone number.

'That's where I live,' Burrisk said, 'and that's my private number. Unlisted. Call me any time, about anything.'

Martin escorted him to the front door. At once the huge Cadillac limousine glided up. After a handshake Burrisk got in and was driven away.

Martin returned thoughtfully to the drawing room, to find his father-in-law pouring himself another whisky.

'What do you make of him?' he asked, without turning.

Martin said, 'A little fishy. I think we should watch our step with him.'

'Oh, I don't know,' the Old Man said. 'What can he hope to get out of us? Besides, judging by the size of his car, and the diamond ring and gold cufflinks and jewelled tie clip, he doesn't need money.'

'A sort of entrepreneur, I suppose,' Martin said. 'Investigations and whisky and literary agencies don't normally go together.'

The Field-Marshal said, 'We've asked him to get some information for us and either he does or he doesn't.' He glanced at the clock. 'We have time for a chat before dinner. Ask Caroline to come down.'

'Caroline?'

'I said she would be my secretary, so she has to be in on everything from now on.'

Martin went slowly upstairs. He had approved of the Old Man's asking Caroline to help him; it would give her something to do and, more important, it showed confidence in her. But he had somehow never thought that she, his own daughter, would be made privy to all the confidential and personal matters which were going to come out. But why had he not foreseen this? The Old Man's purpose from the beginning – egged on by Charles Gibson, perhaps – had been to bring the hidden to light. It would be idiotic to expect that his own children would somehow not know what everyone else in the world was going to know.

He knocked on her door and told her her grandfather wanted to speak to her – to both of them – about the book.

She called, 'I'll be down in a sec, Daddy.'

He returned downstairs and soon she came in, smelling of soap, hair unbraided and brushed, her face clean, her eyes a little red.

The Old Man said, 'Sit down, Caroline. You don't like whisky, do you?'

She made a face and he said, 'There's a bottle of Australian red wine in the cupboard there. Help yourself. Now, Martin, tell us what happened earlier today. You've told us what Henry Bartlett said. Anything else?'

Martin tried to think quickly. Should he tell them about Terrell's order? Caroline was glancing at him over her shoulder, wine bottle in hand. The Old Man's hooded eyes were on him. Years of trained obedience to orders fought in him with a gathering resentment at what was now being done to him, and to the Old Man, by the hierarchy he served.

He made up his mind. 'Sir Victor Terrell ordered me to get the wire recording you told me about.'

'And if you can't . . . or don't?'

'He didn't say, but he sounded threatening.'

'Did Henry give you any orders, too?'

'Not directly. He just repeated that he was sure I could persuade you not to mention certain things.'

'They're blackmailing you,' Caroline broke in indignantly. 'They're saying that if Grandpa doesn't do what they want him to do, they'll sack *you*. Because they can't get at Grandpa!'

'That's what it looks like,' the Old Man said with a slight and vaguely happy smile. 'We do seem to be stirring up the pond. . . . You said that Henry asked what would it matter now if Senator Jordan or Sovik had got away with five million dollars. Did he ask, what if *I* did – meaning himself?'

'No.'

'But clearly he meant you to include that possibility in the other questions. . . . They *are* trying to get at me directly as well as through you. They could use the wire recording, for instance, both defensively and offensively.'

'Where is it, sir?' Martin asked. The Old Man glanced at him and Martin thought he detected a cold glint in the look. 'It ought to be in safe hands,' he finished hurriedly.

'It is,' the Old Man said; then, after a pause, 'We'll continue as planned. Caroline, do you see that row of thick red books up there?'

'*The Official History of the War?*'

'Yes. Read the volumes on Italy up to the end of 1944, and the 1945 Balkan Campaign.'

'All that?' she said, her eyes wide.

'Yes. You can't understand the side lights, or read between the lines of what we're doing until you know the main facts – have read the lines themselves, in other words. Don't try to absorb too much – just keep at it, a little every day without fail. Tomorrow morning I'll make out a chart for you so that you know what a battalion, brigade, division and so on, mean in terms of men and material. . . . We'd better get ready for dinner.'

The girl took down one of the volumes and said, 'I'll start tonight. I never thought I'd be reading military history in bed.'

When she had gone the Field-Marshal said, 'Clive didn't come to the court.'

'I suppose something cropped up . . . an inspection, or something.'

'A pity, when he'd said he would,' the Old Man said. 'I suppose he couldn't see himself, a Guards officer, watching his sister sentenced to jail.'

Martin went to his bedroom and undressed for his bath. Looking at himself in the mirror he thought, that's me, seen by me . . . but I must learn to look at myself as seen by others, such as Caroline. What did Clive and Caroline really think of him? Did they admire him as a person, as a father, as a soldier? Perhaps they didn't admire him at all. Their opinion would be further lowered if they knew the truth about Dick Armstrong and Appreciation R3, for instance. Or ... God, could *that* too come out? Surely not. That was private if anything was. But the Old Man had said flatly that nothing was private or personal when it came to analysing the actions men took. He seemed to see a black hole in his forehead and turned slowly, as though to face the executioner; but it was only a trick of shadow on the door.

CHAPTER SIX

Lois Ruttledge stood in the front window, looking over the feathery tree tops at the river below. Blackfriars Bridge cut diagonally across her line of vision close to the left. Up river, to the right, the flat, pale arches of Waterloo Bridge disappeared into the glass and concrete towers of the south bank.

'Why don't you take up your painting again?' Charles asked, at her elbow.

She hunched quickly, shrugging away the thought. 'I'm not good enough. I hate amateurs.'

'You wouldn't be an amateur if you worked at it. You have talent – more than talent, I think. But you have been stifling it, burying it . . . and other talents of yours, I don't doubt – since you married Martin.'

'I don't want to talk about it. . . . What are you working on now?'

'A couple of portraits, of fat merchants as usual. And more abstractions. Come and look.'

He led her to the other end of the long room, which ran through from front to back of the building. At that end, big skylights faced the northern sky, now heavy with summer clouds, slate-coloured from their burdens of rain.

She stood looking at the portrait on the easel. Incredibly good in the facile style which her generation had been taught to despise, she thought. Charles was bringing out some large canvases which had been stacked against the side wall.

'They made me an R.A. for my portraits,' he said, 'but one day they'll elect me P.R.A. for these.'

She looked at them, wondering. There was no facility here, and the line, which seemed to flow unimpeded from the brush to the canvas in his portraits, was here halting and indecisive. The colours were not as strong as they probably should have been, and the composition ineffective. Altogether, not remarkable . . . yet these meant something to him, the portraits nothing. Here, he was saying to himself and the world, is my immortality.

He was watching her closely. 'Very interesting, Charles,' she mumbled.

'You don't like them,' he said and quickly carried them back to where they had been.

He returned, 'But you will, one day.' He rested a hand lightly on her shoulder. 'Come and see me again. Not just for a sherry.'

She stood undecided. There was an awful lot going on with the catering. Her father didn't think she should have allowed anything to prevent her going to court when Caroline was sentenced.

'All right,' she said.

'Tuesday next week?'

That day was impossible, she thought. There was a job she really couldn't leave to her helpers. 'It'll have to be Wednesday,' she said.

'All right. About twelve. . . . By the way, who's this man Burrisk you gave an introduction to Daddy to?'

'Burrisk? Burrisk? Oh, the Yank who gives me racing tips. I don't know anything about him. He came here twice and we've had a couple of meals together. At the Savoy, and at his expense, of course, in both cases. Why do you ask?'

'He came down the other day. Martin's suspicious of him, but Daddy doesn't seem to be.'

'That's a failing of the very strong. The man might well be as crooked as a corkscrew. But if he sells you the Brooklyn Bridge, don't blame me.'

The taxi deposited her outside the back entrance to St James's Palace at half past twelve and she found her way up the narrow stairs to the dining room without difficulty, for she had been here several times before. Lunching at St James's when Clive was on public duties at first had been a thrill to her, and was now a pleasure, for the palace staff and Guards servants did one very well.

Clive came forward, pecked her on the cheek, and introduced her to the major and ensign of the guard. A servant brought her a glass of sherry. Her son looked good in his blue jumper with the high collar. He was the same height as his grandfather but because his neck was not stooped nor his shoulders bowed he looked taller, and he was burly and bull-like where the Old Man was lean and hawk-like. Now he drew her into a window, a little apart from the other two officers, and said in a low voice, 'I couldn't get to the court last week . . . busy up to my eyes, y'know.'

'It doesn't matter,' she said.

'Caroline was lucky to get off so lightly, eh?'

'I suppose so. . . . You'll never guess what she's doing now – reading *The Official History of the War*.'

'Good God! What on earth for?'

'Grandpa's given her a job as his secretary, to help him and Daddy prepare the Memoirs.'

'She'll know a lot more military history than I do at that rate. Always found it a terrible bore, myself. Damned if I can see how that bow and arrow stuff's going to be any use when the Russkies start throwing atomic shells at us.'

He led her out of the window towards the others who turned, smiling, to face her. They began to talk about horse racing.

The house was empty when she reached home soon after half past four, a pair of parcels weighing her down. The garage doors were open and the Bentley out. She called, 'Caroline!', but there was no answer. He must have taken her out with him. They were becoming thick as thieves, those two. Well, it would do him good to have a young person to talk to, and absorb the young's point of view . . . not that Caroline could be called typical – shooting people. Or could she?

The telephone rang. It was Harry Mullins. He said, 'I've tried the Field-Marshal's phone, Mrs Ruttledge, but he doesn't answer.'

'He's out. Can I take a message?'

There was a pause as though for thought and then the cockney voice said, 'Why not? Do you have a pencil and paper? . . . We've had an anonymous letter. Unsigned. Hand-written. I'll read it to you.

'*Dear sir* – it was addressed to the Editor of the *Sunday Journal*, by the way – *Dear sir I read in the papers that Field-Marshal Durham is going to write his memoirs and tell the truth about everything, because too many things have been concealed for too long. You should ask him about the court martial of Captain David Powell in 1942. Let him tell everyone what he was promised by who for that . . .*

'That's all. We're not going to publish it, of course. . . . I thought the Field-Marshal ought to know about it, in case.'

'In case this person tries to blackmail him, do you mean?'

'In case, anything. I just think he ought to know we've had such a letter.'

'Thank you. I'll tell him.'

She hung the telephone back on its wall bracket in the kitchen and went to the drawing room. Charles, next Wednesday. She'd wear a plain cotton dress, the white one with the small flower pattern, and the white shoes. They'd get rather dirty in the train ... she might drive up. It was getting impossible to park in London and it cost the earth when you did find a garage.

The Bentley burbled past the window and, glancing out, she was astonished to see Caroline in the driver's seat. She herself had never been allowed to drive that green monster. Too hard for a woman, Daddy had said. And now Caroline was perched up there ... turning the wheel, with visible effort, to get the car into the garage ... it was going to be close. She shut her eyes. ... The Bentley had disappeared inside, apparently without a mishap. The Old Man would have had the girl hung, drawn, and quartered if she'd scratched the paint.

They came in and her father said, 'Have a good time in London? ... We've been out for a spin.'

'It might have rained and you'd both have got soaked,' she said reprovingly.

'I like rain,' he said, 'and Caroline doesn't seem to mind. She's certainly not wearing a dress that might get spoiled.'

Caroline giggled, looking down at her patched blue jeans.

The Old Man said, 'She was wearing that damned skirt that looks like a ragwoman's, scraping the ground, and I said if she wanted to drive the Bentley she'd got to get into a short skirt or trousers and reasonable shoes, not those clodhoppers.'

Lois said, 'Mr Mullins rang up. About an anonymous letter they'd had.'

She handed her father her note. The Old Man found his glasses, put them on and read. When he had finished he put the note in his pocket and said, 'I have been wondering about her.'

'Her? Do you know who it is?'

'I think so. After dinner I'll tell you. Meantime, Caroline, while we were out I made up my mind to contact the Yugoslav Government about the Zvornos Collection. Will you draft a letter to their ambassador here telling him what we know about the disappearance of the collection from Zvornos Castle. You've seen my notes in the file?'

'Yes. But I can't quote exactly the letter from Sir Henry Bartlett, can I?'

'No, but you can tell them what I remembered, and wrote

down. Tell the ambassador we will do all we can to learn the truth of the matter. Don't mention Burrisk.'

'Am I to say that Sir Henry hinted to Daddy that Sovik was the man who originally asked for the authorisation?'

The Field-Marshal thought a while, then said, 'No. We can keep that for later. Ask them to give us any information they have, either from that period or later. It would be interesting to know where and when, exactly, they think that some pictures from the Collection have already been sold.'

'All right. I'll do it now, and show you the letter before dinner.'

'Good girl.'

They sat in the drawing room, in a rough circle. The Old Man had his usual deep seat at the right corner of the fireplace. Lois had noticed that it was becoming more difficult for him to get up out of that seat, but he liked it. Two or three nights a week he wasn't down here with them at all, but sitting in the corner of his study upstairs, in winter by an electric fire, thinking, what thoughts? He had a glass of port in his hand now – the old ruby he had always preferred. People didn't drink much port these days, but they'd drunk it when he joined his regiment in 1913, and he still did.

The Old Man said, 'I think her name is Madeleine Phillips, but it was Madeleine Powell. You know, in January 1942 I was appointed DMT at the War Office, and . . .'

Caroline said, 'You'll have to translate, Grandpa. I didn't go to Sandhurst.'

'Director of Military Training. . . . I'd been commanding a division in the Western desert before that. Well, we lived here and I commuted by train – though we didn't call it commuting in those days. Sometimes when the bombing was bad, or I worked late and missed the last train – I was often working till after midnight – I'd go up and sleep the night with Charles. He had the same studio. He'd made good as a young man.'

'How did you first meet him?' Caroline interrupted. Lois said, 'Shh!', but the Old Man answered her. 'He came out to the desert as an official war correspondent. He was very young . . . about twenty-five, and he did some paintings of men in my division. He was at Sidi Bel Sharif and did a good one of a night attack. He was right up there. He had plenty of guts, which made everyone not mind his extraordinary dress and the poses he put on. . . . Well, when I went to the War Office he was back in London and I saw quite a lot of him. It was fun meeting artists and poets and dancers and heaven knows who. It shook up my mind, sometimes gave me new slants on things.'

'Did Grandma enjoy all that, too?' Caroline asked.

The Old Man shook his head. 'She didn't come up to London much – practically never. She was . . . still very sad over Andrew's death.'

Don't I know, Lois thought, a picture of her mother's pale, withdrawn face suddenly as clear as Caroline's in front of her.

Her father continued. 'One day Charles took me aside at a party at his studio . . . I must have been much the oldest person there, and I was only forty-nine then. . . . There were two or three people in uniform, including a private, and of course so was I, a major-general, but that sort of thing was all right at Charles's. . . . As I was saying, he drew me aside and said "I have something rather unpleasant to tell you." I said "What?" He said, "An officer on your staff at the War Office is a homosexual." I said, "I should think there are several." There were at least fifty officers in the Directorate, and unfortunately homosexuality seems to be quite common. Charles said, "It's not ordinary. This chap is in with a bad lot, including some foreigners . . . a Swede and a couple of Dutch. One of them has been had up for blackmailing another man – for the same thing." Then I whistled and began to look at the matter differently. The Military Training Directorate isn't as sensitive as say Intelligence or Operations, but there's a great deal of top secret stuff there, particularly in war. An enemy who knew our training methods, and what we were training for and with, would have a very powerful advantage. I asked for the man's name. Charles said, "David Powell. He's a captain."

'As it happened I knew him quite well, because he was in charge of a project that was particularly concerning me at that time. He was a stocky fellow with dark hair and brown eyes and a sort of rounded plump figure. Charles said, "I may be wrong, but that's what I hear, and, you know, there are a good many homosexuals in any bohemian group . . . including mine." I thanked him and said, "Now that I know where to look, it should be easy." '

He finished his port and put down the glass. Lois noticed that Caroline was making notes on a pad in the half shadow where she sat. Thunder rumbled in the Surrey hills to the south.

The Old Man said, 'I put the Special Investigation Branch on to it. Charles's information was correct. Powell didn't seem to have sold or given away any military secrets. No blackmail had been attempted as yet. His real partner was his own clerk. We caught them in the act. They were both court-martialled in May, 1942. Powell was sentenced to be cashiered.'

'What's that?' Caroline asked.

Martin answered, 'It only applied to officers. It meant that your commission was taken from you and you were dismissed in disgrace. Any medals or orders you had were stripped from you, too.'

'That's unfair!' Caroline said strongly. 'How can they take away the worth of something good you've already done?'

The Old Man said, 'I don't think Powell ever knew that I was responsible for his disgrace. He told me after the court martial that he would change his name and join the Navy at once. You see, once he had been cashiered he would have been conscripted back into the army, as a private, unless he volunteered for something else. He didn't tell me what his new name would be, and I couldn't keep in touch with him. . . . But I did keep in touch with his wife. They had a baby boy, less than a year old. She changed her name to Phillips. I kept up with her for a long time, until about 1955. I got her jobs in War Office installations. During the war she was all right, but afterwards she began to go to pieces. . . . I never met her, you know. . . . She kept getting sacked from jobs I'd got her . . . drunkenness, not turning up for work, once having an affair with a night-watchman actually in the building. . . . Then one day my Christmas card was returned marked "addressee gone away, left no forwarding address". I've never heard of her since.'

Caroline said, 'The baby boy must be about thirty-two now. . . . Why did you keep in touch with her? Did you feel guilty over what you'd done?'

'Caroline!' Lois said sharply.

'Yes,' the Old Man answered, 'I did. Also, Powell had asked me to do what I could for her, as they had no savings. I said I would.'

Martin said, 'But why would she send this letter to the *Journal* – if it was she who wrote it?'

'I am pretty sure it must be . . . I don't know. Unless she learned somehow, and recently, that I was the one who actually put the Special Investigation Branch on to him. Perhaps she has something else on her mind. I'd like to know.'

Caroline said, 'What does she mean about you having been promised something?'

'I don't know. I'd like to find that out, too.'

Lois thought, this has come out really because of the Memoirs; otherwise the woman would surely have continued to keep quiet, as she had for so long. And surely it was the sort of minor scandal that need not figure in them.

The telephone rang in the downstairs study next door and Martin went to answer it. Through the open door she heard him say, 'Yes . . . he's here. . . . I see. Yes. Wait a minute.'

He called out, 'It's Burrisk, the American, you remember. He says he's made a preliminary investigation into the Zvornos Collection business and he does have a lead. He thinks it won't be long before we get some information. Not the whole story, but at least a beginning, he says.'

'Good. Thank him,' the Old Man said.

'He asked if there was anything else he could do for us in the meantime.'

The Old Man said, 'I don't think so,' but Caroline broke in, 'Grandpa, why can't we ask him to trace this Madeleine Powell, or Phillips, for us?'

'I don't see . . .' Lois began, but her father said, 'Very good. Do that please, Martin. . . . Wait! Tell him you'll call him back in a few minutes, with her last known address.'

A moment later Martin came back into the room. The Old Man said, 'You'll find the last address I have in the address book on my desk top, under Phillips.'

'Burrisk asked what she looked like.'

The Old Man said, 'I told you, I've never seen her. I always imagined she looked like a barmaid, but I'm probably quite wrong. She's not young now, either.'

Caroline said, 'Wait a minute, Daddy. Would she be getting a pension? That would help find her.'

The Old Man said, 'Powell would have given Madeleine as his next-of-kin. Perhaps even as his wife. If he was killed, the Navy would be paying a pension to Madeleine. She could tell them any time that her name was Mrs Phillips, provided she could prove that she was the wife of the man they knew under some other name. If Powell survived, he'd only have got a gratuity, which they'd give him direct.'

Caroline said, 'What strange places your Memoirs are leading us into, Grandpa. . . . That was a marvellous thing you and your regiment did at the Sicily landings, Daddy.'

'Oh,' Martin said, 'you didn't know about that before?'

'You never told me,' the young girl said, 'and perhaps I wouldn't have listened if you had.'

Martin said, 'I'll go up and call Burrisk.'

. . . unnaturally warm, for England, these past few days, and dry. The east wind has caused it and sometimes I feel that I am back in Sicily. I have completed my hybridising programme for this season, and now must possess myself in patience. I shall use up all my stock of that important commodity on the roses, leaving none for the rogues and/or fools who are attempting to browbeat me into keeping silent over matters that should be published abroad . . .

. . . I would have been as unhappy as you if I had had time to afford the luxury. Von Heldenmark saved me from that, and I have always been grateful to him for it. I think he wondered at the cordiality of my greeting of him at the Reunion last April. How could he – or anyone – know the true reason?

CHAPTER SEVEN

Martin strolled along at Robert Cunningham's side, enjoying the sun and the warm slight breeze. It had been a good lunch at the Ritz. The grass of Green Park was strewn with couples lying in each other's arms, men dozing under spread newspapers and girls reading paperback novels.

Cunningham said, 'You know, I had another reason for asking you to lunch besides to discuss protection for members. It's about my brother.'

Martin thought and said, 'George?'

Cunningham said, 'No. Arthur.' He turned his head and looked at Martin.

Martin said, 'Oh, the one who . . .'

'Committed suicide in the Balkans in 1945. Yes.'

They walked on, leaving the gravelled paths now and walking directly across the grass under the heavily leaved trees toward the gate at the top of the Mall. Robert Cunningham was a well-built man, bald on top, hair greying at the sides, bright blue eyes. He was a barrister and a Member of Parliament, and in his mid-fifties. The eyes . . . his brother's eyes had been bright blue, too.

Cunningham said, 'It has been suggested to me recently that Arthur did not commit suicide.'

'Oh? I was there. He shot himself.'

'It has been suggested that he was murdered.'

'Is there any evidence for this?' Martin asked.

'Medical. The doctor who examined him at the time now says that the shot could scarcely have been fired by Arthur himself. The angle of entry and exit made it all but impossible.'

Martin wrestled with the turbulent memories jostling through his mind. The building had been a big farmhouse in the hills. The central room had been converted into the map room. A table and chair had been installed for the Old Man, and the walls covered with maps. There was a little side room which had once been perhaps a bedroom or storage room of some kind. He and the doctor were in that little room with the corpse. The doctor was an R.A.M.C. major, young, sandy-haired, wore glasses. He was kneeling, looking down at the holed forehead, the blood and brains oozing out from the back of the head over the stone floor. The stone had been almost white, now it was stained and splashed. The door from the map room was open and the Old Man was standing in the doorway, Eden behind him.

'Tufnell,' Martin said aloud, 'Major Tufnell!'

Cunningham said, 'Roger Tufnell was Field-Marshal Durham's headquarters' doctor at the time, yes.'

'He was the one who declared him dead,' Martin said, 'though there was no doubt about it.'

'Doctor Tufnell's been a G.P. in Great Burford since 1952,' Cunningham said. 'He's a constituent of mine. He's always had a great admiration for the Field-Marshal.'

They stood at the kerb on the Mall, waiting for a gap in the stream of cars and taxis. Once safely across and in St James's Park, Cunningham said, 'I'll tell you frankly, Brigadier ... we don't want anything more to be said or done about the Zvornos Collection.'

'Who is we?' Martin asked belligerently. 'Senator Jordan? Sir Henry Bartlett? Sovik?'

'We are not concerned with personalities, only with policy,' Cunningham said calmly. 'It's the government that's interested. I'm an assistant whip, as you know, and you can take it from me that what I am telling you has the maximum possible weight behind it.'

'Including the Opposition?' Martin asked.

'Including the Opposition. This is not a party matter but a national matter.... When my brother died ... rather, when Doctor Tufnell got there, he found only three people present with the body – you, Lieutenant Eden and the Field-Marshal. We don't want to open an inquiry into the case ...'

'I wouldn't,' Martin siad. 'Some unpleasant facts might emerge.'

'... but we could be forced to it if, say, Tufnell were to go to the papers with his story. He is perturbed because it is strongly rumoured that the Field-Marshal is going to let out all kinds of secrets. It would damage Tufnell professionally if it were published that Arthur was shot by someone else and he, Tufnell, agreed to lie about the cause of death.'

They walked on in silence now, crossing the bridge over the lake. Near Queen Anne's Gate Martin said, 'I'll talk to him about it.'

'Please do,' Cunningham said seriously, 'It'll be best for all of us. It will also enable us to put a damper on the people who are asking that the bribing of Genearl Ballino be enquired into. That pressure *does* come only from the Opposition, by the way, so far. Well, I have to get back to the House, so I suppose we part here.'

'Thanks for the lunch,' Martin said. The other nodded and strode on, his rolled umbrella swinging. Martin walked slowly up the steps of his office, his head down. At three he had an appointment with Sir Victor Terrell, who was going to ask him whether he had yet got the Vojja Lovac wire recording; and he was going to say, no he had not got it. The question was, was he going to have the guts to add that he had no intention of trying to get it?

'Cunningham took me out to lunch today,' he said.

'The M.P.?' the Field-Marshal asked. He was in his shirt sleeves, working in The Factory grafting seedlings on to root-stock. The evening was warm and there was still light, though it was beginning to fade.

'Yes. He talked about his brother Arthur's death. Said that the doctor who examined Arthur, Tufnell, was now telling him it couldn't have been suicide. But if we ... you ... pursue the Zvornos business, Tufnell would feel compelled to write to the papers, to protect his reputation.'

The Field-Marshal said, 'He won't do that. Has nothing to gain by it, because he can't alter the fact that he has kept quiet all these years, knowing it not to be a suicide ... if indeed he did know.'

'He didn't say anything at the time,' Martin said.

'No,' the Field-Marshal said. 'I was standing in the door. You were standing over the body, Tufnell kneeling. I said, "He committed suicide, then ... the best solution, really." Tufnell looked up at me. After a time he said, "Yes, it's suicide." I suppose he could claim now that it was made obvious to him that I wanted it called suicide.'

Martin burst out, 'Have we got to publish this, sir?'

The Field-Marshal said quietly, 'Yes. I think so.'

Martin felt cold and trapped. He cried, 'I don't see why! The man's dead and nothing's going to bring him back to life even if anyone wanted to. Everyone except his brother has forgotten.'

'Brothers,' the Field-Marshal said. 'There's another on the estate in Wiltshire.'

'Everyone except the family has forgotten all about it. His

regiment won't want the massacre brought up when so many people have kept their mouths shut for so long. It'll turn Sam Herrick against us.'

He glared at the Old Man, almost hating him. He had put down his grafting knife and was facing Martin, the grey eyes blurred, the hands gripping the back of an old wooden chair, not from anger, but to support himself, Martin realised. He *was* old, and now he was showing it. Martin didn't care.

He said, 'So I have to face a murder charge just so that you can satisfy your vanity ... the only general who really told it all.'

'Murder?' Caroline's voice behind him was quiet and unsurprised. She might have been asking him whether he'd like a cup of tea. He turned and saw that Caroline and Lois were standing in the door of the greenhouse. Lois's mouth was set and the corners of her mouth downturned.

'What next?' Caroline said. 'You'd better tell us. I gather it's going to come out in the Memoirs, anyway.'

'Not if I can help it,' Martin snapped.

'You can't,' the Field-Marshal said. 'I am sorry, Martin, but if we are setting out to tell what really happened, and why, that's what we must do, at whatever cost to ourselves.'

'To me, you mean,' Martin said angrily.

'My turn will come,' the Field-Marshal said, 'and, of course, the giver of an unlawful order is as responsible as the one who executes it.'

'Tell us,' Caroline said.

The Old Man sank on to the wooden chair, and said to Martin, 'Go on.'

Martin stared furiously at him a while, and then looked away, up the garden path, toward the house. His wife and daughter were waiting, one on either side of the Field-Marshal.

He said, 'It was a village called Mitrovica. The people in the area were reputed to be pro-German and we were making special efforts to placate them, because we couldn't afford to divert large numbers of troops to protect our L. of C.'

'Translate, please.'

'Lines of communication. In the middle of March 1945, the Germans put in a big counter offensive on both sides of Mitrovica. The division holding that part of the front had a very hard time for two solid weeks. During those two weeks the 7th North Wessex lost some men to what was reported as guerrilla snipers behind the lines. Two days after the German offensive

85

was thrown back the North Wessex were taken out of the line – they'd suffered very heavily – and put into billets and bivouacs round Mitrovica. That day and the next they lost three more men. Arthur Cunningham, who was a captain, commanding C Company of the battalion, went mad. He rounded up the entire village and shot forty-seven of the villagers ... including ten women, three of them heavily pregnant ... and two very young children, three or four years of age.'

'That's incredible!' Lois cried.

'Most of the men were as much in a state of shock, frenzy, whatever you want to call it as Cunningham, after their two weeks' hammering, three hundred hours almost without sleep, three hundred hours of shelling, firing. . . . That company had lost eighty-seven men killed and wounded out of a hundred and twenty. All the officers gone except Cunningham. Most of the sergeants and corporals ... then to have three more men assassinated by snipers. The soldiers shot about twenty villagers and then refused to kill any more. Cunningham killed the others, and all the women, and the two children himself. . . . His C.S.M. – company sergeant major – finally knocked him out with a rifle butt and took him straight to the C.O., who was Sam Herrick. Sam had only just been posted to the battalion and the Army commander decided not to hold him responsible for the massacre, otherwise he certainly wouldn't be Chief of the General Staff now. But that was later. At the time, Herrick realised how serious it was and brought Cunningham straight to us. Army Headquarters was about twenty miles behind Mitrovica, outside some small town whose name I can't remember.'

'I can remember it,' the Field-Marshal said, 'I can't pronounce it.' He smiled slightly. How can he smile, Martin thought? His anger had evaporated with the telling of the story, but had been replaced by the same mixture of fear and disgust that had filled him at the time, those twenty-eight years back.

'He ... Herrick ... asked if he could see the Army commander – Grandpa here – urgently, and alone. It was unusual, but the Chief of Staff agreed and he went in. Ten minutes later the Army commander sent for me, told me what had happened, and said, "This man can not be allowed to go for court martial." I didn't need to be told why.'

'Why?' Caroline asked.

'The battalion was in a bad way. The last thing it needed was for one of its officers, and perhaps some of the men, to be court-martialled. What was wanted, from the army's point of view, was to pull the battalion out of the line, get it up to strength, give it a couple of weeks on the Adriatic and plenty of medals for the way it had held the Germans in front of Mitrovica, then some hard training and back. . . .'

The Field-Marshal said, 'But from the point of view of the campaign as a whole, and of England's future relations with the people and whatever government emerged the perpetrators had to be punished. . . . So I said to Martin, "He must commit suicide." '

'I asked, "What if he won't?" '

'I said, "Then you take his own pistol and shoot him. I'll see that it is declared suicide." '

'I went out. Eden went in. The Army commander sent for Herrick and told him to take Cunningham into that room . . . a little room next to the Map Room . . . by the outside door, as he would interview him. I wasn't there, but that was what the Army commander had told me he was going to do. I watched Cunningham going in. He had a pistol, a .38 Smith & Wesson. That was all I was concerned with.'

'What did he look like?' Caroline asked.

'I don't know . . . blue eyes, marching very upright. He had the pistol in his holster. As soon as the door closed, I followed. He was sitting on a bench, his head in his hands. He looked up, saw me, stood up like a man in a daze, or punch drunk. He saluted me . . . I was the B.G.S. – Brigadier, General Staff – and began to say something. "What . . . ?" he began – some question. I didn't let him finish. I took the revolver out of his holster, checked that it was loaded, handed it back to him and said, "I'm going out for ten seconds. When I come back, I do not expect to find you alive." '

'I think you said, "The Army commander does not expect you to be alive",' the Old Man said.

Martin frowned, concentrating. Yes, that was right. He had used the Old Man's rank and position to make Cunningham understand that the orders came from the top.

He continued, 'Then I went out. I counted ten, slowly, but there was no shot. So I went back in, and . . .'

'That was dangerous,' Caroline said, 'he had the pistol.'

'I suppose so. I wasn't thinking of that at the moment, only of what I had to do. I drew my own revolver as I went in, stepped close and shot him between the eyes. Then I changed pistols. The Army commander and Eden came in as I was doing that. They stood in the doorway, there . . . in the doorway, and the Army commander said "He committed suicide." I said "Yes." He said, "We'd better send for Tufnell." I shouted for an orderly and we waited till Tufnell came.'

There was a long silence. Lois said, 'And no one ever talked about it? Or asked questions . . . till now?'

'The massacre at Mitrovicá was never officially mentioned. The Committee of Three partisans had had to keep out of the area because it was, as we had heard, pro-German. They agreed not to ask awkward questions. Of course, everyone in the North Wessex knew of it, and there was a lot of whispering, but soon we were on the offensive, and we all had other things to occupy our minds. It was all buried, forgotten, until . . .' He couldn't finish the sentence. Choking, he hurried out of the greenhouse and up the garden in the gathering twilight to the house.

He stood in the front window of the bedroom, looking unseeingly at the lawn and the trees that separated it from the field. He felt lonely and miserable. If he had a revolver now, as he had had that day, he thought he would use it, on himself.

He heard his wife come into the room, but he did not turn. She said, 'That was the most disgraceful story I've ever heard. That poor man was shellshocked. How could you do it?'

'Because I was ordered to, by your father.'

'Of course he's responsible too, but you actually killed the man. He should have been sent to hospital, not murdered in cold blood.

'Shut up!' he grated.

'I won't,' she said. 'I don't want to share the same room with a murderer. Please take all your things out at once. Go to one of the spare rooms.' She went out.

Martin sat down on the bed. Now, in peace, no one would understand. That was why it was better to let the affair lie, dead and buried, existing only in a few people's memories. He could feel the horror of that moment, but it was no different from a time when he had been working his armoured car's turret and a dozen running Germans had been his target. It was war. The effects of a court martial on Cunningham would have been unthinkable, not for the verdict, but for what the enquiry would have done to the 16th Army at its most important moment, when the Old Man was holding the full weight of the German counter offensive with one third of the attacker's strength, building up the recoil force that would drive the Germans back a hundred miles in ten days and destroy them at Vojja Lovac.

And finding Cunningham innocent, or sending him to hospital – rightly or not – would have cost scores more British lives as the local partisans took to more sniping to avenge Mitrovica. He had done things to be ashamed of – his part in Appreciation R3, for example – but not this. Why, why, why was the Old Man scourging him?

The light had gone altogether from the lawn when he began to take his clothes and toilet articles to the spare room across the passage, at the back, the one farthest from where Lois would now be sleeping alone.

Caroline came running up the stairs while he was carrying a bundle of shirts and socks down the passage. 'What's going on?' she asked.

'Your mother does not want to share a room with me any longer,' he said, not stopping.

The girl hurried along beside him. 'But why, Daddy? Because of what you've just been telling us?'

'Yes.' He began stowing the shirts into a drawer.

'It was a pretty awful story,' Caroline said. 'I'd never have thought it of you ... or Grandpa ... but I don't know why not.'

'We'd never have thought you would be concealing pistols, to shoot people.'

'To protect people,' she said. She sat on the bed, and said, 'It won't make much difference really, will it? I mean, your sleeping in here.'

'What do you mean?' He looked at his daughter, ready to be angry with her. What business was it of hers?

She said, 'Oh, Daddy, it's been pretty obvious for a long time that you and Mummy aren't exactly lovebirds any longer.'

'We don't fight,' he said defensively.

'It would be better if you did, I think. You just don't care. That's what I've thought for years, really.'

He said at last, 'You're right. This only makes it official.'

'Clive won't like it,' she said. 'He likes things to look as they are supposed to look, and to hell with what's inside. . . . Oh, all this put it out of my mind. I came up to tell you that Mr Burrisk called. He has Madeleine Phillips's address. 29 Bishop Street, W.1. That's in Soho. He said she was a sort of part-time call girl. She must be a bit old for it, but I suppose that's what some men like. The son Paul was sent to Borstal for mugging an American in Dean Street ... and later to jail for two years for living off immoral earnings. He's been a printer but is out of work now. He makes some money on the side by doing pornographic pictures for better-known professionals. And the father was queer, wasn't he? What a messed-up lot!'

'Thanks to your grandfather.'

'You mean, because he caused the father's disgrace and the breakup of the family? If he can be blamed for that, then he should be called a murderer too, because Burrisk has found out that David Powell went down in a mine sweeper in the North Sea early in 1943. If it hadn't been for Grandpa, he'd have spent his war in London, with his playmate.'

Martin said, 'I'm thinking of the son. Poor bastard! How can we – society – any of us – expect anything else of a child when he sees his mother selling herself, in the house probably, as soon as he's old enough to understand what's happening? And she wouldn't have started out on that course if the Old Man hadn't listened to Charles Gibson.'

'So Charles is really the one responsible,' Caroline said. 'He's a strange man. . . . I like him, and I don't like him, at the same time.'

'I didn't know you knew him. Oh, of course, you've met him here for birthdays and so on.'

'He gave me a few meals when I was at university,' she said. 'I didn't know.'

Now she would say, you ought to have known; but how could he, or Lois for that matter, know if the girl didn't tell them?

'Have you told Grandpa this, about Mrs Phillips?' he asked.

'Not yet. I'm going to. I wonder what he'll do next.'

'Create more trouble,' Martin said, slamming the drawer shut. 'I wish no one had ever suggested he wrote the bloody Memoirs.'

'And Charles Gibson has encouraged him in that, too,' Caroline said. She stood, looking at her father a long time without speaking. At length she said, 'You said, just now, that you'd never have thought I would be concealing pistols. You never mentioned stolen goods.'

He said, 'I don't believe you knew they were there.'

She said, 'Thank you. Grandpa never did. That's why I've already told him what I'm going to tell you. . . . The chairman of the university branch of T.P.M. gave me the suitcase and told me the police were getting ready to frame him. But he never mentioned the other stuff. I believe he was just a thief.' Her eyes were damp again. Martin put down the suit he was hanging up and put an arm round her shoulder.

'Don't cry, Caroline,' he said gently. 'You were betrayed.'

'Oh, why do people have to spoil things?' she cried, resting her head on his shoulder.

'Forget it,' he said. 'We've all been taken in, one time or another, and it hurts. We know.'

She wept unashamedly and he patted her shoulder, thinking, we haven't been so close since she was a baby.

CHAPTER EIGHT

Number 29 Bishop Street was a narrow door between an Italian delicatessen and a window display of flyblown magazines devoted to whips, high-buttoned boots and rubber underwear. Martin glanced at his watch. She had said five-thirty sharp; he was a minute early. He waited, leaning against the door jamb, then pressed the bell. He heard the shuffle of feet moving downstairs almost at once, and a moment later a bolt was drawn, a key turned, and the door opened.

She was very close to how the Old Man had imagined her ... short, curvy, big bosom, big blue eyes, rather bloodshot, and a mass of golden hair piled on top of her head – either dyed or a wig. Her face was round and her complexion pink and white. The pouches under her eyes and the crow's feet in the corners showed her true age. She must be over fifty, he had worked out, though if you didn't look too closely she could pass for forty plus.

She was wearing a pink dressing gown edged with marabou and pink mules. She waited, one hand still on the door handle as though ready to slam it in his face.

He said, 'I'm Martin Ruttledge. I called.'

'Aaow yes,' she said, her accent a blend of suburban gentility and city cockney. 'Come in.'

He followed her up the stairs and into a room on the right of the landing. It was small and over-furnished, the windows looking out on Bishop Street grimed, the curtains half-drawn. He could see a small kitchen and bathroom through an open door to the left; opposite, two other doors presumably led to bedrooms. She sat down on the large sofa, one of its springs hanging out underneath and its blue and white upholstery torn. Martin sat gingerly on a hard chair opposite.

She said, 'You said you'd come about the letter I wrote to the *Sunday Journal*. How did you know I wrote that letter?'

'We don't know, Mrs Phillips. The editor mentioned it to the Field-Marshal and he guessed.'

'Field-Marshal Durham, eh?' she said. 'Are you one of his officers?'

'I was. I'm married to his daughter. He lives with us in Surrey.'

She was eyeing him more carefully now. He thought, she may be shrewd, but she could not look it however hard she tried. She was too much like the stock character gold digger or barmaid with a heart of gold.

She said, 'And what have you come for now?'

'The Field-Marshal asked me to find out what you meant in the letter ... where you wrote that the public ought to know what the Field-Marshal was promised, by whom, for having Captain Powell court-martialled.'

She said, ' 'Ow much?'

After a pause Martin said, 'I don't quite understand.'

'How much ...' She aspirated the H carefully this time – '... to keep my mouth shut?'

Martin said, 'We don't intend to keep anything secret, Mrs Phillips. The Field-Marshal really does not understand what you meant. He is sure he was not promised anything.'

She got up, the dressing-gown swirling carelessly to reveal shapely calves and a dimpled knee. She found a packet of cigarettes on the mantelpiece over the blocked-off fireplace, and lit one.

'You're not going to pay me anything?' she said, puffing furiously.

'We're only trying to find out what happened.'

'Why should I talk to you for nothing?'

'From your letter, we thought that you wanted the truth to come out. So do we.'

'Like 'ell you do!' She gave him a long stare, then sprawled back on the sofa. The gown fell farther open, showing half one thigh. She was wearing stockings, he saw. She was still looking at him. Was she inviting him, luring him on as a customer? Or daring him? In her lush sexuality she was quite the opposite of Lois – as Lois had been the last twenty years, at least.

He looked away from the curve of plump thigh and said, 'Please tell us.'

She said, 'I'll believe you, though thousands wouldn't. . . . Who told General Durham, as he was then, wasn't he, about David being a pansy?'

Martin said, 'Charles Gibson. He's a . . .'

She said scornfully, 'Don't try to tell *me* who Charles Gibson is! I've been in that studio fifty times ... with and without my clothes on. I was pretty then, see, really pretty. I'm forty now but then, when I was young, I was a picture. . . . I always had the figure, since I was eleven—' she arched her back where she reclined, thrusting out her breasts, 'but then I was slimmer below, in the hips, and of course my face didn't have any of these bloody wrinkles. Charlie-boy I called him, once we got to know each other, if you know what I mean. He was crazy about me.'

'Was this after or before you were married to Captain Powell?'

'After. When he got that job at the War Office. We were short of money and when I saw an ad for models for an artist, I applied. David didn't mind. He wasn't very interested in me for anything except cooking, once Paul was born. Paul was his alibi, see? I ought to have guessed about him, but I didn't. I was innocent then ... But Charlie-boy wanted me to himself. So he found out about David being a pansy, went to General Durham, and said he'd fix it for General Durham to get promoted and get a good command in the battle somewhere if he would get rid of David.'

Martin, listening carefully, thought – she really believes it. She seemed to be less on her guard as she warmed to her story.

He said, 'But I don't see how Charles Gibson could do anything for General Durham. Oh, of course, he was a friend of Winston Churchill.'

'That's it! Charlie-boy painted with Winnie. Winnie used to listen to everything Charlie-boy said, because, Winnie said, Charles Gibson can see everything that's inside a person, particularly what's bad. He liked Charlie-boy to tell him what he was hearing, what he had learned, anything ... because that was the kind of things those toffs in the Cabinet would never hear otherwise. So Charlie-boy dropped a hint to Winnie that General Durham was a smashing general. General Durham got promoted and sent back to Africa wasn't it? And David got court-martialled, and Charlie-boy got me ... David wasn't a bad bloke. Like a lot of them pansies, he was kind, but no use to a woman, if you know what I mean.'

This time the invitation was unmistakable as one handsome rounded breast half fell out of the top of the dressing gown, and she allowed her left leg to fall off the sofa and trail on the carpet, revealing that she was wearing a garter belt with the stockings, but apparently nothing else.

Martin felt a thickening in his head. Was she smoking marijuana? The atmosphere in the room felt dense and strangely scented. My God, he wanted a woman, any woman as long as it wasn't Lois. She was so removed now that the last time they made love, and that was some months ago, he had felt that he was embracing a rubber dummy.

He must control himself, at least a little longer. He said thickly, 'What happened . . . after you went to Charles Gibson?'

'I lived in his studio for a time. Then he got another girl, kicked me out. The new girl was a little taller than me, black haired . . . she wasn't as pretty as me. I saw her once, going into the studio, when I was hanging around outside, hoping he'd see me and see how cold and miserable I was, but he didn't care. Charlie-boy never cares for anyone, does he?'

Martin went to her, stumbled to his knees, reached out, parting the gown. Her twin breasts were magnificent, heavy but not drooping. He fondled the nipples and asked, 'Then?'

'Then . . . I had jobs at the War Office, military places round London. Someone told me that General Durham got them for me. I suppose he thought that'd keep me quiet about what Charlie-boy had done for him . . . but Paul was growing up, and he was a good boy, but wild, you know what I mean. I was drinking too much . . . The usual . . .'

The gown dropped back on both sides. The triangle of her loins was small and golden . . . dyed, he thought, reaching down to caress it.

'Men like it gold, don't they?' she said. He stood up unsteadily and began to take off his trousers. She said, 'Not so fast, lover, boy. I have to buy stockings and clothes, and food's expensive, you know.'

'How much?' he said. The trousers were off and he was urgent and trembling.

'A fiver,' she said, 'for you, because . . .'

He thrust a five pound note from his wallet into her hand and sprawled on top of her, entering her with ease as she swung up her legs and held him round the small of the back. The five pound note crinkled against her ears, when she was clutching it tightly in her hand.

In his other ear she whispered fast – 'Go on . . . Oh, you're big . . . Harder . . . I like it . . . I like it.'

He came suddenly, in gasping spasms, and to his astonishment found himself in helpless tears.

'My!' she said. 'You do make a noise, don't you?'

'It's been a long time,' he said.

'Trouble with the wife? Poor old chap! There, there, Madeleine will always give it a good home, eh?'

After a time she pushed him aside and went to the bathroom. He heard the sound of running water. When she came back she had brushed her hair again and her complexion was a little mottled.

She said, 'Don't worry about anything. I'm clean. . . . I don't do this with just anyone, you know. I have a few gentlemen friends, very rich and important they are, and they . . .'

'Of course,' he said.

He felt less oppressed, and grateful to her. The proverb said *Post coitum omne triste est* – after copulation all is sadness; true, sometimes one did feel disgust, and this could have been such an occasion, for she was certainly a prostitute, whatever words she chose to use to describe her way of life. But he found that he did not despise her, or himself – rather, he despised the man who had made love to Lois when it was obvious that she was only suffering him, not enjoying him, still less sharing a sacrament of marriage. And he rather liked Madeleine Phillips, in addition to finding her sexually stimulating and satisfying. She had had a hard life and been much misused by many men, but still there was a genuine sense of comforting in her, behind the brassy exterior . . . the tart with the heart of gold, he thought wryly. Well, they do exist.

The doorbell rang, twice, a pause, then twice again. 'That's Paul,' she said.

'I'll go.'

'No, wait and meet him. You'll like him.' She hurried out and downstairs.

Martin stood up, checking his clothes and running a hand over his hair. A moment later she returned followed by a man of nearly six feet, with fair hair, pale brown eyes and a small red birthmark on his left cheek.

'My son Paul,' Madeleine Phillips said proudly. Behind Paul on the landing stood a burly young man and a statuesque redhead with a small mouth. Both chewed gum steadily. No one introduced them as they followed Paul Phillips into the room, and stood silent by the door to the kitchen.

'How do you do? I'm Martin Ruttledge,' Martin said, extending his hand to Paul.

Paul was about thirty, well dressed though on the flashy side, coatless, the shirt with a Byronic collar, the trousers very low cut purple hiphuggers.

He said, 'How do you do, Mister . . . but I bet you're an officer. Must be General Ruttledge, sir?'

'Brigadier,' Martin said, thinking – do I look as stereotyped as that? Well, not many people still wore the dark blue suit and there were the rolled umbrella and bowler hat and briefcase as additional evidence, not to mention the military moustache.

'He's married to General Durham's daughter, Paul,' Madeleine said.

'Field-Marshal Durham, Mum,' Paul said.

He had very little of his mother's accent. Perhaps he'd trained himself out of it in his years at Borstal and the Scrubs. The redhead shifted her weight from one outflung hip to the other. Martin suddenly understood that they were going to be Paul's models for some pornographic photography. Madeleine would presumably hold the flash apparatus . . .

He said, 'I must be going. Thank you so much, Mrs Phillips. The Field-Marshal asked me to tell you that he would be writing to you as soon as I had told him what I have learned. But I can assure you now that what you believe is not true.'

'Well, he'll have the 'ell of a job proving it,' Madeleine said, 'Winnie being dead, and Charlie-boy isn't going to talk. And if Charlie-boy does say he had nothing to do with getting General Durham promoted, it'll be just the opposite of what he told me, so what am I going to believe, eh?'

Martin said, 'The Field-Marshal will write.' The son's sardonic eye was on him, his manner both servile and hostile.

To Madeleine, Martin blurted out, 'And I'll call you, if I may. Perhaps we could have . . .'

She reached onto the mantelpiece and gave him a card which he stuffed into his pocket, muttering, 'Don't bother to show me out.'

'I'll come, sir,' Paul said. 'We have to keep the outside door locked and bolted in this neighbourhood, you know.'

He walked at Dick Armstrong's side along the sand. The tide was out, a fresh west wind blew off the Atlantic, and the rollers marched up in steady procession, like endless lines of green-coated white-plumed infantry.

'Not so many people here as usual for a Saturday,' Dick said. He leaned down and slipped the harness off the Alsatian bitch's neck. 'Go, Rachel, go and play!' The dog raced off, gambolling into the water and among the children building sand castles.

Dick was tall and thin, his thick curled brown hair flecked with grey at the temples. His eyes and the deep scar across the bridge of his nose were almost hidden by heavy horn-rimmed tinted glasses. The eyes themselves were gone, irreparably damaged by a shell splinter and afterwards removed by the surgeon. He had been Martin's adjutant when Martin was commanding the 40th Lancers in North Africa, Sicily and Italy.

'Working on any more books, Dick?' he asked.

Dick had a deep-toned voice, with an extraordinarily pleasant timbre.

He answered, 'A little thing called *The Nature of Perception*. I haven't had any offers for the film rights yet.' He laughed and strode out.

Some children were crouched ahead and Rachel, the seeing-eye dog, was not guiding him. Martin was about to catch his arm but he changed direction without being warned. Yet the children had been making no sound. He must have some form of radar, or had developed a sense that the rest of mankind, which still had its eyes, had no use for.

Martin said, 'How long is it since we last met?'

'Three years,' the other said promptly. 'At the regimental reunion. I got Rachel later that year. Maud had been run over by some drunken idiot.'

'You told me in a letter.'

'What's going on with you? You sound strained. Are they finding spies in your office?'

'The Old Man's writing his Memoirs. He's putting in everything. There was some funny business about a collection of paintings at Zvornos Castle. We're trying to ferret out the truth, but the entire government seems to be determined to stop us.'

'I heard something about the Zvornos Collection on the radio. Put a price on your silence, Martin.'

'So much is going to come out that it rather frightens me . . . I've been thinking. I must tell the truth about Appreciation R3.'

'Why bother?' Armstrong said, smiling. 'You're out of the army and whatever fame I have will rest on *The Limits of Pure Reason* and *Critical Metaphysics*, and now *The Nature of Perception*. And that's as it should be.'

'But it's not the truth.'

'The truth can sometimes cause a great deal of trouble. Didn't Oscar Wilde say truth should be used sparingly, like garlic. Or was it Saki?'

Martin said, 'But your whole life has been devoted to finding out what truth really is, these things that I'm damned if I understand . . . perception, immaterialism, immanence, reason, noumena, faith . . .'

'That's pure thought,' Armstrong said. 'Another form of real truth is pure mathematics, which I am studying too, because I'm running into philosophical speculation about it. When deciding how to use mathematics, for example – build a new bridge, invent a new type of heat generator – I would guide myself pragmatically, but the tool – the mathematics itself – must be pure, unaffected by outside considerations, formed of pure truth. The correct application is affected by scores, hundreds of factors . . . public good, private concern and involvement, future effects, past history . . .'

'I have to,' Martin said doggedly.

'I see you feel a hair shirt is needed in your wardrobe. All right, if you must, you must. Just make it clear that it was my suggestion that you claim the Appreciation, not yours.'

'But I agreed to it, and I shouldn't have.'

'I think you should. It did you, and the army, and the country a lot of good. That's what mattered.'

'All kinds of things are coming out,' Martin muttered. 'Things I've been sitting on, inside myself, for twenty, thirty years.'

Armstrong said, 'Tell me, if you'd like to.' He stopped. The sands reached on past the foot of the cliffs at this low state of the tide. 'We'll have to turn back in ten minutes, or we'll get cut off . . . and those cliffs are unclimbable.'

As they walked, north for half a mile, then back the length of Bude sands, then north again while the sun crawled westering across the sky and the tide inched up the beach, Martin told Armstrong of the killing of Arthur Cunningham; and the theft of the Zvornos Collection; and the bribing of General Ballino; and the court martial of Captain Powell. . . .

'What about the bombing of Peskevo?' Armstrong asked quietly.

Martin whistled under his breath. 'I didn't know you knew about that.'

'I was in hospital with an R.A.F. type who was wounded in the raid. Same trouble as me, but his face was much worse than mine. He said he was not supposed to talk, but he did.'

'I suppose the Old Man will insist on bringing that up, in time,' Martin said. 'That'll be worse than anything else so far, for getting the government on us. They'll throw the Official Secrets Acts at him.'

'The Prime Minister is a capable man in many ways,' Armstrong said, 'but he's not very farsighted and he doesn't know how to handle men. The Copenhagen negotiations boiled down finally to a difference of one tenth of one percent in the agreed prices and he wouldn't buy it. We'd all have been better off if he'd accepted. Then look at the West German treaty – shortsighted again. And he's sent the wrong man to Russia. They're always going to be suspicious, but they respect a man who's tough and clean. Bidwell is not, he's devious, and they've caught him out once, in 1956 when he was at the Board of Trade.'

'What would you do with the Old Man, if you were Prime Minister?'

'I'd go down to see him, or ask him to drop in at 10 Downing Street, and tell him the government would give him all the co-operation he needed. That would mean getting him to Yugoslavia to see Sovik, or vice versa. The Prime Minister doesn't seem to understand that whatever horrors might come out could not be worse than having the country believe the government is suppressing relevant truth. . . .

'Personally I have a feeling, from what you tell me, that the Field-Marshal has something else on his mind. Something different. He can't bring himself to let it out, but will be able to do so if he can, so to speak, be forced to. I mean, now he's sayisg, "I'm going to tell the whole truth, even about the killing of Captain Cunningham." Later, he can say to himself, "As a matter of conscience, I must now also tell the truth about—" whatever it is.'

'What on earth can be bigger than the Zvornos Collection business, involving Bartlett, Jordan, and Sovik? Or the bombing of Peskevo?'

'I didn't say bigger . . . different.'

Then they went up towards the house, and sat through the evening and half the night talking about politics and personalities.

The train was swinging through Slough and Martin checked that he had left none of his belongings on the rack or the seat. Not that there was much room for anything, with the whole train jammed with sunburned families returning to London, this Sunday evening, from holidays in Devon and Cornwall. It was good to be wearing country clothes instead of the bureaucrat's uniform he had left in the club after sleeping there

Friday night. He remembered Madeleine and stirred uncomfortably. He knew he'd be calling her sometime ... sometime soon; and that miserable Paul would be leering, thinking, I know what you're doing, I know what my mother is, but if you think you're any better than us, with all your la-di-da accent and bowler hat ...

Better to think about Dick Armstrong. An amazing brain, but that was not so uncommon: the universities were full of brilliant men. What was so wonderful about Dick was his personality. He charmed you by being both interested and interesting. When he talked, he knew what he was talking about. He persuaded you of the validity of his beliefs, and of what he thought ought to be done, by a combination of logic and a certainty that *he* could make that solution work; the certainty originated in him, but was also created inside you, the listener. And in all the time the blind head turning, looking, searching, as though the eyes behind the spectacles were not of glass.

Ealing ... not far now. It was getting dark, though it was only nine o'clock. Now, in the middle of July, the very long days of mid-June were shortening as mid-summer receded. He'd just go to the club, read a bit, have a quiet dinner, then go to bed. Of course he might run into some old friend there, but the country bumpkins didn't usually come up to town on weekends – their wives wanted to do some shopping – unless for a regimental or division reunion. Then tomorrow fold up the tweed coat and flannel trousers, put them with the walking shoes back into the overnight bag, dress in the blue suit, put on the bowler hat, pick up the rolled umbrella, the briefcase, and the overnight bag, go down in the lift, walk down the hall steps, 'Morning, Riddick', a brisk ten minutes' walk and then 'Morning, Giles,' and up to his office.

He hung up his hat and umbrella, put the overnight bag in the corner and opened his briefcase. There were a few papers he'd been working over on Friday night at the club, that he could send down for typing now.

The buzzer on his desk sounded. A female voice said, 'Brigadier Ruttledge, the Secretary would like to see you, please.'

He pressed the lever, 'Coming.'

The Secretary was at his desk when he entered. He looked up and said, 'Martin, I believe you signed a letter to the Yugoslav ambassador a few days ago, asking for information about the Zvornos Collection, and offering what help you could give in tracing what happened to it.'

Martin said, 'I did. On behalf of the Field-Marshal.'

'Quite. Some weeks ago I ordered you to obtain a certain wire recording from the Field-Marshal. Have you done so?'

'No. I . . .'

The Secretary raised one hand. 'No excuses, please. I do not think you can satisfactorily carry out your duties as Chief Government Security Officer while you are in intimate correspondence with a foreign government. Accordingly, I am relieving you of your position, now. You are suspended indefinitely, without pay.'

Martin stared at the Secretary unbelievingly. Sir Victor had taken off his pince-nez and was holding them in his hand. His expression was cold and hostile.

Martin said, slowly, 'You mean, sir, you are sacking me because we might find out the truth about Zvornos?'

The Secretary said, 'I am not compelled to give you any reason for your suspension. Nevertheless, I have already given you one.'

'Do you believe the Field-Marshal will accept it, sir?'

'I have the greatest respect for Field-Marshal Durham – but his opinions on matters within my responsibility are of no concern to me. . . . When you return to your office, you will find Mr Lockhart of my personal staff there. He will take delivery of all your keys and the secret files. Lockhart will also take your special identity and entry cards, and see you out of the building. Remember to take your personal belongings with you.'

The rage was rising in Martin's throat till he was ready to hit the smooth face before him. Then streams of fierce sarcasm came crowding ready to his lips.

But he controlled himself, and said, 'Obviously you are doing what you have been told to do, sir. I am sorry for you.' He turned on his heel and strode out, closing the door carefully behind him.

He parked the car in the garage, picked up his bags and got out. The van was out, the Bentley in. Lois was probably off at the wholesalers. Just as well. He didn't feel like facing her now . . . Monday morning, eleven o'clock, out of work.

As he entered the front hall Caroline peered down at him over the bannister. 'Are you ill, Daddy? We heard the car coming in but couldn't believe it.'

He came up the stairs, passed her and went into the Field-Marshal's study, Caroline at his heels. He saw that a type-writer table had been set up for her by the one window and an angle lamp placed in position.

He said, 'They've sacked me, sir. They call it suspension, but it's really the sack. They say it's because I signed the letter to the Yugoslav ambassador, but that's balls. It's because we're not giving up on the Zvornos Collection, and because I didn't get them the wire recording.'

'Ah,' the Field-Marshal said. He was sitting in a deep chair, his bony hands folded in his lap. He nodded. 'I expected this.'

The Old Man was taking it very calmly, Martin thought – his job gone, his income reduced to a pittance . . . now he'd be more dependent than ever on Lois's success with her catering. But that was the way he was; this is how he had been all during the Balkan campaign – hard-driving during the preparation, intolerant of the slightest mistake, ruthless until the battle had been well and truly joined . . . then calm, tolerant, unmoved, while the reports grew blacker and blacker.

The Field-Marshal said, 'Would you like me to give up the Memoirs, Martin?'

Martin thought. Caroline was watching him like a cat, a notebook clutched in her hand as though ready to take down whatever he said and use it as evidence against him. He remembered Sir Victor's hard demeanour. They thought they'd got him by the balls . . . God damn their bloody bureaucratic eyes!

'Yesterday, I would have said yes,' he said. 'Now, let them go to hell!'

'Right on, Daddy-oh!' Caroline chanted. 'I'm beginning to enjoy this job. I don't want it to stop now.'

'I'll do whatever I can,' Martin continued, 'but I'm going to have to look for work. We can't afford to live the way we have been without some more money coming in.'

The Field-Marshal said, 'That'll throw a heavier load on Caroline, which is good, but it may be too much. . . . Well, we'll have to see how it works out. Did you have a good time down in Cornwall?'

'Marvellous. I had two long talks with Dick Armstrong about . . .' He hesitated, this wasn't the moment to bring up Appreciation R3. 'He's a great man,' he said. 'He could be Prime Minister if he went into politics.'

'And did you find Mrs Phillips?'

'Madeleine?' he said. Caroline looked up, then back to the notebook where she was now doodling. 'Yes. She wrote the letter because she is sure that you had her husband court-martialled in order to get rid of him.'

'But why should I want to get rid of him?'

'Because Charles Gibson wanted Madeleine as his mistress. In return for your getting rid of Powell, Charles would speak well of you to the Prime Minister, indicating that you should be given a corps in a theatre of war.'

Again, the Old Man's reaction surprised Martin. He spoke almost to himself. 'Charles did tell me about Powell . . . He did say he'd speak of me to Winston and Beaverbrook. He knew them all, on the personal level. He was at their parties, when they got drunk, when they gambled . . . but I don't think, in my own mind, that there was any connection between the two.'

'Are you sure there wasn't, subconsciously?' Caroline said.

'Caroline!' Martin burst out. 'Do you realise what you're accusing Grandpa of?'

'Being like David and the wife of Uriah the Hittite, only not for himself,' she said, unabashed.

'It might be true,' the Old Man said, still half to himself. 'I knew Charles had great influence . . . he still does . . . Did I know that he wanted Madeleine? Did he mention it to me, pretending to joke? I don't know. . . . I wanted very badly to get out of that bloody War Office and back to a field command.'

'Why?' Caroline asked.

'I don't know,' the Old Man said. 'It wasn't glory. It wasn't power. I wanted to get away from the War Office more than to get *to* any other place. That building reeked of old men, planning in safety for holocausts that would take place thousands of miles away.'

Martin broke out, 'But most of the people at the War Office *had* been in action, or went out later. You couldn't run the war without a central headquarters.'

'I know,' the Old Man said, nodding his big head wearily, 'but that doesn't alter the fact. A battlefield is real. There are real dangers, real emotions. A battlefield is the truth about war. The War Office isn't. . . . I'll have to talk to Mrs Phillips and tell her I don't know whether she's right or not.'

'It's going to look rather odd in the Memoirs,' Caroline said. 'It'll give the other side something to throw at you. But they'll never be able to prove it.'

'Or we to disprove it,' the Old Man said. 'Do you think she'd come down here?'

Martin said, 'I'm not sure. Probably. . . . I met the son, Paul, too.'

'What's he like?'

'Rather unpleasant, though it's hard to put a finger on just why. He's on the dole, and does a little pornography, according to Burrisk, and from what I saw, that's correct.'

The Field-Marshal said, 'We could employ him here. . . . That will solve the problem of there being too much work for Caroline. Does she have a telephone?'

Martin felt in his pocket and found the card she had given him. It read MADELEINE, and below, 29 *Bishop Street*, and a Gerrard telephone number.

Caroline wrote down the number and the Old Man said, 'I'll call her soon, when I've worked out what to say.'

'But, sir,' Martin said, 'we don't know whether young Phillips – Paul – has any education, or skills. He'd have to live here . . .'

'Yes.'

'He's been to Borstal and jail.'

'All my fault,' the Old Man said. 'I must try to make some amends. You two go on down and have a drink to celebrate Martin's being sacked. . . . Come, man, you didn't *like* that job, did you? You hated it. If we're going to tell the truth about events and personalities outside ourselves, let's face the truths we have inside us, too. . . . I'll be down in a quarter of an hour.'

... *the sea is a mirror today, shining like bronze far below out there. I close my eyes and imagine we are sailing on it, but it is not our little green boat that moves (it is a boat made of lily pads!) but the whole sea slowly revolving round us, lapping at the lilies with a gentle sound, so cool under the sun . . .*

CHAPTER NINE

Lois stood in one of the front windows, looking out over the river and Blackfriars Bridge. It was a close muggy day, threatening rain, the pavements greasy and grey, the sky grey, all the buildings grey, the water grey, grey the tugs sliding down on the tide.

Charles came up from the other end of the huge room and gave her another glass of sherry. 'Did you see all the stuff about Yugoslavia in this morning's paper – *The Times*?'

'No,' she said, 'we take the *Telegraph*.'

'Well, it was pretty interesting in view of what's being whispered about why Martin was sacked. "Usually well-informed sources" are quoted as believing that a subterranean upheaval is going on among the Committee of Three and their chief followers. The sources don't say what is causing the upheaval, but gossip here does – the story is that it's caused by a letter Martin wrote to the Yugoslav ambassador about the Zvornos Collection.'

'He wrote the letter on Daddy's behalf,' she said. She wished Charles would get off the subjects of Yugoslavia, the Zvornos Collection, or the Memoirs. But he wasn't going to.

'Who do *you* think got the Collection?' he asked.

'I don't know,' she said, 'and honestly I don't care. I wish everyone would forget about it. It *was* long ago.'

'But someone got millions,' he said. 'Perhaps several people got millions. Do you know what I think?'

'No.'

'I think the Chancellor of the Duchy of Lancaster is the man ... Sir Henry Bartlett, O.M., G.C.B., K.B.E., M.V.O.'

'I'll never believe that,' she said. 'It was the Count himself, or Sovik, or some American. It was an American truck that took the paintings away.'

'Well, we'll see, if we keep the pot boiling. . . . The other piece was even more interesting, I thought.'

'What other piece?' she asked resignedly.

'The article by the political correspondent. Oh, of course, you don't take *The Times*. It was a background piece, probably ordered by the editor because of the increasing amount of news that's coming out of Yugoslavia. It went into the war, the German invasion, the various groups of partisans and guerrillas, the struggle between the National Freedom Movement who were right wing and the Committee of Three, who were Communist. These two groups were fighting each other even before the war against Germany in the Balkans had been won – at Vojja Lovac. The writer brought out strongly that the final victory of the C.O.T. people would have been much less complete, might even never have come about without two events – the accidental bombing of Peskevo, where a lot of N.F.M. leaders were killed . . . and the seizure of German tanks and other war equipment which the C.O.T. got when it was left on the battlefield of Vojja Lovac.'

'Why was it left?' she asked, puzzled. 'It must have been very valuable . . . at least important to see that no one else got it.'

'That's just the point,' Charles said eagerly. 'A few days after the battle, having sent all the prisoners to the rear, your father pulled the 16th Army back about twelve miles from the positions on which it had received the Germans' surrender – with all their remaining armour, artillery, weapons of every kind; radio, vehicles, quite large stocks of fuel, ammunition, and food. The official explanation – which *The Times* writer quotes here – was that the Old Man was preparing to receive an attack from another German army retreating in front of the Russians . . . but that never happened. Before the 16th Army could move forward again, the war ended. In the meantime the Committee of Three partisans got all the German war material that had been left at Vojja Lovac . . . and promptly used it to annihilate the N.F.M.'

'But surely that's all past, too?' she said.

'Of course. But I find it quite fishy that it's being brought up again. That man – *The Times* writer – is in very close touch with the present government. He as good as said that the stated reasons for pulling back the 16th Army don't ring true.'

'So what are the real reasons supposed to have been?'

He shrugged, 'Political pressure. But from where? More bribery? But by whom?'

'The person bribed, though, would have been . . .'

'The Old Man. Exactly . . .' He seemed to realise then that the discussion did not interest her, and asked, 'Has Martin found a job yet?'

She shook her head. 'He's had a couple of offers, I believe, but not anything he wants.'

'How's your catering coming along?'

'Very well. We're making twelve per cent more money this year than we did last, on feeding about eleven per cent more people.' She heard herself going on, rattling off facts and figures, numbers and prices. Charles watched her, a quizzical smile on his long face, his green eyes glowing. While she talked, he put his glass down on a table, took her by the elbows and kissed her, stifling the flow of words. She resisted a moment, then relaxed in his arms. Here I am, nearly fifty she thought, and I feel like a girl having her first affair . . . well, it had been.

He leaned back from her, shaking the long red hair out of his eyes, 'Lois, why don't you go back to painting?'

She broke free and said, 'I've told you. I don't want to. I'm quite happy as I am.'

'Liar!'

She said, 'I'm as happy as I can be, married to Martin. . . . The catering business is what I live for. It takes up my time, it keeps me busy, it makes money, it's interesting.'

'Liar!'

She stopped. He was right. It wasn't interesting, certainly not now that she had it running so smoothly. But if she did not immerse herself in it, what else was there for her? Dream of a past that she had thought long-buried? Catalogue reasons for despising Martin?

'Paint,' he said, as though the words were on her forehead.

'No,' she said again, 'I . . . don't want to.'

'You daren't,' he said. 'You're afraid. Why don't you take my word for it that you can, with application, be an extremely good painter? You were once, you know, when you had really very little training or practice.'

'That was then,' she said. 'This is now.'

'And now?' he said. 'Well, now . . . is now . . .'

He led her, his arm round her, to the back room where a couch stood under the northern skylights. A half-finished oil of a nude girl stood on one of the two easels across the room. He took the glass from her hand and she began to undress, putting her clothes neatly on the chair at the head of the couch. She had dressed with care, knowing he would see her underclothes. When she was naked, and he was with her, she lay down on the couch, and held out her arms.

'Oh, Charles,' she whispered. 'Why? Why?'

'Because . . . we're us,' he said. His hair fell on her face. His hands began to explore the secrets of her body as his lips descended to caress her swelling nipples.

She came off the 4.08 train at Ashwood, unlocked her van and drove home. A large black official Austin was parked in the drive and before opening the front door she patted her hair into place and, once inside, took a quick look at herself in the mirror of the hall umbrella stand.

Caroline came out of the kitchen and said, 'Sir Victor Terrell's with Grandpa, in his study upstairs.'

Lois asked, 'What's it about?'

'Haven't the foggiest. He's been here about half an hour. Paul, is the kettle boiling?'

'Yes, Miss Ruttledge.' Lois remarked again the upper-class accent in Paul Phillips's voice, but her daughter frowned and said sharply, 'Make tea, then! The small pot . . . Grandpa said not to disturb them.'

They sat round the kitchen table, drinking tea. Lois noticed the bent figure of Vetch working in the vegetable garden and told her daughter to call him in for tea. Paul Phillips raised his cup with the little finger rigidly extended. Vetch slurped his tea with cheerful sucking sounds.

They all heard footsteps coming down the stairs, and men's low voices; then the front door closing. Through the window they watched the black Austin glide round from the front of the house and drive away.

The Field-Marshal came into the kitchen rubbing his hands. 'Ah, tea. Just what I've been wanting.'

'You said I wasn't to disturb you,' Caroline said reproachfully.

'You won't now, will you? Because he's gone.'

Paul sprang to his feet and pulled up another chair. Caroline poured her grandfather a cup of tea. The Field-Marshal began to talk to Vetch about what needed to be done next in the development of the Black Durham.

Fifteen minutes later he looked at Lois. 'Martin not back yet?'

Lois looked at her daughter, for she did not know and had not thought to ask.

Caroline said shortly, 'Daddy's not back.'

The Field-Marshal said, 'Vetch, you get started on those cuttings. The rest of you come to my study – unless you have work to do, Lois.'

She hesitated. Really, she did have quite a lot to do . . . work that she should have completed this morning instead of going to Charles. She had thought she would feel better for her excursion, and perhaps she did . . . certainly she experienced some bodily sense of ease; but in her mind the visit had raised more sensations and emotions than it had quieted and she was going back again next week. It could only be a matter of time before Martin found out. Much better to tell him; or leave him, and then she wouldn't have to explain or inform anyone.

Her father was waiting and she answered, 'No. I'll come.'

Paul hung back as they left the kitchen and the Field-Marshal said, 'You too, Paul.'

Once in his study and settled in his favourite chair, he said, 'Sir Victor came here first to blackmail, then to bribe me, into silence over the Zvornos Collection. He started by saying he was empowered to reinstate Martin in his job. And offer me a life peerage.'

'They should have given you that when you finished being Governor of Gibraltar,' Lois said.

'Well, they didn't. How would you like being the Honourable Mrs Ruttledge?'

'It wouldn't matter one way or the other.' she said, thinking, it's the Mrs Ruttledge that I don't want, not the Honourable that I do want.

The Old Man said, 'Anyway, it's academic. I told Terrell I did not want and could not accept a peerage. What could they pretend they were giving it to me for? I stepped down as Governor of Gibraltar in 1953, twenty years ago. And that was my last active appointment. It would look very fishy indeed. . . . The blackmail was the reiteration of an old threat they've made before, through Martin . . . to reopen the question of what happened to the one hundred thousand pounds in gold we paid to General Ballino. Terrell also said that such an enquiry could not avoid going into other monies spent by me while Army commander.'

'What did he mean?' Caroline asked.

Lois noticed that Paul was sitting upright in his chair, a shorthand notebook on his lap, looking at whoever was speaking, his pencil moving in small easy movements over the paper.

The Field-Marshal said, 'He was referring to money we had for clandestine operations. We spent quite a lot, over the whole period of the Balkans Campaign. It was handled by my I. Staff – Intelligence – working with Civil Affairs and the counter intelligence people. Mostly, very brief records were kept, but in some cases nothing was put down.'

'I can see why,' Caroline said slowly. 'If you recorded that a thousand pounds had been paid to Joe Snooks, with or without his receipt, anyone who saw or knew about the entry would know that Snooks was on your payroll. And it probably wouldn't be very difficult to work out what he was paid for doing. And get rid of him when convenient.'

The Field-Marshal said, 'Quite right, my dear. And whatever documents did exist were collected by our Civil Affairs people at the end of the campaign. God knows what happened to them after that.'

'Civil Affairs was controlled by who?' Caroline asked.

'Supreme Headquarters, Mediterranean, gave out the policy, which had been decided on in consultation by the Allied governments concerned. It was put into effect mainly by political advisers at Army Group and Army level, with Civil Affairs teams down to Corps and division level. My Civil Affairs chief at 16th Army, Johnson, sent all his documents to Jordan at 17th Army Group, when we disbanded.'

'17th Army Group . . . Sir Henry Bartlett.'

'Yes.'

Lois said, 'Have you been taking all this down, Paul?'

'Yes, madam.' Paul always spoke very formally to her.

'Where did you learn shorthand?'

'At school, madam.' Lois noticed Caroline frowning at him.

'It doesn't matter where he learned it, it's a very useful accomplishment,' the Old Man said. 'To continue . . .' he pointed at Caroline – 'let me have the top letter on the desk – that one.' He pulled the letter out of the slit flap and said, 'This is from the Yugoslav Ambassador. You can have a look at it later . . . the salient point is that the ambassador pretends to be very upset that I should even have hinted that Comrade Sovik could have had anything to do with the theft of the Collection. The ambassador trusts that I will not give further credence to this unfortunate and ill-founded rumour by publishing it any shape or form. He begs us, instead, to devote our efforts to helping them find the present whereabouts of the Collection. Or what's left of it, though they don't think much has been sold so far. Only perhaps five paintings in all these years.'

'Whoever's got it is not greedy,' Caroline said.

'Or needy,' Paul added in a low voice.

'He – the ambassador – said they now had had confirmation that the Rembrandt sold in New York in May, which started all this up again, was definitely from the Collection. And now they're sure that some Picasso lithographs sold in London some time late in 1944 were from the Collection, too. A rich Frenchman called Peyraude has them now.'

'Which is strange,' Caroline said, 'because the raid on Zvornos Castle didn't happen till February 1945.'

'That *is* odd,' the Old Man said. He relapsed into silence, frowning.

After a time Lois asked, 'Have you had any calls about the article on the missing German war material, Daddy?'

'What article? I didn't see one in the *Telegraph*,' he said.

'Oh, it was in *The Times*. I bought one at the bookstall to read on the train.'

How easy it was to be caught in a petty lie, she thought; I must get away, free myself from these sordid subterfuges. She continued aloud. 'The writer hinted that the official explanation as to why you pulled the 16th Army back after Vojja Lovac wasn't the whole truth.'

'Ah,' the Old Man said. 'I'm rather surprised at them starting on that – the writer was primed, of course – when they haven't been able to get at and destroy the evidence of the truth. Perhaps the article was commissioned before they realised that they weren't going to get what they want.'

'What *is* the truth, Grandpa?' Caroline asked. 'Tell us.'

'Not yet,' he said cheerfully.

Caroline said, 'Anyway, I don't think we ought just to sit here and let them make all these threats and generally attack while we have to try to defend ourselves. I think we ought to counter attack. I think the person behind all the pressure is Sir Henry Bartlett. We ought to go after him. That's the proper military thing to do, isn't it, Grandpa?'

'Quite right,' he said, chuckling. 'The best defence is an active offence. What do you propose to do to, or with, our Member of Parliament?'

Lois said suddenly, 'We used to know them before the war. He had a girl about my age.'

'She married an Australian and lives out there,' the Field-Marshal said.

'I know. But they weren't living in that huge Rackleigh Manor. They had a small, cheap house – with about an acre, perhaps two.'

'He was only a lieutenant colonel, the same as I was,' her father said.

'Yes,' she said. 'We had this big house because Mother had inherited it from her mother. When was that?'

'1936.'

'But Sir Henry Bartlett bought Rackleigh Manor not long after the war – about 1946.'

'You mean, where did the money come from?' Caroline asked.

'Of course, he was a general by then, though retired,' the Old Man said thoughtfully. 'But that's not enough to explain the great change in his circumstances that occurred about that time. One did not inquire too closely, but I believe his wife inherited a considerable sum from relatives in Canada.'

Paul said, 'Excuse me, sir ... I don't know the gentleman you are talking about, but he might have given out that his wealth came from an inheritance to hide its true source.'

Caroline looked at him sharply. – 'And what might that have been?'

'I don't know, miss ... something that would have been taxable, perhaps, only he didn't want to pay taxes or death duties on it ... something improper, like taking bribes ... something shameful, even, that he wouldn't like to come out, especially if he was going into politics ... something ...'

Caroline interrupted him. 'Let's find out, Grandpa. Let's rake up all the dirt we can and get the *Journal* to publish it!'

'We'd better be sure it's true first,' the Old Man said, 'and on matters of public interest. Besides, we are not out to "get" Henry at any price but to find what happened to the Zvornos Collection. If Henry did acquire a lot of money at the relevant time, that is a legitimate line of enquiry. We'll call Burrisk and see if he has any leads yet. Caroline, will you do that, please? I'm going down to see how Vetch is getting on.'

He pulled himself slowly to his feet and went out, head bent forward. Caroline sat at the telephone and dialled. Lois thought, I should be getting to work now but I'll just listen. Paul slipped out apologetically, with a half bow towards her, closing the door silently behind him.

Caroline was saying, 'Caroline Ruttledge here, Mr Burrisk – Field-Marshal Durham's grand-daughter. He told me to ask you whether you had learned anything more about the Zvornos Collection?'

She listened a long time, making notes while the earpiece

buzzed. Lois could detect the American accent, but not any words.

After five minutes she said, 'That's very interesting. Now, Grandfather also asked if you have any way of finding out whether Sir Henry Bartlett's wife – she died a few years ago – really did inherit money from relatives in Canada in 1945 or 1946 and if so, how much, and what was the source of the relatives' wealth. . . . Sir Henry Bartlett, Member of Parliament for Rackleigh-and-Hawkford, retired full general, in the Cabinet, lots of orders and decorations – Rackleigh Manor, Rackleigh, Surrey. It's only four miles from here. . . . I can't imagine how you will find out what the wife's maiden name was, and where the relatives live in Canada. . . . Oh, I see. Well, that's wonderful. . . . Yes, he's here. . . . No, he went out. In his own room, probably. . . . Daddy saw them and thought the same as you do. . . . That was Grandpa's doing. He insisted, out of a sense of guilt, I'm sure. . . . I will. Thank you.'

She hung up, turning to her mother, 'Do you know what that last bit was about?'

'Paul, I suppose,' Lois said.

'Yes. He said, don't trust him. He wanted to know why he was here, and I told him.'

'I heard. What did he say about the Zvornos Collection?'

'*Very* interesting! The last Count Zvornos arrived in New York in the middle of 1939. Saw the war coming, obviously. He seemed to have plenty of money, stayed at an expensive hotel and had endless mistresses. Late in 1944 he left and went to Italy. How he got there, in the middle of the war . . . ? Ah, I get it. He was flown over to give advice on the planning of the invasion of the Balkans – Operation Wolfpack. I've just got to that in the *History* . . .'

Lois said, 'People in his position, with his money, can do a lot of things that are impossible to the rest of us, even in war.'

'Well, he was there till soon after the end of the war in Europe. Then – early in June, 1945 – he returned to New York. A month later he disappeared. And a month later again, in August, 1945, his roped-up corpse was found in an old refrigerator in New York harbour. Burrisk says he was obviously working with a gang. During his first, long stay he contacted them and told them he had pictures which would be worth a lot if they could be got out of Yugoslavia. But no one could do anything while the Germans still held the country. Then the Count either heard about the idea of an invasion, or worked out the likelihood for himself and got himself to Italy, where he would be in a position to plan the raid with the gang's people on the spot. And that wouldn't be difficult because all those American gangsters are Italians, aren't they? And then when the pictures had been stolen . . .'

'But we still don't know whether anyone was bribed to let the truck through,' Lois said. 'That was the vital part of the plan.'

'No, we don't know. Then back in America the Count was killed because he was asking for too much from the gang. Or perhaps wouldn't let them in on the share they were supposed to get. . . . Mr Burrisk is flying to New York tomorrow on business, for a week. He doesn't think he'll have much trouble finding out about Lady Bartlett's inheritance – if any.'

'I wonder where he gets all his information.'

'I don't know. I like his warning us to keep an eye on Paul – he's rather a fishy character himself, if you ask me!'

'How's Paul doing?'

'He's useful,' Caroline said grudgingly. 'He hasn't been here long enough to learn where things are . . . and he doesn't know the first thing about history. Not just military history – *any* history. Anything before about 1960 didn't happen. I'm making him read the *Official History*, so that at least he'll have heard that there was a war. . . . He gives me the creeps, calling me Miss Ruttledge all the time and wiping his hands on invisible soap. The servility's our fault, the class system's, I know, but – anyway, I think he'd stab any of us in the back if he got half a chance. . . . Have a good time in town, Mummy?'

'Oh, yes,' she said, getting up. 'It's a change.'

She went downstairs. As she reached the hall the front door opened and Martin came in, striding fast. He took off his hat and flung it at the hatstand. It landed on a peg as he thrust his umbrella into the stand below and ran up the stairs.

'Sir . . . Hullo, Caroline! I've got a job – selling shirts! No, no, not at Austin Reed's – with Tommy Proctor's firm, that makes them. Their main business is with big institutions – the Birmingham police force, British Rail, British Airways, that sort of thing. That'll be my end of it . . .'

She heard his footsteps firm and fast along the upper landing. He didn't even see me, she thought.

CHAPTER TEN

Martin drove to work that Friday, July 27, in a good mood. He missed the twenty-four minutes that he used to have on the train from Ashwood to Waterloo, and back in the evening, as it was a familiar friendly routine, chatting with long-time acquaintances on the platform, buying a paper, folding it narrowly, getting the crossword puzzle at least three-quarters done before beginning to collect himself as the train rocked through Vauxhall. Now he had to drive every day, for Proctor's factory was on the Great West Road near Slough, and there was no train connection from Ashwood.

He felt unusually good in his new routine today because the day before he had settled a deal for the sale of five hundred shirts to the police force of Reading, and already this morning, before setting out for Proctor's, he had had a useful hour's talk with the head of the Southern Counties bus fleet. After dropping in at the main office to tell Tommy Proctor what he'd done, he'd be going on up to town for a talk with the people at British Airways. Five hundred shirts wasn't much of a job for a firm geared, like Proctor's, to handle orders in the thousands, but it was a beginning ... and he was finding salesmanship a good deal more interesting than being a prop of the bureaucracy.

The machines were whirring and clacking as he passed through the manufacturing floor toward the offices one floor up at the back. There was no other way to get at the executive offices, because Tommy Proctor wouldn't have it any other way.

'I want everyone of us office-bound chaps to realise, at least twice a day, that we live by making shirts,' he'd said. 'Not by drinking dry martinis with buyers – by making good shirts.'

Martin swung up the two flights of stairs and walked briskly into Tommy's outer office. The secretary was a tall blonde, attractive though not young.

'Oh, Brigadier ... I was trying to get you,' she said. 'Mr Proctor wants to speak to you.'

'Can I go in?'

'I'll tell him you're here.'

A moment later Martin walked into the owner's large deeply-carpeted office.

'Good news, Tommy,' he said, as he sat down in the leather chair opposite the desk, 'I've sold five hundred shirts to the City of Reading, for the police force. Here are the specifications. They seem perfectly ordinary, from what your people were teaching me.'

'Good work,' Tommy Proctor said automatically, reaching out for the paper. He read it. 'No problem there, and that's a reasonable price. We won't make a lot out of it, but we'll make something . . . and perhaps we'll get a reputation outside the government – if we're allowed to.'

'What do you mean?' Martin asked.

'You've just arrived? Did you pass a big man in a dark grey hat and blue and black striped tie, going out?'

'I passed a man in the machine room passage. I didn't really look at him.'

'That fellow was from the Department of Defence. They're not going to confirm the provisional order they gave us for 30,000 shirts for the Navy, last month.'

'But they can't . . .' Martin began.

'They can,' Tommy Proctor said. 'It was a provisional order, due for confirmation next week if they didn't find some reason not to proceed. They have found such a reason.'

'But what . . . ?'

'They don't have to explain', Proctor said, 'but Mr Snodgrass or whatever his bloody name was did in fact make it clear that the order was not being confirmed because we were employing you.'

'Christ!' Martin said violently, the word forced explosively out of him by a sudden blast of rage.

Proctor continued, 'And we will get no more government contracts as long as we continue to employ you.'

'Christ!' Martin said again. 'This is . . . absolutely outrageous!'

'It is,' Proctor said, 'and for the moment I'm not going to knuckle under. I know our M.P. well and I'm going to see him over the weekend. We're due to play golf tomorrow. Throwing a thousand of his constituents out of work isn't going to help him at the next election. I'll see what can be done. . . . Didn't you tell me the other day that you were going to give someone at British Airways lunch today?'

'Yes.'

'Well, I think it would be better if you don't. They're a government corporation and whoever's after you could bring considerable pressure onto them too ... not quite as directly as with the Department of Defence, but enough. I'll phone them, say you're ill, and send Bill instead.'

'What do you want me to do?' Martin asked.

Proctor said, 'For the moment, nothing. Go home. Have a couple of drinks. I'll know more after the weekend.' He nodded in sign of dismissal and Martin went out.

Christ! he exploded to himself, walking along the passage to his office. Christ! This was like being a hunted fox ... but instead of hounds and horses and red coats and blaring horns, it was a cold front, faceless voices uttering polite threats, without reason given or excuse accepted. Security ... necessity ... he'd done some things himself under those banners, but in war, in foreign campaigns, when lives were literally at stake. Here, the traffic roaring along the Great West Road, garish signs advertising a hundred peacetime products, it was impossible. He couldn't face it. So what? Go home? To Lois and the Old Man?

He took the telephone and dialled a number, 'Madeleine? Martin here. . . . Martin Ruttledge. Can I come and see you? . . . Inside an hour. And afterwards I'll take you out to lunch.'

He'd make love to Madeleine, and tell her everything. If they thought they were going to keep these things secret by hounding him, they were making a mistake. What he knew would soon be all over London, funnelling out from Soho through a hundred mouths. Madeleine knew a lot of people, intimately.

When he was ten minutes from home, driving down the by-pass well ahead of the evening rush hour traffic, he slowed from the fast pace he had maintained all the way from the West End. Madeleine was a woman practised in the art, or business, of pleasing men sexually; and she was not expensive ... but what was he doing, at his age, trying to find reliefs from his frustrations in her? What was he doing living in the big house that belonged to his wife, a minor planet in the orbit of the Field-Marshal? What was the point of continuing the charade with Lois? Neither of them was getting any of the spiritual or physical benefits of marriage, only the irritations and annoying restrictions. Better walk away from it all – house, Old Man, Lois, the damned Memoirs ... and Caroline? She wasn't exactly a new girl since starting to work with her grandfather, but she was certainly different from what she had been. She had even talked to him, in the evenings, about politics, sport, little unimportant things, mere gossip sometimes ... but until this, to all intents she had not communicated with any of them since she was thirteen.

She came out of the front door as he was walking back from the garage, and said, 'I want to talk to you, Daddy. ... You look funny? Did something happen at Proctor's?'

'I'll tell you later,' he said. He was going to add – 'What's on your mind? And make it quick, because I'm tired ' – but stopped himself. In truth he was in no hurry, nor was he tired. If he didn't give her the opportunity now to say what she had to, she wouldn't come to him next time.

He said, 'What's your problem?'

She said, 'Paul Phillips is a thief, and perhaps worse.'

Martin sighed. More trouble in the household. 'How do you know?'

'I've been missing a few things since he came. Small change ... a brooch ... nothing valuable, and I couldn't even have been sure because I don't count my silver every time I empty my purse and I haven't worn that brooch for ages. Anyway I suspected Paul. He looks shifty, and he's been to jail.'

Martin thought, she's probably right. The fellow's been raised in an atmosphere where theft is no crime, simply something one does if one can get away with it.

Caroline continued, 'This morning I dropped a pound note where I knew he'd find it, and think it had fallen out of someone's pocket. It disappeared. He's got it.'

'Do you know that?'

'I'm *sure*, Daddy!' She was so vehement that Martin did not question her as to why she was sure. It sounded unpleasantly like a personal vendetta, or a case of 'give a dog a bad name', yet, still, her instinct was probably right.

'What do you think we should do?' he asked.

'Ask him to empty his pockets. Of course, he might have put it away somewhere, but he's the sort of person who would think I'd search his room, so he'll still have it on him. I have the number of the note.'

'All right,' Martin said. 'Let's get it over with. Where is he?'

'Working in Grandpa's study.'

'Is Grandpa there?'

'No, he's in the Factory.'

They turned into the house. Martin left his briefcase on the hall table and went straight upstairs, Caroline at his heels. Paul Phillips was bent over the typewriter by the window, and seemed to be typing back shorthand notes.

Martin said, 'Paul . . .'

The young man turned round, 'Yes, sir?'

'Caroline here thinks you have some money that doesn't belong to you.'

A convincing expression blended of pained surprise and hurt feelings spread over Paul's face, 'Miss Ruttledge does, sir?'

'Yes. May we examine your wallet?'

'My wallet, sir?'

'Yes.'

He was playing for time, and perhaps from the corners of his eyes searching for a place he could hide the note, if he could get it out of his wallet. Having seen that that was impossible, Paul said, 'This isn't a very nice thing to ask a man, sir.'

Martin said, 'We have no right to *demand* to see your wallet, Paul. We're asking, to clear the air.'

Paul felt in the inside pocket of his coat and handed over a long thin brown leather wallet.

'Everything in it's mine, got from the bank only two days ago when I cashed my last pay cheque . . . Oh, and there's a quid I found in the hall this morning.'

'And you were keeping it,' Caroline broke in angrily.

'No, Miss Ruttledge. I was waiting to give it to Mrs Ruttledge.'

'She's not here?' Martin asked.

Caroline said briefly, 'No. She went to London. . . . You're lying, Paul. This is the note I dropped for you, because I knew you'd steal it. There's the number. You're just a thief, and I think you're a traitor, too.'

'What do you mean?' Martin asked.

'I think he wants to hurt Grandpa. He didn't take this job to help, but to find out how he could hurt.'

'I don't 'ave to stand any more of this shit,' Paul said with sudden violence. The birthmark on his cheek stood out a more inflamed red, and he was half crouching, like a cornered animal, or . . . a man getting ready to draw a knife, Martin thought. They used knives a lot in Soho.

'If you think I like working in this 'ole you're mistaken,' he snarled, the cockney accent now plain. 'Listening to your la-di-da talking all day long, no one doing an 'and's turn of work, and then accusing me of stealing just because there was no one 'ere I could 'and the money over to. One lousy, fucking quid!'

'Paul!' Martin said sharply.

'That's not true,' Caroline said quietly, 'I've been here all day.'

'Why should I hand it over to you? It might not have been yours, either. If no one claimed it, it would have been mine.'

'It wouldn't,' Caroline said. 'If it wasn't yours to begin with, it never could be afterwards.'

'I don't care!' Paul cried, flaring up anew. 'You're all down on me because you know I've been to prison and Borstal. And whose fault was it that we weren't living a decent life . . . that old swine in the garden.

He stormed out of the room, slamming the door behind him.

In the silence Martin said, 'Quite a well-executed smoke screen of righteous indignation. We should feel guilty because we're kicking a man when he's down. A nasty piece of work, I'm afraid. We'll talk to Grandpa about him. He has to go.'

'I like him better when he's angry, than when he's so . . . smarmy and servile,' Caroline said thoughtfully. 'I wouldn't mind so much about the stealing, by itself. It serves us right for being so careless of money. But I've been watching Paul for two weeks now. He makes notes of things that aren't really his business. He has a full file of all the bad things that Grandpa has talked about, or mentioned, but he's not in the least interested in the good things – how Grandpa fooled the Germans with his Wolfpack plan, how he was everywhere in the heaviest fighting at Vojja Lovac, risking his life twenty times a day. . . . Paul's mother hates Grandpa, and she's been nursing that all these years, and obviously teaching it to Paul. You heard him burst out about that "old swine". I don't know why he stays if he hates Ashwood, and hates the job and hates us, and hates Grandpa . . . unless he has some ulterior motive. At any rate, it would be much safer to get rid of him.'

'Come along,' Martin said.

They found the Field-Marshal cleaning and putting away his tools in the greenhouse. Caroline told him of the trap she had laid, and Martin described the confrontation with Paul.

He ended, 'I think we must dismiss him.'

The Old Man's heavy white brows bent. 'We? *I* hired him, Martin. . . . So he's a petty thief. I don't suppose he really knows what that means. And there's the chance that he'd forgotten about the pound, after he'd realised that Lois wasn't here.'

'He could have given it to you,' Martin said doggedly. 'At any rate, he certainly shouldn't have kept it. There aren't that many people in the house. It's not the same as finding a pound in Oxford Circus underground station.'

'I don't think he'll do it again,' the Field-Marshal said.

Martin looked at Caroline, shrugging.

She said, 'I'm not sure what side he's on, Grandpa.'

'There aren't any sides,' he answered at once. 'I'm trying to publish the truth, and if I don't know it, to find it. What use people make of that truth is nothing to do with me. . . . I mean, I shall not complain at any use people make of that truth. . . . I don't want to send him away now. I'm going to wait till Monday, when everyone will have had time to think things over, then have a talk with him. You say he claims he's unhappy here? He may *want* to leave.'

Caroline said, 'I think he does, for himself. But his mother won't let him. And he has no other job to go to.'

'Well, we'll find out on Monday.'

Martin said, 'Very well, sir. . . . They're after Proctor's now. Because they employed me.'

The Old Man shook his head, 'They're really frightened, aren't they?'

The three of them entered the house by the garden door just as Lois came in at the front. She looked flushed, Martin thought, as though from a good lunch; but she must have finished lunch a long time ago. She went upstairs without speaking to him.

Martin stared at himself in his shaving mirror. Saturday morning and he'd lain in late. They didn't want him at Proctor's on Saturdays. Some Saturdays the machine floor was working, but there was nothing for a salesman to do, unless he was playing golf with a prospective buyer . . . such as some big wheel in the Ministry of Defence. He wondered what Tommy Proctor would find out from his M.P. today. His own M.P. was Henry Bartlett; he wouldn't get much satisfaction from him.

It was a hot day, the sun blazing down with almost Indian intensity from a coppery sky, no clouds in sight, the trees the dark green of high summer, the slate-blue shade heavy on the grass under them. After breakfast he read the paper from front to back, making it last, then strolled down the garden path toward the Factory. The Old Man was digging in the ordinary rose garden, in his shirt sleeves, wearing a stained old brown hat. The sweat ran down his bare arms and dripped off his chin and nose.

When he saw Martin he straightened up slowly, a hand on his back, 'By God, it's hot!'

'You should have asked Vetch to come if there was all that digging to do.'

The Field-Marshal shook his head. 'I don't ask him to come on Saturday unless there's some big do on.'

'Come into the house. There's some cold lemonade in the kitchen.'

The Field-Marshal looked at his watch, 'And Mr Burrisk coming in half an hour.'

'I didn't know that.'

'Oh, he called me yesterday evening. He has some news for us.' He picked his jacket off the back of the battered old chair and walked with Martin up the path.

Lois met them as they came in – 'Visitors,' she said.

'Burrisk? He's early.'

'No. Mrs Phillips. I put her in the drawing room. Paul's with her.'

The Field-Marshal said, 'You go and speak to them for a minute, Martin. I'll wash up.'

Madeleine was sitting by the fireplace, curiously examining the signed silver-framed photographs on the mantelpiece, including ones of the Queen and the Duke of Edinburgh, Churchill, Maitland Wilson, and half a dozen other field-marshals and American generals, the soldiers in uniform and appearing as they had been in the years immediately after the war. She turned, as Paul stood up quickly from his seat on the sofa.

'Mrs Phillips,' he said. 'How nice to see you here.' What was she going to do or say, he wondered. She was looking subtly different from the way she appeared in Soho. Her clothes could not be described as in good taste but they were a great deal better than he would have feared if she had given him time to wonder about it.

'You can call me Madeleine, Martin,' she said, trying to smile, but no smile came.

So that's it, he thought: blackmail. She is emphasising our other relationship. It was less than twenty-four hours since she'd been sprawled on her bed in Soho, her florid female charms exposed for him.

Paul said, 'I didn't want my mother to come down, sir. I told her everything would be all right, but she insisted she must see the Field-Marshal.'

He had regained control of his accent, Martin noticed. Was there a hint of greater ease in his manner, less of the bowing and scraping that so annoyed Caroline?

The Field-Marshal came in and went straight to Madeleine, walking slowly, his hand out. 'Mrs Phillips. I'm John Durham.'

'I know,' she said. 'I've seen your picture in the paper. Everyone has.'

The Field-Marshal motioned her to the sofa and sat down opposite on a hard windsor chair. 'What can I do for you?'

She arranged her back hair and fiddled with the big hand-bag resting on her lap. 'Paul called me in the night,' she said, 'about the pound note. He said he was afraid you were going to give him the sack.'

The Field-Marshal said, 'The first thing I intended to find out was whether he wanted to stay here. It's not a very exciting place for a young man.'

'He's not all that young,' she said. 'He's thirty-one, you know. Time he settled down, really. . . . He told me about Miss Ruttledge accusing him of stealing the pound when all he'd done was pick it up. I'd like to ask her how she knew he meant to keep it.'

The Field-Marshal said, 'Caroline's not here. She's gone up to London for the day.'

Madeleine sniffed. 'Well, it doesn't seem right to me. . . . My boy's not a thief, sir. He's learning a lot here. He's got no other job to go to, and not likely he can get one. If he can work with you on this book, and you can give him a good recommendation when it's done, that'll mean a lot. If he can show a recommendation from Field-Marshal Sir John Durham, everyone's going to take notice. He'll have a better chance. He hasn't had much of a chance so far.

'No,' the Field-Marshal said, 'I would not like to deprive him of such an opportunity on such slender grounds.'

Madeleine turned to Martin, 'You wouldn't want to see him out on the streets, would you, Martin? You know what we've been through and how hard it is to make ends meet these days.'

'I know,' Martin muttered. It was, after all, a sort of black-mail: put in your word for Paul, see that he keeps the job — or else I'll tell about us. She didn't realise what sort of a man the Field-Marshal was. Nor that he, Martin, didn't care a damn whether Lois knew about his sleeping with her or not. But Clive would be shocked. And Caroline? What would Caroline think?

He thought he heard the front door bell ring and a moment later Lois came in. 'Mr Burrisk's here,' she announced.

'Show him in, please,' the Field-Marshal said.

Burrisk strode in, preceded by a waft of eau-de-cologne. He had the same even sun-lamp tan, and he was still wearing a white-on-white shirt and a large pair of dark glasses. The Field-Marshal did the introductions, and Martin noticed that Burrisk examined Madeleine carefully from behind his glasses.

The Field-Marshal said, 'We were talking about whether Paul Phillips should continue to work here. . . . Mr Burrisk is also helping me with the Memoirs, so there's no reason why he should not share our discussions. Paul, tell me honestly, do you want to stay here and continue working on the Memoirs?'

Paul hesitated and then said, 'Yes, I do. But Miss Ruttledge doesn't like me. It's awkward.'

'We have to work together, even though we don't all agree on everything,' the Field-Marshal said. 'You can stay. I'll speak to Caroline.'

'Thank you, sir,' Madeleine broke out. 'I knew you were too much of a gentleman to pick on Paul just because . . . he's been in trouble.'

'And he'll be in trouble again if he goes back to photographing thirteen-year-old chicks screwing with spades,' Burrisk growled.

'I never . . .' Paul began.

Burrisk said, 'Don't waste your breath, sonny. The police were ready to jump when you quit to take this job. I guess you knew, and that's why you took it . . . I'm just back from New York, like I said on the phone last night.' He wiped his brow – 'Man, is it hot in here? They told me it was never hot in England. Mind if I take off my jacket?'

'Not a bit.'

Burrisk stood up and began to shrug out of his summer-weight jacket; then said, 'Heck, I'm used to it,' and shrugged back into the coat, but not before Martin had noticed the leather strap of a shoulder holster under his left armpit.

Burrisk sat down again. 'We found something . . . Sir Bartlett's wife came from Edmonton, Alberta. Her father owned a lot of shares in a big oil corporation, that struck it rich early in 1945. A month or two later the father died, leaving his money equally between the two children – Mrs Bartlett and her brother.'

'That would explain where Henry got his wealth from, at that time,' the Field-Marshal said.

'It would,' Burrisk continued, 'except that the old man had secretly sold out nearly all his shares just *before* the gushers came in, when they were worth very little. The children didn't get a cent, well, no more than a thousand bucks apiece.'

'But,' the Field-Marshal said, 'I remember Henry mentioning that his brother-in-law, his wife's brother, had come into a lot of money, with the inference that his wife had also.'

'The brother didn't come into any dough, Marshal. He made it himself, about the same time. But he never gave a cent to his sister. Our guys in Edmonton report there was a feud of some kind between them. They're both dead now.'

Martin whistled thoughtfully. If the source of Sir Henry Bartlett's wealth was not the Canadian wife, what was it?'

Burrisk was saying, 'I'm going to start on having my guys look into Sir Bartlett's life a hell of a lot more closely. All we need to do is find a few of his enemies. They'll point in the right direction.'

Madeleine was on her feet. 'Well, sir,' she began awkwardly, 'I'm sorry to have bothered you.'

The Field-Marshal stood up, towering over her, 'I'm sorry we had never met before.'

Madeleine said, 'You were so high up, and David was so low . . .'

'You didn't attend the court martial?'

She shook her head and said in a low voice, 'I didn't want to. . . . I must be going back. I have to catch the train, I think it's at 12.17.'

Burrisk stood up, 'You can come back with me.'

'Oh, well . . . thank you very much.'

Martin said, 'Anything else, Mr Burrisk, about Zvornos?'

Burrisk shook his head. 'We're working on finding out who put the Count in the refrigerator. That'll only be the beginning.'

Then they were going out and Madeleine was pressing his hand, saying, 'Thank you, Martin. I know Paul wants to go on working here.'

'Come along, ma'am,' Burrisk said; and in a low aside out of the corner of his mouth to Martin, 'Keep an eye on that Paul.

... Goodbye, Marshal. Expect I'll be seeing you again soon.'

The huge limousine swished out of the drive and then Martin and Paul went back into the house, in time to see the Field-Marshal already at the top of the stairs on the way to his study.

They followed him up, and Paul said, 'I'd like to thank you, sir, for what . . .'

The Old Man waved a bony hand. 'Nothing. Just keep at the work.'

Paul sidled past and took up his usual position at the type-writer, which began to click.

The Old Man said to Martin, 'You know Mrs Phillips quite well, I see.'

'Yes,' Martin said, 'I've seen her two or three times.'

He was about to say that he had been getting information from her, but stopped himself short. The Old Man might think what he had said odd, with no further explanation, but what the hell, he was past caring. If the Old Man was hiding nothing, he might as well follow suit.

He said, 'You know what I was telling you about yesterday, sir?'

'About Proctor's losing the contract?'

'Yes. I think I may have to resign from them. I can't stay on if it would mean men being thrown out of work. Anyway, Tommy would have to sacrifice me rather than risk that.'

'You'll hear on Monday, won't you?'

'Only what he's been able to learn from the Slough M.P., which may not be much by then. I can't just hang on, while no one actually says anything, but the firm keeps losing contracts. I'll resign after I've spoken to Tommy. Then I'll leave here and try to get work on my own.'

'Not associated with me, you mean?'

'Yes, sir,' Martin said. It was the truth and the time had come to see it, and say it.

'Will Lois go with you?'

'I won't ask her,' he said.

'I'm sorry,' the Old Man said. Martin thought, he doesn't sound or seem sorry. He must have recognised the failure of their marriage a long time ago, and been expecting the open break to come: now it had.

The telephone rang and Paul leaned to answer it. 'Field-Marshal Durham's office here,' He turned to the Field-Marshal. 'It's Mr Mullins of the *Journal*, sir.'

The Field-Marshal said, 'Martin, you take it.' He lowered

himself into a chair and closed his eyes. 'Don't type for a bit, Paul. Martin can't hear properly when you do.'

Martin took the phone. Mullins's voice at the other end was loud and cheerful. 'We're a bit short of hard news for tomorrow,' he said. 'Anything hot from the Old Man?'

Martin looked back at the Field-Marshal. The old bastard had been taking a sort of devilish delight in springing surprises on them, letting off his bombs one at a time, without warning, and always when least expected. It was time he had a taste of his own medicine. He said, 'He's going to tell the truth about the bombing of Peskevo.'

'Peskevo? Wait a sec. That was the time we got the wrong information and some bombs hit a Yugoslav village that was on our side.'

The Old Man was nodding encouragingly. Damn him! There was no way to get under his skin.

Martin said, 'It wasn't a few bombs. It was a hell of a lot. And it wasn't a mistake. It was done on purpose.'

He heard the loud whistle at the other end. 'Ordered by whom? Why?'

The Field-Marshal raised his voice. 'Tell him he'll be able to publish the details in due course, when he serialises the Memoirs. All he needs to say now is that I am going to do so.'

In the earphone Mullins's voice said, 'I heard that. He's right. We want to whet the public's appetite, not force-feed it. . . . Anything else?'

'Yes,' Martin said. 'This is rather technical, but it's important – to me, at any rate. *The Official History* and all other historians record that the main idea of the Balkan Campaign – its overall purpose and its co-ordination with the campaigns in Italy, France, and South Russia – was set out in a paper called Appreciation R3.'

'I've never heard of it,' Mullins said.

'You're not a military historian. . . . It is stated that Appreciation R3 was the work of then Lieutenant Colonel Martin Ruttledge, 40th Lancers, Indian Army.'

'You?'

'Yes. Of course, it was reworked and the draft that was finally submitted to the War Cabinet was not quite the same as the original, and by then it had become the official appreciation of the Supreme Commander, Mediterranean Theatre. On the strength of R3 I was put onto General Durham's staff in XIV Corps, and later made Brigadier, General Staff, 16th Army.

But Appreciation R3 was not my work. It was originated by my adjutant, Captain Richard Armstrong.'

Mullins said, 'The author of *The Limits of Pure Reason* and *Critical Metaphysics*?'

'Yes. . . . He gave me the appreciation one day, in Italy, and said "That's what we ought to do. Will you submit it? Only send it in your own name," he said. "No one's going to listen to what a captain has to say." I didn't agree. I knew that no one was going to listen to what the C.O. of an armoured car regiment had to say, either. . . . Two days later, his car was hit by an 88, and he was blinded. The last thing he said to me as they were taking him back was to send in the appreciation, in my name. I couldn't make up my mind for a week. Then I did. I called it R3 – Ruttledge No. 3 – because I'd done two others before. It should have been Armstrong 1.'

'Very interesting,' Mullins said. 'But, as you say, it's not exactly a matter of great public concern. Most of us don't know what the hell an appreciation is.'

Martin said, 'You ought to send someone down to see Dick Armstrong. He's quite amazing. The books show he's brainy, but he has a breadth of understanding which makes me feel as though I'm wearing blinkers.'

'H'mm!' He heard Mullins musing at the other end, *'Blinded war hero wins overdue recognition* . . . It might do. Does he have a seeing-eye dog?'

'Yes.'

'Great! I can't do it in time for tomorrow, but next week, unless something crops up, it'll make a nice paragraph. Give me his address, please, and phone number if you have it.' Martin did so, and then hung up.

'I was going to tell you,' he said to the Field-Marshal.

'I knew,' the Old Man said.

'That Dick Armstrong wrote that appreciation?'

'At first, of course, I assumed you had. But after you'd been in my headquarters a few weeks I knew you couldn't. You have a good mind, Martin, but it's rather like mine – dependent on experience for much of its strength. That appreciation was the work of a genius, whose mind could and did work out the correct answer to problems *without* having any experience of them.'

'It's been on my mind a long time – worse than shooting Cunningham. I felt that *that* was duty, this was cowardice. I made excuses – no one would read it unless I put my name to it – Dick wanted me to. Nothing helped. I lied, out of ambition.'

'I got all that down, what you and Mr Mullins said on the telephone,' Paul said. 'Do you want me to type it up?'

The Field-Marshal broke in. 'Not until I give you the details about the bombing of Peskevo. Meantime—' he looked at his watch '—we have a few minutes before lunch. Hand me that notebook there please, Martin.' He turned over a couple of pages, adjusted his glasses and began to speak from what Martin saw were brief notes, recently made.

'Take this down, Paul. . . . Early on 26th April, 1945, while with my Tactical Headquarters near Vojja Lovac, Yugoslavia, I received a signal informing me that the Army Group Commander, General Sir Henry Bartlett, and his chief Civil Affairs adviser, Mr Matthew Jordan, were flying in to see me at eleven a.m. The signal gave no indication as to the purpose of their visit. They arrived as indicated and I met them at the light airstrip we had prepared. General Bartlett told me that the three of us were to confer in private, without any other persons present. After briefly introducing the visitors to my principal staff officers and corps commanders, whom I had called in, in case General Bartlett had come to give me new orders, we went to my command caravan. Being entirely alone, we discussed supply matters. I was told of secret German peace feelers in Sweden and the probable surrender of Germany on all fronts within a week or two. Then Mr Jordan informed me that it was vital that the Committee of Three form the government of Yugoslavia after the war. Great damage had been done to the opposition National Freedom Movement in the bombing of Peskevo, but more was needed. He and General Bartlett had agreed that if the Committee of Three partisans could have the use of the German war material recently surrendered to my army, they would be in position to wipe out the N.F.M. within a month, and so stabilise the country, avoid a prolonged civil war, and establish in power a political party which, though not particularly friendly to the democracies, was at least better than the N.F.M., which was fascist in outlook, though anti-German from nationalistic reasons. I had no reason to question the motives behind this suggestion, which was then translated into a verbal order from General Bartlett, under which I was to withdraw my Army twelve miles, leaving the captured war material *in situ*. The movements of German forces farther to the east offered a possible, though unduly cautious motive for such a withdrawal. After General Bartlett and Mr Jordan had left, I gave brief orders to the Corps commanders. The withdrawal began the next day and was completed the day after – 28th April. That day one of my staff officers revealed to me that when he had heard that my meeting with General Bartlett and Mr Jordan was to be entirely in private, he had quickly got possession of a wire recorder that was used in the Signal Section, concealed it in my command caravan, and set it in operation. He showed me the machine, and asked whether I had received any written confirmation of the orders given to me. I said that I had not, for it was the kind of thing that often has to be done off the record; but that we were all gentlemen and no one would deny what had been said, if a competent authority later asked us to testify about it. The staff officer said, "Quite, sir. All the same, I think we should keep this wire." And we have. A transcript was made of it, which I kept in my personal files. That was seized by the police, here, on 29th May, 1973. . . . That's all.'

After waiting a minute, Martin asked, 'Who was the staff officer, sir?'

'You ought to be able to work that out,' the Field-Marshal said. He rose carefully. 'Lunch, and I'm hungry.' He went out.

Martin tried to think back. Who had been there when Bartlett and Jordan flew in? He himself had been at Tac H.Q., and didn't go to the airfield to meet them with the Old Man. Did the C.O.S. go? The M.G.A.? Johnson, the Civil Affairs man?

He couldn't remember. He felt vaguely better though and couldn't think why. What was there to feel better about? Sacked from one job and now being forced to resign from another?

He had come out with the truth about R3. That must be it. Now he'd have to tell Caroline. Or perhaps she'd read it in the transcript and understands a little more of how it had been, how they had all been, in those days of war, before she was born.

CHAPTER ELEVEN

The train drew away from the platform at Surbiton, snaked out onto the fast line and headed into the deep, curved cutting. Next stop – Waterloo. Caroline folded away the newspaper and threw it up on the rack opposite. The carriage was nearly empty, for few people went to London on Saturdays and those who did went a little later.

Her father had been in an odd mood yesterday. The business about someone in the government cancelling a shirt contract because of him would be enough to upset anyone, if he were as innocent about the realities of how the system worked as Daddy was; but she had felt that there was something else, too. He'd been somehow more aware of her mother, in an unpleasant way, and defiant of Grandpa, whom he was afraid of. But everyone was changing, becoming more defiant, more like their real selves, perhaps, as the preparation of the Memoirs continued.

Even Paul. She had almost liked him when he turned at bay on them about the pound note. He was guilty, of course. It was rot to pretend he had been keeping the money until he found someone he could give it to. But when he'd snarled at them for being snobs, down on him because of his class and history, he was quite right. The atmosphere of Ashwood House must be very difficult for him – Vetch touching his forelock to Grandpa like a mediaeval retainer, Daddy calling Grandpa *sir*, the many rooms and big windows and shaded lawn and giant trees, practically every visitor a Sir at least, and the famous Field-Marshal searching for the Philosopher's Stone down in the Factory, for everyone knew it was impossible to breed an absolutely black flower. All this would be enough to make anyone in Paul's position act subservient, all the while suppressing a wish to spit on it, show it up for the out-of-date nonsense it was. Now, if she could meet him in some other surroundings . . . Soho perhaps, or better, the university, or in a crowd of artists and writers, creative people somewhere near their own age – above all, people without money or privilege – then he might turn out to be someone different, and better.

But he was a criminal, Borstal, and then prison – for pimping, of all things. And, she was sure, a secret enemy of her family. She should not be thinking of him, certainly not of meeting him. He was a criminal. . . . So what? What were her father, and grandfather, and apparently Sir Henry Bartlett, and heaven knew how many other pillars of the Establishment? She wasn't going to let their bourgeois ideas govern her life. And yet . . . and yet, it was hard to wipe out all traces of your upbringing.

She had not been surprised, or accusatory, when Harry asked her to take the suitcase with the pistols and ammunition down to Ashwood; but she'd found herself shocked to the core, really outraged, by the fact that he was a thief . . . and she still felt that way. He'd left the university now and T.P.M. was in other hands, she'd heard. She ought to make contact with them again. But all that seemed a very long time ago now and, to tell the truth, rather petty compared with what she was becoming involved with through the Memoirs. She must have outgrown them. They seemed undirected and, worse, amateur. Working with Grandpa she was learning the meaning of the word 'professional'.

Paul must have a girl friend in London, or several. He lived off their earnings. But he didn't seem to have any money except what Grandpa was paying him. The girls would be lonely as he could only get off one day a week. Or they'd keep themselves in practice with other men. They'd have hearts of gold. They all did.

Burrisk called her 'sweetheart' when he spoke to her on the phone. He pronounced the word in an extraordinary way, and of course it didn't mean anything. He was an extraordinary man in lots of ways. She wished she could have stayed at home long enough to see him and hear what he had to say about his investigations. Paul would tell her when she got back. . . .

The train was squealing slowly round the last curves, under the glass roofs of Waterloo. She looked at the clock and decided to walk across Waterloo Bridge and then along the Embankment. Twenty minutes later she rang Charles Gibson's doorbell.

She leaned against a tall chest of drawers, one elbow rested on it, her head tilted to rest on one cupped hand, the other hand on her hip. A glass of wine stood on a side table beside her. She was naked, and it felt better that way than in her clothes, for it had turned hot and close, and there were murmurings of distant thunder in the east. The skylights high above bathed her in light; at the far end of the long room the curtains were drawn on the windows that looked out over the Thames.

Charles said, 'Take a drink whenever you want to, but try

not to move anything except your right hand.'

She took the hand off her hip, reached out, and drank. She said, 'Mr Burrisk's found out something.'

'About what?'

'The Zvornos Collection theft, I suppose. He's down in Ashwood now, telling Grandpa whatever it is. We did ask him to find out about Sir Henry Bartlett's Canadian money, too.'

'And he said he could do all these things?'

'He's the European manager of an investigation service – Investigations and Information, Inc, 43 Cadwallader Street, W.2. Four Eyes, he calls it. Didn't you know? You're the one who gave him the introduction to Grandpa.'

'My dear child, if I tried to find out the boring background and sordid means of livelihood of everyone who gives me racing tips – or telephone numbers of likely models, come to that – I'd have no time for painting . . . 43 Cadwallader Street? I seem to have heard that address before. Hold on a sec. Sit down, if you like.'

She stepped down from the low dais where she had been posing and sprawled on the sofa beside it. She ought to cover herself now that she wasn't actually posing: professional models did, she'd heard. What did it matter? Besides, she was hot.

Charles came back with a phone book, the E to K section. He turned the pages, peered, and said, 'As I thought. That is also the address of the Essex Club.'

'I've never heard of it,' she said lazily, sipping her wine.

'There's no reason why you should have. It doesn't cater for the young, unless they're very rich and foolish. It's a gaming club. Do you remember Burrisk's phone number?'

'Yes,' she said, '483 9044. It's unlisted.'

'That's not the number of the Essex Club. He must have separate quarters inside the Club. Which is very interesting . . . very interesting, indeed. And it explains some things which would be hard to explain otherwise.'

'What do you mean?'

'The Essex Club is owned and run, under various legal and financial subterfuges, by a New York Mafia family. If Burrisk is connected with them, that would explain how he can get information. They are everywhere and will help each other, for a price, provided there isn't an inter-family war on.' He laughed loudly, slapping his thigh as he put the telephone book away. 'My Burrisk is a hood! This Investigations corporation has been set up to find out what opportunities there are in Europe, and handle the buying and selling from this end. And perhaps to carry out contracts on this side. Burrisk ferrets out the victims, who probably think they're safe here, and makes them an offer they can't refuse.'

'I saw *The Godfather*,' she said. 'Do you think Burrisk is some family's godfather?'

'I'm sure he isn't. The top man will stay in New York. But he may be high up in the family. You'd better tell the Old Man what we've discovered, when you get home.'

'Are you sure you didn't know before?' she said, looking at him suspiciously. Charles Gibson was someone you automatically distrusted . . . and kept on seeing.

He said, 'And deliberately introduced a snake into the bosom of the family? Though, I must say, he seems to be a very useful snake. Anyway, tell your grandfather. I expect it'll make him laugh. . . . We'd better get on with this. Can you stand another half hour?'

She took her pose again. Charles adjusted the position of her elbow slightly and returned to his easel. 'How's everyone at Bleak House?' he asked, his brush moving fast over the hidden canvas, his eyes down.

'All right,' she said. She frowned. 'That's not true. They're not all right at all. Daddy's in a state because after he got sacked from the security job, and got a job with Proctor's, they lost a contract because of him.'

Charles said, 'Your father's a very capable man – brilliant at times . . .'

'So I'm learning from the *Official History* and Grandpa's war diaries.'

'. . . but he has always needed someone stronger to lean on, or look up to. For a long time now it has been your grandfather. I wonder what will happen to him when the Old Man dies.'

'He's drinking rather a lot. Mummy made him move into one of the spare rooms after he'd told us about something he'd done in the war.'

'Killing Captain Cunningham?' Charles asked, still without looking up from his canvas.

'Yes. How did you know?'

'The Old Man told me about it long ago.'

'Mother's acting odd, too. She's moody, gets cross with the women who help her with the catering. And snaps at me all the time – but that's not new, just worse than usual.'

'Perhaps she's having the change of life.'

'I think she's about over that. She doesn't talk to me. . . . No, she's behaving rather as though she doesn't know where she is, or who.'

Charles said, 'Her mother, Margaret Durham, was much the same to her, only worse. You know there was a boy, your mother's brother, who died at ten, at prep school?'

'Yes.'

'That broke Margaret to pieces, practically destroyed her. She had lived for and in that boy, the Old Man told me.'

'Not for her daughter,' Caroline said bitterly. 'That's the way it always is, isn't it? And now Mother's carrying on the good work.'

'I tell you, you're not having it anything like as bad as Lois did. The Old Man was in Palestine when the boy died. He came home the next year to find Margaret completely withdrawn physically and mentally. Neither he nor Lois, your mother, could make any human contact with her.'

'That's what Mother's been like to me, as long as I can remember,' Caroline said, 'but *she* hasn't lost a son. . Clive's alive and posing happily.'

'She might have lost a lover, or something,' Charles said.

Caroline raised her head, startled, 'What? You mean Mummy has . . . ?'

'I didn't say anything,' he said, laughing. 'I am only suggesting one possible cause of her withdrawal from you and Martin. But, the way Margaret treated her, anything can be excused. Margaret's death was a blessing to her.'

'Grandpa was incredibly lucky to escape,' she said.

'He's not so sure.'

'How do you know all this? You didn't meet Grandpa till sometime in the war, did you?'

'1941, in the Western Desert,' he said. 'Your grandfather was . . . is . . . a lonely man. He needed someone to talk to – someone who was neither in the army, nor his family. He talked to me.'

'About an affair of Mother's? And I bet you spread it around.' She finished her glass of wine and stepped down from the dais. She felt unaccountably mischievous. 'Daddy's talked about you,' she said. 'You're a troublemaker. Now I see how. But why do you do it? Isn't Grandpa your friend?'

'Yes,' he said. She stepped round behind him and saw that his leaning figure of her was slightly exaggerated as to the length of her already long legs and torso, and the eyes had been slanted. The face was barely brushed in yet, but someone who knew her body well enough, and the shape of her breasts and loins, might guess who the model had been, in spite of the exaggeration.

'After Modigliani,' Charles said briefly. 'A long way after, I'm afraid. It's an experiment. I really ought to do either a straight nude, or a complete abstract. . . . Caroline, the world is full of sham. A still calm pond is not really still or calm, but a seething mass of bacteria, animalcules – cannibalism, fear, sex, and death. Some of this becomes apparent if you throw in a big stone, or stir up the bottom with a long stick. All sorts of vile smells are released, the water clouds up, tiny things rush about eating, mating, dying. It isn't as pretty as it was before, but it's much more true, and more interesting.'

'And you like to stir the pools of people's lives?'

He nodded. 'I like truth, that's why. I'm not interested – no painter should be – in whatever pretence people choose to cloak themselves in, only in the reality. I like to see the dirt rising, the fish darting, the frogs swimming for their lives. The Old Man does, too. He's got the U.S. Embassy in a tizzy now.'

'What about?'

'He's refusing to keep quiet about something dreadful that happened to the 798th U.S. Infantry. The ambassador told me last night.' He turned and put his arm round her waist. 'Wouldn't it be nice if something dreadful were to happen to you,' he said. 'Like being made love to by an eminent Royal Academician on that couch?'

He was facing her now, the other hand gliding cool and smooth across her torso. Her nipples tingled and swelled as his hand brushed the top of her pubic hair. His face came close to hers. She'd always known he would do this, sooner or later. For a time, when he first took her out from the university, she had longed for the moment to come, sure that she would soften in his arms, surrender, and become the willing object of his desire. He was electric in magnetism then, at the beginning . . . still was, the green eyes glowing close, the hair touching her cheek.

The hair was dyed. And now, she wasn't sure. She felt the thrust of desire in her body and leaned away from him. 'This is part of stirring up the pond?' she asked.

'Could be,' he whispered. 'I am a close friend of the family. Your father and mother would be outraged. You so young, me so old. It would be more exciting than falling in love with a man your own age.'

'Who for? And who's going to fall in love?'

'Me now. You later. That's the usual form.'

He touched his parted lips to hers and then she knew that she did not want him, not now. Later, perhaps; some other time or place, perhaps. But not here, not now. She stepped back. He did not try to follow her, but let his hands fall.

He looked at her a long moment and said, 'You're very nearly a woman now. And very beautiful. If you'd only dress like a woman instead of a tramp, what a stunner you'd be. Put on your clothes and let's go and have lunch. Do you like Greek food?'

She was in a bad mood when she reached home that evening. Charles had made no further attempts to seduce her, and by mid-afternoon, full of retsina, she had rather been wishing he would. Now she had a small headache and all the way down on the train had held a peevish conversation with herself – if you wanted him to make love to you, why didn't you give him some sign? It isn't supposed to be difficult. But I don't want to become his lover, on a permanent basis. Why not? I don't know ... He *is* old. Nearly sixty. He doesn't look it. Yes, he does. It's the dyed hair. That doesn't account for his energy. Do you know any young man as full of life? All right, but I don't think I like him. And I'm sure I don't trust him ... and so round and round, as the train whirred down the long trail toward the south west.

She found Paul locked in the small lavatory off her grandfather's study, with a notice on the door: DO NOT OPEN DOOR DARK ROOM OPERATIONS IN PROGRESS. She called, 'I'm back. What did Burrisk have to tell us?'

'I'll be out in a minute,' he said.

She felt an urge to sting him. 'What photographs are you developing in there? Dirty pictures?'

He did not answer; but came out five minutes later, looked at her and said, 'That was a nasty crack, Caroline. What have I done to make you try to hurt me?'

'Oh nothing,' she said, 'it was only a joke. 'But she felt better, because he had called her Caroline. 'What *have* you been doing?'

He handed her a still wet print. 'Hold it by the corner, there.'

'Finger prints!' she exclaimed.

'Mr Burrisk's.'

'Who told you to get them?'

'I've been suspicious about him ever since I heard about how he came here. He finds out things too easily. He knows too much. I think Burrisk is not his real name. I decided to get his prints as a first step. Then, if the Field-Marshal will use his influence with the Chief Constable – he told me he served under him in the desert – we can find out here and in the States whether Mr Burrisk has a criminal record, and what his real name is. I thought your father would disapprove, but when I told him, he said I had done right, because he saw this morning that Burrisk was carrying a gun in a shoulder holster.'

'And I learned that he lives at the Essex Club, with a private phone number there.'

'Mafia! The Mob,' Paul said thoughtfully. 'This could be dangerous, miss . . . Caroline. I live in Soho, and I know.'

'But why did he get an introduction to Grandpa? We don't have any money. At least not the sort of money the Mafia are interested in.'

'I don't know,' Paul said. 'We'd better find out. Carefully. I tell you, those people are dangerous, even here in England.'

Her father came in. He leaned against the door and said, 'I thought I heard you come in, then you vanished. Had a good time in town?'

'Yes.'

'What did you do?' His speech was slurred and he was rocking slightly where he stood against the door. She looked at him curiously. She had seen him tipsy a few times after regimental reunions and the like, but not recently, and never like this – blurred and dull instead of high.

'Oh, saw some old friends – girl friends,' she said. 'Went to the flicks.'

'What did you see?'

No name came into her mind. What was running? Paul was looking at her curiously.

'*The Godfather*,' she blurted out at last.

'Very appropriate,' Paul murmured.

'Eh?' her father said. 'Why?'

'We think Burrisk is a Mafioso. That's what they're called.'

'Might be,' her father said. 'He carries a pistol. Wears the right kind of suits and shirts. And suntan.' He sat down heavily in the swivel chair behind the desk, swung it round and said, 'I'm out of work. Resigned half an hour ago.'

'Did you call Mr Proctor?' she asked.

He nodded. 'Tommy said the M.P. was cagey. Wouldn't promise anything. Tommy was sure he wasn't going to raise the thing in the House. So I resigned. Can't throw all those chaps out of work for my sake.'

'What will you do, Daddy?'

'I don't know. I ought to leave, you know. Change my name . . . like Powell . . . go to sea . . . I've got to get away.'

'Don't run away,' she said. 'We're going to beat them! Get Grandpa's Memoirs published, in full. Aren't we, Paul?'

'I hope so,' Paul muttered, 'I'm doing my best.'

She sat down opposite her father. 'Half an hour before bath time. Daddy, what happened to the 798th American infantry?'

He leaned forward. 'I've had a drink or two. Or four. I won't be too clear. It's not very complicated . . . the Old Man told me, but it was a long time ago. Lessee, now . . .'

'Let me tell them,' a voice said in the door. 'Secondary evidence is not admissible when the primary evidence is available.'

The Field-Marshal came in slowly, smiling. He squeezed Caroline's shoulder. 'Had a good time in London? You ought to go up more often. You don't want to shut yourself up here with a lot of old squares like us.'

'Not so square,' she murmured, smiling back. He sank into the swivel chair which her father had vacated.

'I think I'll go to bed,' her father said, 'I don't feel so good.'

'Do that,' the Field-Marshal said. 'Take a couple of aspirins and we'll talk in the morning.' When the door had closed behind her father, the Field-Marshal said, 'It was April 4th, 1944. I've checked in my diary. We were having a hard time pushing the Germans back. My XIV Corps was on the British left. The U.S. LXV Corp was on my left. We were advancing up the line of the mountains, with the crest of the range the dividing line between us and the Americans. We were all having a bad time . . . Tigers dug in on shallow reverse slopes were knocking out our tanks by the dozen, so we had to push infantry out ahead. That slowed the advance, and kept everyone for longer periods under shellfire. It was raining, deep mud everywhere, an icy north wind blowing day and night . . .'

'Your objective was San Prospero,' Caroline broke in, a page of *The Official History* suddenly recreating itself before her eyes, spread open for her to read.

'The line San Prospero to Farolo,' her grandfather said. 'San Prospero was in the valley on our side, Farolo about opposite in the valley on the American side. We were working together, but because of the nature of the ground, all our artillery was in the floor of our valley, and the Americans' in their valley. So our guns could only support our men, and theirs only theirs. ... Pour me a drink, Paul, please. A whisky and soda. No, I don't have ice. Thank you. ... I could see San Prospero ahead when I went up to the headquarters of my left-hand division. Storm clouds over it ... the cathedral campanile disappearing into the clouds ... dead Germans everywhere ... and dead British ...'

His eyes were open, but hooded and far seeing, as though looking through the wall.

'The division commander got a message that the American battalion nearest to him – the 2nd battalion of the 798th Infantry Regiment – wanted to come over the crest to outflank a very tough Hun position their side and on the crest itself. That was all right with us, but we would have to give them artillery support, as the Americans could only support them with mortars and a few howitzers.'

'Why?' Caroline asked.

'Guns have a flat trajectory. Any shell that missed the crest would land miles on our side, among my leading troops, who were almost in the outskirts of San Prospero. Mortar bombs and howitzer shells go high in the air and come steeply down. ... We sent a gunner party of F.O.O.s – forward observation officers – up to them, and they began their advance. I went back to my headquarters and was just about to set out to look at my right division when we got a frantic call from the division on the left, where I'd just come from. The senior F.O.O. we'd sent up to the 798th wanted to speak to the C.C.R.A. – Commander, Corps Royal Artillery – urgently and in secret. He was an Indian, and the C.C.R.A. told him to speak in Hindustani, but slowly and clearly – it was a long time since the C.C.R.A. had learned it. I listened to the conversation on another set – I can speak Hindustani, too. The F.O.O. said the Germans were counter-attacking very ferociously, with tanks. The Americans were mostly very young, he said, and were tired. The battalion had had very heavy casualties and seemed in a bad way all round, dispirited officers, sullen men. He thought they were on the point of breaking and running. The battalion commander had lost his nerve and was cowering in a foxhole. His second-in-command, who might have saved them, had just been killed. I asked how long he thought they would hold. He said, perhaps half an hour, no more.'

Caroline saw, down the garden, that it was raining. Low clouds obscured the darkening sky and the thunder that had boomed subterraneously from the east when she was in Charles's studio, now crashed about the sky, shaking the trees and rattling the old Georgian windows in their frames.

The Field-Marshal raised his voice: 'My American liaison officer was with his own corps. I tried for ten minutes to get through to the American division commander. There was no radio contact. The weather was like this . . . San Prospero was hidden now by the rain and the driving clouds . . . I looked at my air adviser and he shook his head. A waste of time even to think of air support. The Germans attacking the 798th were so close to them, even mixed with them, that artillery support was no longer possible . . . I ordered my C.C.R.A. to switch all artillery within range from other targets and bring down a barrage behind the Americans, to last for an hour. I ordered my left-hand division – 29th Indian – to counter attack the Germans that were attacking the Americans, with the support of a tank regiment I had in Corps reserve, the attack to start in an hour . . .'

His voice had been cracking, but not, Caroline thought, with emotion. He had had to raise it to be heard above the thunder, and he had done it. He was a man who did what had to be done, without thinking much about the morality or even the reason of it, she realised. She was seeing him for the first time, as he sat there, sipping his whisky to clear his throat, as a man, not as a grandfather, not as a Field-Marshal.

'It worked,' the Old Man continued at last, his voice hoarse. 'The American battalion saw that there was much worse behind than in front – my God, we had over three hundred guns in that barrage – and they held their positions. The counter attack was able to use them as a pivot and catch the Huns in flank. It was a considerable local victory . . . I believe the 798th Regiment got a battle pennant for it. When my American liaison officer returned I sent him straight to their corps commander to explain. He sent back verbally, thanking me, and saying he would certainly have agreed to what I'd done, if I'd been able to ask him. But he didn't want the truth to come out, as the battalion had had six men killed and twenty wounded by our shelling. It could be written off as a mistake – fog of war – and would soon be forgotten, but if it were known we had done it on purpose, there might be hell to pay in the U.S. I agreed. There was some talk, but it soon died. . . . I wrote to the next of kin of the six Americans killed by our artillery fire . . . got the names and addresses through the Liaison Officer.'

He swivelled the chair to one side, opened a drawer in his desk and rummaged among the papers there. 'These are some of the unofficial mementoes I've kept . . . here's a letter from Ted Crandall's sister – I'd been getting quite fond of her, but after Le Cateau – Ted was killed there – she never wrote again . . . this is a drawing a fusilier did of Dick Newby a week before he was killed on the Somme. It doesn't look anything like Dick, but . . . I keep it. This is the letter Jimmy Livingstone had in his pocket, ready to send off to his mother, when he was gassed at Ypres . . . Here we are.'

He handed over a sheet of paper. It was a U.S. Army message form, on which had been written in a careful script six names : —

Pvt Austin, John B.
Pfc Belprato, John G.
Sgt Dunnagan, James R.
Pvt Herrera, Ricardo F.
Pfc Hessinger, Michael K.
2/Lt O'Malley, Francis X.

The Old Man said, 'Those are the names of the killed. I didn't keep the names of the next of kin, after I'd written to them.'

He got up from the chair, holding out his hand for the list. Caroline returned it to him and he put it away in the same drawer.

'Bath time,' he said.

Paul put down his shorthand pad and said, 'Sir . . . I've made photos of Mr Burrisk's fingerprints, as I suspect he may not be what he seems. To find out, we will have to have help from the police.'

'What's wrong with Burrisk?' the Old Man asked quietly.

Caroline and Paul, speaking in turns, told him about the shoulder holster, the Essex Club address, and his mysterious sources of information.

At length the Field-Marshal said, 'I'll call the Chief Constable. I'll arrange for you to take your photographs to him, and he'll find out what he can about Burrisk.'

'Here and in America, sir,' Paul said.

'Of course. Then perhaps we'll learn whether Charles did us a good turn, or a bad one, in introducing the fellow.'

CHAPTER TWELVE

The Field-Marshal pressed quickly down on the accelerator, let up for a fraction of a second and rammed the gear into third without using the clutch. He pressed down hard on the accelerator again, and the Bentley bounded forward, its exhausts burbling throatily. As soon as he had passed the two cars that had been in front, he slipped back into top, again without using the clutch, and slowed to a sedate fifty-five. He felt good. In the old days he never used the clutch, but now sometimes he missed the gear and there was a painful sound of grinding teeth in the gearbox.

Old age was a nuisance, sometimes painful, and always frustrating, because you couldn't use your old skills, enjoy the pleasures you had been trained on, and you were unable to train yourself in any others; at least, he was, though some old men seemed to get as much value out of stamp collecting as they once had out of fox hunting. He was lucky that roses had always been an interest, almost a passion of his. Wars did not go on for ever, and a time came when even the peacetime army had no further use for you – then what did you do with your mind, your hands?

A driver hooted at him crossly and he realised that he had been drifting farther toward the middle of the road than was safe. Must concentrate . . .

Perhaps writing the Memoirs had become a new pleasure for him. More like a surgical operation on an interesting body – his own. Real pleasure, and the capacity for it, had left him much earlier . . . he kneeling in the shell hole before Passchendaele, looking down at what had been Peter Curran; yet Peter's death was more the accumulation of all that had gone before, not so horrible in itself, nor so indelibly graven into his mind as Jimmy Livingstone's. Seeing that letter four days ago, mud-stained in his drawer, the stains nearly sixty years old, had made him think of it again, and he had not slept well since. And, more often, his hands had seemed to glow red. He yawned. Some old men needed little sleep; he seemed to be needing more . . . Jimmy, staggering out of the morning mist toward him, coughing helplessly, reeling from side to side, suddenly the vomit pouring out over his tunic, obliterating the badges and buttons of the Royal Oxford Fusiliers in a torrent of yellow-green mucus and blood ... falling on forward, stumbling, staggering half upright again, falling finally onto his face, the vomit that was his lung tissue bubbling out under his face, one last effort to rise, three unendurable minutes of heaving and jerking ... final stillness; and he, holding Jimmy with one arm, had found his pistol drawn in his other hand, ready, for it was indecent that any man should suffer like that, above all not Jimmy, Jimmy the One they used to call him for his jokes and ...

Two car drivers hooted at him, one passing and shouting something unintelligible as he went by. The Field-Marshal slowed and returned again to his proper lane. There was too much traffic, too many cars, too many lights and signs. Too many people, by far. There used to be a fundamental good humour and decency, because there was room for it, except perhaps in the big city slums. Now – snap, snarl, bite ... like Caroline at Paul this morning, for no reason that he could see. The young had no business to waste their youth in anger, or guilt. . . . The road signs began to proliferate as he approached London. He had driven the road often enough so that he did not have to slow to read them; but, he thought, if ever six months pass when I don't drive up, they'll have altered things so that I won't know my way. Once every six months! He laughed quietly to himself – I should be worrying about the passing of this day, not of the next six months.

The wind was no longer clean but full of exhaust fumes. The trees and grasslands and playing fields of Surrey had given place to rows of houses and spaced lights on tall poles. He pushed his airman's goggles up onto the crown of his peaked tweed cap and began to hum a tune from *The Co-Optimists*. When had he seen that? Leave in 1916, was it, or ... ? He cursed himself and wiped his mind clean of everything but the road and his driving.

From where he sat, opposite Charles at the table in the middle of the room, he looked past Charles's shoulder at the life size nude on the easel.

'Good-looking body that girl has,' he said, nodding at the painting. He helped himself to the excellent cold roast beef.

Charles said, 'Not bad.'

'Nice life you lead,' the Field-Marshal said, 'looking at naked women, young 'uns too, when most men your age have to be satisfied with their middle-aged wives – with middle-aged spread. And not only look at them, I'm sure.'

'It has been known to happen that the purely artistic interest is temporarily superseded by some other,' Charles said, pouring some more burgundy.

'What do you mean, it has been known to happen? I know damned well you were sleeping with half the girls I used to meet here back in forty-two.'

'I was younger then. Much younger.'

'Lois used to paint,' the Field-Marshal said.

'I know,' Charles said, 'I saw some of her work when I first went down to your house. Of course she was very young then, and had had no training – but the talent was obvious. Perhaps more than talent.'

'I never knew why she gave it up,' the Field-Marshal said, shaking his head. 'But after – the trouble – she never touched a brush again, as far as I know. Then I was sure she would start again after she was married, when Martin was B.G.S. FARELF. So much colour out there, so much light and movement, the sort of things that used to excite her when she was a girl. . . . Well, we can't account for everything that women do.'

'Thank heaven!'

The Field-Marshal pushed away his plate and said, 'Now, I told you why I wanted to see you.'

'Yes.'

'About those ten drawings, or sketches – I don't know what they were.'

'They were lithographs, the third set of three.'

'Did you see the letter in the *Courier*?'

'No, I don't read it, but I was told about it.'

'Someone wrote to the editor saying that as I was going to tell the truth about other people in my Memoirs, he hoped I would tell the truth about the Picassos looted – that's the word he used – in the Balkans. Do you know how I did get them?'

'No. They no longer existed, so I didn't think it worth asking. But when I saw them the Balkan invasion hadn't started.'

'Exactly. . . . I was warned early in September of forty-four that I would be given command of the new 16th Army that was going to be formed as part of the 17th Army Group for the invasion of the Balkans – Operation *Wolfpack*. On September 27 I moved into the Casa Grimani on the outskirts of Ancona with a skeleton staff – Wilfred Eden, Vetch, and a padre, Soapy Woodham, were all I had for the first week. The Casa Grimani was empty when we got there ... a big house in a walled estate, with two cottages. I learned later that one was used as a sort of dower house, and the other for the head gardener and his family. As far as I could tell nothing had been looted, and there was not much war damage, but things were in a mess ... papers lying about, chairs damaged, firewood and discarded motor tyres in the hallways. I decided that we would occupy one of the cottages, and use the main house as the headquarters building. There were four rooms – two upstairs and two downstairs. I had one, the padre had one, Vetch and Wilfred shared one, and we used the fourth as an office, and also ate there. I'd left my old command caravan with XIV Corps and hadn't got a new one yet. The second day Soapy Woodham came to me and said he'd been cleaning up his room and found, fallen behind a chest of drawers, some filthy pictures. Blushing, he unrolled this rather dirty roll of thick paper covered with cobwebs and dust. They were ...'

'Margaret showed them to me,' Charles said. 'They were erotic lithographs, in a style that could have been Picasso's – they were unsigned – or someone imitating him pretty well.'

'I know nothing about art,' the Field-Marshal said, 'except that I like that sort—' he nodded at the long-legged nude '—but I thought it would be nice to have these. I thought they might bring Margaret back to some sort of ... personal affection. The padre said he didn't want them, and hurried off as though he'd committed some terrible crime by looking at them, even by finding them. He was an awful ass. Died a few years ago.... I got the lithographs taken home by a pilot who I knew, and he gave them to Margaret. That was September 30, 1944.'

'Margaret brought them to me,' Charles said, 'asking me whether they were valuable, as she thought they were disgusting, and didn't want to keep them in the house where Lois might find them.'

'A bit late by then,' the Field-Marshal said.

'Quite ... I told her they might be Picassos, when they would be worth a lot of money, or they might be imitations, when they would be worth nothing. It would need an expert opinion to tell. A week later she told me she had decided to burn them, and had done so.'

'That's what she told me in a letter,' the Field-Marshal said, 'but this fellow who wrote to the *Courier* says he has information that the lithographs I looted have been located in the collection of a French multi-millionaire and are valued at twenty thousand pounds.'

'And the Yugoslavs insist that a set of ten Picasso lithographs are known to have been in the Zvornos Collection.'

'Which was still in Zvornos Castle when Soapy brought me these lithographs. I can't understand any of it . . . unless this fellow's deliberately lying.'

'He might be, as part of the counter-offensive against you. It's unfortunate for you that the lithographs might somehow be from the Zvornos Collection, as that brings you under suspicion in that matter, too. Now they're in a stronger position to say, "It might be Jordan, it might be Bartlett, it might be Sovik, it might even be our revered Field-Marshal Durham, or God knows who else . . . so let's bury the whole matter." . . . These lithographs that have been located in France – they might be another of the three sets that were originally made. Whoever the artist was had marked each lithograph "3/3", meaning the third set of three. Where are the first and second sets? Or is it possible that Margaret did not burn them as she said she had?'

The Field-Marshal looked up sharply. What was Charles getting at now? The green eyes seemed innocent, but he knew the man behind them well. Charles was never innocent.

He said, 'For money? She had no vices . . . didn't like jewels, or mink coats . . . spent very little on dress. She didn't gamble or buy antiques. Her mother had left her a little. What would she want money for? A lot of money.'

'She was seeing a great deal of Madame Olga.'

'Ah! That bitch!'

'Yes, but Margaret never saw through her, and wouldn't hear a word against her.'

'She spent a lot on her even when I was at home. While I was overseas . . . God knows.'

'Mind, I'm not saying that Margaret did sell the lithographs. I'm only pointing out that we don't have to believe her when she says she burned them.'

'She wouldn't lie to me,' the Field-Marshal said aloud; but to himself, he was saying, at that time in her life she might have done anything, and not even known what she was doing.

Charles said, 'When I told her they might be Picassos I gave her the name of a man who would tell her, and if she wanted, give her a good price for them. He's dead now.'

'That's a pity,' the Field-Marshal said. 'I shall have to write to the *Courier* telling them all that I know about the lithographs . . . Of course, I never dreamed they might be valuable, let alone by Picasso . . . and it would help if I could tell them at least that I had talked to this dealer, though she might have gone to someone else.'

'The man's dead, but his son's still running the business,' Charles said, 'Isaac Benoliel, 20 Maddox Street.'

'I'll talk to him. Or get Martin to.'

They rose from the table and walked toward the front windows. The Field-Marshal sank into an easy chair and let his head rest. 'I'll be dozing off any minute. Got to prepare myself for the drive back.'

'Go ahead. I'll do some more work on that abstraction, and wake you in, what, an hour?'

'Fine. . . . Mullins is very excited about this blind man who was Martin's adjutant, Richard Armstrong. Says he's going to give him a column of notes and comment every week . . . on anything he cares to write about – politics, religion, sport, fashion – anything. Says he has the best intellect he's ever come across. . . . I wonder if he guessed the truth about the *Bushmaster* plans and the sacking of Stephen Ross.'

He settled himself more comfortably. The wine was warm in his belly and even his hands, which were often cold nowadays, were warm where they rested on the arms of the chair. . . . Those dirty drawings had been well done. Funny and sexy at the same time. Now it turned out they were probably Picassos . . . if Margaret had sold them she'd have got, what, five, ten thousand pounds? Perhaps tax was due. In any case they'd belonged to Stefanie's husband. Or Stefanie. Why hadn't she asked about them when she and her husband came back to the Casa Grimani? She must know something about them.

He had not many years, perhaps even months, or days, to live. He must see her again. He would ask her about the lithographs, and tell her he'd pay what he owed, and that would be sufficient excuse for him. And he'd go and find Ballino and talk to him, as one old soldier to another. But tell no one he was going.

He felt the approach of sleep and saw her face, as it had been these nearly thirty years back, golden-haired, dark eyes vibrant, lips parted. He had told himself so often, in the years between, that it was only a physical need that had held him to her; but that was a deliberate lie. In truth she had given him not only sexual fulfilment but strong inner peace, for the first time in his life. That strength had given him the firmness to carry out Vojja Lovac. The memory of it had borne him through good times and bad ever since. Then why, why had he not gone back to her? What did duty, country, profession, children matter compared to that . . . ?

Slowly, sleep came.

... *the fifty-ninth anniversary of the outbreak of the Great War. I spent that evening drinking with friends in our regimental mess in Aldershot. We were looking forward excitedly to the war.*

But why do I waste your time with this? It is also my grandson Clive's 26th birthday.

The Memoirs keep me busy. Some of the information I want doesn't seem to be available here, and I may have to go abroad to look for it, if it exists. I used to love travelling but recently have become lazy. It will do me good to stir myself again. I must be careful not to sink into valetudinarianism, just because I am 80.

It is a lonely business, living.

'Peskevo,' the Air Marshal said, lowering his voice, 'Where can we talk? I don't have to disturb him yet. Shall we walk up and down here?'

Martin fell into step beside the other. The Air Marshal said, 'Martin, you've got to persuade him to publish nothing about the bombing of Peskevo.'

Martin said, 'He has made up his mind that the truth must come out.'

'Well, the government have decided that it must not, and they are prepared to go to any lengths to ensure that it doesn't – including putting the Old Man in prison and keeping him there until he undertakes not to publish the facts, in violation of the Official Secrets Acts.'

'People will talk. They're talking now.'

'I know. But talk – gossip – rumour – is not the same as a flat statement by the man who requested the operation.'

'Why's the goverement so upset?'

'Mainly Sovik . . . He's our friend, as you know. He has done a lot for us, and for the Americans, that is public knowledge – and more that we do not publicise because it would weaken his position in the Committee of Three. It's already being rumoured that he was the man behind the theft of the Zvornos Collection . . . and now this.'

'But the people who were bombed at Peskevo were the National Freedom Movement partisans. Why would it be so bad for it to be known that Sovik had had a hand in destroying them? His Committee of Three were their enemies.'

'That's not the way it would be seen now. Peskevo is in Montenegro and most of the people killed there in the raid, apart from the N.F.M. leaders, were Montenegrins. There's been unrest among all the minorities in Yugoslavia recently, and the Committee of Three's trying desperately to stop separatist movements that are gaining strength there. If this comes out it will make Sovik very unpopular not only with Montenegrins, but with all minorities. The other two – Panaz and Mallac – will get rid of him.'

' . . . and then they won't buy the ten Tridents they said they might. I don't think you'll be able to change the Old Man's mind on those grounds.'

'It's not only our national interest,' the other said heatedly. 'It's personal! Damn it, I was on that raid, leading a squadron of Stirlings. I knew, and the other squadron leaders and the Yanks knew, that we were going to destroy Peskevo because it

155

contained at that moment all the leaders of the N.F.M., and the Committee of Three had told us they would not co-operate with our forces any more unless we wiped out the N.F.M.'

Martin said, 'We tried to work out an operation to do it with a parachute brigade. It would have been much better . . . but it wasn't on. The Old Man said, "We've got to have the partisans working on the German flanks. It's part of the plan." So he asked for the bombing.'

'We did it. And we've kept our mouths shut all this time because we knew it was a dirty, necessary job. Now the Old Man's going to blacken our faces, brand us as liars to our pilots, just so that he can cleanse his own soul. Why should he feel guilty, anyway? *We* all know it was necessary.'

'I think,' Martin said slowly, 'that if that's the case, he feels that the country, the world should know, and why. He thinks they will agree, too.'

'The Yanks are going to be furious. Kissinger's trying like hell to get a better working relationship with the Committee of Three. The Pentagon boys are going to be badly hurt if this comes out . . . and they'll take it out on us . . . less co-operation, fewer test facilities, everything. I wish now that the Joint Chiefs hadn't insisted on the Americans taking part in the raid. It seemed wise at the time . . . it *was* wise, so that the Yanks couldn't claim later that *they* never harmed any nice Yugo-slavs . . . but now, if the Old Man makes it public, we'll get into hot water with two people instead of one.'

Martin said, 'You'd better speak to the Old Man. He's in the greenhouse. This way.'

'I'll go by myself, Martin. And find my way back to the car. You go on with whatever you were doing.'

Martin wandered back to the front lawn. 'Nothing' was what he had been doing and would continue to do. Clive came to-ward him, putter in hand.

'Finished?' Martin asked.

'Yes. Want to borrow my putter?'

'No. I'm going to get the lawn mower and . . .'

'Brigadier Ruttledge!' Paul was leaning out of an open window upstairs. 'Telephone.'

'For the Field-Marshal? Who is it?'

'For you. It's General Herrick.'

'Tell him I'm coming.' He went into the house, his son at his heels. In the study Paul handed him the telephone and picked up an extension. Martin said, 'Martin Ruttledge here.'

'The Chief of the General Staff here, Martin ... Sam Herrick. But I'm not speaking from the Ministry of Defence. I'm at home.'

'I should hope so, on a lovely day like this,' Martin said.

'I want to get you back into the service, Martin. You're wasted selling shirts.'

'I wasn't allowed to sell shirts. By the Navy.'

'I heard about that. That security job must have been pretty boring, too. I can't put you back with troops even if you wanted to go, but I can give you a job carrying major-general's rank and pay.'

'In England?' Martin asked, glancing at his son. Clive was looking out of the window; Paul's hand glided over his pad as he took down both sides of the conversation.

'In the U.S.A., as Deputy Head of our Joint Military Mission there. It would be for five years.'

Martin thought, of course there's a requirement ... that I shut up the Old Man. He'd love the job – but the Old Man would not keep quiet for his sake.

He said, 'You know, Sam, I can't promise to persuade the Old Man to do anything he doesn't want to. No one can.'

'I know that,' the General said. 'Come and talk with me. Monday suit you? Twelve at the M.O.D., then we'll have lunch.'

Martin put down the telephone. Clive turned, leaning against the window jamb, and said, 'We are moving in august military circles today. Wasn't that Air Marshal Makepeace? And now the C.G.S.'

'He's offering me a job ... on condition that I persuade your grandfather to keep his mouth shut,' Martin said briefly.

'I wish you could,' Clive said. 'The fellows are giving me quite a hard time ... all in fun of course, but it gets wearisome. Having a field-marshal as a grandfather is not what it's cracked up to be – at least, not this field-marshal.'

Paul said, 'There was another phone message earlier. From the Chief Constable.' He handed Martin a note.

Martin read: *No record of the fingerprints in Britain; am sending them to Washington.*

The telephone rang and Paul picked it up. He listened a moment, handed it to Martin and hooked his own extension onto his head.

'Hullo ... Martin? Charles Gibson here. I'm in the middle

of painting a luscious long-legged nude, but the call of duty comes first. You know Robert Cunningham, the M.P.?'

'Quite well,' Martin said, noticing that this time Clive was leaning over Paul, so that he too could hear what was being said.

'Well, I saw him yesterday and he told me he's going to ask a question in the House about the events in 206 R.A.C.'

206 R.A.C., Martin thought. A Sherman tank regiment, part of an armoured brigade, in the 11th Armoured Division in the Balkan Campaign. Ah, he remembered.

'One squadron of that regiment mutinied,' he said.

'Yes. And were driven back by American tanks.'

'That was said at the time. There were two American tank battalions very close but the squadron, which was going to the rear in their tanks, their officers dead or wounded or, in one case, going along with the mutiny, were actually stopped by 35th Dragoons of ours, under a direct order from the Old Man.'

'You'd better be able to prove it,' Charles's voice said cheerfully from the other end. 'Cunningham's out for the Old Man's blood . . . yours too, it seems. Thought you'd better know what's in the wind. Now, excuse me, I've got to get back to this bird.'

Martin gave the phone back to Paul. They can't do anything to the Old Man now, he thought, even if it were true that he'd called in American tanks to stop the mutiny. But it would make him very unpopular: 206 R.A.C. had lost a dozen men killed in that business.

'*The Official History* doesn't mention that incident,' Paul said.

'I know . . . 206 R.A.C. had had a very bad time, and they were convinced that the armour in their tanks was inferior to other tanks. They'd lost so many brewed up . . . mainly their own fault – but they couldn't think of any other explanation. The Armoured Division was supporting XXII Corps when this happened, and the Old Man was at the Corps Headquarters, 35th Dragoons were in reserve, and he put them across the path the squadron of 206 R.A.C. were taking toward the rear. 35th Dragoons waited, turret down, while their C.O. went out with a white flag telling them to stop. They didn't . . . they ran over him, as a matter of fact. . . . As soon as the 206 R.A.C. tanks got to a place where the road was on an embankment, 35th Dragoons let them have it, from the flank . . . brewed up three at once then stopped firing. The others surrendered. Then the Yank tanks came by on their way to the front. They had to use our roads for a spell there.'

'What a messy business,' Clive drawled. 'The Dragoons won't like that to come out at all. They didn't do anything else in the war. They're very touchy about their war record.'

'They had bad luck,' Martin said. 'Whenever anything exciting happened, they were somewhere else. Whenever they were put into the thick of battle, to gain some glory, the thick of the battle turned out to be in another place . . . 206th R.A.C. has been disbanded long since, of course, so there'll be no kickback from them.' My God . . . he thought for a moment. 'Yes. I'm sure. The C.O. of 206 R.A.C. at that time was George Cunningham, the M.P.'s other brother. I've met him occasionally in the Cavalry Club. And the C.O. of 35th Dragoons was – he was killed, of course – the second-in-command, the man who finally did the job, and did it very well, was Tom Langford. He's also Cavalry Club. Runs a restaurant and night club in Maidenhead now . . . The Golden Goose. Get the number for me please, Paul.'

Clive said, 'Messier and messier.' He had a look of languid distaste on his handsome, rather heavy features. He glanced out of the window. 'The Air Marshal's coming into the house, with Grandpa.'

Paul gave Martin a number and said, 'Shall I get him for you?'

'Yes please. Major Langford.'

A minute later, Langford was on the phone. Martin said, 'Martin Ruttledge here, Langford. You may have heard that my father-in-law, Field-Marshal Durham, is writing his Memoirs. I'm helping him and I'm going to need some facts about the trouble we had with 206 R.A.C. in March '45. Do you remember?'

'Oh yes, a spot of bother,' the other said, the voice drawling but – was he imagining it – guarded.

'Will you have lunch with me at Quag's tomorrow?'

'Sunday's a pretty busy day here, but . . . dash it, if I can't leave the place to run itself for a few hours, I don't deserve to stay in business. What time?'

'Noon do you? . . . Fine.' He hung up. 'Now all I need is to get him to sign a little statement, perhaps, and we're in the clear. Paul, will you type out three copies of a short statement saying simply that on an occasion in March 1945, near the village of, what was it called? . . . Jastrec – 35th Dragoons, acting under the direct order of General Durham, fired on 206 R.A.C.'

'I'll draft it, and show it to you before typing it fair,' Paul said.

'I wish we could drop the whole business,' Clive said. 'It was sordid to begin with, and it's getting sordider . . . and spreading like a beastly fungus. Someone ought to do something about it.'

The Field-Marshal strode in, his face set. He stood in the middle of the floor, his rolled shirt sleeves showing the corded muscles in his thin white-haired arms. 'Makepeace has been talking to me about Peskevo. I told him he could do what he damned well liked, I was going to do what I see as my duty. He didn't like it.'

'The C.G.S. called,' Martin said. 'He's offering me a job – Deputy Head of the Joint Military Mission to Washington, as a major-general.'

'On conditions, of course?'

'It must be. We're having lunch on Monday.'

'Did he call from the M.O.D., or from home? This is too bloody much. Paul, look in that little black book, under Herrick, Sam, residence. . . . Get General Herrick and tell him Field-Marshal Durham wants to speak to him.'

He sat down, drumming his long fingers on the desk top. They all waited. Paul handed him the phone.

'Sam, John Durham here. Look, I won't have any more of this pestering and bullying of myself and my family. I have a public duty to perform, and it does not, repeat not, include protecting the reputation of your regiment or yourself. . . . Don't interrupt. . . . You would have been damned lucky to reach the rank of brigadier, let alone full general, after Mitrovica. . . . If this harassment continues I shall ask the Queen to relieve me of my rank and all orders and decorations because I do not wish to have any further association with a service that is assisting, through its chief, in attempts to browbeat and blackmail one of its own most senior officers. . . . I know damned well you're acting under instructions. What do you think is the honourable and proper thing for a British general to do when he is given a disgraceful order? You lack moral fibre. I made a mistake in giving you a reprieve. I am ashamed of you.' He hung up.

Martin felt quite warm and trembly. Full generals who were also the professional heads of armies didn't often get that sort of verbal whipping, and the Field-Marshal had been so cold throughout – a swear word here and there, but the voice even and hard, certainly with no trace of age in it.

The Field-Marshal leaned back in his chair. 'Give me a drink, Paul. How's life at Chelsea Barracks, Clive? I've hardly had a word with you since you arrived last night.'

Martin rocked with the motion of the train, the folded *Sunday Journal* in his hands, his small overnight suitcase on the rack. This was Dick Armstrong's first column for the paper and Mullins had given him an outside one on the second page. Martin had read the piece at breakfast, but now began to read it again. It was dedicated to the future course of Britain – more particularly as regarded her internal politics and social policies. Dick had done an amazing job of making complex ideas easy to grasp, without over-simplifying. At the same time he had turned what was by nature a heavy, serious subject into something light and yet sharp. The ideas themselves . . . cut down on Britain's ancient but now outdated centralisation; more freedom and self government for various regions of the country; a different allocation of responsibilities as between local and the new regional governments; a whole new system of state education embodying what was already in existence, reshaping it and pointing it toward new goals . . .

He rested the paper on his lap. If only Dick had eyes, he should be in Parliament, driving these great ideas through from theory into practice; and there would be more to come, for next week he was going to analyse Britain's future in the world. There would be so much to do . . . the private interests of so many people to be considered, but blended into the common good, ancient and rusted minds to be broken free and made to work again. He could sense the enthusiasm these ideas would generate, among the young particularly.

Caroline had read the column at breakfast, too, and exclaimed afterwards, 'Now there's a man who *could* make this system work, even if he had to turn it inside out to do it'; and Clive, languid to the last, had said, 'Brainy chap.'

He picked up the paper again. Cricket results . . . a murder . . . N.A.T.O. meeting in Brussels. . . . Here was a little squib to the effect that Mr Robert Cunningham M.P. had announced that as soon as Parliament reassembled he intended to ask the Minister of Defence to make an official inquiry into the death of his brother Captain Arthur Cunningham, North Wessex

Regiment, in 1945 during the Balkan Campaign.

That was all. The only man who could give any information was that doctor, Tufnell, who'd examined the corpse: and the C.O. who'd brought Cunningham in – Sam Herrick. And now it looked as though Herrick would swear to whatever the Government wanted.

He thought of what Herrick would be offering him tomorrow: the Washington job; a major-general's rank; and no questions about the death of Captain Cunningham. It was a tempting package. It was all very well for the Old Man to call it bribery and attempted corruption – *his* neck wasn't in danger. Technically he was equally guilty, but perhaps he was too old to care. He, Martin, on the other hand, had obeyed that order, knowing it to be illegal. Anyway, he would never say that the Old Man had given him the order, so he'd be on his own: but the Old Man *would* say so; which wouldn't help: so back to Square One. . . .

Isaac Benoliel's gallery was small but extremely expensive-looking. A young man in striped trousers and black coat showed Martin past the paintings – nearly all abstract and unintelligible to him – to the back, where he was introduced to Mr Benoliel, who was also wearing striped trousers and a black coat. He was in his low sixties and very like the cartoons of Disraeli, Martin thought, plus ornate side whiskers. The curled hair was obviously dyed a shiny black, and his fingers were loaded with jewelled rings.

He indicated a chair and they both sat. Martin said, 'I hope you didn't come here on Sunday just for me.'

'Oh no,' the other said. 'Sunday is one of our most important days. We don't usually open on Monday, unless some important client or would-be client wants to come round. My father was a very unorthodox Jew, and believed that business came first – even on our Sabbath, I fear. . . . Field-Marshal Durham's note was waiting for me when I returned from New York the day before yesterday, and as you know I called at once. You are indeed his son-in-law?'

Martin found his driver's licence and showed it. 'Quite so.' Mr Benoliel said, 'Now . . . ?'

Martin said, 'Some time in October, 1944, my late mother-in-law, Lady Durham, may have brought a set of lithographs to you for valuation or sale . . .'

'Not me,' Mr Benoliel murmured, 'I was playing at soldiers in France – 17th Lancers. My father was running the business single-handed then.'

'I see. It was a set of ten erotic lithographs, the third set of three. Charles Gibson, who's a friend of the family, had told my mother-in-law that they might be by Picasso.'

'Ah, Charles. He had recommended us to Lady Durham?'

'Yes.'

Mr Benoliel got up and walked to a bookcase lining one wall of his elegant retreat. He selected a heavy volume, brought it down and began to thumb through its pages.

'This is part of our filing system. We file by clients, and also by artists. If a Picasso passes through our hands, we list here what happened to it. As a matter of fact we have information about a great many paintings that did not pass through our hands. And if Charles thought these lithographs might be Picassos, they probably were. I only wonder why he didn't tell Lady Durham one way or the other, at the time. I don't think he could have been in doubt.... H'm ... lithographs ... Picasso did quite a lot of erotic work, you know, not all of it adequately catalogued ... H'm ... very interesting, *very* interesting.' He read aloud – '*Set of ten unsigned lithographs of sexual scenes, mostly of women with men, some of women with animals or birds, unsigned. Executed July 1924, 3 sets. 1/3 sold to Mr John Avropoulos, price unknown; 2/3 kept by artist; 3/3 given to Mr Pierre Fantas.*' He looked up. 'Avropoulos was a Greek shipping millionaire. His son probably still has that set. The Picasso estate will have set two.... Fantas was a hanger-on around Picasso for a time in the twenties. He probably sold the set Picasso gave him, to get drinking money.' He returned to the big tome: '*October 12, 1944. Series of ten lithographs, marked 3/3, probably the above, bought from Lady Durham, Ashwood House, Surrey, for cash. Ten thousand guineas.* And below that, this, made only a week or two ago: *Yugoslav Govt claiming Picasso lithos, probably one of these sets, was in Zvornos Collection at Zvornos Castle, before 1939. Could be 3/3 of above.*' He closed the book. 'How they could have got from Fantas to the Zvornos Collection, I don't know.'

Martin said, 'But the Field-Marshal was given them before the Zvornos Collection was stolen! They were in a house in Ancona, Italy.'

'Very mysterious,' Benoliel said smoothly.

'Where are they now?'

'I couldn't divulge that ... even if I knew. I have no information beyond the name of the person to whom my father resold them.'

Martin said, 'I don't think it's important, for the moment. They've apparently finished up with a French multi-millionaire, Georges Peyraude. The Field-Marshal might have to get the information later.'

'The courts could issue an order, in certain circumstances. ... The interesting point, if I may say so, is how the writer of that letter to the *Courier* knew that the lithographs had ever been through the Field-Marshal's hands. The information was certainly not given out from this establishment.'

Who knew? Martin thought. Soapy Woodham – dead: the pilot who'd brought them home – no trace: and anyway he'd probably only been given a paper-wrapped roll: Margaret Durham – keeping them secret: the Benoliels – discreet as tombs: and Charles Gibson ...

'How did the Field-Marshal acquire them, if I may ask?' Benoliel said.

Martin briefly told the story and Mr Benoliel shook his head sadly, 'I really thought the clergy of the Church of England were a little more sophisticated than that ... not to mention generals.'

As they rose, Martin said, 'There's a Rembrandt recently come to light in a private collection in America, which the Yugoslav government think was part of the Zvornos Collection. Could you find out anything for us about where that came from? We're trying to clear up the mystery, in which some people are trying to involve the Field-Marshal.'

Mr Benoliel said, 'I never had the privilege of serving under Field-Marshal Durham, but I have always admired him. I will do what I can.'

Martin walked along the street toward the Cavalry Club, thinking hard. The Old Man's wife had got ten thousand guineas in cash, but told him she had burned the lithographs. So she had in effect stolen the money. What would the Old Man think of this? Or did he suspect already? And it was almost certainly Charles Gibson who had let this particular cat out of the bag. The man was really a two-faced scoundrel. He couldn't think what women saw in him. ... And there was still one major mystery: how did the Picassos get to Ancona when they were supposed to have been in Zvornos Castle until four months later?

Tom Langford was impeccably tailored, partly bald, and wore a monocle on a wide black ribbon. They took their pink gins to a quiet table, where Martin said at once, 'The reason I've dragged you up from the country, and your hotel, is that my father-in-law, Field-Marshal Durham, needs public proof of the fact that when B Squadron of 206 R.A.C. mutinied at Jastrec, it was not American troops that stopped them, but ours ... the 35th Dragoons, your regiment.'

'Poor Bill,' Langford said, 'such a good chap. He was the C.O., you know.'

'Yes.'

'All the guts in the world. When that squadron came down off the road, he got out of his tank and walked toward them, waving a white handkerchief. The blighters ran right over him. After that—' He shrugged and took a sip of his drink. 'I'm afraid I couldn't swear to anything.'

Martin looked at him in astonishment. 'But you were there! You were the second-in-command. The Army commander had you in the next day and congratulated you and your regiment on doing a very tricky job very well.'

'Did he?' Langford said. 'I can't remember.'

Martin's surprise changed to anger. He said, 'You mean, you've been told not to remember? Who by? Cunningham?'

'My dear chap,' Langford said plaintively, 'I was with the regiment throughout the rest of the campaign. I got blown up once and brewed up twice. Weeks of terrible noise. Sordid food. Ill-mannered types, Germans and so on. I don't remember a lot of things that happened, and frankly I don't want to. . . . I have a vague recollection of an engagement that day, and of seeing American tanks. That's all.'

Martin stared at him a long time in silence. The other said, 'Really, old boy, it's no use.'

Martin got up without another word and went to a telephone. A moment later he was speaking to the hall porter at the Cavalry Club—

'Fred, can you give me the home address of Mr George Cunningham?'

'Certainly, sir. We forward quite a bit of mail to him ... Maybourne Court, Marlborough, Wiltshire. Telephone Maybourne 7.'

Martin stood a moment, wondering whether he should call to make an appointment. But then Cunningham might refuse to see him. This needed to be done face to face, and it needed to be done now. He'd probably have to spend the night in Marlborough, but what did that matter? He hailed a taxi and said, 'Paddington, please.'

Maybourne Court was three miles outside the old market town, a huge grey stone pile of Queen Anne's period. The owner, Mr George Cunningham – the elder brother of the M.P., and of the Arthur Cunningham whom Martin had shot – greeted him in the study. He was in his sixties, and looked very like his brother – average sort of figure, grey hair curling over his ears, shiny bald on top, eyes bolting blue.

Martin said, 'I've come to ask if you'll make a public statement to the effect that when B Squadron of 206 R.A.C. mutinied in forty-five at Jastrec, and tried to go to the rear, they were stopped by the 35th Dragoons.'

The other stroked his drooping grey moustache. 'I was commanding 206 then,' he said.

'I know,' Martin said impatiently. 'That's why I've come to you. It's being said that the Field-Marshal – Durham – used American tanks to stop the rot. It's being said only to embarrass the Field-Marshal and rouse public opinion against him. He says he would have used American tanks if he'd had to, but that's not the point. He actually used British and he would like that substantiated.'

'I wasn't there,' George Cunningham said. 'I was forward with the rest of the regiment.'

'But you went back right afterwards. You were there within ten minutes. You spoke to the men. What did they tell you? What did you see?'

'I saw the 35th Dragoons. I saw a lot of Yankee tanks going forward. Some of the men in B Squadron said one thing, some said another.'

'But . . .'

'The point is, Ruttledge,' the other said heavily, 'that I can't *swear* to anything, because I don't know. If you can find some of the men in that squadron – they might give you the evidence you want. Or they might contradict it. All I can give you is hearsay. As you know, the 35th Dragoons had Shermans – so did the Yanks.'

Martin seemed to hear in his head the ticking of the meter

of the taxi that had brought him out. What could he say to make this pompous ass tell what he knew to be the truth, whatever legalisms he chose to hide behind at the moment?

George Cunningham said, 'Don't you think it would be wiser if the Field-Marshal forgot about his Memoirs – the same way everyone has forgotten about the trouble in 206 R.A.C.?'

Martin got up. 'Thank you,' he said coldly. 'I have to be getting back now.'

To the taximan outside he said, 'Ashwood, Surrey, please. I've got enough money to pay.' He gave the man a five pound note. 'That's to start with.'

It was near midnight when he returned to Ashwood House. The lights were on and to his surprise he found the whole family waiting for him in the drawing-room.

The Field-Marshal said, 'What did you find out?'

Martin poured himself a stiff whisky. 'A lot,' he said. 'George Cunningham has been got at by his brother, and will say nothing about 206 R.A.C. Nor will Langford, who's been got at by one of the Cunninghams. Robert, the M.P., could give him a hard time with that hotel if he wanted to. And Lady Durham didn't burn those lithographs. She sold them for ten thousand guineas.'

Lois cried. '*What!* I don't believe it!'

The Field-Marshal said, 'I'm afraid it's true.'

'But I was here. Mother didn't buy furs, or jewels, or spend a lot of money on anything. She was quite mean, really.'

'We'll never know,' the Field-Marshal said, his face grim. 'But she probably gave it to Madame Olga, who's long since vanished, and is probably dead. She was older than me.'

'Who was Madame Olga?' Clive asked.

The Field-Marshal answered – 'A fortune teller ... a medium ... a quack, I always thought, but didn't dare tell Margaret that. She said she could put us in touch with Andrew. I didn't believe her, of course, but Margaret said she had spoken with Andrew, at a seance Madame Olga had arranged. She told me that in a letter, early in the war.'

'Madame Olga *was* a quack,' Lois said viciously. 'Mother spent all her time with her, and thought of no one else. She had her down to stay, often. . . . When did you first meet her?'

'Some time early in thirty-seven,' the Field-Marshal said.

'And Andrew had died in November, thirty-six. Madame Olga was the sort of person who reads the death notices in *The*

Times and battens on the families.'

Martin asked, 'Is it worth trying to find her?'

'No. Even if she's alive and has some of the money, we'll never get it. . . . Margaret should have paid taxes on that money, I'm sure. Something like five thousand pounds, it will be.'

'It *will* be?' Caroline asked, her voice rising in pitch. 'You mean, we're going to pay the tax?'

'If Margaret should have, I will,' the Field-Marshal said briefly.

Paul Phillips said, 'Excuse me, sir, but I'm positive you're not liable. First, even if Lady Durham should have paid tax, you're protected by the Statute of Limitations. And I'm positive that the sale of paintings, like that, would not have been taxable at that time, unless the seller was an art dealer.'

Martin said, 'I'll speak to Forsythe, shall I, sir?'

The Field-Marshal grunted. 'All right. But make it clear I'm not going to try to wangle out through any loophole. If an honourable man would have paid the tax in 1944, I shall pay it now. Where I shall get the money, all at once, is another matter. I'll think about it while I'm abroad.'

'Abroad?' Martin repeated, hearing Lois and Clive and Caroline also repeating the word in various tones of astonishment.

'I'm catching the night ferry from Victoria tomorrow,' the Field-Marshal said. 'Caroline can drive me up. I shall be away about ten days.'

He rose a little unsteadily, and went out, shoulders bowed but jaw sticking forward.

'Where on earth's he going to go?' Martin asked. 'Has he talked about this to any of you?'

Lois said, 'No. And it doesn't matter, does it?'

CHAPTER FOURTEEN

The Field-Marshal looked out of the window as the train slowed, and saw the station name board glide by – *Falconara.* That was only a few miles up the coast from Ancona. In fact, the Villa Grimani was in the direction of Falconara, but set three miles in from the coast on the low hills. The train stopped and he lit a cigarette. It was a bad habit and he'd all but conquered it years ago, but today, so short a time to wait, he needed one more than his usual ration of three a day.

He settled back. Rome was becoming impossible, the traffic quite out of control, the city in a state of mechanical anarchy. He'd been glad to leave this morning after a fruitless but somehow comforting discussion with General Ballino yesterday. Ballino had been most polite to 'the great Marischalo del Regno, nobler than the Romans of old;' but behind the suavity John Durham thought he had been laughed at. Of course General Ballino remembered the contacts made to him soon after the Allies crossed the Straits of Messina. Let us see, he was Military Governor of Caltera at the time, and the great Marischalo was ... of course, commander of the British XIV Corps. Quite so. He had sent a senior officer to the agreed rendezvous, in spite of severe danger that, had the Germans discovered what was going on, he, General Ballino, would have been shot out of hand. But no one came from the British side, so his emissary reported.

'I went myself, and handed over the gold,' the Field-Marshal had said, half smiling, for he couldn't help admiring Ballino's gall. They were of an age, too; but Ballino had a plump dark-haired girl of about twenty living in his big flat, with obvious though unstated duties.

Ballino threw up his hands. 'Then my emissary lied to me! Or are we all, my dear Marischalo, suffering from hallucinations brought on by the passage of the years? I certainly never received the money, which I planned to distribute to the poor. How much was it?'

'One hundred thousand pounds, in gold bullion.'

'What a haul someone made! Still, we were blowing that much into nothingness every few minutes those days, were we not?'

Half an hour more of polite, evasive talk. Another glass of Punt e Mes on ice. A hint that General Ballino thought nothing less of the great Marischalo del Regno for having got away with one hundred thousand pounds of the British taxpayers' money, in fact increased admiration, for the sternness of British accounting systems was well known. Profusely congratulatory leave takings . . .

The train had started while the Field-Marshal was in his reverie, and was now again slowing. *Ancona.* Down there were the docks, whence he had sailed for the Balkans on board a British destroyer, on the night of December 5th, 1944, the second day of Operation *Wolfpack.*

The taxi waited while a girl came out of the gatehouse and opened one of the tall wrought iron gates. That used to be the head gardener's house. If it still was, the girl would be one of his daughters. That house, at least, hadn't changed since he drove out through these gates, then guarded by a detachment of Military Police, that December evening long ago.

'Drive slowly now, please,' he said to the taxi driver. '*Lento, lento per favore.*'

The taxi's wheels crunched on the gravel. A row of tall cypress trees blocked the view of the Villa Grimani from here . . . round this next corner, he'd see it. The Dower House was on the right, tucked back, its own small lawn in front. That was where Soapy had found the Picassos . . . where he'd lived – at first with Soapy and Vetch, later with Grimani and Stefanie and of course Wilfred Eden. It had been his house, his household.

How would she look? He experienced a moment of panic. Would she recognise him? She knew he was coming, for he had sent a telegram from Rome and her reply was unambiguous: *Please come.* Worse, would he not recognise her, and go forward to greet perhaps her maid or the cook? That was silly. Stefanie had savoir faire. She would allow no chance of mistake or embarrassment for either of them. In those two short months of his happiness here she had never made him feel in the smallest degree embarrassed in front of her husband, or, as far as he could tell, vice-versa; and that was a remarkable accomplishment, considering that Grimani knew he and Stefanie were lovers. Grimani more than knew, he actively connived.

The taxi drew up under the portico. It was a hot August afternoon, cooled by a hint of sea mist blowing off the Adriatic toward the hills. A manservant ran down the three steps, and bowing, held the taxi door open and offered an arm to help the Field-Marshal out. The driver hustled round to hand out the suitcase and the small toilet bag.

She was standing in the open doorway at the top of the steps, smiling. Her hair was golden still, with a silvery grey tone shining through. Her eyes were dark and flashing, the skin crinkled at the corners of her smile. Her face seemed to have been untouched by time. He went slowly up the steps. As he reached her she held out her hand. The response came naturally to him, though he had not done it for nearly thirty years. He lifted the hand to his lips and kissed her on the back of the wrist.

'Giovanni,' she said softly. 'Welcome home.'

He stood a while looking down at her, for she was more than half a foot shorter than he. She was still slender, though not thin, for her shape was womanly. Now that he was close he saw that of course she was no longer thirty, but near sixty. What did it matter? She was still smiling, her eyes alight. The manservant had gone upstairs and she said, 'He has paid the taxi driver. Come.'

She led into the house and into the first room on the left. This used to be the G.S. Operations Room, he remembered; but now it was an ornate red drawing room, and she had turned. She whispered 'Giovanno!' and laid her head against his shoulder. Her body melted against him, following the shape exactly so that they seemed to touch from her toes to her head. He stroked her hair, murmuring 'Stefanie . . . Stefanie.' After a time she raised her head and he bent down and kissed her on the warm parted lips.

She stood away from him – 'You look wonderful, Giovanni . . . better than ever.'

'I am old, Stefanie.'

'So am I. But in those days you looked stern. Angry.'

'I was commaning an army. I was planning to kill people. Thousands of them.'

'And now, what are you doing?'

'Trying to grow roses.'

'We'll look at mine.'

'You had wonderful roses then.'

'They're better now. It's my hobby, too. You taught me about roses.'

171

'You taught me how to love. I'm afraid I've forgotten, though.'

She looked at him and said, 'You're pale, Giovanni. It's a tiring journey, and on that train you have to change at Orte, don't you?' She looked at the grandfather clock ticking in the corner, its brass pendulum swinging weightily. 'Half past four. Would you like to take a nap?'

He yawned. 'To tell you the truth, I would. I do at home in the afternoons, when I can.'

'Come upstairs. I'll show you your room. Afterwards, we'll have a quiet supper, with a little *polenta al forno*. You used to love that. Angelo was a Venetian, of course, and he really knew how to make it. Mine is not so good, but I learned, and it is all right . . . and tomorrow we'll look at the roses and you can tell me why my Red Radiances are coming out such a strange colour.'

It was cooler still next morning, house and garden bathed in the drifting swathes of thin golden mist, so that sometimes the house loomed over them like a giant monument of antiquity, and sometimes it had vanished and they walked alone, side by side, between the dew-washed roses in a universe of mist.

'These are the Red Radiances,' she said.

'They *are* a funny colour. They should be light crimson.' He knelt and felt the earth, picked up some, crumbled it through his hands, and sniffed it. 'Have you had a soil analysis done?'

'Yes, but it was a long time ago. I don't like strangers coming here more than necessary.'

'You'd better have it done again. The alkali ratio could have changed with the use of fertilisers. I see you still have Il Trovatore—' he gestured toward a grey spotted donkey standing tethered to a fruit tree by a well in a far corner.

'Il Trovatore's grandson,' she said laughing, 'but with the same deplorable habits.'

He said abruptly, 'Stefanie, when I first arrived here, before you and Angelo came back, one of my officers found some lithographs in the Dower House. He brought them to me and I sent them to my wife. It turns out that they were Picassos and worth a lot of money. I owe you that money.'

'Do you still have the lithographs?' she asked.

He shook his head. 'My wife sold them.'

She looked up at him, questioningly. When he added

nothing, she said no more. She understood, without it having to be spelled out.

He said, 'I should have told you about them, when you came. I don't know why I didn't. Perhaps I was ashamed of keeping them, because they were pornographic. We didn't know each other then.'

'You didn't know me. I knew you from the first moment you shook my hand . . . such an English hand, and a soldier's eye, and a man's heart.'

He persisted. 'I should have told you that I'd taken them. Why didn't you ask? You must have known they were there.'

She said, 'I hid them there originally, when we had to leave here in a hurry, about two months before the British first came. I thought the Germans had got them. A German colonel lived in the big house for a time, and perhaps he had some staff in the Dower House. Or it might have been the first British who got them.'

'Did you suspect me?'

'Not you, Giovanni. It was obviously possible that your people had found them, as much as it was possible the Germans or the first British had. But there was nothing I could do about it. If it was anyone else, I could never have got them back. If it was you – I wanted you to have them, as a gift from me. I am sorry you do not still have them. Sometimes, as I lay awake alone in bed these long years, I dared to hope that you had them, and were thinking of me.'

He interrupted her. 'How did you get them?'

She looked up, the big brown eyes met his. 'I was mistress of the last Count Zvornos.'

He said nothing, Mistress of Count Zvornos. Before she was married to Grimani, presumably. She was a Yugoslav by birth, born Stefanie Cupril, so would have met him there.

'Are you jealous?'

'No,' he said. 'I don't think so. I have no right to be, anyway.'

'You do, because . . . you know why.'

'No, I'm not jealous. I wish I'd known before, though.'

'I don't think you would have liked to know then. And we had no time to talk or think of the past – or the future. Only the present. . . . I met him when I was a music student in Belgrade. He had a big town house there. I was nineteen . . . I stayed with him in Belgrade, and in Zvornos Castle off and on until shortly before I came to Italy and married Angelo. It was in 1934 that he gave me the Picassos. He never gave me any money. I would not have taken it, of course.'

'And you brought the lithographs with you when you came here to marry Angelo?'

She nodded. 'Yes. That was 1936. I never showed them to Angelo. He would have tried to sell them. He was always greedy for money.'

'I thought he was very rich – the fleet of fishing boats, the cannery, this—' he waved his hand at the great house, then shining above the mist, the two gardeners now working by the well, the ordered flower garden and manicured lawns.

'He was,' she said, 'until a week or two before he was killed. But he always wanted more.'

'What happened just before he was killed?'

'He lost twelve fishing boats in a storm . . . the bad two weeks before Christmas 1944. Forty-one men were drowned, too, but Angelo didn't worry about that.'

'I remember,' the Field Marshal said. The storm had been so severe, though short, that for forty-eight hours the support shipping for *Wolfpack*, and the ships that were bringing in the material to enable the armies to break out of the bridgehead on *Bushmaster*, had not been able to leave Ancona or land at the Yugoslav assault harbours.'

'He was not insured. Then the Communists burned down his cannery – he was not insured there, either. When they killed him, he was almost penniless.'

Almost penniless, the Field-Marshal repeated to himself. The moon was shining in through the window, for he had drawn back the curtains before getting into the high old-fashioned bed. This had been one of the Q offices in '44, and there'd been no bathroom attached. All the bedrooms had their own bathrooms now, and that must have cost a lot of money, for the work had been done with taste, and the best materials. But Grimani had died almost penniless. Where had Stefanie's money come from?

Wilfred Eden had told him, not long after the event, that a Communist mob had lynched Grimani. He'd written to Stefanie offering his formal condolences – formal because he knew that Angelo Grimani had long since ceased to mean anything to her, if he ever had. It was lucky they had no children.

If he had known about Grimani's death, then, why had he first pushed it to the back of his mind, then out altogether?

He'd rationalised by telling himself the campaign required all his energy; which was partly true, but there would have been enough to spare to acknowledge that in fact Angelo Grimani had only survived after the Germans had been driven out, through his – John Durham's – protection: as soon as he and his army had sailed on Wolfpack, the Communists moved. Why had he protected Grimani, knowing him to be a Fascist? For he had to admit, now, that he had known. The Civil Affairs people had told him twice, at least.

The answer was that Grimani's connivance was necessary for his love of Stefanie, and hers for him, to find any sort of fulfilment. More than his connivance – his actual co-operation. So she came every night to his room, and slept there in his arms until before dawn. And Wilfred Eden knew and Angelo Grimani knew, but no one else, for there was no one else there, only the sentries on the main gate, and the Inlying Patrol that every night wandered the grounds with tommy guns, blackened faces, and police dogs.

The moon used to shine in on them in the Dower House, too. Her hair turned a paler gold in those moments, almost as it was now silvered.

He waited, the next night, until they were alone in the drawing room, cups of coffee and glasses of Marsala wine beside them. Then he said, 'How do you live, Stefanie?'

'Quietly,' she said, smiling. 'Few people come – and the fewer the better. I go out little, though I might go more if I was invited to ride in a Red Label Bentley. Do you still have that car?'

'Yes.'

'I knew you would. You talked about it, in the Dower House, until I became jealous of it.'

'Tell me.'

She finished her coffee and stood up. 'Come, Giovanni. . . . What do you think of our paintings here? This one? This one?'

She walked round the room, through the door, into the dining room beyond, out into the hall. They were all lined with paintings of various sizes in heavy, mostly gilt, frames. There were a few portraits, but most were landscapes – lakes with fishermen in the foreground, mountains with a stag in the foreground, rustic bridges with a washergirl in the foreground.

The Field-Marshal said, 'I like that one . . . the horse is well drawn there . . . that sunset's pretty.'

She laughed. 'Giovanni, don't ever think of collecting art, please! All these paintings are bad, and some are terrible. Not even the Germans wanted to take any of them. Oh, some drunken soldier seems to have stuck a bayonet into this, but otherwise they are just as Angelo bought them, and had them hung ... Now try to turn one round, back to front. That one, it's small.'

The Field-Marshal tried, but could not. The frame was apparently screwed to the wall rather than hung from a hook.

Stefanie said, 'Here's a screwdriver. You can just get at the screws. Unscrew this one. I'll hold it when you've got the two bottom screws loose.'

Ten minutes later the Field-Marshal set the painting down on a sofa. Stefanie turned it round. The back showed a luminous river in a misty grey-green dawn light, and dark-leaved trees, and two young girls. He recognized at once that it was of quite a different class from the banal scene on the front.

Stefanie said, 'Corot. We'll put it back as it was now. It's worth about fifty thousand pounds – as long as no one knows it's here.'

When they had finished, and returned to the drawing room, she said, 'Alex – that's Count Zvornos – drove in here in a truck early in March 1945. I was alone except for our old butler who's died since. Alex told me that he'd managed to get more of the paintings he'd had in Zvornos Castle out of Yugoslavia and into Italy.'

'They were taken on February 16,' the Field-Marshal said.

'He said he'd had to pay a lot of money to manage it, and kill two men, and he'd still have to pay something to people in New York, but not as much as they, the people in New York, thought he was going to. He had the paintings in the truck, not framed, of course. We three carried them inside and over the next few days we tacked them onto the backs of the pictures we had, and screwed the frames to the wall, so that if a wire broke, or some inquisitive person tried to turn a frame round, nothing would be given away. When he was ready, he told me to look after the paintings until he got back, when he'd marry me and we'd live like millionaires the rest of our lives.

'You loved him?'

'Then? How could I, Giovanni? It was after I had met you. But he thought I did, for I had loved him before, when I was his mistress, or imagined I did, as young girls do. . . . I said I would do my best. I knew that if the Communists came to power in Yugoslavia they would confiscate all that he had – his houses, castle, paintings, land – everything. He went away about the middle of the month, in the truck, which he had altered a lot in appearance, and it had an Italian number now. I never heard from him again. I don't know what happened to him.'

'He was murdered in New York in July or August, 1945.'

She shook her head, her eyes down. 'It was not in the papers here. He was not known in Italy. . . . Early in 1946, nearly a year later, I was getting desperate for money. I could have sold this place, but would have got very little for it. And I did not want to sell it. I knew your wife had died, and I kept hoping you would come to me. . . . I took down one of the paintings, took it to Paris. Under a false name I sold it, for cash, to a dealer who promised to ask no questions, and answer none, about me. I have sold one every three or four years since. I do not need more money than to keep up this place.'

The Field-Marshal drank some more Marsala. A very sweet wine, and one he never touched in England. But here, in this Italian night, looking across at Stefanie, it was right.

He said, 'I still owe you the ten thousand guineas, and I shall pay it.'

She looked up and seeing his eyes on her, she moved with sudden grace to kneel at his side, her head turned sideways resting on his lap. She asked, 'Are you happy, Giovanni?'

He thought a while and said, 'No . . . My daughter and son-in-law are going different ways. My grandson is – well, I don't know what he is, I have never found a real person inside his rather imposing body. My granddaughter – she's the best of the lot, but an eighty-year-old man can't build his life round a twenty-year-old girl – a very modern girl – nor vice versa. As I mentioned, I am writing my Memoirs. They have been causing great difficulties for all of us with the Government, because I want to tell the truth.'

'Will you tell about us?'

'Of course not!'

'I am sorry. It was beautiful. I am not ashamed.'

'I couldn't do it . . . No, I'm not happy. It is not that I feel old. Much of the time, I don't. I am not wanted, but I am used to that . . . I live for your letters.'

'And your family still think they really come from a French-woman in Marseille?'

'Why not? Your sister has not made a mistake all these years, when she forwards them.'

'She is sure that they are full of passionate love poems, torrid endearments. . . . I don't know why no one should know I write to you, and you to me.'

'They might guess . . . the rest.'

'I would not care. I was – am – proud of it.'

He put down his wine and stroked her hair. She rose to her feet with a lithe grace that women half her age would have been proud of. She said, 'Let us go upstairse now, Giovanni. In half an hour, I will come to you.'

'Just like you used to, in the Dower House. But I am thirty years older now, my dearest.'

'Not too old for my arms,' she said, bending down to kiss him on the lips as he looked up.

She's right, he thought, rising; she could always do anything she wanted with me.

Below the Trident's wing he could see the Dover harbour-works and piers. A stewardess on the intercom announced, 'We are starting our descent for London, Heathrow Airport.' The Field-Marshal checked that his seat belt was fastened and leaned back. . . . He had most of the truth about the Zvornos Collection now, except the one factor that was most sensitive to all the British, American, and Yugoslav officials concerned – who actually arranged for the Count and his henchmen to get at the collection, presumably in consideration of a large sum of money. On the other hand, he couldn't publish any of what he knew because it would lead to Stefanie losing the paintings and perhaps being accused of stealing them. He'd have to work out a cover plan which would allow the investigations to continue without any danger that the trail would lead to Stefanie.

What could he say he'd been doing, when he got back to Ashwood? Passing the happiest week of his life. Rediscovering love. Acknowledging it, more truly, for he had tried to tell himself that those wartime nights had been in part therapeutic – making love to Stefanie had relieved him of the tensions of his days. And to a certain extent, at that time, any woman would have done; but not this past week at the Villa Grimani. Only Stefanie could have been his lover and only Stefanie could have made him hers. Of course the lovemaking had not the frequency or urgency of the old days, but because of that there was more beauty and infinitely more tenderness. Best of all had been the daylight hours, lunching in the loggia, sitting on the lawn, working among the roses; for in 1944, by day, they had never exchanged more than the most formal conversation, always with others present, mostly about what the General would like for lunch, and would the General be good enough to request the staff officers up at the big house to use some other material than the hall carpet for blackout curtains.

The truth was that he had been loved as no man had been loved before. She would always have done anything for him. Why could he not say as much about himself? For he knew that there was much he would not have done for her . . . betray his military responsibilities, or his country, for example. Now he was not so sure: and the thought gave him an oddly exciting *frisson* of fear.

He muttered to himself, 'She loves me.' The man in the next seat glanced at him, and quickly returned to his magazine. He thinks I'm in my dotage, the Field-Marshal mused.

He wouldn't tell anyone a bloody thing about where he'd been or what he'd been doing. He opened his toilet bag and made sure the wire was in a prominent position. He'd bought it yesterday in Paris; it was an ancient recording of a man imitating first one then gradually more and more farmyard noises. The security people doubtless waiting at Heathrow to give him a thorough checking, as they had at Victoria a fortnight ago, would find it interesting. He chuckled to himself. His neighbour stirred uneasily.

CHAPTER FIFTEEN

'Hullo? It's Caroline ... I was calling to tell you I won't be able to come on Saturday.'

Lois, coming in at the front door, paused to listen to her daughter, who was speaking on the telephone in Martin's study, beyond the drawing room.

'Charles, I can't,' Caroline said. Lois stiffened.

'... next week? Well, I think so. All right. Same time.'

Lois heard the phone being put down, then Caroline came out, brushing back her hair which she was now wearing long and loose over her shoulders. She paused on seeing her mother, then came on.

Lois said, 'Was that Charles Gibson you were talking to?'

Caroline shrugged. 'It might have been. I know several men called Charles, including the Prince of Wales.'

'Answer me, Caroline!'

'*Why* are you hanging around listening to my telephone conversations? I'm twenty-one and I've lived alone in London for over two years.'

Lois said, 'Charles is old enough to be your father, and then some more. And he's ... he doesn't have a good reputation with young girls.'

'I can look after myself, thank you.'

'That's what they all say. Caroline, please ...'

Caroline brushed past her and ran down the hall and out of the garden door. Lois stood looking after her for a time, then sighed and went into the kitchen. Charles ought to be ashamed of himself. But he'd never change and nor would the girls ... the women. He looked at them, and for all his affectations and the obvious falsities of his character, there was no hope; they were taken in. She ought to tell Caroline that Madeleine Phillips had been Charles's mistress, once. She had never thought to see again that disconsolate figure she remembered hanging round outside the studio so long ago; but Paul's mother was definitely the same Madeleine.... What good would it do to tell Caroline that, hoping to put her off Charles? They'd all been young then, and Caroline would realise it.

Two of her helpers were working in the kitchen when she got there. They had done a lot since she had given them their work and gone out shopping an hour ago. She glanced at the calendar on the wall: wedding, 60, Saturday; garden party, 80, Sunday ... those were both well in train. Dinner party, 12, Tuesday ... that was the no-expense-spared affair for the Markhams to impress an important client of his. Cricket club tea, Saturday week, but they couldn't tell her for how many yet; and it had to be under 20p a head – a tall order. Perhaps something could be saved from the garden party, that would cut down the cost. To do that, food would have to be kept for six days; but if expense was the cricket club's main consideration they'd have to put up with some not too fresh items.

Faintly she heard the comfortable whirr of the lawnmower from the front of the house where Vetch was mowing the lawn and putting green. Her father was at work in the Factory. Sometimes she could see his white hair glimmering through the glass down there, more often there was merely a sense of occupation, a changing of the patterns of light and shade inside. He at least was happy – especially since his return from his trip abroad. She wondered where he had been and what he had done. Talked to rose growers in France, probably. Whatever it was, it had done him a great deal of good.

Martin was anything but happy. She wondered what he was doing now. He was about somewhere, but doing – what? He had wanted to live somewhere else, but her father had talked him out of that, for the time being at any rate. That was a pity, probably. It was awkward, the two of them being in the same house, but not in the same room any more, pretending to be married yet really having given up even the pretence. He would be better off away from her father. He was too strong a man, and had been too powerful an influence over Martin for him ever to feel quite free, or able to make his own decisions, in his presence.

'Mrs Ruttledge,' one of the helpers broke in tentatively, '—about this sliced bread. I think . . .'

She turned wearily. 'Sliced bread? Oh, I see. Perhaps we could . . .'

Through the open kitchen windows she distinctly heard a woman's scream – 'Help! Come quickly!'

Some instinct from her early days of motherhood sent a message racing to her brain – that's Caroline, in trouble. She saw her father come out of the Factory door and peer across the garden toward the two big oaks that stood in the far corner of the rose garden, bordering Old Barn Lane and the wall which separated the Ashwood House property from the converted farm behind it.

Paul Phillips came in, saying, 'Do you know where Brigadier Ruttledge is, because . . .'

'Come with me, Paul,' she cried. 'Get a golf club, anything! Caroline's screaming for help down there.'

Paul ran ahead of her out of the house, a kitchen knife in his hand and was past the Factory, catching up with her father, when she was barely out of the door. She arrived at the oak trees, panting, a few moments later, to find Caroline, breathing deeply, a short-barrelled automatic pistol in her hand, held steadily pointed at the back of Mr Burrisk's head. Burrisk was standing with his face and body pressed against one of the oaks, his hands over his head. In Old Barn Lane a car accelerated away from close by.

Paul ran to the low wall, looked over and said, 'Stop him! That's the car I saw!'

'Get its number!'

'It's covered.' Paul came back to the others. 'It's gone. Perhaps Mr Burrisk will be able to tell us something about it.'

They stood in a circle round Caroline and her prisoner.

'Can I put my hands down now, lady?' Burrisk said.

'Search him, Paul,' the Field-Marshal said. Paul did so, his hands moving with expert facility, Lois thought; but of course with his background he'd probably done this sort of thing plenty of times, and also had it done to him.

'Let me have the gun, Caroline. . . . Put your hands down. Turn round. Now, what's all this about?'

Burrisk's hair was dishevelled and there was mud on his white shirt, leaves on his coat. His trousers were stained, and there was a bruise on his cheek.

He said, 'Marshal, I was just . . .'

'Be quiet!' Caroline said angrily. 'I was in the tree house, Grandpa. . .' Lois looked up. There it was, practically invisible in the dense summer foliage, unused for – how many years now? Not so many. Caroline was only twenty-one which wasn't far from fourteen.

'What were you doing up there?' the Field-Marshal asked.

Caroline tossed her head defiantly. 'Thinking . . . Clive and I spent a lot of time there while he was making me play lawyers, or cooks, or abandoned families, or whatever it was at the time. . . . I . . . Mother and I . . .'

'We had an argument in the hall,' Lois said.

'Yes. I didn't want to speak to anyone. I went up into the tree house and thought . . . about all sorts of things. People . . . love. Hate . . . life. One of the people I was thinking about was Mr Burrisk, because we haven't heard yet from the Chief Constable about his fingerprints. I was looking down all the time, you know, looking at that bit of the wall, but not seeing it, when suddenly I saw Mr Burrisk. He cut the barbed wire on top of the wall with a pair of wire cutters, which he then dropped behind him. Then he came over the wall into the garden. By this time I was really here, I mean, I knew where I was. Right under the tree house he stopped and pulled this pistol out from his shoulder holster. He was putting it into his coat pocket when I jumped onto him.'

'From the tree house?' Lois said, startled. 'It must be nearly twenty feet.'

'At least,' Burrisk said morosely. 'She's no fairy. Goddamn near six feet tall and landed on me like I felt I'd been tackled by Dick Butkus.'

'I knocked him down, out, really, because he couldn't move and his eyes were open but he seemed to be concussed or something. While he was lying there I took the pistol and started shouting.'

'Where's Martin?' Lois said. 'Why isn't he here, when his own daughter. . . . ?'

'He's in the village,' her father said brusquely. 'Now, Burrisk, what's your story?'

'Marshal, I wanted to talk to you. We – I – have enemies. I heard they might be out to get me today. I came here by a different route, in a different car, with a different driver. I climbed over the wall here instead of coming in the front door. These guys could be waiting for me anywhere. I always carry a gun.'

'It's a tallish story,' the Field-Marshal said. 'I wouldn't believe it for a moment if someone could tell me what motive he has for killing me, or any of us?'

Lois noticed that Caroline had got round behind Burrisk. Now she said sharply, 'Belprato!'

Burrisk started and turned, saying 'Yes?'

Caroline's hair shook in a fury of triumph. 'I was right! I told you I was thinking about you while I was in the tree house! What relation to you was the man killed at San Prospero?'

Burrisk was glaring at her, brows drawn. He looked very dangerous suddenly, the violent animal showing beneath the manicure, the suntan, the perfume. Her grandfather had noticed and the automatic in his hand dropped a little, pointing now at the pit of Burrisk's stomach.

Burrisk said, 'You're too damned smart for your own good. Yeah, I'm Peter Belprato.'

'That's why I was looking for the Brigadier,' Paul said. 'The Chief Constable's office called to tell us that they'd just had the report in from America about the fingerprints. They belong to a man called Pietro Belprato, of New York. He's been arrested twice, once for robbery and once for murder, but both times got away with hung juries. He was fined five thousand dollars for tax evasion, too. He's high up in the Mafia.'

Burrisk/Belprato said, 'That was my brother you killed in front of San Prospero, Marshal.'

'There's the motive!' Caroline cried. 'We would have guessed it earlier, only it's taken such a time to get the identity of those fingerprints from America.'

'We have friends there,' Belprato said dryly. 'The photo was lost a while . . . then delayed a while . . . then lost again. Someone slipped up, though – the report wasn't supposed to get back here till next week.'

A realisation of what had so nearly happened flooded over Lois and she said, 'Call the police, Caroline! You . . . you swine . . .' – her voice rose, out of control – '. . . sneaking in here with Charles's introduction, then trying to murder . . .'

The Field-Marshal interrupted gently, 'Relax, Lois. I'm alive, and Mr Belprato, who has already helped us a great deal, even if it was only to ingratiate himself among us, will now be blackmailed, by us, into helping us a great deal more.'

He looked down at the gun in his hand, then with a click took out the magazine, dropped it into his pocket, cleared the breech, and handed the weapon back to Belprato; he finished '. . . though attempting to murder me would not be regarded as a crime these days. If the Home Office heard about it, so far from throwing you into jail, they'd give you a free pardon, and a medal. Come inside.'

Belprato was drinking whisky on the rocks, sitting hunched by the empty fireplace, staring at the Field-Marshal. Paul was behind Lois somewhere, and she knew he had his pad on his lap. Caroline was leaning on the door jamb, arms folded, like a wardress. She was still flushed and triumphant, over half an hour after she had jumped on Belprato from the tree house. She ought to be proud of her daughter, for it was Caroline, by pure intellect and knowledge of human nature, who had guessed the motive for the attempted murder; and it was Caroline's physical courage that had thwarted it; singlehanded she had captured an armed and dangerous man. She should be proud indeed of her, but all she felt was jealousy, disguised as concern for her moral well-being. It was herself she should be concerned for – long married, even though unhappily, nearly fifty years of age, going back to Charles like a . . . foolish, desperately lonely girl of nineteen, long ago.

Her father was saying, '. . . so you see, I can't swear that it was necessary. Nor that I was ordered to do it. There was no one within a hundred miles with the power to give me such an order. I can only say that in my military judgment, I thought it was necessary, and I did give the order . . . just as, nearly a year later, I ordered one of our tank regiments to fire on another. Twelve men were killed.'

'You did that?' Belprato said, his face altering.

Paul interrupted, 'Yes. Some people believe that he ordered American tanks to fire on the British squadron which had mutinied, but that isn't true.'

'But would you have done *that*?' Belprato said. 'Had your own men shot down by our guys?'

'If I had believed it was the best course open to me at the moment, yes,' the Field-Marshal said.

Belprato shook his head and said, 'It's hard to believe. Papa won't believe it. That's my father, the head of our family, if you know what I mean.'

'The Godfather!' Caroline said.

Belprato said, 'That crap! . . . Johnny, the one who was killed, was the apple of Papa's eye. He tried to stop him from going off to the war, but Johnny was obstinate as hell, and he enlisted and he got killed there at San Prospero, and Papa got a letter from the Marshal here – only we'd never heard of him, then – saying how sorry he was about the accident. But we heard stories that it wasn't an accident, and one night Papa said "I swear by the Virgin Mary" – he's a very religious man – "that if some Limey killed Johnny on purpose, I'll get him." Then it was published in the papers over there that the Marshal was going to write his Memoirs and a columnist wrote that maybe now we'd hear the truth about our boys being shelled by the British on purpose to stop them getting to some town before the British.'

'That was quite untrue, of course,' the Field-Marshal said.

'Yeah, but Papa believed it. . . . Let me come clean.'

'It's about time', Caroline said.

'Papa told me to fly back and talk to him. When I got to New York he said, "Pietro, get to meet this Marshal Durham. Find out if he killed Johnny. If he did, kill him." There's nothing more important to Papa than our family, not even money. So I flew back here, got that artist guy to give me the introduction. Then I learned about these paintings that someone's got away with, and I wrote to Papa saying I was pretty sure that the Marshal had given the orders about the shelling; but there was a chance that we might get into a lot of dough, if we could find out about these paintings. So Papa said, O.K., I could wait a few months, but then I was to do what I'd been told. I didn't want to, Marshal, because I've become like a friend, right?'

'Wrong,' Caroline said.

Belprato ignored her. 'I like you, Marshal. And I still think we can get our hands on those paintings, and make some millions, but Papa said now they've got your fingerprints, go ahead and kill him. So I tried.'

'Now we've got you!' Caroline said. 'One word from us and you'll be deported, at the least. Presumably the police here don't know that Burrisk is the same man as Belprato?'

'We didn't know when we sent the fingerprint photos to the Chief Constable,' Paul said.

'What do you want me to do?' Belprato asked.

Caroline said, 'Find out more about the Zvornos Collection.'

The Field-Marshal cut in, 'I don't care where the paintings are, you understand. I don't want time or money wasted trying to find them. All I want to know is, who is responsible for letting the thieves through.'

'I'm going over to New York again soon,' Belprato said. 'I'll find out what our boys have learned. . . . I guess I have to apologise, Marshal. I never thought the job would turn out like this when Papa told me what I had to do. . . . I never liked the military much. But just being on the outskirts of preparing these Memoirs, finding out what you had to do, and did, was making me feel a heel. There was something rotten somewhere, but it wasn't in you, like I'd expected. Maybe it was in the war itself. We do some hard things in my family's business. Guys get rubbed out, you might say, and you don't think anything of it. It's business. But you never rub out a guy who's on your side, in your family, and loyal. For him, you have to risk your own life ... everything you own. That's loyalty.'

'We have loyalty, too,' the Field-Marshal said, 'but our family is very large. I was commanding a quarter of a million men in the Balkans. Sometimes loyalty to the majority, to the task you've been given, forces you to act against others.'

'I'll have to persuade Papa, and that won't be easy. He's a hard man to persuade, but I'll tell him you've got me by the balls — pardon me, ma'am — and he'll understand. ... I didn't think I was going to need to give you the information, but my people have found out something about Sir Bartlett. When he got money, in June 1945, it came in cash — British one pound and five pound notes. That's how he paid it into his bank. A hundred and fifty thousand pounds. That's all we've been able to get on that. ... Everyone seems to say he's snobby but otherwise a good enough guy — except a lord, Lord Stockbridge.'

'How did you come to talk to him?'

'There was talk from old timers that Bartlett and his wife used to know the previous Lord Stockbridge's daughter, the Hon. Daphne Fuller, though why in hell she isn't called Stockbridge or him Lord Fuller, I'm goddamned if I'll ever understand. ... This lord said he personally had nothing against Bartlett, but he had an old aunt who swore the guy was a crook and a heel and a thief and God knows what else. But she won't tell anyone why. My people have tried to talk to her — got nowhere. Maybe one of you should try.'

'I will,' Caroline said. 'What's her name and address?'

'Miss Janet Parmentier ... hold on a minute ... 24 Madrid Road, Barnes.'

'I've got it.'

Belprato said, 'Let me know what you find out. ... I heard you were a little short of cash, Marshal. Something to do with the government on your back for taxes on the sale of some paintings.'

Caroline said, 'He doesn't owe any taxes. We've found out that the sale was not taxable. But Grandpa feels he must give the money back to whoever owned the lithographs.'

'How much?'

The Field-Marshal said, 'Ten thousand guineas. That's ten thousand five hundred pounds. But half of that is being advanced to me by the people who are going to publish the

Memoirs, the Mermaid Press and the *Sunday Journal*.'

'So you're still short five thousand pounds, that's, what, twelve thousand dollars. I'd be happy . . .'

The Field-Marshal waved his hand. 'No, Mr Belprato, I'll find the money somehow. For one thing, I'm getting good royalties from the Red Durham and if I can just perfect the Black, there'll be a great deal more. Now, let's have some lunch. Lois, you can feed Mr Belprato, I expect?'

'Yes,' said Lois, getting up. 'And his driver, if he's come back.'

Belprato got up, laughing grimly. 'Hell no, ma'am, he's in London, busy getting his friends to swear he was with them all morning.'

They sat in the drawing room, watching television. Lois had never met Dick Armstrong, only seen the picture of him the *Journal* published every Sunday at the head of his column. That, being a still, gave no idea of his animation, the way he moved his head a little as he spoke, the firm economical gestures he made with his hands to emphasise his point. This was the first of what was planned to be a regular Tuesday evening talk on ITV, and his subject was industrial relations.

Martin said, 'He's right, but the trade unions will never buy it.'

The Field-Marshal said, 'They would, if they can be shown that what he suggests is better for them than the old ways.'

Caroline said, 'Shhh, please, Grandpa, I want to hear him.' Later she said, 'He's absolutely great. What a shame he's blind. If he could see, he could be anything, do anything.'

Lois agreed. Industrial relations, trade unions, strikes, lock-outs and the like had never interested her at all, except in so far as they interfered with her daily routine, but Armstrong was keeping her attention riveted; more than that, she believed him. She couldn't imagine anyone not being convinced.

There was a ring at the front door. Lois looked round, realised that she was the only one who had heard it, and got up. She found three men waiting outside beside a black limousine. All were in uniform. One was a full general, the others a brigadier and a major of Military Police.

The general said, 'Is Field-Marshal Sir John Durham in, madam?'

'My father? Yes.'

'I am General Braithewait, the Adjutant General. I have here an order of the Army Board to arrest the Field-Marshal.'

She stared at him under the porch light. She thought she had met him somewhere, while Martin was still serving – but that was a long time ago. 'Did you say ... arrest? My father?' The words sounded ridiculous.

'Yes, madam. He is charged with an offence against Section 70 of the Army Act 1955, that is, an offence contrary to Section 2 of the Official Secrets Act 1911.'

'Oh,' Lois said, 'come in. Where are you going to take him?'

'The Tower of London, madam. He should pack a suitcase now, please, and he should change into uniform.'

... *can I go on as I have for these nearly thirty years? You have changed physically, of course, as I have, and I suppose we have both changed in ourselves, for one cannot go so long suppressing the fundamental truth of one's life without suffering for it. I am only half a person, and those few days made me realise it again ...*

CHAPTER SIXTEEN

The courtroom was one of the old-fashioned kind, a large amount of the small space available taken up by the dais and desk for the three judges, with the ornately carved and painted royal coat of arms on the oak-panelled wall behind it. There was a dock, but the Field-Marshal had been allowed to sit in a chair, with a cushion under his thin buttocks. He was wearing Service dress uniform, with his five rows of medal ribbons, cap and cane in his lap. Martin sat on another chair beside him. To the judges' left the Solicitor-General of Great Britain was on his feet, finishing his submission of the Crown's case as to why a writ of *Habeas Corpus* should not be issued.

The Field-Marshal's eyes wandered. The old Beefeater they had appointed to be his body servant had come with him from the Tower and now sat in the back of the court, listening anxiously, his head tilted, for he was rather deaf. Two detectives stood with their backs to the closed door, and outside he knew there were two more, ensuring that no one came close enough to hear what was being said inside the court.

The senior judge, Mr Justice Owens, leaned forward, his be-wigged head resting on his left elbow, either making notes or doodling with his right hand. Through the windows, set high along one wall above the panelling, the Field-Marshal saw blue sky and drifting white clouds. A nice day, and just a month since they'd arrested him . . .

'M'lords, I suggest that there can be no question but that the Field-Marshal has committed acts preparatory to the commission of an offence under the Official Secrets Act 1911. I suggest that we have proved that great harm will be done to this country if the facts of the bombing of Peskevo are published, and vouched for by someone in the Field-Marshal's position. The question before your lordships is whether the military authorities are unreasonably detaining him in close arrest, and incommunicado, before his court martial.' He leaned down and took a sip of water from the glass on the table beside him. He straightened and repeated, 'before his court martial. But to ask the question in this case is surely to answer it. We are trying to prevent damage to the nation, not punish the Field-Marshal. The fact that your lordships agreed to hold this hearing *in camera* enabled us to present the facts of the Peskevo affair, and relevant documents in the secret archives of the Cabinet Secretariat. We believe . . .'

The senior judge interrupted, raising his hand. 'How long do the military authorities propose to keep the Field-Marshal in custody, Sir Ernest?'

'Until they can adequately prepare his trial, m'lord. Or until the Field-Marshal agrees not to publish anything connected with the bombing of Peskevo, which they earnestly hope he will, rather than put the army and indeed the nation through the trauma of a court martial of such an eminent and respected figure.'

The three judges bent over and conferred in low voices. The Field-Marshal could not hear what they were saying and did not strain his ears to try.

Mr Justice Owens said, 'It appears that as there is no military equivalent of "bail", if we directed that the Field-Marshal be released from custody he would be returned to his home but under "open" rather than "close" arrest, would not be guarded, and would be free to go about his business in the normal way, until the court martial.'

'Precisely, m'lord.'

The judge turned to the Field-Marshal. 'Have you been deprived of opportunity to see and confer with your legal advisers?'

The Field-Marshal said, 'No, my lord. As I said at the beginning of this hearing, I do not wish to be represented by counsel.'

The judge turned back to the Solicitor-General. 'How are you going to see that the Field-Marshal keeps his promise?'

'We believe him to be an honourable man, m'lord. The Army Board is sure that if he gives his word, he will keep it, both on his own behalf and on behalf of his family. Of course, if he didn't, and published, we would feel compelled to bring him to court martial, and push the case with all possible vigour. Among other considerations, the example would be disastrous. If a man of such stature as the Field-Marshal can do these things, and go unpunished, what is to prevent every clerk, underling, and junior official in government service from selling what he knows?'

'I see. Have you finished your submission?'

'Yes, m'lord.'

The judge turned to the Field-Marshal. 'Are you ready to state your case, Field-Marshal?'

'Yes, m'lord.' He pushed himself carefully upright. His quarters in the Tower were comfortable enough, but the air in that gloomy old pile was always damp, and his bones felt chilled all the time.

The judge said, 'I am sorry you wouldn't take my advice and get counsel to represent you. And sit down, please.'

The Field-Marshal said, 'Thank you. I don't want the clarity of my purpose to be muddied by legalities. . . . What I am trying to do is tell the truth about commanding a Corps and an Army in war. The whole truth. The events I am preparing to recount took place nearly thirty years ago. Many of the people who took part in those events are dead. When I decided to write my Memoirs I felt that the only new element I could add to the mountains that have already been published was this factor of truth – personal truth. Command in war is not exercised by robots over robots, but by men over men. Men get stomach aches, jealousies, hangovers. They get homesick, over-optimistic, careless, frightened. They make mistakes and those mistakes cause more mistakes. Sometimes what has to be done is not what ought to be done. . . . I am determined to tell the truth, not only about the bombing of Peskevo, but about many lesser matters . . . the death of Captain Cunningham – the dismissal of Lieutenant-General Ross – the mutiny in 206 R.A.C. – the deliberate shelling of the 798th U.S. Infantry by our artillery – the attempted bribing of General Ballino – the . . .'

The junior judge said, 'I believe a question is to be asked about that in the House of Commons.'

The Solicitor-General rose. 'It is, m'lord. Mr Robert Cunningham, the Member for Great Burford, is to ask whether the Minister of Defence will institute an inquiry to find out whether there is any connection between the disappearance of the gold, which was supposed to be used for bribing General Ballino, and Field-Marshal Durham's acquisition of some valuable lithographs by Picasso.'

The Field-Marshal said, 'The gold was handed over to General Ballino's representative on September 6, 1943. I was present. The lithographs were brought to me by my chief padre late in September, 1944. I cannot prove that he gave them to me, as he is dead, and as they were erotic in nature I didn't show them to anyone else, including the pilot who flew the roll back to England and handed it over to my wife. I cannot prove, at this late date, that the gold was actually handed over to General Ballino. We might unearth the driver, but he did not know what was in the vehicle. . . . I am also attempting to find out who made it possible for someone to steal the Zvornos Collection of art from Zvornos Castle on February 16, 1945. I have reason to believe that the actual thief, if such a word can be applied to the rightful owner, was Count Zvornos and that he managed to take the paintings to America. But I do not know yet through whom he acted. . . . And I have been told, in a roundabout way, that murder charges will be brought against my son-in-law and myself if I do not cease these enquiries.'

'Is this true, Sir Ernest?'

'I cannot believe it is, m'lord.'

'Who told you that, Field-Marshal?'

The Field-Marshal thought. It was a small, oldish man in a dark suit and dark felt hat, a mousy little man, who'd come to his quarters with letters that had been picked up at Ashwood, examined, and now brought to him. The man had not given his name – just handed over the letters, and in a small bland voice made his threat, and bowed himself out.

'It doesn't matter,' he said at last. 'He'll never come forward, and the government will never produce him.'

The senior judge waited: then said, 'Is that all? . . . I see. . . . Field-Marshal, I would like to hear what, if anything, you have to say in rebuttal of the Solicitor-General's contention that the publication of all this – specifically, he has been basing his case on the bombing of Peskevo – will do great harm to the nation.'

The Field-Marshal said slowly, 'I could say that we must punish people who have done wrong . . . study the mistakes and plan to avoid them in future . . . put the records straight . . . reinstate those who have been maligned, pull down those who have been wrongly set up, or have so set themselves up. . . . All that is true. But just as you can't get a big calculation right if on the first line you have written that two plus two is three, so there is an abstract case for truth. Things . . . the world . . . life . . . don't come out right without it. With it, there is unhappiness, God knows, but there is hope of something . . . the right answer. The solution. The finished shape. There comes a time when truth has to be. As far as my part in the events of 1944 and 1945 is concerned, that time has come. That's all.'

Again the judges waited a long time, Mr Justice Owens peering anxiously down at the Field-Marshal, as though hoping he would say something more. At last he said, 'The court will adjourn until . . . eleven thirty.' The judges rose, the court usher hurriedly crying, 'All stand!'

The Field-Marshall struggled to his feet. Martin said, 'We're supposed to wait in a cell downstairs, but the clerk of the court says we can stay here.'

The Field-Marshal nodded and sat down again. Nearly eleven o'clock. He wondered whether Vetch was keeping an eye on the cotyledons of this spring's crosses. And there was always so much pruning, tidying, throwing out, recording, which none but himself could do. Being shut up in the Tower might set back the Black Durham by a full year. . . . The roses were in full bloom along the hedge where Dick Newby lay, by High Wood on the chalky downland above the Somme. Windrows of his Fusiliers lay along the hedge there, caught by the German machine guns in enfilade on the second day of the Somme battle. The trenches showed white in the chalk, the barbed wire was a giant rusty python crawling down the valleys, over the downs, through the woods. Six bullets he'd counted in Dick, after he'd wiped his own face. They started in the left side of the forehead then came down across the face, the last one was through the right shoulder. Instant death – twenty-three years old, one of the Musketeers, the second oldest friend among them, for he and Dick had been at Cheltenham together, then the R.M.C., then the regiment. He himself had won the M.C. that day. A pretty medal, the prettiest ribbon of them all, with its white and purple shot silk, a well-designed medal too, the shape of the cross stark and silvery.

They had left Dick lying there all day, for the wounded had to be brought in before the dead. After dark he'd gone out with a party and brought him in. Dick was stiff by then, and wouldn't bend. His hands and face were cold, though it was a hot night. Next morning, over the top again. That had been a good day, a long section of German trench captured . . . but by then Ted Crandall was already gone, at Le Cateau; Jimmy Livingstone, outside Ypres; now Dick Newby, lying there. The lips had been ice cold to his, and caked with dust.

'All stand!' He started up. He must have been dozing. A useful accomplishment, in an upright chair like this.

Mr Justice Owens said, 'Field-Marshal, will you give the undertaking the Solicitor-General has asked of you? It is understood that Brigadier Ruttledge must give the same undertaking, and all members of your family to whom you have revealed what are still Official Secrets.'

The Field-Marshal said, 'I am sorry, my lord, I cannot give that undertaking.'

The judge said, 'Then we must, with great regret, agree with the Solicitor-General's contention, that you must continue to be confined until you do give the required promise, or are brought to trial by court martial. But this court would advise the military authorities that one or the other must come about within the next thirty days, or oppression will have been inflicted on the Field-Marshal. You will so advise them, please, Sir Ernest.'

'I shall, m'lord.'

The judge looked at the Solicitor-General over the top of his glasses – 'Sir Ernest, what is the Government proposing to do about Brigadier Ruttledge, who has been assisting the Field-Marshal in the preparation of his Memoirs? And the grand-daughter, Miss Ruttledge, and a Mr Paul Phillips, all of whom, it appears, are in possession of Official Secrets?'

The Solicitor-General said, 'None of them is subject to military law, m'lord. The appropriate authorities do not think, yet, that they have committed acts preparatory to an offence against the Official Secrets Acts – on their own, that is, without the instructions of the Field-Marshal, their employer. However, they have all been warned that if they do, so to speak, continue on their own, on the course they were following under the Field-Marshal, then they are liable to arrest and trial under Section 2 of the Official Secrets Act 1911.'

The second judge said, 'Once the facts are made public, I should think the government would find it very difficult to prosecute, in this case. Miss Ruttledge and Mr Phillips are not here, of course. Do you propose, on your own account, to publish what the Field-Marshal has told you, Brigadier?'

The Field-Marshal did not let his son-in-law answer, but cut in, 'I don't want you to do that, Martin. The truth that I want to make known is my truth, not yours.'

'I will not publish,' Martin then said.

Mr Justice Owens said, 'Good. Take the Field-Marshal back to the Tower. . . . You will be released at any time, by sending me a message that you will give the promise the Army Board has asked for.'

The Field-Marshal said, 'I understand. I propose to appeal against your decision, my lords.'

'You may. But you'll have to get counsel for that.'

'All rise!' the usher intoned.

The black Austin was drawn up at the kerb when the Field-Marshal went out, walking between the same Military Police officers who had come down to Ashwood to arrest him a month ago. The Beefeater was waiting by the car, his hand at the salute. About two hundred spectators were gathered, held back by policemen to leave a lane between them. The Field-Marshal glanced at their faces as he walked down. Mostly old people, mostly men. Perhaps they had served under him in the Desert, or Italy, or the Balkans. They were silent, though, watching. No boos, no cheers – silence. It had been very different a month ago. They'd got him into the Tower before anyone knew what was happening; but afterwards, according to the papers, there'd been tremendous public arousal – thousands of people standing outside the Tower, special launch excursions on the river, portentous leading articles in all the papers, huge headlines recalling the Baillie Stewart case of the late thirties; only now it wasn't THE OFFICER IN THE TOWER, it was THE FIELD-MARSHAL IN THE TOWER. . . . That had died down. What were these people experiencing, as they watched a knight and a Field-Marshal go back to jail? Silent delight? Silent worry? Silent sorrow? They didn't say.

Before getting into the car he said to Martin, 'Keep up the enquiries. And talk to Forsythe about the appeal.'

'Yes, sir.'

'Give my love to Lois and Caroline – and Clive, if you see him. He must be hating this.'

Martin didn't reply and the Field-Marshal climbed into the car. The Military Police and the Beefeater took their places. The car glided off.

Belprato was back from New York, and had some information, Martin had told him on one of his frequent visits to the Tower. It would be appalling if he'd found a trail that could eventually lead back to Stefanie. Those gangster people had such resources, and of course didn't hesitate to use torture to make people talk. Belprato was also sure that someone close to himself was leaking information to those who did not want the Memoirs published. If this person leaked the information that Burrisk was Belprato, he'd be deported . . . so Belprato/Burrisk was now Mr Peter Bigelow, complete with another passport, another address, another phone number.

Stefanie . . . she'd know he was in the Tower because the Italian papers would have published the news. Every newspaper in the world seemed to have published it. Sitting alone in his room, looking out through a narrow window on an inner courtyard, he had spent lonely hours composing letters to her. but he would never write them, or send them, or ever go back. The best, the only, things he could do, were protect her reputation by ensuring that no one knew of his relationship with her besides the one other living person who already did – Wilfred Eden, his ex A.D.C.; and protect her possession of the Zvornos paintings, the means by which she could live out her old age in ease, among her roses. To achieve those aims, he'd lie like a trooper . . . already had, as a matter of fact. So much for the truth, when it cuts close to your *own* heart.

CHAPTER SEVENTEEN

Harry Mullins, the editor, lounged back in his swivel chair, his feet up on the desk. Beside him a secretary sat with pencil and pad ready.

Caroline said, 'You know they refused to let Grandpa out at the hearing yesterday?'

'Yes.'

'Well, Paul and I decided to tell you the story, and ask you to publish it.'

'This is the story of Peskevo?'

'Yes.'

'O.K. Let's have it.'

Caroline cleared her throat. 'We have a draft of the chapter in which Grandpa is going to describe it, but he hasn't seen it yet, so we don't want to give it as though it were official ... his. These are the notes we made when he was telling us about it, from which we prepared the draft.' Beside her, Paul nodded agreement.

Mullins said, 'I understand. If we publish we won't say that this is the Field-Marshal's story – simply that this is what happened, and that the Field-Marshal's book will describe the whole thing in more detail. Go ahead.'

Caroline opened the file. 'On February 22, 1945, partisans came to Grandpa's headquarters and told him that Draja Sovik, one of the communist Committee of Three, wanted to talk to him. At that time Grandpa's army was advancing through the mountains to the plain of the Morava. Grandpa said he would be happy to meet Sovik at any time. The staff – my father, Brigadier Ruttledge, was in on it – arranged a place where Sovik could be picked up. Very little of Yugoslavia had been liberated from the Germans by then, but our air forces could operate almost without opposition. Three days later, on February 25, Sovik was picked up by a light aircraft and brought to Grandpa's headquarters.'

'Brigadier Ruttledge went in the light plane,' Paul added.

'Yes. Grandpa saw Sovik, with Peter Johnson, who was Chief Civil Affairs adviser to Grandpa. Sovik wanted to know when the Allies were going to break out into the plains, as the partisans weren't going to risk coming out of their hiding places and mountain refuges unless the German main forces in the plains were going to be kept fully occupied with the Allies. Grandpa, of course, was very anxious to break out as soon as possible . . .'

'Did he tell Sovik this, or is this something he has told you, for the Memoirs?'

'He didn't tell Sovik anything at that time. . . . He was anxious because the Magitor Range separated his own 16th Army from the American 11th Army. While they were in this position the Germans could have attacked either army in superior force, and the other could not have come to its help.'

'I remember that time,' Mullins said. 'I was windy as hell, but the Old Man – your grandfather – didn't seem worried.'

'Well, he says he was, really. The separation of the two armies was partly forced on them by the shape of the ground, and partly it was a matter of choice – it gave the Allies a chance to outflank the Germans along the Morava. The risk of the Germans being able to strike was great, but both Army commanders, and General Bartlett, who was commanding over-all, thought our air forces could delay or prevent the Germans mounting an effective counter stroke while the British and Americans were so separated. . . . Please don't think I really understand all this, Mr Mullins, or that these are my words. I'm not a Field-Marshal.'

'Don't worry. Go on.'

She turned to Paul, 'You go on. I'm getting hoarse.'

Paul said, 'General Durham, as he then was, wanted the partisans to do two things . . . first, get accurate information to him about German troop movements. This was an immediate and continuing requirement. Second, when he gave the signal he wanted them to attack every German rear installation; base, railway, road, garrison, et cetera. For the first job, the partisans had to avoid battle, keep out of view, just watch, and use their secret transmitters. For the second, they had to come out and fight. Sovik agreed to co-operate, on certain terms . . . he wanted more radio transmitters of small size, that could easily be carried and hidden, with all the related equipment, like spare parts, generators, petrol, plus half a dozen expert repair and maintenance men. General Durham agreed to that at once. Sovik then asked for more of certain types of arms . . . anti-tank mines, rocket launchers, demolition explosive, shaped charges, plastic explosives, fuses, incendiary grenades, things like that. He asked for a lot – we don't have the exact figures but when General Durham seemed amazed at the amount, Sovik said, "General, the Committee of Three has two hundred and eighty thousand men, women, and children under its orders." General Durham said he could spare some of the stores from his own 16th Army reserves, but he would have to get most through Army Group Headquarters, as he was likely to need most of his own, which he had been piling up ready for the time when he broke into the plains. Actually, he later sent Brigadier Ruttledge to General Bartlett's headquarters, and it was agreed to supply everything that Sovik had asked for. It was also arranged where and how they should be dropped by our air forces.'

Caroline took over. 'Grandpa thought that was all Sovik wanted, but he said, "There is one more condition. The National Freedom Movement must be destroyed." '

'I remember them,' Mullins said. 'Their leader was a fellow called Danilo Elbasan. In the early part of the war, after the Germans had invaded Yugoslavia, they were almost as powerful as the Committee of Three.'

'Grandpa asked Sovik why he wanted that done. They were, after all, fighting the Germans, too.'

'The Old Man must have been playing for time,' Mullins said, 'because the answer's obvious. Everyone knew that the war would not last much longer. In countries that were then occupied by the Germans, the question was, who is going to be in the stronger position when they're kicked out.'

Caroline said, 'Grandpa took his Civil Affairs man away and they talked privately. When they met again with Sovik, they wanted more information ... why should they do this, how could it be done, and so on. Sovik said, that as far as why they should do it – his Committee of Three partisans were ready to risk their lives against the Germans, but inevitably many of them would get killed. They would use up ammunition and lose equipment and in general be weakened. This would make it easier for Elbasan's N.F.M. to sieze power after the German defeat. Unless Grandpa agreed to what he asked, his people would do nothing. They would neither provide information, nor would they act. They would save themselves for action later – against N.F.M. He was sure the Allies would be able to push the Germans back, but it would be a longer business and it would cost thousands more British and American lives. Grandpa knew that was true, so he asked, how can it be done? Sovik said that the centre and head of the whole N.F.M. movement was Peskevo. It was a small town in a remote valley and the N.F.M. had taken it from the Germans in a mass assault a few weeks before. It wasn't on any important line of communication and the Germans had only put some troops to watch it. They had not diverted any force to recapture it, presumably because they thought it was not worth while, and they needed the troops for other work. Sovik said that Elbasan and most of the other N.F.M. leaders were there, with nearly all their reserves of ammunition, rifles, grenades, arms, all kinds of things. He wanted it wiped out by a big bombing raid.'

Paul said, 'General Durham had some fighter bombers directly in support of his Army, but the heavy bombers were based in Italy, under the control of the Joint Chiefs of Staff as to overall policy of allocations, but under the Supreme Commander, Mediterranean as to missions and targets. Brigadier Ruttledge took Sovik to another place while General Durham and Peter Johnson discussed this. General Durham thought we'd have to do it. It would have to be kept out of the press and absolutely secret, but it would have to be done, unless Sovik and the Committee of Three could be persuaded to forego the requirement. Mr Johnson thought they would stick to their demand – blackmail, he called it.

'Then they saw Sovik again and said he must stay at General Durham's headquarters while the matter was decided. Two days later there was a conference at General Bartlett's headquarters, with Brigadier Ruttledge representing General Durham, and Air Marshal Shaftesbury representing the Supreme Commander, Mediterranean. Matt Jordan and Peter Johnson were there, and General Bartlett. The Air Marshal said they could put four hundred heavy bombers on to the target if it was done soon. General Bartlett said it was imperative for political reasons that both British and American aircraft should take part. He said there could be no raid unless that was agreed upon. Matt Jordan agreed, and said he was sure he could get the American Chiefs of Staff to agree. Neither he nor Peter Johnson liked the idea of the raid, but they agreed that if it would improve our military situation, it should be done. The conference ended and everyone returned to his own headquarters.

'Three days later the Combined Chiefs of Staff – that's the Joint Chiefs of both Britain and the U.S.A. – agreed. The raid was laid on for the night of March 5th/6th. Originally the air planners planned to have Pathfinders drop their markers on

Peskevo in mistake for another target, but then they decided it would be much simpler and less likely to go wrong if they made Peskevo the target, on the basis of "false" intelligence that the Germans had driven out the N.F.M., and were occupying the town in force.'

Mullins said, 'On the night of March 5th, Peskevo disappeared under two thousand tons of high explosive and incendiary . . .'

Paul said, 'Out of the twenty top leaders of the N.F.M., our Intelligence later learned that sixteen had been killed, including Danilo Elbasan – besides two thousand others, men, women, and children. Many of these were N.F.M. members, but many were not. General Durham estimated that the later actions of Sovik's partisans saved his army four thousand casualties . . .'

'Two to one in our favour,' Mullins said, 'and the Committee of Three in due course took over the country, which promptly disappeared behind the Iron Curtain. Quite a story.'

He got up and walked round the table to peer down into the sluggish red and black river of traffic in Fleet Street. 'They'll probably put me in jail for breaking the Official Secrets Acts if we publish,' he said. 'But I could cable this to the *World* in New York – we have an agreement with them – then they'd publish tomorrow, which is Sunday . . . then everyone would feel free to publish. But *we'd* be too late for tomorrow, and would have to wait till the next Sunday, by which time the dailies would have flogged the story to death.'

He paused, looked at Caroline, and said, 'Damn it, if the Field-Marshal is willing to go to jail, so am I. We'll publish. Tomorrow. And so will the *World* in New York, I'll bet. Senator Jordan is not going to like this at all.'

A little later Caroline and Paul were out in Fleet Street. Paul said, 'Well, there's one thing Mullins forgot to say – that we'll probably be going to jail, too.'

'Nonsense,' Caroline said. 'Once it's out, they'll give up. It would cause far too much controversy to have trials about it now.'

'It's all very well for you to talk,' Paul grumbled, 'but I don't want to go to clink. I've been there. . . . Look here, Caroline, like to come and have lunch with me? Nothing posh, but I do know of lots of places in Soho.'

Caroline looked at her wrist watch. It would be fun to say Yes. Not exactly fun but – a good thing to do. Paul might open up. He was so sensitive, about his birth, his birthmark, his father's shame, his mother . . . and Charles would be furious. That would do him good. It wouldn't really, because he'd just laugh and shrug it off. There were lots of other models, other girls.

'I'm sorry,' she said, 'I can't. I have an appointment.'

He turned away, muttering, 'O.K.'

'Wait,' she said, 'could we have tea together? Before we go back to Ashwood?'

'I'm not going back. I'm having tomorrow off.'

'Let's have tea,' she repeated. 'Where?'

He looked at her suspiciously. His face cleared. 'O.K. Lyons in the Strand, next to Charing Cross Station.'

'Fine,' she said, 'four o'clock.'

She stood leaning against the table, naked. From the direction of Charles's glances she thought he was painting her face in fully today. It had been, so far, a formalised shape, faintly oriental, while he concentrated on the pose of her body and legs. She took another puff of the joint and set it down in the ashtray.

'That's good,' Charles said, 'nothing like pot to give a girl that dreamy look.'

She had smoked pot before but infrequently. She didn't particularly care for it, but she didn't want to cut herself off completely from the other young people she knew. Yet she was finding that her ways of thought and theirs were becoming increasingly divergent. Was it Grandpa, the army background which she couldn't shake off, however much she might have fought it? If you're black, you're black. . . . This joint in her hand had been more or less pushed on her. Charles had insisted she would look more as he wanted, a sort of weary voluptuousness, a sense of well-being. Sometimes it happened like that; sometimes only a hot dry mouth and near nausea, like the first time she had smoked an ordinary cigarette.

'Not much longer now,' Charles said. 'Then we'll have a drink and lunch. By the way, did you see in the paper today that General Ross had died?'

'No, but Mrs Ross telephoned early this morning. Grandpa will be sad because he won't be able to go to the funeral.'

'That won't upset Hilda Ross one bit. She cordially hates the Old Man.'

'She's a funny old thing, always drunk. I can't think why

Mummy has her down so often, and goes to see her. Grandpa keeps saying he's going to tell something about General Ross in the Memoirs, but he hasn't yet. And now it's too late.'

Charles said nothing and she shifted her pose slightly, keeping her head at the same angle. Really, if he was just doing her head she could have kept on her blue jeans and perhaps her shirt. That was silly. She was modelling, and being paid good money for it. Whether she took her clothes off or not was for the artist to say, not the model.

Fifteen minutes later Charles carefully laid down his brush and palette and came forward. He held up his arms. 'There, it's done .Come and take a look.'

She stepped down, walked away from the easel and studied herself as Charles had painted her. It was a good composition, it was erotic, but not selling her as a piece of female merchandise. She really seemed to have a good body; the face . . . unmistakably her now, though still slightly orientalised, the lips just parted and the dreamy look Charles had been wanting – not dreamy, remote, as though she were thinking of a lover, with whom she had spent last night.

Charles's arm was round her waist. 'Now we've finished the work,' he said, 'let's play.'

He turned her round and his lips met hers. His jacket felt rough against her belly and his trousers against her thighs. He smelled of cigar smoke and the sherry of which he'd had a few sips while painting. Why not, she thought? He might be good. He must have made love to five hundred women, perhaps he knows something I don't. Perhaps the joint's getting to me. His tongue was exploring her mouth. He was old, of course, but honestly that didn't seem to matter. It never had, with her. Paul was at least ten years older than her, come to that, and she never thought of that. Paul seemed older than Charles, most of the time. Charles's breath came deeper, as one hand moved down into her loins, the other on to her buttock.

It simply wasn't there. He was full of lust, but she felt not the smallest stir of it. She stepped out of his arms.

'How does Mummy fuck?' she asked.

Charles's face was suffused, and for a moment he looked really angry, a personal and true emotion escaping. She had never seen that, she thought; usually whatever he showed was what he had decided was the right thing to show – rather like Clive. He took a furious step toward her, but when she held up her hand, he turned, found a cigar, lit it and picked up his sherry glass. 'Sherry, Caroline?'

'Wine, please. Red.'

He poured her a glass of claret. 'Jealous?'

She shook her head. 'I think Mummy is.'

'All women are jealous of their daughters, unless they're deformed. . . . She comes here.'

'Only recently. She never used to go away from Ashwood, unless she went shopping with me, or went with Grandpa to London for something. She's been coming here since . . .'

'Grandpa started to write his Memoirs,' Charles said. 'And she decided to send Martin to sleep in another room.'

Caroline said, 'Poor Daddy.'

'He has found some consolation, not that there was much to miss in his relations with your mother, recently, I understand. He has been visiting Madeleine Phillips.'

Caroline was shocked then. 'Paul's mother?' she said. 'But she's no more than a tart!'

'By appointment only,' Charles said. 'When you get to know men better you'll realise that there's a lot about tarts that makes them very attractive to men. They are the beginning and ending – each act – in itself. Wives and lovers are like icebergs, most of the relationship emerges later, often for the worse . . . or fuses, which you light, but you don't know what the other end is attached to. . . . Martin's been having a very hard time and the one thing he doesn't need is involvement with another woman. Not until he has settled who he is and what he is going to do. Madeleine Phillips is not an involvement.'

'At his age,' Caroline said, 'Daddy must know who he is.'

'He thought he did. Now he's learned that he's been deliberately fooling himself, to make life easier. The Old Man's smoked him out of that, unintentionally, as a by-product of the Memoirs.'

Caroline began to dress. Charles was intelligent, and more sensitive than one might think. He knew it was no good returning to his attempted seduction of her. Some other time, he was saying to himself. But she thought not.

He said, 'How's the rest of the family? Clive? Didn't I hear he was on leave in St Tropez?'

'Yes. This week he's decided to be the Guardee Jet Setter. He's taken some Duke's daughter down there. I don't think he even likes her, really, but she suggested it, and they went off.'

'Is she paying for it?'

'She could. She's rolling . . . but that would be a different scene, wouldn't it? That would be Lady Ermyntrude and the Gigolo.'

'I expect Clive could do that part, too.'

'Of course he could – but it would conflict with the part of Captain Clive Ruttledge, Scots Guards.'

'The Ouida Hero,' Charles cut in, laughing.

'Who? . . . I've never heard of her. . . . I don't know what Clive ought to be but it certainly isn't that. Really, he hates the army. When we were kids, we used to spend hours pretending . . . I was seven and he was about twelve and of course I worshipped him, my big brother. And it was fun, for a time . . . in the bedroom, in the nursery, in the day nursery, in the garden, up in the treehouse, always pretending, we were. When I was about ten it got boring. . . . I remember once he said he was Prince Albert and I was Queen Victoria. I had to tell him to open the door, and he refused; then I had to weep and say I was not the Queen, but his wife; then he opened the door.'

'A well-known story from the royal Victorian legend,' Charles said. 'Are you ready?'

'Yes. . . . How did you know about Daddy going to see Mrs Phillips?'

Charles looked at her a long time, then said, 'Wait there.' He disappeared through a side door where Caroline knew he stored canvas, stretchers, and old paintings. There must have been hundreds, the time she had got a glimpse through the half-open door once while she was posing. She heard much rummaging and then Charles emerged, dusting off a painting about four feet by five. He set it up. It was a nude, a busty curvy blonde with cornflower-blue eyes and Cupid's-bow lips and big erect areolas and luxuriant golden pubic hair. She was carrying a basket of violets, and holding a bunch out to the viewer, laughing. It was a cockney flower seller to the life, but with no clothes on.

'Good God!' Caroline said. 'Madeleine! But do you still . . . ?'

He laughed, and took the painting away.

Paul was waiting at a little table in the middle of the crowded café, looking toward the door. He had a pot of tea and a pile of hot buttered toast in front of him. His face altered subtly when he saw her hurrying in, finding her way between the tables. He didn't believe I was going to come, she thought. What a life! What a way to expect the world to behave! She sat down.

He said defensively, 'I had to order something or they wouldn't have given me a table.'

'I love hot toast,' she said. 'Mustn't eat too much though. It's not exactly slimming.'

The clatter of plates and rattle of conversation were very loud. Buses roared and growled and ground through their gears as they thundered down into Trafalgar Square. The floor trembled to the deep passage of underground trains.

'There's going to be some excitement this time tomorrow,' Paul said.

'About the Peskevo story? I wonder what Daddy will say? He said that the judges asked whether he intended to publish anything on his own account, and Grandpa told him not to. But we weren't there, were we? Grandpa didn't tell *us*.'

'I don't know whether he'll approve, though.'

'I think he will, as long as we don't say that it is his story. And they'll have to let him out. Once it's published they can't pretend they're keeping him in the Tower in order to save the country.'

Paul was eating toast, his eyes down. He said, 'You know, you might get a double sentence.'

'How?'

'You're under a suspended sentence. If you're found guilty this time, they can tack the two years on to whatever they give you for this. Remember, that man who came down a few days ago warned you.'

She tossed her head. 'Let them try!'

After a while he said, 'How are you getting on with Miss Parmentier?'

Caroline laughed. 'She's rather an old dear. Dotty, you know, but at heart she's kind. I haven't got round to business yet – that'll take two or three more meetings, but she's beginning to trust me. She was madly in love with Grandpa . . . no, no, she never met him, just his picture, as a war hero. And, as Belprato told us, she despises Bartlett . . . but hasn't hinted why . . . yet.'

He said nothing while he ate and drank, his head still down. Then he said, 'You're nice, Caroline.'

'Thank you.'

'I didn't think you were, at first . . .'

'Ditto.'

'You were ... snooty. At least, I thought you were. I think that about most people.'

'I know.'

'I've got good reason. Most people are, as soon as they know something about us.'

'I know. We all would have been, if we'd all got what we deserved. Grandpa. Daddy. Me. Probably Mummy ... everyone. That's what I'm learning from the Memoirs.'

'My mother's no better than a prossie,' he said suddenly, looking up, the birth mark flaming.

'Has she been a good mother?'

'I think so. Yes.'

'Mine hasn't. And she's been sleeping with someone else, too. Not for money. Not for love, either. For her own pleasure. To make herself feel better. So what's the difference? They both despise themselves, I expect. That doesn't give anyone else the right to despise them.'

Paul's eyes filled with tears. Oh God she thought, now what can I do? He'll hate me and himself if he breaks down now. But he pulled out a handkerchief and blew his nose unashamedly. Looking round she realised that no one else in the big crowded restaurant had observed, or would have cared a damn if they had. Paul didn't have her bourgeois concern with appearances, or her inherited military penchant for the stiff upper lip.

He whispered, 'Caroline, I love you.'

She stared at him, dumb. What could she say? Or do?

He misinterpreted her look and said, 'I'll leave. I won't come back to Ashwood. I just had to tell you.'

She said hurriedly, 'You come back, Paul. ... Thank you. ... I don't know what to say ... so don't let's say anything more, now, eh? Later, we can talk.'

'I got back a week ago,' the New York accented voice was saying, 'and told the Brigadier here that I had some news, but I'd prefer to tell it to the Marshal in person, when he was let out. Well, they didn't let him out, so I came down ...'

What was his name now, Caroline tried to remember – Burrisk first, then Belprato, which was his real name; now he'd changed it again. Bigelow, that was it. Peter Bigelow.

'I got the dope ... most of it, except where the loot is,' Bigelow said. He was smoking a cigar, very short, chewing the stub rather than smoking it; it smelled vile. 'It was the Orlando mob. The man who was padrone of the family in forty-five died long since – but I know the present padrone well, and Papa even better, of course. They're not great friends of our family, in fact we had to negotiate with them once, but that was a long time ago. This fellow, Tim Orlando, told me what he knew, or as much as I needed. . . . October, forty-four, a Yugoslav guy who later turned out to be Count Zvornos contacted Tim and asked him to introduce him to the padrone. Tim fixed it and the Count asked the padrone if he could help him get his family paintings out of Yugoslavia. They were worth about eight million bucks, he said. It wasn't the kind of deal that our family would have gotten into any time, but the Orlandos were always offbeat – partly because they never really got their foot into any of the better businesses in New York, Chicago, or any place else. They were on the outside, and being kept out, so they dealt in things like art. They were one of the first to go into drugs, too. . . . The Count gave the Orlandos details so they could check up on his story, which they did and found he was speaking the truth. The Count told the Orlandos that he was working as adviser to some Civil Affairs set-up in Italy, but was being transferred to another bunch, under Matt Jordan, that was going to go with the armies when they invaded Yugoslavia. The Count said there'd be pay-offs to make, about a million and a half, he thought. Then there'd be the costs of doing the job – maybe three hundred thousand. He wanted Orlando to put up the money. In return he'd split the take down the middle, from the sale of the paintings. Orlando said, after we've deducted all the expenses, to be shared between us, we split it. So that was agreed. They'd each have cleared three million one, if the estimates were right. . . . The Count went back to Italy and early in January 1945 sent a message through the Orlandos' top guy there that half a million was to be paid into each of three numbered accounts at the Glauber Bank, in Zurich, Switzerland.'

'Does Orlando have the numbers?' Martin broke in quickly.

'Yeah. *And* they gave them to me, on a percentage basis, if we can get anything out of it. The Orlandos have turned over the whole operation to us, the Belpratos.'

'Why? Don't they have the paintings?'

Bigelow shook his head triumphantly, threw his cigar stub into the fireplace and pulled out another. 'They do not! They thought they were covered, having their guys in Italy the men who actually pulled the job, but this Count was a hell of a lot smarter than they reckoned. He turned up in New York in June of forty-five, and told Orlando he wanted three quarters of the money from the sale of the paintings. Where were they, Orlando asked him. The Count said, wouldn't you like to know? That's where he wasn't so smart, after all, because one day they took the Count away in a limousine to a big house they have on Long Island, and tried to persuade him to talk. They spent a long time on it, a couple of weeks, and maybe he would have, in time, maybe he wouldn't, but one of the gorillas squeezed too hard, and he croaked on them. So . . . the two Orlando guys who'd worked with the Count in Italy were dead – it turned out he'd killed them. The Count was dead. No one knew where the paintings were. No one even knew whether they were in the U.S.A. or still in Italy.'

Caroline said, 'The Count wasn't a bit smart. He was stupid.'

'And greedy, miss,' Bigelow said. 'That's a combination that never pays off.'

Martin said, 'We must find out who owns those numbered accounts.'

Bigelow said, 'Yeah, except it's impossible.'

'It's got to be possible!' Caroline said.

'The Swiss bankers will never talk,' Bigelow said. 'I know. It's more than their jobs are worth, even their lives. A lot of those numbered accounts belong to people who are in a position to have every damned employee of the bank rubbed out, if they told. And the Swiss Government would probably finish off anyone they missed. Billions of dollars depend on that secrecy.'

'Well, if the other people can use threats, so can we,' Caroline said. 'We should find out who in the Glauber Bank is in a position to know the actual names of the owners of these numbered accounts, and get him to talk.'

'How on earth can we do that?' her father said wearily.

'Kidnap him,' she said. 'Torture him, a little . . .'

'Caroline!'

Caroline persisted. 'Mr Bigelow said he'd help us. In fact, he's got to, or we tell the police about him. You have agents in Switzerland, don't you?'

'Sure.'

'Well, get them to find out what they can about the Glauber Bank – who in it would be in a position to give us the information we want. Then, when Grandpa comes back, he can decide what we should do about it.'

Bigelow said, 'I can do that. We'll have to watch our step, though. Trouble is, even if we find out who owns these accounts, and so who got paid off, it won't tell us where the paintings are.'

'Grandpa said that didn't interest him,' Caroline said.

'It sure interests me, though,' Bigelow said.

... *you will realise from your newspapers, I imagine that the delay in my writing has been caused by a period of incarceration in the Tower of London, a romantic but singularly damp dwelling. I found your letter of August 26 waiting for me when I came home after my release. My grand-daughter, who is a very bright girl, realised that it would be wiser not to have it sent up to me in the Tower. When I asked her why she thought that, she said 'It's your French lady love, isn't it? We don't want any more scandal, do we?' The minx ... I suppose the family did once think my correspondent in France was or had been a lover, but when so many years passed and I never went to see her, or she to visit me, they accepted what I told them – that our shared love was only for roses.*

I do not know whether it was a wise decision after all to write my Memoirs. I seem to be making so many people unhappy, and there now looms up the possibility that I shall have to do just what I promised I would not – take off my underwear and dance in public to make a spectacle. You know about it. But you shall not be involved – that I promise, so have no fear.

CHAPTER EIGHTEEN

The sun still shone on the long sand, as it had when he was down in July. The row of little houses and small hotels lined the front, and the cliffs rose up severe and gaunt to the north, topped by rolling grass where sheep grazed. But the beach was all but deserted now, only the two of them walking side by side on the sand, Rachel bounding ahead, her guide harness swinging free in Dick's hand; and the ocean was an October ocean, a dark slate blue under the sky, its voice slower and deeper, and heavy with the forewarning of storm. To north and south the surf towered up the cliffs where those powerful rollers struck the granite, hesitated, then began to climb the cliff, at first solid walls of water, breaking, white fingers clawing higher, dissolving, falling back into the arms of the next; and again, and again . . .

'Your column in last Sunday's *Journal* was wonderful, we thought,' Martin said.

'You would,' Dick Armstrong said, laughing. 'It was all on your side.'

'Yes,' Martin admitted, 'but you gave reasons that everyone I know who read it agreed with. Lots of people know what's right, or what ought to be done. I've never met anyone who can make others believe it, and fire them to do something about it, the way you can. I knew you were something extraordinary when I inherited you as adjutant of the regiment.'

'We were pretty young then, weren't we? Babes in arms, entrusted with the lives of other babes in arms.'

'We didn't do too badly.'

'Because we were being guided by men like the Field-Marshal. I don't say he had the best brains, or even skill, but he knew how to use other people's for the common good. And he had the guts, the inner power, to stand against very strong destructive pressures, some from outside, some from inside.'

'It's easier if you're a full general,' Martin said.

'Not if the people you have to stand up against are presidents and prime ministers and other full generals. Or, as I say, if the destructive force is coming from inside. Anyway, I'm glad he's out. The Tower is not supposed to be the most healthy place in the world for old gentlemen.'

'Your piece did it.' Martin said.

'That, and the publication of the Peskevo story in the *Journal* and in America. No judge could possibly agree that the government had any validity in their case when it was all out.'

'I thought they'd charge Caroline. She stuck her neck out a long way. Damned if I'd have the guts. . . . They did try a combination of threats and blackmail on her, you know.'

'What did they do?'

'She was told she'd be charged unless she found out where the Old Man has hidden the recording that was made of a meeting at Vojja Lovac, after the battle. But if she did tell them, they'd give her a full pardon for the stolen goods business, and two thousand quid into the bargain. She said she had no idea where the recording was and that her grandfather was not the sort of man who'd let the information out by mistake. They'd been bluffing, of course.'

'She's a brave girl, and a wise one. . . . What's the situation on the Zvornos Collection?'

Martin explained the information that Bigelow had brought back from New York, and added, 'The Old Man's toying with the idea of forcing one of the Glauber Bank officers to divulge the names of the three numbered account holders. I think he's getting obsessed. You can't go around kidnapping respectable Swiss bankers and presumably torturing them.'

'Why not?' Armstrong said. 'These numbered accounts are indefensible, morally. If a man has nothing to hide about his account – if he's paying taxes where he is supposed to – what is the justification for them? Many of them exist only to enable people like Latin American dictators or North American gangsters to keep money they've stolen from people. . . . Sheikhs and kings and commissars feather their own nests at the expense of their subjects. The Field-Marshal has the right idea. I'm not sure that he will be able actually to do it, but a way might be found. An angel might appear and convert Mr Glauber to Total Disclosure!'

They turned at the north end of the beach, where the surf was mantling the rocks, and started back into the strengthening breeze.

Martin said, 'I've heard a couple of your ITV talks now. What are you going to talk about next Tuesday?'

'Tribalism,' Armstrong said. 'What we gain from our individual heritages as Scots, or English, even as men of Wessex, or

Cornishmen . . . how we can keep this in our way of government and life.'

'If we could do that, without losing the strength of central government,' Martin said, 'we'd be much happier . . . especially the Scots and Welsh.'

'The minorities,' Armstrong said. 'Yes . . . the ITV people are coming down on Sunday to tape the show. They're pressing me to go up to London instead – say they'll pay my travel expenses and accommodation, everything, in addition to what they pay for the show itself.'

'It would be cheaper for them than having to send the crew down here and back every week. Perhaps you ought to go. It's wonderful here, but it's a bit remote, once you come out of your philosophical studies into the world. You'd be in things much more in London. You'd hear more, see more . . . sorry.'

'Don't be silly, Martin . . . I'm thinking about it. I've had approaches from half a dozen political personages, too, you know. They all seem to think I'm in their party – whatever it is.'

'What *are* you?'

'Ah! What colour I really am, and what colour I should wear in my buttonhole are two entirely different things, and often have to be, as long as there is no deception of the observer – the public.'

They walked on in silence for a while. The waves swept remorselessly in. The steady thunder caught at Martin's brain so that for a while he could think of nothing, his mind simply absorbing that majestic rhythm. He shook his mind free: Dick Armstrong had everything the nation needed – brains, guts, compassion – but he couldn't see. He was blind, and all that energy and genius had been turned inwards, studying the mathematics of metaphysics as reflected in the cells of his own brain. To direct them outwards he needed human eyes to work for him, to see and execute for him. As he gave Rachel guidance as to where he wanted to go, and she took him there, avoiding dangers he could not see, so there should be some intelligent person to help him carry his policies into action.

Why not himself? Dick knew him and trusted him. He didn't have Dick's startling genius, but he was not an idiot, he had dealt with responsibility in his time; and he knew the ins and outs of government.

The gulls were flying high, shrieking . . . shrieking their disdain. What a hope! What would he live on! He ought to do what he'd said he'd do when he resigned from Proctor's — leave Ashwood and Lois and start again miles away, not a son-in-law of the Field-Marshal, not a retired brigadier, just Martin Ruttledge.

'We'd better be starting back,' he said. 'It's a hell of a long drive for me tomorrow, and we've got a big lunch party.'

They were eating in the dining room. Outside a steady October drizzle was falling on the trees and the lawn, which was strewn with gold and yellow and ochre-coloured leaves. The Field-Marshal sat on one side of the table, Hilda Ross across from him, Caroline on his right, Clive faced Paul, Lois was at one end, Martin at the other, Martin drank some beer from the silver tankard, half listening, part of his mind elsewhere. . . . It was Friday. Tomorrow Caroline would be taking the day off and going up to London. To see a boy friend, presumably. Who? Perhaps not, this time, as she had said she was going up with Paul. What on earth did young people do these days . . . art gallery? one of those porno flicks? subterranean juke box cafeteria in Leicester Square? Christ, why hadn't he spoken to Dick Armstrong of what was in his mind?

'The Man of the Year! Let's drink to that!' He looked up. Hilda Ross's voice had become sharper and louder than usual. She was wearing a black dress with a white collar. How long was it since the old general had died? Nearly two weeks. He and Lois had gone to the funeral and Lois had cried. It was the first time he'd ever seen her cry, that he could remember.

Hilda was on her third or fourth whisky. She must be damned nearly eighty herself. People of that age couldn't hold their liquor. Well, Hilda had never been able to, he admitted; at least not for as long as he'd known her. And that was since 1945, when he first came home after the war and the Old Man started introducing him round to his family and friends, including Lois.

The Field-Marshal nodded in acknowledgment as everyone round the table drank.

'You, too, Vetch!' Hilda cried. 'Here, take a drink from this.'

'Very good, madam,' Vetch said apprehensively. He took the glass. 'Your very good health, sir.' He took a genteel sip. 'Thank you, madam.' He slid out of the door.

The Field-Marshal said, 'It looks as though something of the sort might happen. The *Journal* people are publicising me and the Memoirs for all their worth. I can't blame them. They're putting up a lot of money ... but I don't want to be declared Man of the Year. All I want is to leave an untouched and unsmudged footprint in the sand. A lot of people are trying to prevent me. Some time ago I told Sam Herrick that if they didn't leave me and my family alone I'd make a formal application to resign my commission. No Field-Marshal's ever done that.'

Caroline said, 'But I don't understand why you don't just retire, Grandpa.'

Hilda Ross cried, 'Twenty-one years old and raised in an army family – two army families – and you don't know that Field-Marshals don't retire!'

Caroline said defensively, 'I've been reading the history of the campaigns, but I've never learned about ranks and all that. I didn't want to.'

'And no one bothered to tell you. Well, a Field-Marshal is always on the active list. He may not be given any military employment, but that doesn't mean he's retired. That's why it means so much to be made a Field-Marshal. When they're not militarily employed, they get half pay, not retired pay. Others want it because it's a great honour, the top of the tree ... more orders, decorations ...'

The Field-Marshal said quietly, 'I have told Sam that I would ask Her Majesty to allow me to return all mine, if this went on.'

Hilda Ross's face was mottled, not the normal mottling of old age, but something harsher. Her eyes were small and suffused and her hand trembling on the table cloth. She said, and the bitterness was unmistakable in her voice, 'You may not want the rank and orders now, John, but that's easy for you – you've had them. Stephen never did, because ...'

'Please, Hilda,' the Field-Marshal said gently.

She ignored him and burst on – 'You saw to it that he didn't! You relieved him of command of his Corps because he didn't approve of your plan ... then you used *his* plan! Why don't you put that into your Memoirs? Because you don't want anyone to know that the great *Bushmaster* plan was not yours, but his. ... So Stephen retires as a lieutenant-general, with a C.B. – nothing else. We go to a few reunions, and that's all. No one recognises *him* on the street, nor his name in the paper ... and it only gets *there* because he's chairman of our local British Legion, or some piffling thing like that. I'm Mrs Ross, every

other lieutenant-general's wife is Lady something. I kept hoping that somehow you'd make amends. And now he's dead.
... After all that I ... we ... did for this family.'

She relapsed into silence, staring down at her empty plate.
She lifted her glass and took a big gulp. She put the glass down
with a defiant bang.

The Field-Marshal said, 'The truth about *Bushmaster* is
going to come out, Hilda.'

'Too late,' she said.

The Field-Marshal continued. 'I admit that I didn't do
enough to get Stephen reinstated after I had relieved him. It
was not all my fault. There were other factors ... no Corps
commanders were failing, or being replaced at that stage in
the war. None of the Army commanders anywhere wanted to
exchange the people they had for Stephen. Soon, it was too
late. But I could have done more.'

Caroline said, 'It's still raining. We can't go out. Tell us what
really happened, Grandpa.'

Martin noticed that Paul surreptitiously produced his shorthand pad from his pocket and made ready to write on it on his
lap.

'I'll go and start washing up,' Lois said.

'No,' her father said, 'you should listen. ... After Appreciation R3 had been accepted and 17th Army Group had given
the overall directive, the two Army commanders were left to
work out their own plans. My 16th Army was to be on the left
– north – directed more at Montenegro, and the American 11th
Army on the right – south – directed at Albania. This was all
Operation *Wolfpack*, the crossing of the Adriatic and the
establishment of a bridgehead the other side. The Americans
were to land first, partly so that we could use the same landing
craft and naval and air support, partly to draw the Germans
south. If I could advance reasonably rapidly, I would then cut
them off. I was allotted two Corps VIII and XXII, which was
Stephen's, plus the 11th Armoured Division as Army Troops.
D Day for us was December 4th, 1944, and though we had
some fairly heavy fighting on the beaches, all went well, and
we began to establish the bridgehead, rebuild the ports, and in
every way make ready for the next operation, breaking out of
the bridgehead, which was codenamed *Bushmaster*.'

Vetch had come in and was hovering in the background. Lois
waved him out, but the Field-Marshal said, 'Fill my glass before you go, Vetch. Thank you. ... A range of mountains,

about forty miles square lay to the left front of my Army's landing zones. There was a good wide valley to the right – south – of it, more or less directly ahead of us, and the obvious thing to do was advance the whole Army up this valley on a broad front . . .'

'Going straight at the Germans, who had excellent defensive positions at the head of the valley,' Martin murmured. The conferences on this were coming back to him sharp and clear. The Villa Grimani outside Ancona. The Old Man's map room, the glasses of red Italian wine, the cold stone floor, a bell tolling nearby, the Old Man, the C.O.S., the M.G.A., the Air Marshal, and himself arguing, scribbling on pieces of paper, doing calculations, burning the papers in the open fire. The Old Man had been at his very best all that time – confident, decisive, approachable.

The Field-Marshal continued, 'There was a way round the back of the range – a poor road and a narrow steep valley that swung round far to the left – the north.' He looked suddenly at Paul, his white eyebrows beetling. 'Ever heard of a book called *Grand Tactics*, Paul?'

Paul looked up, startled. 'No, sir.'

'Look around in the library. It's there. It's by a fellow called Durham – Lieutenant-Colonel John Durham, Royal Oxford Fusiliers – published in 1937, just before this Durham, who was supposed to be a coming young man, took over as G.1 of the 3rd Division in Aldershot. You haven't read it . . . Caroline hasn't read it . . . Lois hasn't read it . . .'

'I've read it,' Martin said. 'After the war, though.'

'Field-Marshal Ritter von Heldenmark had read it, before the war. I didn't *know* he had, but I assumed he had, as I knew he was a great student of war theory, and was an instructor at the German General Staff school at that time. . . . In *Grand Tactics* I laid down certain rules for the interrelation of large bodies of troops. The balance between offence and surprise on the one hand and defence and security on the other, was what mainly concerned me in the principal section of the book. I wrote that in general the requirements of security must come first; that is, a force must balance itself thoroughly before it advances, and it must not be caught off balance or widely separated in the advance itself. . . . Now the two alternatives open to me would also be quite clear to von Heldenmark as soon as he learned the extent and positions of our landings. He would try to guess what I would do. My own teaching, my own theory, expounded in *Grand Tactics*, was to make sure of not being caught off balance, then go like hell. We could not be caught off balance if we went up the broad valley. All parts of my Army could quickly support all other parts. General Durham would certainly follow that course, von Heldenmark must conclude.'

'Unless you were bluffing,' Caroline broke in excitedly. 'The German might think that you would know that he knew, so . . . I never knew war was so interesting.'

'It is, very,' her grandfather said grimly. 'Bluffing was always a possibility. But I don't have the reputation of a bluffer. Surprises, yes . . . but surprise in the weight of the attack, new use of weapons, new minor tactics, speed . . . tremendously tight and fast battle drills right down to section level – that's my reputation. I decided that von Heldenmark would conclude that I was going to go straight ahead, and all together, if I gave him any evidence to support that idea.

'At this point Stephen came to me with a plan strongly advising me to send one corps round the flank of the range, by this difficult route, to get behind the main German defences. Stephen had not published any books on strategy, but when he was commanding his Corps in Italy, and before that when commanding a division in the Western Desert campaigns, he had carried out several daring wide sweeps. He had surprised the enemy not by the weight of his attack, but by the place it appeared from. In each case he safely got through a period of some danger, when his force had been off balance, and a German counter stroke would have caught him unsupported and unsupportable by anything except air action . . . I listened to Stephen's proposal carefully, and said I'd let him know. I talked his idea over with my chief staff officers. Finally, I decided that my principles as laid down in *Grand Tactics* were the right ones, and I would follow them. Von Heldenmark would very likely guess what we were going to do, but by the use of minor tactics, air power, speed, and so on, I'd see that he couldn't stop us.

'Then on December 21st I fell sick – it turned out to be a form of pneumonia – and was evacuated from our Balkan beachhead and flown back to England. Stephen took temporary command of 16th Army. I returned to my headquarters on January 18th, 1945. Everything was ready for the break out. Before returning to his Corps, Stephen begged me to change the *Bushmaster* plan and split the Army, as he had recommended.

He thought we might be held up totally on the German defence line, which had been made very strong. In any case, we were going to lose men and material which the country could not afford. I told him I'd think it over. Henry Bartlett set D Day for both Armies as January 23rd. On January 21st Stephen came back and begged me again to change the plan – which we could do up till the last moment, as we were poised ready to go either way, in such a manner that no German air or other reconnaissance could tell by our dispositions how we intended to move. I asked Stephen at last, point blank, whether he had confidence in my plan. He said no he had not. I then relieved him of command of his Corps. If a general has no confidence in the plan he is to carry out, he won't carry it out well, so justifying his lack of confidence in it. The failure won't be deliberate, at least not in this day and age. It's happened often enough in the past, and in other countries . . . but it'll be failure just the same.'

He sipped his whisky. Paul flipped over a page of his note-pad. Hilda Ross seemed to have fallen asleep, slumped forward on to her elbow.

The Field-Marshal continued, 'Stephen was sent back to England at once. . . . The day after he'd gone – the day before D Day – I ordered that the advance of 16th Army would be by the two routes, VIII Corps the main valley, XXII Corps the left hook.'

'Two routes?' Caroline said, her face showing her astonishment. 'But you've just been explaining why . . .'

The Field-Marshal said, 'My child, didn't know what I was saying.'

Martin looked up. 'I don't understand,' he said.

'Just what I say. I didn't know what I was saying. I had cracked up. No one noticed.'

Martin thought back. They were inside the camouflage-netted caravan, and that parked in the lee of a shattered house at the edge of the village, a mile in from the sea. Just the five of them in the crowded space, the light flickering because the generator wasn't working well. The Old Man standing at the map, his face white . . . damp, he'd thought, damp from sweat, tears, what? Everyone was thinking of the single straight ahead advance – then the shattering announcement: the left hook. The other four had stood there like men turned into pillars, mouths open. All of them were trying to say something. In his own case he remembered that what he wanted to get out was that he hadn't indented for enough maps of the northern valley to provide XXII Corps with what they'd need. The others must have been trying to say similar things; but the Army Commander's voice had been harsh, his face taut. And in a moment, like light flowering from a starshell, all of them simultaneously realised that here was a stroke of genius. Certainly there was a great deal to be done, but it could be done, and it would be. He remembered the Chief of Staff saying 'Shall I get General Bartlett's O.K. on this, sir, or will you? Or has he already given it?'

'We don't need it,' the Old Man had said.

'Then shall I tell the Americans?'

'Yes.'

That was all. He remembered them all saluting, not a word more, then out into the early daylight, looking at each other, and the C.O.S. speaking for all of them. 'The Old Man's really going to blast von Heldenmark out of his jackboots this time. Let's get to work. And, Martin, you'll have to find a way for the Germans to get to know about General Ross's dismissal, in a hurry.'

That moment was the first climactic point of his book, *The Balkan Campaign, 1945*. He'd gone into all the Old Man's calculations of von Heldenmark's character and of his own, of how carefully he had balanced the risks, and then the master stroke of dismissing General Ross, the proponent of wide sweeping movements. It had been hard on Ross, for he'd been a victim of war. Everyone in the professional army knew that, even if the civilian population didn't, and he himself had made it clear in his book that Ross's dismissal had only one purpose – to reinforce von Heldenmark's conviction that the Old Man would follow his own principles. Then he'd done what Ross had obviously been dismissed for urging him to do – make a wide northern sweep. This was an example of the theme of his book – the great generalship of John Durham. Now the Old Man was saying he hadn't known what he was doing.

The Field-Marshal said, 'The planning of *Wolfpack* had been very hard work. The Italian campaign before that had put a considerable strain on me. Generals are not supposed to feel things like that, but they do. Then I got pneumonia. When they let me out of Millbank to convalesce here, I was very weak for a few days. Then I got stronger, but there were other worries . . . and Margaret was not well. There were money problems. Finally, the accident. When I came to, I couldn't find any bones broken. I was bleeding a little here and there – my arm hurt, leg hurt, head hurt, my skin was scraped, clothes torn ... I was in a hedge. Margaret was dead, her skull crushed against the high wall there. We'd both been thrown out of the car, of course. I was put back in Millbank, but raving to get out. *Bushmaster* was due in fifteen days, fourteen.... I was examined by the top doctors every day. Winston came to see me and he practically ordered the doctors to certify me as fit ... I thought I was, but really I wasn't ... I flew out ... my head ached all the time, everything hurt, but I was commanding the 16th Army. Everyone was asking questions, what to do about this, about that, about the other thing ... I didn't care a damn what they did. What anyone did. Margaret was dead, like Ted and Jimmy and Dick and Peter ... and I was alive. I lost my temper with Stephen when he came to me the last time about his plan. It wasn't a calculated thing, as it's said to be. I simply lost my temper. I could barely put two words together and he was trying to make me face a complicated decision. After a time I'd forgotten what he was talking about ... I sacked him. Then everyone kept away from me, as much as possible. They thought they were keeping the work load off me, while my head was full of mighty thoughts of strategy and grand tactics. It wasn't. My mind was a blank – often a black blank, sometimes shaken with livid light. Then one morning early you, Martin, came and reminded me final orders for *Bushmaster* had to go out before ten a.m. I'd been asleep. Eden woke me up and you suggested nine o'clock for the orders conference. ... When you four came, I remember staring at you, and thinking what do they want? What am I supposed to say? Words shuttled back and forth in my head, and I knew we were supposed to go somewhere. I gave an order, and five seconds later didn't know what it had been. You all went out. Eden came in. He saw that something was wrong with me. He'd suspected it all along. He was closer than any of you ... and not just business, like you. We used to talk about roses ... cars ... funny legal cases of his.... He got some medicine for me, pretending it was for himself, and put me to bed.'

That was another thing they'd all marvelled at, Martin remembered – the Old Man sleeping like a baby while these tremendous torrents of men and machinery moved to his will. God, how people would laugh at his pompous explanations of the Old Man's genius in *The Balkan Campaign, 1945* when all this came out. And poor old Ross hadn't lost his career by the chances of war, but as the act of a man temporarily out of his senses.

He'd expected the Old Man would be getting tired by now, for about this time he'd usually be ready for a nap; but he was visibly filled with new life. He looked again as he had in Italy and at Vojja Lovac – alert, commanding, only white where he had been grizzled, bent where he had stood like a tough tree against the winds and the whistling shells.

The Old Man said, 'A couple of days more, and I was all right . . . at least, I knew what I was doing. My mind had recovered. Whether other parts had . . . the spirit – I don't know. But much of me had been dead, or mortally wounded, for years before.'

Clive said, 'Grandfather, when you came out of Millbank the first time, you said that Grandma was ill, and you had other worries . . .'

Hilda Ross raised her head and said thickly, 'He certainly did. Lois was pregnant.'

In the stunned silence she continued, falling over her words. 'You say you want the truth? Let 'em have it. . . . When John got here, Lois was pregnant. Margaret hadn't noticed. She never noticed anything about Lois, did she?' Martin was staring at his wife. He didn't believe it, yet he did. She was looking down at the table, impassive. Caroline was staring dumbfounded at Hilda Ross.

Hilda continued, 'John found out . . . came to me to ask if I'd look after her. . . . We were their oldest friends, weren't we? When Margaret was killed Lois came to live with me. Three weeks later, so did Stephen, sacked by John . . . a nice thank you present.'

'Is this true?' Martin burst out.

Lois nodded.

'Who was the father?'

The Field-Marshal said, 'She's never said, Martin. It's best not to ask.'

Clive pushed back his chair with a loud screech. 'I have to get back to London.' He hurried out, head down.

Caroline said, 'Poor Clive. . . . Poor Mummy. I wish I'd known.'

Hilda Ross was on her feet. 'I'm going. Clive can drive me up.' She went out.

'I shall take the Bentley for a spin,' the Field-Marshal said. 'My head needs clearing. Then I shall have a nap.'

Caroline and Paul went out together, silent. Lois still sat, her head down. Martin was on his feet. He felt cold and angry.

'Don't you think,' he said bitterly, 'you might have told me about this child?'

'I should have.'

'What happened to it? Where is it?'

'Farmed out. Hilda Ross fixed it all. I don't know where it – he – is. I never have.'

'Well, you've certainly made Clive's day,' he stormed. But it was hard to quarrel with her. He felt an irrational wish to stoop and touch her short greying hair, tell her it didn't matter, it was past. She must have been in love, and very young, the Old Man away at war, her mother absorbed in sorrow for the dead son. Lois surely had memories of love, which she must cherish, for there had been little more.

She looked up. 'Get out.'

He started, bit his lip and crossed the hall to the study. He picked up the telephone and dialled. When the familiar genteel cockney voice answered he said, 'Madeleine, it's Martin here. I'd like to take you out to dinner.'

Madeleine said, 'Oh dear, Martin, I'm afraid I can't to-night.'

'Tomorrow then,' he said. What was the difference; he could wait another twenty-four hours for the physical release.

Madeleine sounded uneasy. 'Well, you see, not then either. Not at all.'

'What *do* you mean?'

'There's a gentleman, Martin . . . an American gentleman. I've been seeing a lot of him. You know him. He doesn't want me to see any other gentlemen. He's a very generous gentleman . . .' She sounded pleading.

'All right,' Martin said, 'I understand.' He hung up slowly. Should he laugh or cry? The care and feeding of Madeleine Phillips had been assumed by Peter Burrisk/Belprato-Bigelow. They'd suit each other perfectly.

CHAPTER NINETEEN

'Well, I wouldn't have done it, I'm positive,' Caroline's voice was high, clear and scornful. Five days had passed since Hilda Ross had exploded her lunchtime bomb and Martin and his daughter were returning from a shopping expedition in the village.

'There was no pill in those days,' Martin said. 'None of us can be sure what we might or might not have done.'

'I don't mean having the baby,' Caroline said. 'I mean letting people talk her into getting rid of it. If I had a baby, no one would take it away from me.'

Martin said, 'Surely the circumstances would affect it? If you'd been raped, for instance. Or if you'd found that the man was really a stinker, you might be afraid the child would grow up like him.'

Caroline, who was driving, said nothing, but sniffed. She obviously thought her mother had been weak, even wicked, in getting rid of her child. Things were different in those days, Martin thought. Young people didn't live together, unmarried. Babies without fathers, mothers without husbands, found life anything but pleasant, especially in the society where Lois had lived and moved.

He was still thinking of Lois twenty minutes later when he sat down at his desk and continued his rewrite of one whole chapter of *The Balkan Campaign, 1945*. He stared at the sheets of paper: he'd been working on this since the day of the terrible lunch party, but whether the new work would ever be published was doubtful. He had called the house that had published the book back in 1950 and it had taken a long time to find anyone there who knew what he was talking about or who he was. Then, after he'd explained what he wanted – needed – to do, they said they'd call back. When they called, it was to explain that in principle they didn't believe there would be enough interest in the Balkan Campaign, at this late date, to make a revised edition worth while. But the publicity surrounding Field-Marshal Durham and his forthcoming Memoirs might make a paperback pamphlet, to be published by itself as a correction to, or exposé of the original work, financially feasible.

'General Durham landed at Kojar airfield in the early hours of January 18, 1945. To those who met him, including the present writer, nothing seemed unusual about his manner. But in fact the Army commander was suffering from extreme strain, brought about by his recent illness, and months of tension as a division and corps commander, all aggravated by personal tragedies that had arisen during his brief stay in England.'

He looked at what he had written, and read it again. What problems, the readers would reasonably ask? Well, he wasn't going to tell them. It would come out, apparently, in the Old Man's Memoirs, but not here. He was damned if he was going to tell the world that his own wife had had an illegitimate baby, even if it was before he knew her. It happened to plenty of girls, but that didn't mean it had to be shouted from the rooftops. He ought to write it all down though, just to see how it would look.

The main cause of the general's condition was that on January 2 he had been involved in a motor accident near his home, in which his wife had been killed. The general, who was driving, miraculously escaped with minor injuries, as far as his body was concerned. In fact, with the approval of the doctors at Millbank Hospital, and at the urging of the Prime Minister, he was released from hospital on January 9 and left England in a converted Liberator of the R.A.F. on January 16.

Another contributing cause was that the general had discovered, during his convalescence, that his unmarried daughter was pregnant.

He looked at what he had typed, re-read it, and finally tore it out of the machine, scrumpled it up and threw it into the waste paper basket. He couldn't do it. Let it come out in the Memoirs, if it had to. He frowned at the typewriter. There was something else about this story, beyond it being a betrayal of Lois's secret. It was wrong . . . false. He had a clear picture in his mind of the Army commander in those days both before and after his illness and flight to England. He was a strong man, equable in the face of adversity, a man who supported others when they were eaten by doubts, a man who faced all kinds of personal tragedies and losses without faltering in his purpose. He was not a puritan about sexual matters. It was finally impossible to imagine him breaking down simply because his daughter had gone the way so many young women went.

There had to be more. Of course there was the death of Lady

Durham, but even that didn't seem enough. That marriage, he knew, had not deeply engaged the Old Man's emotions for many years – only his sense of duty.

The Old Man was holding something back from him – even lying, perhaps. He regarded the idea with surprising shock. But that was where his thoughts had led him. He couldn't avoid it. He'd have to find out the truth.

He got up and went upstairs to the Field-Marshal's rooms. He was in his study, writing; Paul was typing from a tape machine that he was working with a foot pedal.

Martin said, 'Sir, can I speak to you privately?'

The Old Man looked up. He seemed old today, the fire that had infused him at the lunch party long since died down. He said, 'Is it about the Memoirs?'

Martin said, 'Yes.'

'Then we'd better take it down. What is it?'

Martin looked at Paul. Why didn't the bastard get out? Couldn't he see he wanted to talk privately? But Paul was setting the microphone of the tape recorder up on the table where it would catch all that he and the Old Man said. I have my orders, his manner seemed to say.

Martin sat down, 'It's about your state when you came back from England in January forty-five,' he began. 'You'd found that Lois was pregnant. Lady Durham was killed in the accident.' He braced himself. 'I find it hard to believe that these two things, even with your own earlier illness, would have caused the state of shock . . . loss of mind . . . I don't know what the right word is . . . that you told us you were suffering from when you dismissed General Ross and later changed the axis of advance for *Bushmaster*. I think there must have been something else, which you haven't told us about.'

The Field-Marshal's formidable eyebrows bent down while Martin was speaking and the etched lines round the mouth and jaw grew deeper. He remembered that look two or three times in the war, and the tongue lashings that had followed, leaving major-generals white and shaking. But he was determined: the Old Man was the one who had forced the search for truth, and he'd have to take it. He reached the end of what he had needed to say and waited for the storm.

The Field-Marshal said at last, 'Something I didn't tell you about . . . that's right. I've been trying to dodge it. Trying to persuade myself I didn't need to bring it out. Now you've made it clear that I do, which I knew all the time, really. Margaret was mad, that's the fact. One fact. She had an obsession about Andrew, our dead son. While I'd been away, first in the Desert, then in Italy, she'd been feeding this obsession in every way she could. I didn't find out the whole truth . . . I still haven't and probably never will, but by pretending to be sympathetic, to believe her even when she was talking rot, I learned some things. She was spending her time and money getting in touch with Andrew through a fortune teller and self-styled medium called Madame Olga. Every now and then Madame Olga would "get through" to Andrew for her, at great expense. I knew she gave that charlatan a lot but I never guessed how much until I learned about the Picasso lithographs last month.'

Believing she could communicate with her dead son seemed a harmless enough aberration, Martin thought, except for the money. If Lady Durham had been happy because of it, so much the better.

'I could have put up with that, not knowing then how much money she had spent,' the Field-Marshal continued, 'except for the effect on Lois. She was twelve when Andrew died. When the war began she was fifteen. These are important years for a young girl. Her mother neglected her. . . . That's not the right word; she actively resented her, because she was in the way, she obscured Margaret's vision of Andrew. She had to feed her, buy clothes for her, even talk to her sometimes . . . all this she resented. Lois had always got on well with me, and now I realised why. I was her only hope in the family . . . and when I wasn't there, as I wasn't for months, years on end, her life was hell. I saw the paintings she'd been doing. She brought them out to show me. I thought they were bad. I'm not an art expert. I can't read emotion into paintings . . . I couldn't then, at any rate, but even I realised that those paintings were a sign that there was something wrong about a twenty-year-old girl – I'm talking about my Christmas 1944 sick leave now – doing those paintings. They were like what you'd expect to find on the walls of a prison cell, or a lunatic asylum.'

'Where are they?' Martin interjected.

'The paintings? I believe they're in the attic. I put them there when Lois went to Hilda Ross. . . . Of course, when she brought the paintings for me to look at, she was trying to tell me something, but I only guessed a part of it. Perhaps it was enough, because the next morning I had a good look at her, and saw that her breasts had swollen up, and she was wearing a very loose dress. . . . She was six months gone, she told me, when I asked her if she was pregnant. . . .'

'Did you ask her who the man was?' Martin said. Paul's head was down. How the bastard must be gloating over all this dirty linen coming out of the spotless bedrooms of the upper class! Above all, out of the house of the man who'd broken his father's life – and indirectly killed him – for immorality.

'I told her she could tell me, if she wanted to,' the Old Man said, 'and I would do whatever she wanted about getting him to marry her, acknowledge the child, pay upkeep for it, and so on . . . that is, if she were pregnant and we couldn't get her an abortion. Then I called our doctor – he's dead now – and asked him to make a test on Lois as soon as possible.'

'Was Lady Durham here all this time?' Martin asked.

The Old Man nodded. 'Yes. But she didn't know anything. She hadn't seen, she hadn't guessed, or asked. And I decided not to tell her. It would not have helped – only turned her more against Lois, whom she would now see as actually demanding attention for herself and the baby. . . . Doctor Kingsbury came round a couple of days later – he didn't want to use the telephone – and told me Lois was pregnant, and it was too late to think of an abortion. Then he asked me whether Margaret had talked to me. I said no, thinking he meant about Lois being pregnant. Then he said, "Margaret has cancer, John. Advanced carcinoma of the breast – both of them." It was inoperable. Her life would drag out in increasing agony. He had not told her because she was in an unstable frame of mind. He had been planning to go to the War Office and get a private message out to me about it somehow.'

The Old Man was looking out of the window, his face calmer than Martin had seen it for a long time, the watery blue eyes unfocused. His voice was musing, as though talking to himself. 'After Kingsbury had gone and Lois was in bed, that night, I looked at the situation. Margaret was mad and she was destroying Lois. Lois had to be got away from her . . . or vice versa. Margaret was also dying. If Lois was going to have to spend a year, two years watching her die, hating her, feeling guilty because of it, she would be destroyed, finally and irrevocably. I believed she would become as insane, as deranged, as her mother. . . . I was emotionally empty. I had felt little deeply since 1917, anyway. Most of what had made me a person, a human being rather than a commander, had died in that war – bled to death through my friends' wounds, coughed up in the lungs of the gassed outside Ypres, drowned in putrid mud at

231

Passchendaele. I didn't want to live because I might gain new depths of feeling, through caring for Lois, and then I'd suffer again, as I had in 1914 to 1918. . . .

'I decided to kill Margaret and myself. I made plans. I should have shot her, and myself. It would have been sure, and I was not afraid to do it. But I didn't want Lois to grow up with that on her conscience, because she might believe I'd done it on account of the disgrace of her pregnancy. . . . I decided a car accident would be best. I reconnoitred and chose Hawkford Hill. There's that long wall on one side. I'd go down, lose control, hit the wall at sixty or more and there'd be no chance – certain and instant death. . . . I had difficulty getting Margaret to come with me when the time came, because she was working on taro cards Madam Olga had sent her. I finally persuaded her. . . . We hit the wall at over seventy. When I came to, I was lying there, beside the road. I knew at once I had survived . . . with all the violent death I'd seen I ought to have known better than to think anyone could forecast the effects of a crash. . . . Do you know, a pilot jumped from a Spitfire in that war and his parachute didn't open. He fell two thousand feet on to grass and didn't break a bone in his body. He was dead, from shock, but nothing broken or damaged. . . . I was a bit like that. The shock was there. . . . Margaret was dead, half smiling. Perhaps she'd been thinking of Andrew at the moment we hit. . . . They took me back to Millbank. Three, four days of rest, examinations of all kinds . . . they looked for internal injuries, real shock, concussion . . . nothing, but the few cuts and bruises I had. They said, all right, convalesce at home for a week and if nothing else comes up, you can go back. . . . Winston came – I told you. He sat in a chair, by the bed, and said – you know the way he liked to make these grand gestures? – lisped, "General, a field-marshal's baton awaits you inside the walls of Bucharest." I thanked him, thinking it was a hell of a long way to go for my baton. He'd told Alex his was awaiting him inside the walls of Rome, I believe. . . .

'All the time I was in Millbank, and afterwards, I was feeling very strange. I was able to answer questions, pass tests, and so on. I hurt . . . but I didn't tell the doctors, because I couldn't tell them, apart from a bruise on the head, where I hurt. It kept moving . . . it was in my hips, my chest, behind my eyes. I'd see things when I was supposed to, other times, not. I felt a failure. I had determined to destroy myself, and I had failed. Charles Gibson came and I told him everything.'

'Everything? The truth?' Martin asked.

'Yes. I needed to tell someone, so someone would know that I was a failure ... then I had to prove it. I went back to the war. I'd killed Margaret and I thought I could finish the job on myself properly. I tried to shoot myself in my caravan, right after I'd sacked Stephen Ross. You remember I carried a Mauser I'd taken off a dead Boche in the Desert? I put it to my head and pulled the trigger. It jammed without firing. I was sitting at my desk, looking at it, when Wilfred Eden came in. He knew at once, I think, and took it from my hand and said, "I'll clean it for you, sir." Failed again.... Then came the conference. I didn't know what I was saying, but I had to say something. And at the back of my mind there was a feeling that whatever I said would be so wrong that someone – you probably – would recognise that I'd broken down. The C.O.S. would call Bartlett and I'd be flown out in an ambulance plane. But no one noticed anything. You just did what I told you – obeyed the words that had come out of my mouth, though I didn't know what they had been. The medicine Wilfred gave me, and more rest, began to pull me round. And then I had a strange feeling that I was being preserved for some purpose ...'

'To win Vojja Lovac,' Martin murmured.

'Perhaps. Or to write these Memoirs. At all events, I felt like Clive of India. You know, he tried three times to commit suicide and after the pistol misfired the third time, he exclaimed that his life must have been preserved for great things. In another day or two I was myself again – General Sir John Durham, K.C.B., K.B.E., D.S.O., M.C., Commander of the 16th Army ... murderer and would-be suicide.'

Martin thought, what he has told us now, explains it. His breakdown in January '45 at Kojar had not been due to the pneumonia, or the accident, or even Lois's pregnancy, but because he was facing the guilt of a deliberate murder. Yet, he had done it for Lois's sake, and to save Margaret pain, so why should he feel that he was a murderer? And on several other occasions he had deliberately caused the death of his own people for a greater cause – look at the shelling of the Americans, the breaking of the mutiny in 206 R.A.C. And he hadn't really loved his wife. So ... but it was no use speculating further.

He said, 'Why didn't you use the Bentley, in the accident, sir? You would have been more likely to get killed in an open car.'

'Why didn't I use the Bentley?' the Old Man repeated. The blue eyes turned and looked long at Martin, 'I don't know.'

'The Field-Marshal couldn't bring himself to damage it,' Paul broke in.

The Old Man shook his head irritably, 'No, it wasn't that . . . I don't know.'

Martin thought, can it be possible that he expected or hoped to survive the crash, subconsciously perhaps? And that, in that case, he would want to have the Bentley afterwards? But it sounded as if he'd made up his mind he had nothing to live for, except more pain. Perhaps that wasn't quite true, either.

Martin stood up in the attic and carried the sacking-covered paintings to a place under one of the lights. The dust was thick on the sacking, and made a dark cloud as he beat it off. No one had moved these for years. He was surprised that Lois had never wanted to look at them; but she had put all this early time of her life firmly behind her, refusing to look back. He began to undo the wrappings that protected the canvases.

There were a dozen of them, all stretched but unframed. They were oils, blacks and greys mostly, here and there streaks of red, green, yellow. The colours were not bright and strong, as they could have been, but dulled and painful. The compositions were more indicative even than the colouring. The painter had seen tunnels, with no steady light, only painful flashes, at the end of them. Or walls of darkness, which were unclimbable and beyond which there was no brightness. And rivers, which did not give rest or peace, but pain, onward flowing toward greyness. There were no human figures in any of them, only shapes that might have been animals or rocks, or dark clouds twisted by invisible storms.

He stayed a long time, looking at the pictures, then repacked them and put them back where he had found them. Then he climbed carefully down the attic stairs, and went to look for his wife. It was afternoon, and he found her in the kitchen, working at accounts.

He said, 'I've been looking at your paintings . . . the ones in the attic.'

'Oh,' she said, without looking up, 'I meant to burn them long ago. I thought I had.'

I don't believe that, Martin thought. She'd know perfectly well if she'd burned them. She had decided to keep them for some reason; perhaps as a memory of that age of her life, which would somehow be lost if the paintings were actually destroyed.

'I think they're very good,' he said. 'They're powerful.'

She put down her pencil and looked pensively out of the window. The garden was empty and the October sun low. 'Pain makes powerful art,' she said, 'if there's any talent there for it to be expressed through. And some technique.'

'They're full of pain. . . . Were you very lonely then?'

She nodded, 'And frightened. Mummy was madder than Daddy knew, even. He could have had her certified without any trouble, if he'd known all that she did and said to me, right from the time Andrew died.'

'Why didn't you tell anyone?'

'Who was there to tell? Daddy was in England for a couple of years, but he was always at work, or on manoeuvres or conferences. Then he went overseas. I loved him, but I was afraid of him, at that time.'

'Did you know that he deliberately ran into that wall, with your mother?'

'Has he said so now? I always knew, in myself. I never told anyone, of course. That was when I really came to love him, and wasn't afraid of him any more.'

'That's odd, when he'd just killed your mother.'

'Whom I hated, by then. I felt that if he decided to kill me, it would be the best thing for me, and he'd do it the best way possible.'

'That's how everyone's always felt about him, except those who are jealous of him. . . . You must have done many other paintings before you gave it up.'

'Disasters of the war,' she cut in, smiling. 'Yes.'

'Could I see them? Where are they?'

'No. I burned everything, except those, when we got married.'

'Couldn't you start painting again? It's a shame, it's wrong, for you not to, when you have so much talent.'

'I don't know . . . I swore to myself, then, that I'd never touch a brush again. Now, I'm not quite so sure. It's Daddy's Memoirs, I think. He has something to say, and it's making me think, perhaps I do, too. In paint, not in words. . . . Run along now, Martin. I have to finish these accounts. And thank you for trying to defend me against Caroline's contempt. She told me what she'd said – about not keeping the baby – and what you'd said. She didn't want me to think she'd say anything against me behind my back. . . . I try to get closer to her, but I don't succeed. I only pray that I haven't done to her what my mother did to me.'

'I don't think so,' Martin said slowly. 'She's tougher than you were, for one thing.'

'You don't think I'm tough?'

'You've been trying to be. So have I.... Couldn't we try the other?'

'Being tender? I don't know ...'

... thought of you all the time when I read that you had been put in the Tower of London. You know that you have enemies in our government, even after so long, who are pleased to print such news about you, even after all you did to liberate the country. But why do I write that I thought of you when you were in the Tower, when I think of you all the time? I am miserable, Giovanni. I should not have let you come to visit me. I don't think I can bear even to write any more letters, for each word is a wound and a reminder of a wound. No more, Giovanni, no more. Remember me.

CHAPTER TWENTY

Clive Ruttledge came silently into the house, noting that the front door was not locked. He had seen that his mother's van was not in the garage, nor the Bentley. He looked into the kitchen: no one there. No one in the vegetable garden ... or the rose garden. It would be a bore if they'd all gone out for the day, just when he had chosen to come down. He should have telephoned, Grandpa would say. Probably right, but telephoning was a bit of a bore, too. The family never went out on Sundays at this time of year. Of course they could be down the village somewhere. He went upstairs and now did hear voices, faintly, from behind the closed door of his grandfather's study. He listened – there was only one voice, Grandpa's, speaking a few phrases, then stopping. But if Grandpa was in his study, who had taken out the Bentley? He didn't allow anyone to drive it but himself, except Caroline ... he'd given Caroline some lessons on it during this summer. A bit of favouritism, that. He himself was just as good a driver as Caroline, or better, and would cause quite a stir burbling up to the barracks in the Green Monster. He couldn't hear what his grandfather was saying, so knocked, and opened the door. He paused in surprise. His grandfather wasn't there, only Paul Phillips, at a typewriter in the corner, with a tape machine, no, two tape machines.

'Morning,' he drawled.

Paul looked up quickly, reached out to press switches, and stopped the tape machines. 'Hullo, Clive,' he said, 'I didn't know you were coming down today.'

'It wasn't arranged,' Clive said. 'A date I had fell through, so I thought I'd come down.'

'Give the old folks a treat, eh? I didn't hear your car.'

'It's having a tune up. I came down by train, and walked from the station.... I thought I heard Grandpa talking.'

'You did, Clive,' Paul said. 'I'm making a duplicate tape of him recording something. He told me to.'

'Oh,' Clive said. The fellow had a nerve calling him Clive when he'd hardly met him and he was only a secretary or typist or whatever you'd call his job. 'Where is he – my grandfather?'

'Took the Bentley out, with Caroline. Your dad went for a long walk – won't be back till evening, he said. Your mum's visiting someone in Portsmouth, she said. Our Mafia adviser's in Italy, on our business, he says. Will you be in for lunch?'

'Lunch? Oh, yes.'

'It's cold cuts. I'll open another tin of spaghetti to go with them.'

'Not for me, thanks,' Clive said, with a shudder.

He went out, closing the door carefully behind him. As he started downstairs, he heard the tape machine starting up again.

That fellow Phillips knew everything about the family now. God knows what horror Grandpa had recorded, that he was duplicating. It didn't matter; what was already out was enough to make anyone blush for shame. The latest, that Mrs Ross had let out in spite at that lunch, about his mother having had an illegitimate baby, was the worst. Just like some wretched housemaid or shopgirl. A field-marshal's daughter ... grand-daughter of a lieutenant-colonel of his own regiment, the Scots Guards. He'd had a hard enough time with all the other matters the fellows had ragged him about – but this would be the end. If this came out, he'd have to resign his commission or apply for a transfer to the Transport Corps. He'd probably be asked to if he didn't do it himself first.

He found himself in the room his mother used for her work room. He knew it well, the shape of it, the exact placing of the windows, how the light fell at every season, the shape of the tree outside – though it was bigger now – the view down the rose graden. This had been the day nursery. He'd grown up here, reading, dreaming, playing with Caroline. The furnishings were different now, of course, except for a big play table they'd had, which his mother had kept ... and some of the pictures, including a big one of Winnie the Pooh talking to Tigger.

He sat down at his mother's desk. The wall opposite was hung with a calendar, names and numbers pencilled in on many of the dates for the rest of the month; but fewer than it would have been last month. It was autumn. The wedding and banquet and club lunch season was over.

Somewhere he had a bastard half-brother. If he'd been farmed out soon enough, and his foster parents had kept their mouths shut, the man would never know who his mother had really been. There was no reason why he should know. But, Clive thought, he probably does know. His shoulders hunched ... *the world has a down on me. It's not my fault that my mother got caught. You hurt me and I'll hurt you back. I*

239

don't care . . . He straightened up. It might be the other way round . . . *the reason my father didn't marry my mother was because his family wouldn't allow it. You mean . . . ? Yes. The prince! Pheeeew! You do look a bit like him, now that I know. Cor, we ought to call you, Your Royal Highness . . . Your Grace, at least.* If the king had a child by a mistress he used to be surnamed Fitzroy, but what about a prince? Fitz-prince didn't sound quite right.

He shook his head. Who could the father have been? It was very hard to imagine Mother carried away by passion; so hard that no particular sort of lover came to mind as being the natural one for her. He thought of Guards officers, like himself, wounded Battle of Britain pilots, American Negro G.I.s, long-haired poets. None fitted.

He opened the desk drawer and started looking through the papers there. On top were bills and a long typed letter from a wholesale wine merchant. Below that was a letter in his mother's handwriting, dated, with no address, and starting *Dearest Charles* . . .

He took the letter slowly out and began to read it. *Dearest Charles* . . . His mind refused to read the letter straight through from beginning to end, in sequence, but recorded a phrase, then jumped several lines, recorded another, then back again, getting it all in fits and starts, like a painting that had not been painted systematically, but haphazardly, eventually becoming complete.

it was better last time . . . no feeling of guilt . . . didn't know I was missing sex . . . the light in your studio on my naked body . . . no need to make excuses or tell lies, because . . . when I think of what we have been to each other . . . light against darkness, sun out of shadow . . . August 15, 1973.

That was the date of the letter. Two months ago. That was about the time she'd made Dad move to one of the spare rooms. Which came first – her having the affair with Charles Gibson, or the fight with Dad? They must be connected.

It didn't matter. The point was that she was at it again, at her age! It was indecent, incredible! The chaps wouldn't just snicker now, they'd double up with laughter. He'd never find out now who the father of the bastard had been, but the present lover was Charles Gibson, no doubt about that. He wondered what Gibson had made of the letter. But it had never been sent. It was a big sheet of vellum notepaper, but it had not been folded.

He rummaged deeper into the drawer, and at the bottom found two more letters. One, written in July, was more tentative, expressing a sense of guilt at what she was doing; the other, written in September, seemed to be withdrawing somewhat from the raptures of this August letter; and neither had been sent, but over all, they confirmed the fact – his mother was having an affair with Charles Gibson.

The immediate reaction of his brother officers – of anyone who heard about it, the man in the street reading of it in the yellow press, of the clubmen gossiping over their drinks at the bar, of the typists whispering in the trains – would be laughter, giggles. But it was not funny. The Ruttledges were an old and honourable family, going back to before the Conquest. The Durhams were nearly as old. His maternal grandmother had been a Craig, of the great Scottish family. His mother was dragging all that splendour into the mire. He felt as though he had been forced to roll in dogshit, in his scarlet full dress. It must be put a stop to – at once.

But who was to do it? Grandpa? He couldn't tell him that he had been searching his mother's private papers. Before he could say what he'd learned Grandpa would say, I don't want to hear another word. His father? But you could hardly tell a man his wife was being unfaithful to him, especially not if the man was your father. . . . He might confront her himself, and plead with her. No, not that – *tell* her! Give her an order. End this disgusting liaison with Charles Gibson! *It's disgraceful to you and degrading to the rest of us, and the family as a whole.* . . . Gibson might be a good painter, and an R.A., but everyone knew he was the son of a plumber from Birmingham. How *could* she?

She wouldn't listen to him. Obviously she was infatuated, and she had no reason to fear or obey him. It might be different if Grandpa spoke to her, but that was out. Unless he wrote the Old Man an anonymous letter. But he wouldn't read it . . .

Gibson was the person. Someone should tell Gibson. Threaten him with a beating if he didn't stop it. Or even take a revolver along, pull it out and – *It's either that, Gibson . . . or this.* But why be ineffectual? Threats didn't usually work on people like that. He had no sense of honour, or shame, so he'd probably say whatever he thought you wanted him to say, and after you'd gone call the police, and continue the affair. It would be best to go straight in, pull out the pistol, and – *Gibson, you are having an affair with my mother.* He shrinks back against the table. There's a painting on an easel in the background. *Stand still and listen . . . for the last time. My family's honour is being stained and all of us made objects of ridicule*. That's all. Then fire. He falls, clutching his stomach, a look of agony on his face. Take three steps forward, lean down, press the pistol against his heart and fire again to put him out of his misery. Lay the pistol carefully down on the table and stalk to the telephone. Dial 999. *Police? This is Captain Clive Ruttledge of the Scots Guards speaking from . . .*' What was Gibson's address?

He looked hurriedly round the top of the cluttered desk, found an address book, and looked up Gibson.

. . . 88 Blackfriars. I have just shot and killed Mr Charles Gibson. I am speaking from his studio.

Then at the trial, he'd say nothing. There'd be no motive. Of course, he'd be found guilty, but nothing would come out about his mother's shame.

He looked at his watch. Lunch in half an hour. Damn lunch. Let Phillips eat the cold cuts and his disgusting tinned spaghetti by himself. The next train to London was the 12.38. He'd catch it easily, if he walked fast.

It was four o'clock when he climbed the three flights of stairs and rang Gibson's bell. It only struck him then, as he waited, that Gibson might be out. He would look an ass, and feel worse, He should have telephoned from his quarters in the barracks; but he'd never doubted that Gibson would be there, to take what was coming to him.

Gibson opened the door and exclaimed in surprise, 'Hullo, Clive! What brings you here . . . delighted to see you, though.' He held the door open and Clive walked in. The door closed. The lights were on, for it was a dull overcast afternoon, the river flowing oily dark beyond the plane trees and the row of tall lamp standards. Now was the moment. Waste no more time. The pistol was heavy in his pocket and must be bulging out. Gibson was staring at him. 'You look a bit peaked, Clive. Anything happened?'

Clive pulled the pistol out of his pocket. It caught in the flap and he had to struggle with it for what seemed an age before it came free. He said, 'Gibson, you're having an affair with my mother.'

There was a painting on an easel in the background of the long room. It was a nude. Good God, it was Caroline, unmistakably his sister! Was the man having an affair with her, too? But, of course, it was childish to imagine that artists made love to every girl who modelled for them.

'Yes,' Gibson said, 'I am. Now please don't point that gun at me, Clive.'

Clive tore his attention away from his glowing, erotically posed, naked sister. 'Our family will be disgraced,' he said.

'No, it won't,' Gibson said. 'At least, not by me, or Lois. By you, perhaps, if you do something silly now. Murder to avenge the family honour is not considered noble in this country any more, you know – only laughably quaint.'

Clive's legs felt weak. His finger was on the trigger, but . . . Gibson was right. It wouldn't turn out at all as he had imagined. The last sound he heard would not be approving murmurs, but laughter, again.

'Christ!' he said violently, and threw the gun onto the sofa beside him.

'You need a drink,' Gibson said. The green eyes were glowing, the hair flying like a halo round his head and he was laughing. Or was he? A moment ago Clive could have sworn he was, but he wasn't now.

Gibson brought a tumbler half full of whisky, and another for himself. 'Sit down, Clive. Here's to you.'

'Thanks,' Clive said, taking a gulp. The whisky burned down his throat and in his chest. He sat down heavily. 'I wish Mummy wouldn't do it, though.'

'Do you feel degraded?'

'Exactly!' he said. Gibson understood. 'She . . . you're both old. If anyone gets to know, they'll laugh.'

'Some will,' Gibson said, nodding. 'Older people won't, because everyone who reaches our age realises that you don't feel any different, inside yourself. You love, just as much as you did twenty, thirty years before. It may look absurd, from outside, but it doesn't seem so, inside.'

Clive drank again. 'I found some letters to you, in her drawer, that she never posted.'

'I see. I've only had one letter. I wondered whether she might have written more, but decided she probably thought it was too dangerous.'

'Daddy never goes into that room, except when he has to see her. I don't think she'd care if he did find out, anyway, not since they separated . . . started to sleep in different rooms.'

'When did that happen?'

'Two months ago, about. I know – it was soon after Grandpa began the Memoirs and Mummy learned that Dad had shot Captain Cunningham. She was disgusted.'

'Or made that her excuse.' The eyes on his were sparkling now, and he was definitely half smiling. 'Women are not always quite straightforward in their motivations – not even one's mother. I know mine certainly wasn't.'

Clive nodded. That could be true. His mother and father had really been mentally separated for a long time. The business about the bedrooms was no more than a final statement. And if Dad had gone to live somewhere else, not many people would think Mummy was acting disgracefully in having an affair.

Gibson said judiciously, 'I don't know how much longer this will last, Clive. I'm very fond of your mother, but the last week or two I've been feeling that she no longer needs me quite the way she did. When this started, she felt lost . . . abandoned . . . lonely . . . insecure of herself as a woman. She's going through the change of life, too . . . probably about finished, but it's been difficult. It's hard for all women. They need help.'

Clive nodded. He'd heard and read about that.

Gibson continued: '. . . especially when the marriage hasn't been all it should be. A woman feels then that the last of her womanhood is going – and that it was never appreciated or fulfilled.' Clive nodded again. Gibson understood human nature very well. He felt sorry for his mother, sorry for Gibson too. She'd used him and now he was going to be dropped. He was suffering, but too much of a gentleman to say so.

Gibson said, 'I assure you we're being discreet, and, as I say, I have a feeling that soon . . . the flame will be out.' He snapped his fingers. 'I shall no longer be able to warm my hands before what has been, for me, a very real fire of love . . . and affection. Let's talk no more about it. How's everyone at Ashwood?'

'Oh, all right,' Clive said. 'The Memoirs get more awful every time I hear about them, but I suppose nothing can be done about that.'

Gibson said, 'I'm surprised no one's tried to silence the Old Man . . . make him an offer he can't refuse.'

'Burrisk did.'

'Good Lord! Tell me about it.'

Clive launched into the tale of Burrisk/Belprato and the attempted murder and Caroline's part in thwarting it, as it had been told to him. At the end, he said, 'That's Caroline, isn't it?' He jerked his chin toward the nude.

Charles Gibson glanced over his shoulder at the painting. 'Yes.' He turned back, his eyes twinkling. 'I paid her full model rates, but you don't have to, usually. Lots of females are only too delighted to take their clothes off. Proud of their figures, I suppose.'

'Caroline's got a good figure,' Clive said. 'I never noticed it.'

'There's a brother speaking!'

Clive looked more closely at the painting. The pose was provocative and so was the look in her eye.

Gibson said, 'And young girls also sometimes find older men attractive . . . thank God.'

Clive nodded. So Caroline had been his mistress, or still was. He felt an unexpected surge of sexual excitement, as though an attractive woman had that instant offered him her body. Why did this revelation excite him, when she was his sister? He ought to feel as outraged as over his mother. But it was different. Caroline must have thrown herself at Charles's head. You couldn't blame Charles for taking advantage of it.

Gibson said, 'You know, Clive, I'd like to paint a portrait of you, if I may. . . . Good God no, not in the nude!'

'Full dress?' Clive asked. He thought of the painting of his grandfather in the dining room. Everyone remarked on that, partly because it was Grandpa, but also at the power of the work, the striking light, and the composition. It would be marvellous to see himself in such a painting.

Gibson said, 'I hadn't thought. It's a matter of how you see yourself.'

Clive drank some more whisky. This was his third and they had not been small. How did he see himself? In scarlet, seated by a window, his bearskin on a table at his side, the Tudor chimneys of St James's Palace visible outside? No, that would be wrong. One always wore blue in the dining room. Service dress perhaps, as though on a drill parade at Pirbright. Or in ribboned frock coat as the duty officer at Wellington Barracks, inspecting the New Guard with the R.S.M.? He shook his head. They would all look pretty silly set beside Grandpa at Vojja Lovac. That was real: this, any of his ideas, would be pretending.

'I shall paint you as Hamlet,' Gibson said suddenly. 'Black tights, skull in hand – the works. Now, look, Clive, I have a date. So you'll have to run along. I'll give you a call tomorrow to fix a time for your first sitting. . . . Don't leave your gun.'

CHAPTER TWENTY-ONE

. . . a wound and a reminder of a wound. No more, Giovanni, no more. Remember me . . .

The words throbbed in his head so that it ached. It had been so nearly every hour since the letter arrived. What was he to do? Now he had hurt the person he most cared about in the world, perhaps the only one he really loved, or ever had. Was everything he touched doomed to wither, and misery and death follow always in his footsteps?

He closed his eyes, and willed his brain to bring him other messages – anything rather than the repetition, *no more, Giovanni, no more, remember me . . .*

He looked up and saw the calendar: October 24 . . . less than three weeks to Armistice Day. That was the date in 1918, when at the eleventh hour of the eleventh day of the eleventh month the guns at last fell silent in Flanders. He remembered himself and his company commanders handing round a bottle of rum, and three fusiliers slapping him on the back and yelling, 'It's over! It's over . . . and we're alive!'

He remembered, much more clearly, the eleventh hour of the eleventh day of the eleventh month a year earlier, 1917. Peter Curran had died. The last of the four to go: all killed at his hands, he felt. Why else would they have come to him in his dreams and daytime musings for so long? Why else were his hands so often red? Ted Crandall at Le Cateau: they'd both been platoon commanders in B Company, but the company commander was dead and it was he who'd told Ted to move his platoon to the corner of the hedges, where death found him. At 2nd Ypres it was his company that had been supposed to be in the line, but he'd had violent diarrhoea and the C.O. had sent Jimmy Livingstone instead, to die under the gas attack. On the Somme he'd just been pulled out of his company to act as second-in-command of the battalion, and it was Dick Newby who took his place . . . where the German machine guns swept the edge of High Wood.

The garden and the Factory basked under an autumn sun. Paul was typing in his corner, Caroline working on a thick pile of notes. He ought to be seeing them, and the familiar furnishings of his study – the book-lined shelves, the portraits, von Heldenmark's sword . . . but he saw only the muddy crater outside Passchendaele and Peter lying in it, face down, a dozen other bodies around him, all fantastically shredded by ripping steel fragments.

He closed his eyes.

When he turned Peter over he saw that he had no stomach and only half a face. One arm was gone and half one leg, and his uniform was ripped in twenty other places. Pools of blood lay everywhere, for not all the men who had been in the crater had died at once. They'd been there over twenty-four hours before anyone could get to them. And the mud – it was more horrible than the shattered corpses, or the rats eating the flesh under his feet, unafraid. He was up to his knees in it. All round, in the bottom and sides of the crater, and out in the open among the tangled thickets of barbed wire, hands stuck out of it, and a horse's hoofs, the barrel and twisted wheel of a German gun, cigarette packets, pails, boots with feet in them, ammunition belts, a loaf of sodden bread, the side of a British tank like a discarded house sinking in an ocean . . . and Peter, his very first friend . . . and his last. They'd met at prep school, at eight years of age. And fought, of course. Fought all the time, and bird-nested together, ragged, played. . . . Peter had been his second-in-command at Passchendaele. His name was on the war memorial at Hawkford, at the top of the hill where he had killed Margaret.

November 11: he must remember to order his usual wreath of British Legion poppies. The villagers and the vicar thought, when he laid his unlabelled wreath at the foot of the stone cross he was placing it there in memory of the dead of both wars. There was nothing on it to indicate otherwise. But it wasn't – it was in memory only of the five, who had been friends, the Musketeers: Ted Crandall, Jimmy Livingstone, Dick Newby, Peter Curran . . . and for the soul of John Durham.

'I think I heard a car,' Caroline said. She got up and looked out of the east window. 'Yes. He's arrived.'

The Field-Marshal frowned. Who had arrived? Caroline said, 'You remember, Grandpa, we're waiting for Mr Bigelow – Burrisk – Belprato. He called last night to ask if he could come down.' She hurried out of the room.

'Ah, yes,' the Field-Marshal said. The cogs of one's memory had lost a few teeth at his age. There he was, recalling every detail of a shattered piece of Belgian landscape that he hadn't seen for fifty-six years, but he'd forgotten that he spoke to Bigelow last night.

Caroline returned with Bigelow. 'Sit down,' the Field-Marshal said. 'You had a good day for the drive down.'

'Sure did,' the other mumbled. He looked uncomfortable, the Field-Marshal thought, which he certainly never had before. He fiddled with a magazine on the low table in front of him, then fished in his pocket and pulled out a folded sheet of paper. He handed it to the Field-Marshal.

'That's Item Number One, Marshal – a confession by General Ballino, signed and witnessed, that he kept the hundred thousand pounds in gold that you gave his emissary on September 6, 1943 – less ten thousand that the emissary was to keep for himself. Ballino said he was unable to do anything about surrendering his troops, though he wanted to, because the Germans were on top of him with superior forces, and watching him closely. But he kept the money anyway.'

'I can't read Italian, more than a few words,' the Field-Marshal said, 'but thank you, very much. How did you manage it? I thought nothing would make General Ballino talk.'

'So did he,' Bigelow said grimly, 'but we changed his mind. He's old, but not old enough.'

The Field-Marshal wondered whether he should ask if Bigelow had made any progress in his inquiries about the Zvornos Collection. If he had tacitly given up the search, so much the better. But Bigelow was shrewd and suspicious – he had to be – and if he himself suddenly seemed to lose interest, Bigelow would want to know why.

He said, 'Anything further on the Zvornos Collection?'

Bigelow shook his head. 'Not a damned thing. Our guys in Italy have been trying to trace what happened to the truck after the Count killed Orlando's. I went to Ancona myself, and looked around. That was where all the military shipping to and from the Balkans was operating, but it was hopeless, after so many years. I did learn one thing, Marshal.'

'What?' the Field-Marshal asked. He knew he was frowning because the mention of Ancona had worried him.

'Nothing important,' Bigelow said hastily. 'Just, I ran into a couple of guys in Italy who said you weren't too popular there, not with the leftists and Commies anyway. Said you'd protected Fascists during the war. Just thought you'd like to know. . . . Well, we've drawn a blank in Italy, and I can't go into Yugloslavia . . . ran into a little trouble there four, five years ago, and they'd throw me straight into jail . . . but in New York we got some information. Papa contacted some art experts and they think that at least five paintings from the collection have appeared on the market since 1945 – one in London, one in New York and three in Paris, and they think the great agent who sells them for whoever's got them is a woman, but that's all. One big trouble is that there never was a catalogue of the Collection, apparently, or if there was, the Count had the only copy.'

'What about the numbered bank accounts?' the Field-Marshal asked. He felt lighter and younger. Stefanie had hidden her tracks perfectly. They'd never find her, unless she became greedy and tried to sell several paintings at once, or failed to give the dealer a good price in return for his co-operation in concealing the truth about his purchase.

'Nothing yet,' Bigelow said, 'Our boys in Zurich are still making enquiries. Like I said, we've got to be very careful there. . . . Marshal, I'd like to speak to you in private.'

The Field-Marshal looked at him. He knew his brows had come down, and Bigelow would think he was frowning at him; but he wasn't – it was a habit he had got into many years ago as a young man, to frown when he was thinking. It had done him no harm, and frightened quite a few juniors into admissions they needn't have made. Bigelow was looking very uneasy. His palms were sweating and he was rubbing them on his handkerchief. And this was an American gangster, a man who had killed, probably quite often. Such people were tough, but apt to be prudish, he'd heard.

It could only be one thing. He felt a great lightening, as though some heavy substance had been pumped out of his arteries and replaced by a light and sparkling wine. The warmth flowed through him.

'No secrets, Mr Bigelow. Whatever it is, we all have to know.'

'Honest, Marshal, I think it would be better if . . .'

The Field-Marshal shook his head – 'Sorry, let's have it.'

From the inside pocket of his jacket Bigelow produced an envelope and out of the envelope drew a postcard-sized black and white photograph. He said, 'Madeleine Phillips gave me that.'

The Field-Marshal knew for certain now. He took the photograph and looked at it. He hadn't seen it for nearly twenty-five years, when he'd burned his copy before going to Gibraltar:

Wilfred Eden and himself, on a sandy beach, by some rocks, their arms around each other's waists, naked.

'May I see?' Caroline asked.

He handed it over. 'Show it to Paul, too.'

He thought, most people would think Charles was a rotter of the first water for doing this; but for himself, he was glad. He couldn't have done it on his own, yet knew it ought to be done. The enormous relief still crackled in his veins.

Paul and Caroline were looking at the photograph. Caroline had turned pale. Paul glanced at it quickly and handed it back. The Field-Marshal thought, he's seen it before; but of course he would have, if this was his mother's.

Caroline turned on Paul, her voice trembling with fury. 'You stole it from Grandpa's papers! You're always grouting about, poking your nose in everywhere.'

'I didn't,' Paul said sullenly.

'Well, how did your mother get it?'

'He gave it to her,' Bigelow said. 'She told me.'

Paul looked from Caroline to Bigelow – 'So she's told you, 'as she? Of course, you're her fancy man. One of them.'

Bigelow slid out of his chair in one easy movement and before the Field-Marshal could take in what was happening had smashed two punches to Paul's belly, and another to his nose. Blood spouted. Groaning, Paul found his handkerchief and clapped it to his nose. 'I'll sue you for thadd,' he cried through the handkerchief.

Bigelow said, 'Not if you know what's good for you.'

'Where *did* you get the photo?' Caroline persisted. The Field-Marshal waited.

Paul said, 'The negative came for me here in the post. There wasn't any letter with it, nothing at all. A London E.C.4 postmark.'

'Fleet Street, the Field-Marshal thought; close to Black-friars. Charles wasn't interested in hiding his traces.

Caroline said, 'You expect us to believe that?'

'It's the truth!'

'How many copies did you make?' Bigelow cut in.

'Two.'

'Who for?'

'One for myself and one for my mother.'

Bigelow got up again. From his outside jacket jocket he produced a knuckleduster and slipped it on.

The Field-Marshal said sharply, 'He didn't get the negative

from inside this house. I didn't have it.'

'That's not what I'm interested in, Marshal. He's made more than two copies, and I want to know where they've gone.' He faced Paul. 'I want the whole truth now, sonny boy. Your mother won't like it if you come home with your face looking like a plate of raspberry jello, will she?'

'Sir Henry Bartlett,' Paul said. 'He got hold of me a month after I . . .'

Caroline rushed at him, her fists flailing. 'You traitor!' she cried. 'You unutterable swine! We should have sacked you when I found you stealing the money!'

Paul tried to defend himself, dropped his handkerchief, and she hit him on the nose again. He yelled in pain and Bigelow kicked viciously at his groin. He fell to the floor, doubled up, groaning.

The Field-Marshal raised his voice. 'That's enough, Paul, go into my bathroom and clean yourself up. Then come back here and explain yourself.'

Paul stumbled out. After a while the Field-Marshal said, 'I suppose Mrs Phillips proposes to use this photograph for purposes of blackmail.'

Bigelow said, 'Paul might have liked to, if he thought you had enough money to make it worthwhile. And if he hasn't learned that you're not the sort of guy who's going to allow himself to be blackmailed, no matter what. . . . She – Madeleine – told me that a few weeks ago that photograph would have been the best present she'd ever have got in her life. She'd have had it published somewhere, for revenge. It would be something, wouldn't it, seeing what you had her husband court-martialled for? But for the past month, since I got to know her well, she's changed her mind about you, Marshal . . . about all of you, come to that. She just wants to give it back. She didn't know there were any other copies. Paul didn't tell her. But I know that kind of jerk. He has to have made other copies. I didn't know till now that he has the negative.'

Paul came back, the handkerchief close below his nose, one eye swollen and his cheek bruised.

'Sit down,' the Field-Marshal said. 'You were telling us about Sir Henry Bartlett when Caroline . . . interrupted you.'

Paul mumbled thickly, 'He got hold of me a month after I came to work here and said he'd pay me well for things like that. Of course, he didn't know what there might be then. He'd pay me for any information I could give him about what was going to come out in the Memoirs, with the names and addresses of anyone you were talking to about them, or getting information from. And my mother wanted to know all the dirt, too.'

'You *are* a swine,' Caroline said, but almost in sorrow now. 'I suppose you really can't help it. It's a disease, like being an alcoholic.'

'If you'd been made to live the way we've been, you'd be no different,' Paul said with sudden anger. 'And you're so bloody stupid – bringing me into the house without getting something on me first. I need the money. You don't think I can live on what you pay me here, now that I'm out of the photo business? Don't be daft! You ought to have found me out ages ago, because Clive actually caught me in here one day making a duplicate of a tape for Bartlett. He didn't suspect anything. What the hell else other reason would there be? Bloody idiots. What reason do I have to be *faithful* and *loyal* to *you*, any of you?'

Caroline said, wearily 'Calm down, Paul.... Tell us about it, Grandpa.'

'The photograph? It was in Italy, a little beach south of Porto d'Ascoli. It was August, 1944. My Corps was resting in reserve, ready for the Gothic Line battles. I took the day off with Wilfred. He knew of this beach . . . a hundred-yard stretch of sand, with low rock cliffs cutting it off at both ends. The only way you could reach it was to swim past the rock point at the south end, where there was another longer beach with a grassy track leading to it through the woods. . . . We swam round, naked, all our food and wine and clothes in watertight bags we dragged behind us. We played on the sand like children. I forgot all my troubles, all my worries. . . . Margaret – this was before I killed her, but she had been a worry to me for eight years before this . . . the Gothic Line . . . even all that I had seen and felt in the Great War. . . . Then we ate sausage and bread and drank wine. I propped the camera on a rock and took the photo with the delay mechanism.'

'You're supporting the other man – Wilfred,' Caroline said. 'He's only got one foot.'

'The other was blown off at Tobruk,' the Field-Marshal said. 'That's why I took him as my A.D.C. He was unfit for active service but didn't want to sit at a desk.'

'You look good, Grandpa,' she murmured. 'Look how hard and lean you are. How old were you?'

'Fifty-one. That's the scar I got at Villers Bretonneux in -sixteen and that one at Hill 60, in -seventeen. . . . Wilfred was thirty-five or thirty-six.'

'He's plump, everything soft and curved, compared with you. Is this – what this photograph implies – true, Grandpa?' She spoke very gently, looking at him.

He said, 'Yes. I could deny it, the photo's not definite evidence – but I don't want to. I want to tell the truth. . . . The sex was only a few times. I wasn't a homosexual, I don't think, except insofar as everyone is, in part. The experts say that, I believe.'

'They do,' Caroline said. 'I think it's true, too.'

'Wilfred may have been. I don't know. . . . It was loneliness. A Corps commander is always a lonely person. Thinking of Margaret, even being with her, only made me more lonely, and had for years. I didn't have time to get close to Lois. Since 1918 I'd had no close friends. No one was close to me and they knew it, and I knew it. . . . Wilfred became my A.D.C. in North Africa. He was good at his job. He made me relax. I could talk to him in a way that I could with no one else. We became friends, as much as a lieutenant-general can be friends with a lieutenant. Then, soon after Cassino fell, our relationship suddenly changed. It wasn't friendship any more, though it looked just the same to anyone else. It was love . . . a sort of love. I had to admit it. Wilfred knew. He felt the same. . . . He'd always had a bunk in my sleeping caravan, so that I wouldn't have to go out to get anyone in the middle of the night, and as a bodyguard.'

He fell silent, thinking back.

Caroline said, 'And this went on till when?'

'Only till Ancona,' he said.

He realised at once that he had made a mistake, as Bigelow said, 'What happened at Ancona?'

He said, 'It ended, that's all. We realised that we were heading for disaster, which would have meant a lot to me at that time. We returned to being friends, really friends this time. The differences in rank and age meant nothing. He stayed on as my A.D.C. to the end of the war, but the day after von Heldenmark surrendered he came to me and asked if I would send him back to England. I did. I haven't seen him from that day to this. No letters, no Christmas cards, nothing.'

He thought they had believed him – Bigelow certainly,

253

Caroline he was not so sure of. She was an extraordinarily acute young woman.

She asked now, 'Where does he live?'

'If he is still alive, Great Hallerby, Yorkshire, I suppose. He was a solicitor there when the war began and I know he was planning to go back to his practice. He'll get a shock when I call him.'

'Are you going to?'

'Yes. I'll have to tell him what's going to come out.'

'But, Grandpa, you can't publish this!'

'I want to,' the Field-Marshal said. 'It's been a weight on my mind for many years, not in itself but because I was ashamed to let anyone know that I had once loved another man, for however brief a time. And it didn't affect my command of my Corps. People need to know that. . . . In any case, Henry Bartlett has a copy of this photograph. He'll threaten to publish it if I publish anything about the meeting after Vojja Lovac. I shall refuse to be blackmailed, so he'll publish.'

Yes, he thought, he'd have to go to Yorkshire and talk with Wilfred himself. Wilfred was the only person who knew about Stefanie. He'd have to be made to realise that the truth was going to come out one way or another, and that the important thing was to protect Stefanie. Perhaps they could agree to pretend that their relationship had lasted through the Ancona time, and right up to Vojja Lovac. God, perhaps some people believed it anyway, knowing that Wilfred had always slept in the same place with him – either in the sleeping caravan or occasional farmhouses, or, in Ancona, in the Dower House.

He said, 'There's another reason I must go to see him. He is the man who made the wire recording of the secret meeting in my command caravan after Vojja Lovac, where I was told to leave captured German arms for the Committee of Three partisans to get hold of. He was what people would call a hi-fi fanatic nowadays. He is the one who secreted the recorder there and started it running while I was bringing Henry and Jordan up from the air strip. He had the wire.'

'What?' Caroline cried.

The Field-Marshal nodded. 'Yes. I want a tape copy made of that wire – perhaps two or three. You shall come with me, with the necessary machines, Paul,'

'Don't trust him!' Caroline cried.

'I'm going to,' the Field-Marshal said. 'He'll never trust us, otherwise. . . . When we get back, Paul, you shall pass information to Henry Bartlett that there are no copies, only the original wire, and that Eden has it.'

'What will that do, Grandpa?'

'Bring our opponents into the open, because they will think they have both the evidence against them – the wire – and the evidence against me – the photograph. In fact we will have our artillery – the tape copies of the wire – ranged in and ready to be fired when we wish. And their photograph is no more effective against me than a peashooter against a tank, because I no longer care who knows that I once had a homosexual relationship. They can't understand that.'

Caroline slid her arms round his neck from behind his chair, and her cheek was wet on his. 'Grandpa, you're awful,' she whispered, 'I love you.'

CHAPTER TWENTY-TWO

Just as Lois was about to speak to him, Martin said, 'I see that Senator Jordan is being mentioned as a strong possibility to be appointed Vice-President.' He was reading the *Sunday Journal* in his usual chair in the dining room. 'That'll cause some excitement, if he is finally implicated in the Zvornos Collection business, seeing what the previous chap was forced to resign for.'

'It already has,' Lois said. 'The American ambassador called Daddy yesterday, and asked just what he was going to say and what he could prove about Jordan. The President wants to know. Daddy told him he had no proof of wrong-doing on anyone's part – but there was a mystery and he was still trying to solve it. . . . Martin, what are you going to do, about a job?'

Her husband lowered the *Journal*, and said, 'Keep reading the advertisements until I see something I want. What else can I do?'

'Go out and look,' she said. 'You'll never find anything for someone of your age and experience in the paper. You know plenty of people . . .'

'And if I go near them, they'll suffer,' Martin said bitterly. 'I have a damned good mind to go and offer to fight for the Arabs . . . or the Jews . . . I don't mind which. They have plenty of eager young fellows but they could probably do with an experienced type for the main headquarters or planning staffs. . . . Are you trying to get rid of me?'

'No,' she said, 'I felt like that once . . . that it would be more comfortable for all of us if you weren't living here, but I don't think that now. I used to feel that this was bad and that was good, make judgments all the time on what you were doing, what Caroline was doing. . . . Now I feel more that we're all in the same boat, and that somehow we're all going through the same things, whether they actually happen to us or to someone else in the family.'

'I'll go as soon as I can,' Martin said. 'By the way, tomorrow's your birthday. Forty-nine. Would you like to have lunch at the Lion in Rackleigh with me?'

She hesitated. Martin had not cared about her last ten birthdays, so why was he suddenly showing this interest now? But she ought to accept, as it was an olive branch, but ... I'm sorry,' she said, 'I have an appointment in town.'

'Oh,' he said. He looked up belligerently. 'Are you going to see Charles Gibson?'

Again she hesitated; but the time for lying between them was surely past. She said, 'Yes.'

'I forbid you to see him again,' Martin said, glaring at her. 'He's a ... a bounder. An old-fashioned word, I know, for an old-fashioned idea ... but it's the right word. Your reputation will be mud.'

She wondered whether she should tell him that his daughter had been seeing Charles too; but Caroline should tell him that herself, if she wanted to.

She said, 'We can't forbid each other to do things at this stage, Martin. We've got to make it between us so that I don't want to see – whoever I see – and you don't want to go off to – whoever you go off to – at least only as a change, not as a relief, an outlet for frustrations.'

She got up and went out. In the old day nursery she sat down at her desk and stared out of the window. Poor Martin. He'd definitely been visiting some other woman in the past few months. She wondered idly what sort of a woman it was ... widow? tart? typist looking for stocking money? What did it matter?

But it did because she realised that for all her efforts to emphasise the negative side of their marriage, she did care about Martin, what he felt, what he did, what others, men or women, did to him. And he cared for her ... enough to issue that lordly prohibition from seeing Charles. She should really have accepted the lunch invitation and rung Charles to tell him she couldn't make it.

Business, can't waste time. She pulled out her looseleaf notebook, the tables of quantities, and her menu book. Tuesday, November 13: Locksley-Holdens: banquet for 20, to celebrate the old couple's golden wedding. Wines: champagne, of course, a non-vintage *brut* probably. Red wine: the wine merchant had a special offer on Vosne Romanée this month. She'd have to buy within the next two days. Make a note to do it tomorrow before going up to London. Usual liqueurs: the Locksley-Holdens weren't the ones for anything exotic, in that line ... or any other line ...

Paul's face as he looked at Caroline ... what did that expression mean? Love? Hate? And Caroline's, when she was talking to him? The same. They'd had another fierce quarrel only yesterday, but for all the arguing, they were never far apart. Frankly, she couldn't think what Caroline saw in him. She was sorry for him, perhaps, and felt guilty that anyone should have had such an unfortunate upbringing while she herself had been lapped in comfort and respectability.

Charles tomorrow. After nearly two weeks without going to his studio. She felt an uncomfortable shiver of expectation running down her spine. Good heavens, was she trembling, like a virgin? At the thought of lying in the arms of her lover? It didn't feel sexual, at least not sexually exciting. More like looking over the edge of a cliff.

Locksley-Holdens ... damn the Locksley-Holdens! It was past eleven and Bigelow would be coming with Paul's mother in an hour. Lunch for seven. Tomato soup; lamb chops with frozen broad beans; treacle tart, Daddy's favourite.

Her father was talking: 'Paul and I took the train to Great Hallerby, and got rooms in a small hotel there. Next morning I called on Wilfred in his office.'

'Wouldn't it have bèen better to have gone to his home, Grandpa?' Caroline asked.

The Old Man shook his head. 'I don't think so. He might have been married, and then he'd have had to make explanations to his wife or children, before he'd had time to think.'

Lois glanced up and down the table to see that everyone's glass was full. Madeleine Phillips' face was flushed; she was getting what she probably called tiddly; but the wine was freeing her from inhibitions she had seemed to feel in their company. Bigelow frequently patted her hand, or even held it as it rested on the table. They were a well-matched couple – not exactly gross, or earthy, but living on the same level of appreciation: what one liked, the other would like, in the same way and to the same extent. Paul was watching them, a slight smile half hidden on his face ... of amusement, tolerance, contempt? All three probably.

Her father said, 'We talked. I told him what I was going to do ... had to do. He didn't think it would come as much of a surprise to the people of Great Hallerby – he's been living with another man, about his own age, since 1950.'

'How old is he now?' Caroline asked.

'Sixty-four. ... He urged me to think again about telling the truth, for my own sake. He's been doing legal work on behalf of homosexuals for years. He's always been a homosexual, he told me. I never knew.'

Lois noticed Madeleine shaking her head. First, her husband, then the Field-Marshal, now these two men in Yorkshire ... and the world full of willing women, amateur and professional. What were men coming to?

'I told him that security people would soon came with a warrant and take the wire, but I wanted to make copies first, which he was not to tell anyone about. He laughed, then. ... On the way back through London on Friday I saw Sam Herrick at the Ministry of Defence. He'd heard rumours about this photograph, and begged me to make peace with Henry Bartlett and the government over Zvornos and everything else. Then, he'd been assured, nothing would be published about it. And, of course, the reputation of his bloody North Wessex Regiment would remain secure. I said I was going to publish what I knew. He said it would do great harm to the army's reputation if this came out. It would be a sad scandal, affecting morale. I said I had to do it, because it was true. We have to start from there, and deal with the consequences – not say, "We'd like such and such consequences, now let's see what story will bring them about." That's the way President Nixon operates, and in the end the consequences aren't what you want, but what you've been trying to avoid, or worse ...'

After a long pause, Caroline asked, 'So what did General Herrick say, then?'

'Didn't I tell you? No, I meant to. I told Martin ... and Paul. He said that if it did come out, he'd have to move to disown me as far as the army is concerned, for the good of the service ... ask me to resign my commission, get the Queen to deprive me of my decorations and kick me out of my orders. He knows I've been thinking of doing that on my own account, but would prefer me not to, because it would be thought that I was fed up with the whole system, or had had some disagreement about national policy, which wouldn't be true. I told Sam I hope he doesn't do it either, because my original purpose – one purpose – in writing these Memoirs, is to show that it is not saints, or heroes, or supermen, who become field-marshals, win great battles, get covered in orders and ribbons ... but men, human beings, with failings, weaknesses, vices. If I have a policy to put forward it is that in future people be rewarded for what they do and have done, not for what they are, good or bad.'

'Hear, hear!' Madeleine Phillips cried suddenly in a loud voice. She lifted her glass. 'I drink your health, sir!' She drank and put the glass down heavily. 'Is there any more wine? It's lovely.'

Bigelow said, 'Take it easy now, honey . . .'

'I'm feeling fine, Peter . . . and I want to say something. This is the reason I asked if Petey and I could come down.' Martin had refilled her glass. 'Thanks, ducks. I drink your health, too.' She raised her glass and leaned across the table, her bosom cleavage deep above the bright dress, and waited till Martin had picked up his glass and clinked it with hers. Lois had a sudden certainty, from her look at him, and his shamefaced response, that he had made love to her.

Madeleine said, 'As I was saying, I want to say something . . . that sounds funny, doesn't it? You know, when I first wrote that letter to the editor of the *Journal*, telling them to find out what you got for getting rid of David, I wanted to drag you down the way I was dragged down . . . the way poor Paul there was dragged down, and him just an innocent baby.'

'Take it easy, honey,' Bigelow said, patting her hand.

'When you wanted Paul to come and work for you, it seemed too good to be true. I mean, we'd get to know all the dirt, and use it when the time was ripe. But try as I could, I couldn't keep on hating you, especially when Paul came home, week after week, and told me what you were doing to yourself and your family. I don't know why you're doing it. *I* wouldn't, I can tell you that. And then Petey here told me what a fine gentleman you are. So now, whatever happens, we're your friends, me and Paul, aren't we, Paul?'

'Take it easy, honey.'

'Now that's off my chest, God bless us all! Let's drink to that, eh?' She raised her glass triumphantly.

'Thank you,' the Field-Marshal said. 'Paul has been a great help to me.'

They all drank. As Bigelow put down his glass he said, 'Now it's my turn to make an announcement. I'm sorry to tell you, Marshal, I won't be able to help you with the Memoirs much longer. Papa wants me back home and he's sending someone else over to run this end. I don't know when he'll arrive, but probably inside a couple of weeks, Papa says. I'm real sorry about having to go, and especially about not working with you, Marshal — it's been an honour and a privilege, and I've learned a hell of a lot I never knew before. . . . Before I go I'd like to clear up any loose ends that I can. What's the unfinished business, as far as I am concerned?'

The Field-Marshal said, 'You've done enough for us, Mr Bigelow. I appreciate it very much ... though I'm certainly glad Caroline was in the tree house when she was. The Memoirs would only have been half finished, otherwise.'

'That was a booboo,' Bigelow said, shaking his head. 'I sure as hell bungled that, and I shouldn't have been doing it in the first place.'

Martin said, 'There are a couple of matters where we can't get the proofs we want – the business about the mutiny of 206 R.A.C. and who fired on them, the 35th Dragoons or an American tank regiment. Miss Parmentier hasn't told us anything useful yet. But that's nothing to do with you, really. We still hope to persuade someone to come out with the truth.... And the matter of the Picasso lithographs, which Lady Durham sold. The Yugoslav government have now produced proof that those lithographs were in the Zvornos Collection, at Zvornos Castle, in 1930.'

Bigelow rubbed his chin, where the smooth skin was blue under the layer of talc. 'Interesting. The lithographs were found by a priest in some house in Ancona, weren't they, Marshal?'

'Yes,' the Old Man said briefly.

Martin said, 'It was in a small house called the Dower House, in the grounds of the Villa Grimani. The whole place was empty at the time, except for one old gardener who was caretaking till the family came back.'

'What the hell is the link between Zvornos Castle and this villa place? Might be worth having our boys in Italy check out. ... And we're still interested in getting the names of the guys who own those three numbered accounts in the Glauber Bank, right?' He drummed on the table, staring at the ceiling. 'I'll talk to our Zurich people.... I have to take the little lady back to London soon, Marshal. You did say Paul could come back with us?'

'Yes,' the Old Man said. 'He can have three days off. He's been working very hard.'

Paul said quietly, 'Would you like to come with us, Caroline, if the Field-Marshal can spare you?'

Caroline started, looking first instinctively at her mother. The Old Man said, 'She can have three days off, too.'

Lois said, 'Do you want to go, Caroline?'

'Caroline turned to Paul. He's challenging her, Lois thought – come and live my life for a while, and you'll understand why I am what I am and do what I do. But should she, Lois, permit it?'

'Don't you worry, dearie,' Madeleine said, 'I'll look after her.'

Fat lot of good that'll do, Lois thought; but Caroline was speaking: 'I'll come.'

Charles was wearing moccasins and a paint-spattered shirt hanging outside his blue jeans when she reached his studio the following morning. His easel was set up in the usual place and as soon as he had opened the door for her went back to it, picked up his brushes, and said, 'Make yourself at home, sweetie pie. You know where everything is.'

She took off her coat and walked over to stand a little behind him. The portrait on which he was working was a full-length oil of a young man in black tights and doublet, holding a skull in his hand, the traditional dress and pose of Hamlet.

The portrait was only blocked in against a lowering background lit by shafts of sunlight, and two birds on a rock. She could not tell what the birds were supposed to be, but she was sure she would recognise the face when Charles had done some more work on it.

'Clive,' he said briefly, seeming to sense her thoughts.

'My . . . our Clive?'

Charles nodded. 'He came in here a couple of weeks ago with a damned great pistol. He was going to shoot me, to wipe out the stain on his escutcheon.'

'Oh God!' Lois said, 'because of . . . ?'

'No, because of your recent visits. . . . Forget it. Clive was playing a part. I persuaded him, without much difficulty and with the help of a little flattery, not to carry it through. That's where he'd be dangerous – he's always living a part.'

'That's what Caroline says,' Lois said, half to herself. 'She says he's always been like that. Why haven't I noticed?'

'Caroline should know. . . . There – that's all I can do till he comes back for another sitting. . . . You're looking worried. About Clive?'

She said nothing; she didn't know. She was looking past him, past the painting on the easel. The nude she had seen before was propped against the wall now and suddenly the girl's face leaped out at her . . . Caroline. He had completed it since her last visit.

Charles had followed the direction of her look. 'She's beautiful, you know,' he said.

I was never as lovely as that, Lois thought. I had the bloom of youth once, of course, but never those long gently curved lines, the firm grace of a Diana; and because she was naked the eye wasn't distracted from her graceful femaleness by her granny dresses, men's marching boots, or the other affectations of her time.

Charles's hands were round her shoulders, turning her to him. One hand slipped round to cup her breast. 'Take them off,' he whispered in her ear. 'The wine is red in the glass.' She felt herself relaxing into acceptance. So often he had approached her like this, so often had she responded to the gentle expert guidance. And today was the anniversary of the first time – her eighteenth birthday, the searchlight fingers stabbing the night sky and the distant crash of bombs as a German raid hit somewhere on the southern edge of the outskirts of the city ... his hand on her breasts, just like this, her breath coming fast and shallow, the feeling of absolute surrender.

With a giant effort she found strength in her legs and stood away from him. 'It's over, Charles,' she said. 'That's what I came to tell you.'

'Again?'

'It's over. I came back to you from need, not love. You know that. Now I don't need you any more.'

'So you're throwing me out.'

'You're not one to be able to complain about that. Besides, there will be plenty more, younger, and better for you in every way. . . . Though you will lose Caroline soon, I think.'

'If I ever had her,' he said. 'She's as self-contained as you have been the opposite. Have some sherry.'

'Thanks.'

He took off his paint-spattered shirt and shrugged into a clean blue one. 'We'll go out soon. . . . Did you see the government statement in the papers about how the Committee of Three partisans got their weapons at the end of the war?'

'No. I didn't read the paper this morning. I was thinking of what I would say to you.'

'Well, you know there's been a National Freedom Movement group of Yugoslav exiles operating mostly from Italy, ever since the Committee of Three got power. They've been saying all along that the British and American governments, acting through Jordan, Bartlett and the Old Man, deliberately gave arms and tanks to the Committee of Three, their rivals. Today the government formally denied the charges. They repeat the old story, that the captured German war material was left on the field of Vojja Lovac because of military necessity. . . . Any idea why they would publish that, again, at this time, when there have been rumours to the contrary?'

'Yes,' she said. 'They think they've destroyed the only evidence of the truth – a wire recording that was made, secretly, by one of Daddy's staff officers.'

'And they haven't? A copy exists?' He laughed. 'The Old Man may be eighty, but his hand has not lost its cunning. I suppose they're trying to help Jordan get the Vice Presidency. There'd be a fearful outcry over there, even at this late date, if it were known that he had helped Communists destroy anti-communist opposition. . . . Have you heard the other rumour going round about the Old Man?'

'I've heard nothing, but I imagine it's about him having had a love affair with his A.D.C.'

'He's let that cat out of the bag at home, has he? I've been waiting, ever since he started writing the Memoirs, to see whether he'd bring it up.'

'He might not have if you hadn't sent Paul the negative of the picture you took,' she said.

Charles's face altered abruptly, his lips drawing back in an instinctive snarl. Then he recovered himself, and the snarl became the familiar elfin grin. 'And I suppose you think he's furious with me for doing such a despicable thing?'

She shook her head, 'I would have been, but Daddy says he's relieved you did. He'll forgive you anything. I have never understood it.'

'How did you know I took the photo?'

'Caroline noticed what looked like the shadow of a man's head on the rocks to one side, very faint and hard to make out. She thought it must be you because you were the only person who'd send the negative to Paul. She looked at the album of your war art that we have, and saw that the date was all right – you were in Italy at that time . . . and we both agreed that Daddy wouldn't let anyone else take that photograph – it had to be either himself, Eden, or you. And I suppose he lied to protect you.'

'Very clever,' he said. 'That daughter of yours is going to be a public menace – that body—' he nodded at the nude '—and those brains. . . . I went overseas for the second time in June forty-four, to the Old Man's Corps in Italy.'

Leaving me pregnant, Lois thought; though I wasn't sure of it till August – about the time of her father's excursion to the sandy beach by Porto d'Ascoli.

Charles continued, 'I'd been with him when he was commanding the 8th Division in the Western Desert, and of course seen a lot of him when we were both in London in forty-two. When I got out to Italy I found he'd changed. Not outwardly – inwardly. I'm a painter, a portraitist, and a damned good one, and I could tell. The poor bugger was getting desperate for someone on whom he could release some emotion, some faculty other than his power of command ... someone who represented a holiday from his sense of responsibility. Eden was close, efficient, compatible and a homosexual, though he never showed a trace of it to anyone else. No one else even remotely suspected, because the only John Durham they met was the other – the powerful eye, the strong sure mind, the cold true vision. What I saw, wanting to paint him, was the warmth of affection in his look at Eden. I don't think anyone else noticed. Did Martin suspect at all?'

'He wouldn't have told me if he did ... but I'm sure he didn't.'

Charles said, 'I went back to England in mid-September ... to find a Dear John letter from you telling me you'd fallen in love with someone else. Why didn't you tell me the truth?'

'It wouldn't have helped,' she said. 'You wouldn't have married me. By then, I didn't want to marry you. Or any man, perhaps.'

Charles said, 'Poor Martin ... I went overseas once more, in March, forty-five, and joined the Old Man a month before Vojja Lovac. He had changed again. Eden was still there, but he no longer needed him. He wasn't desperate any more. Sated I suppose, or feeling guilty.'

Or, Lois thought, Caroline is right and something happened in those three months in Ancona when he was preparing for the invasion of the Balkans. Her daughter had raised the possibility while they were looking at the photograph and discussing the strange shadow. But they had agreed that it would be wiser to say nothing. If the Old Man wanted to tell them, he would; if he didn't, they knew by now that he would have good reasons.

'Shall we go to lunch?' Charles said.

Lois shook her head. 'Thanks all the same, Charles, I want to go home.'

CHAPTER TWENTY-THREE

Peter Belprato, as he always thought of himself, whatever other name circumstances might compel him to use from time to time, glanced at his watch and saw that it was eleven o'clock. Good time. He returned to his reverie . . . there was something fishy about those Picasso lithographs being at this villa in Ancona months before the paintings were taken from Zvornos Castle. Suppose the Count had owned the villa? Lots of rich foreigners liked to have a place in Italy. It would need looking into, and might be a better lead than the action already taken in Switzerland. Rudolf Glauber, the owner of the bank, and his son Willi were prisoners now, and sooner or later they'd give the information the old Marshal wanted. That was all that interested *him* – who had arranged the theft. He wasn't at all interested in finding the paintings, in fact seemed to have been discouraging any more efforts in that direction. But to him, Peter Belprato, the whereabouts of what was left of the Collection was much more interesting than who'd been paid off to enable it to be stolen, and that twenty-eight years ago. There was money there, a lot of money.

'This it?' the driver asked.

Belprato looked up, and said, 'Yeah.' This was the place. The car glided to a stop and Belprato lit a cigar. The name GOLDEN GOOSE was set up in metal gilt letters across the front of the building. It was three stories high, brick, with white-painted window sills and neon lighting for night display. Big parking lot – room for maybe two hundred cars. He could see the river behind, gliding past the right side of the building. There'd be a lot of overhead here and a big organisation to run the place. The owner would be a man you could reason with.

When he had got out of the car he said, 'Just wait here, boys. I don't expect to be long.'

'Don't you want one of us to come in with you, or at least be where we can hear if you call?'

Belprato shook his head – 'It's not going to be like that . . . not today.'

He walked in. The doorman was dressed as a Hungarian gipsy. 'Where's the boss's office?' he asked.

'Major Langford? Down there, second door on the right, sir.'

He nodded and strolled down the passage indicated. The door had no marking and he knocked once, then opened it. He was in an outer office, obviously the secretary's. Through another door opposite, also unmarked, he heard someone talking, probably on the telephone. He walked across, knocked on that door and, again without waiting, walked in.

The man at the telephone was about sixty, partly bald, dressed like those guys you saw in Piccadilly and St James's, well-cut suit, tie with stripes on it, gold cufflinks. This one, who was glancing up at him as he spoke, had a monocle dangling on a broad silk ribbon from his buttonhole. After a few more words, he put down the telephone and smiled at Belprato, rising to his feet, his hand coming out. 'I don't think I've had . . .'

'Peter Belprato,' Belprato said. It was no use telling this guy he was called Bigelow – it would mean nothing to him. 'I'm connected with the people who own the Essex Club, on Cadwallader Street.'

'Oh,' the other said. 'Sit down.' His eyes had grown wary. He knows, Belprato saw. He's been in the business a long time, and he knows his way around. They'll have girls upstairs . . . very discreet girls. And a guy will be able to get a room any time. Gambling maybe, at times, and for very special customers. The office looked out across a green lawn sloping down to the Thames a hundred feet away. To the right a few people were sitting in a glass-enclosed patio, drinking cocktails.

'I do apologise that my secretary isn't here,' Langford said. 'We keep the place open Saturdays and Sundays all the year round, but not the secretarial staff. . . . What can I do for you, Mr Belprato?' He picked up his monocle and stuck it in his right eye.

Peter surveyed him without expression. Looked a lot more la-di-da than he was. He'd fought in the war, killed guys. Not face to face – but at a mile, in a tank. Still, it wouldn't do to write him off as a Limey fag.

He said, 'What I've come about has nothing to do with your business here, and I hope it never will.'

Langford looked puzzled, but still wary.

Peter said, 'On March 20, 1945, you were a major in a tank outfit called . . .' he fished a notebook out of his pocket, looked in it, and ended '. . . the 35th Dragoons. In the Balkans.' He looked up. 'Is that correct?'

Langford said. 'Yes.' He still looked puzzled, but there was a dawning of awareness behind his eyes.

Peter continued. 'On orders from General Durham, you ordered your outfit to fire on another British tank outfit – the 206th R.A.C. . . . because some of them had mutinied and were heading for the rear.'

He looked up again. By now Langford understood. He said, 'The orders were not given by me, but by my C.O. – Lieutenant-Colonel Burke. He was killed a few moments later. I didn't change the orders.'

'O.K., Burke gave the order. But you were there? Right?'

Langford said at last, 'Yes. I was there.'

'You saw the action? You saw your tanks firing on the others . . . the 206 R.A.C.? And when they'd surrendered, what was left of them, your Dragoons stopped firing.'

'Yes.'

Peter leaned back. 'That's all, major. Just write that down, bring in one of your staff to witness your signature, and give it to me. Put in the place and the approximate time where this happened, as well as the date.'

Langford stood up and walked toward the window. He put his hands behind his back – and spoke still with his back to Peter. 'I'd like to help you, Mr Belprato . . . but you realise I am under considerable pressure from other quarters.'

'To keep your mouth shut? I know.'

'It's very difficult. These people – the others – can make things most awkward for us. It only takes a couple of police raids, however unjustified – and even if they find nothing – to ruin a business like mine.'

'Yeah.'

He waited, pulling carefully on the big cigar. Sure, police raids were bad for business; but nothing like as bad as having a few customers beaten up, food delivery vans vanish a couple of times, or maybe have an incendiary bomb go off in the bar. With some guys it would have been necessary to explain these things; but not with this glass-eyed operator.

Langford turned, sat quickly at his desk, and began to write. After a time he rang a bell; a waiter came in and Langford said, 'Witness my signature, please, Henri. . . . Sign there.'

'Certainly, sir. Thank you, sir.' He backed out, bowing.

Langford handed over the paper. Belprato read it carefully. It was O.K. He folded it carefully, put it away and pulled out his cigar case. He offered it to Langford. Langford took one, hesitatingly, and Belprato lit it for him.

He stood up. 'Any time you visit the Essex Club, ask for Johnny. Tell him Peter sent you. We'll look after you.'

'Thank you,' Langford said. 'That's very good of you.'

Belprato waved away the thanks with a glint of gold and gems in the electric light. 'I must be going back now,' he said. 'And, major, one thing . . . just leave this thing lay, eh? There's no need to tell anyone I came, or that you signed this paper. . . . And you wouldn't want to say at any time that you were threatened into writing this paper, because then people would be able to say, what he wrote isn't true, he was forced to write it, like in those Commie trials where everyone confesses to everything, eh? We don't want that to happen, because what you wrote *is* true . . . *isn't it*?' he barked suddenly.

'Yes,' Langford said, jumping.

As the car hurried through the bare Wiltshire downland, Belprato was thinking . . . perhaps a link could be found between the owners of the numbered accounts and the whereabouts of the remaining Zvornos paintings. Suppose one of them turned out to be this guy Bartlett, for instance. You could go to him and ask him, with suitable inducements to help him remember, what exactly Count Zvornos had told him about his subsequent plans. Of course Zvornos might have sworn he was going to hand the paintings to some government agency, like this Civil Affairs setup they talked about, to look after till their eventual ownership could be decided . . . but up to that point the Count himself was the only legal owner. Still, it was a line, that and sniffing around Ancona. He ought to find out first whether anyone still lived in the Villa Grimani, and if so whether they were the same people who had had it in 1944–45.

'This it?' the driver asked. Bigelow motioned him to pull up. This was quite a different sort of joint, and there'd be a different sort of guy living in it. The name was Maybourne Court, but it wasn't written up anywhere, not in conspicuous letters of gold nor in small letters of wrought iron, nor in any other way. Here, you were supposed to know that it was Maybourne Court, the home of Lieutenant-Colonel George Cunningham, and, here, you probably did. The drive stretched away up a slight rise, topped by the big square house . . . grey stone, big windows, not little ones with lots of lead in, and not the old twisty chimneys and none of those bits of wood let in that people went crazy about; but old, and massive, and rich.

'O.K.,' he said, 'let's go.'

The Rover crunched to a stop outside the front door and Bigelow got out. There was a bell and he rang it. After a time he heard footsteps from inside and the door opened. A short man in shirt sleeves and an apron was looking up at him.

'Is Lieutenant-Colonel Cunningham in?' he said pleasantly.

'Yes, sir. He's in the study. What name shall I give?'

Peter handed the man a card, on which was printed *Mr Stephen Otis Askew, 300 Park Avenue, New York, N.Y. 10017: Dealer in Fine Arts*; with a telephone number. All the information was fictitious, and of the type that could be checked up in a moment; but, in this particular case, and for his present purpose, it would do.

The servant came back. 'This way, sir.' As he led him along the passage, Peter glanced at the paintings hung on either side. He'd have to get to the point quickly, or this guy would ask him questions about art; and he'd very quickly be found out.

The man who rose from the big desk by the window was six feet, more heavily built than Langford, about the same age, quite bald and shiny on top with grey hair above his ears, and prominent blue eyes. He was wearing a tweed suit and another striped tie, but with different stripes. He stooped slightly and he didn't have a monocle hanging on a ribbon; only a pair of glasses, left on the desk, showed that he used them to read with.

'Mr Askew?' he said.

'Colonel Cunningham?' Peter said. He shook the other's hand heartily.

Cunningham was holding his card in his hand, and was now looking at it shortsightedly. 'You are an art dealer, Mr Askew?'

'Yes, sir.'

'From New York, I see. I am amazed that you knew so soon of my intentions.'

What the hell is this, Peter said to himself. 'In our business, one has to keep an ear close to the ground,' he said, playing for time.

'I only spoke to Mr Benoliel three days ago – last Friday, to be precise.'

Peter understood then. By coincidence, Cunningham had decided to put some of his pictures on the market. That made it a little easier, because he had called himself an art dealer and it might be useful to know that Cunningham needed money; but for the moment the quicker he could get to business, the better.

He leaned forward. 'Colonel, I'm not here about art. I'm here to get a written statement from you about what happened to your tank outfit when it mutinied in the Balkans in 1945.'

Cunningham stiffened and took a half step back. 'What . . . ?' he began. 'Do you mean to say . . . ?'

Peter said, 'I mean just what I say. You sit down there at your desk and write.' He sprang suddenly forward and seized the other by the throat. From his pocket he produced a gag and whipped it tight round Cunningham's head and in his mouth. Cunningham struggled but a heavy blow on the ear from Peter's fist sent him reeling. Peter locked the door behind him and pushed and pulled the reeling Cunningham to his desk.

'Now,' he said, fitting on his knuckle duster, 'write . . . or else.'

The man was a dull shade of grey and he thought, I've seen that before, on a guy with heart trouble. He eased the gag a little and said, 'Now, I don't want you to drop dead from over exertion, and I guess you don't want to, either . . . so do what I am telling you. It's only the truth I want.'

He took the pen Cunningham had been writing with, swept the papers and account books to one side, and set out a clean sheet of paper. 'I know what happened,' he said, 'I want you to confirm it.'

He waited. The man seemed to be in a state of shock. Things like this didn't happen to the landed gents of England. A clock struck and he thought, can't stay here all day. He gauged his blow carefully and hit Cunningham hard on the same ear. His head jerked over and a strangled gasp escaped from inside the gag.

'Write!' Peter said, more sharply, but the voice still soft. No one passing by should hear voices raised in anger.

Cunningham began to write. When he had finished, Peter read it. This was the truth. B Squadron of 206 R.A.C. had mutinied and driven toward the rear. Cunningham, then their commanding officer, had followed them with his adjutant and three other tanks. He had come up in time to see the leading tank run over and kill an officer from 35th Dragoons; and he'd seen the rest of 35th Dragoons firing into B Squadron, causing three tanks to burn. Twelve men were killed. He took the surrender of the rest personally. The whole affair was over before he saw any American tanks.

Peter adjusted the gag, took the length of thin strong rope from round his waist under his jacket, and tied Cunningham firmly to the desk. It was very heavy. Finally he raised his fist and said, 'Don't try anything too soon, Colonel.'

He took off the knuckle duster. Cunningham was watching him, the blue eyes watering, one bloodshot, his cheek cut and bruised. He's still in shock, Peter thought, and perhaps his heart was hurting and he was scared. He'd better not die though, that would complicate things a lot.

'Take it easy,' he said, 'you'll be free soon enough.'

He slipped out, saying conversationally over his shoulder, 'Don't bother, Colonel, I can find my way.' He closed the door carefully behind him. No sign of the servant. Less than thirty seconds later he was bowling down the drive and out of the unguarded gates. Five minutes after that the Rover's number plates had been changed; three hours after that he was passing through the flight search routines at Heathrow Airport, tickets for two on an Alitalia flight to Milan in his hand, and Madeleine Phillips, ecstatic in a new mink coat, hanging on his arm.

Peter lit another cigar and said, 'So when did you start working on him?'

'Last night,' the shorter of the two men said, 'as soon as they phoned that you'd reached Milan O.K. Nothing serious, just roughing him up a little, using the rubber. Also, we ain't fed him.'

Peter looked musingly at the newspaper. Screaming black headlines still covered the front page, with pictures of a large building, a house by some water, and two men – one middle-aged and one young. Peter couldn't understand German, but it didn't need that to read the names GLAUBER prominently repeated in the headlines and subheads. Of course, everyone thought they'd been kidnapped for ransom. He looked more carefully at the portraits. The older man must be Rudolf, the owner. He might be a tough nut. He had a hard face, direct eyes, straight determined mouth, and he looked very fit. He sure as hell didn't resemble any banker he'd met in New York.

'He's a mountain climber,' the short man said, 'or was. He's fifty-six now. Those guys are all nuts, if you ask me.'

Peter grunted. Nuts, maybe; but the sort of obstinate nuts

that made life difficult – because they wouldn't see reason and they were used to pain.

The short man said, 'The kid's eighteen ... a bit sissified, like he eats too much and don't run around any more than he has to.'

Peter grunted again. Judging from the portrait, Willi would be easier to work with than old Rudolf – but Willi wouldn't know the bank numbers and couldn't get them. No way.

'They've been here three days,' the short man said. 'We got 'em when they were going off on a trip to some mountain cabin together, so no one raised the alarm for over six hours ...'

'Who's been working on him?'

'This guy they sent from Milan. I don't know what his name is. I call him Fat Boy, because he's so thin, see?' He laughed heartily.

'Yeah,' Peter said. He looked the thin man up and down.

'He don't understand English,' the short man said. 'Only Italian, I guess. Or maybe he's dumb.'

Peter spoke a short phrase in his Sicilian dialect. The thin man nodded and answered. Peter said, 'He's not dumb.'

'They haven't seen either of our faces,' the short man said. 'They haven't seen me at all, after we nabbed them. Fat Boy has been working on them, like I said, and he's wearing a hood. I'll have to spell him now.'

'O.K.,' Peter said. 'You told them you'd start on 'em again at eleven, didn't you?'

'Yeah.'

'It's eleven. Get going.'

He rummaged about in the drawer, pulled out the pack of cards he'd stowed there earlier, and began to play patience.

The short man poured Peter a glass of the Italian brandy on the table, and another for himself. The wall clock showed eight. The man was sweating and looked tired.

'Son of a bitch is tough,' he said. 'Jeezus, this stuff is god awful. Why don't we get us some bourbon?'

'Buying bourbon's too risky, here. And disposing of the bottles. They're conspicuous.'

'I know. .... We're getting to them, I can see, but it'll take more time. Do you want us to go on all night?'

Peter shook his head. Jeezus, the short guy was right. The brandy tasted like mouldy old socks. He said, 'Leave them under the light. No sleep. One of you watching to prod 'em awake. And some time like five or six, when it gets light, start in hard on the kid. Don't do anything to the father. Just make him watch.'

'That's it! He loves that boy. The only one. He'll talk before breakfast, I guarantee it.'

'O.K. One of you get some sleep and the other go get back in there.'

Alone, he gulped down the rest of his brandy with a grimace. Rudolf Glauber would break down soon. Obviously he couldn't just tell them the names of the three account holders, because he couldn't possibly have the names of all the bank's clients in his head. So he'd be taken to the centre of Milan, and left blindfolded, gagged and tied in a car there at three in the morning. Someone would soon find him and he'd be released. Then he'd go back to Zurich and find the wanted names. Peter would call him from a public phone box in Milan at exactly noon the day after that. If he didn't give the names instantly, he'd never see his son Willi again; and in any case Willi would be kept prisoner in this house on the outskirts of Milan until the names had been checked out, and Peter was safely back in New York, where his alibi was even now being established, in case of need. He got out his wallet and checked again that he had the three account numbers which he would give Glauber when the latter agreed to do what he was told.

Half past eight. Time to go out and get a meal. The papers seemed to think that the Glaubers were still in Switzerland. Not surprising, really, for the police there believed that the kidnapping had taken place at two in the morning, not at eight the previous evening, as it actually had. By the time they'd issued orders to search all vehicles leaving Switzerland, the trussed and gagged Glaubers were already over the border.

He stubbed out his cigar. The telephone rang and he surveyed it dispassionately. After six rings, it stopped. He waited. Exactly one minute later, it rang again. After three rings, it stopped. Exactly one minute later it rang again. He picked it up.

The voice at the other end said, 'Pietro?'

'Yeah.'

'You've got to quit what you're doing.'

'What do you mean? Someone on to us?'

'No. Your papa phoned five minutes back. He said, quit. We're getting out of the picture business, altogether, finally, he said. So quit, cold turkey.'

'There's a lot of money round the corner here.'

'D'you think Papa don't know? He says quit, and he says he don't want to hear no arguing.'

The man at the other end hung up. Peter leaned back, scratching his chin. Papa was getting out of the art business; the only art the family was into was this Zvornos deal. So what Papa was saying was, we're quitting on the Zvornos deal. Why? He might have been offered a lot of money to get out, and reckoned that a bird in the hand was worth a whole flock in the bush. And if he'd promised, he'd keep his word. Papa Belprato's word was as good as anyone else's signed cheque. Or he might have been threatened – not directly – just, keep your nose out of this business, or I'll make things rough for you. There weren't a whole lot of people who could say that to Papa and make it stick . . . the Governor, the Mayor and the Police Commissioner of the City, one or two men in Washington . . . Matt Jordan, for instance. Sighing, he got up and went to wash his hands. As far as he was concerned, the Zvornos affair was over. Pietro Belprato did not intend to finish up inside another refrigerator, in the East River. Madeleine was too good a lay, for one thing.

CHAPTER TWENTY-FOUR

The typescript was headed *Honesty is not a policy . . . it's a fact*. It was beautifully typed, not a mistake or erasion in it. Martin had watched Dick Armstrong working on it the evening before, his fingers going like a pianist's, fast and light, the blind head swinging slightly, rocking from side to side, as though it were indeed music, not words on paper, coming out, and he could hear it. Martin read it through again. It always paid to read Dick's pieces at least twice; not that you didn't understand very plainly the first time, but the second and third times you became aware of subtleties and humours, of shafts of wit and insight, that you had missed in your eagerness the first time. It would be a powerful column when it appeared in its usual place in the *Journal* tomorrow . . . a powerful defence of truth as an abstract necessity, keyed to what the public had heard, was hearing, and would hear about Field-Marshal Sir John Durham. Dick didn't attack those who wanted parts of the Memoirs suppressed; he pointed out with compelling logic that truth could not in fact be suppressed and that incalculable human harm was done where the attempt was made, and tainted situations allowed to fester until a plain breath of fresh air was not enough to heal the ulcer. And, he wrote, there is the fatal consequence of basing norms of behaviour on what we would know are not norms, if we knew the truth.

He rested the paper. It was hard to believe that Dick could not see. There he sat, by the window, for all the world as though he were looking out. It was an autumnal day, the air misty, smoke from leaf bonfires hanging in the far corner of the damp lawn, the bare-armed trees reaching over the wall. Martin could have sworn that his friend was enjoying the autumnal calm of the scene. Perhaps he was. He had had his sight until he was twenty-six. He had known the seasons, and in that great brain could recall in its totality the experience of them.

Dick swung half round, 'Finished? How do you like it?'

'Wonderful. I don't know if it will make Bartlett and the government get off the Old Man's back, but it certainly should.'

'I'll take that copy up when I see Tim Hopwood this afternoon.'

'Do you know what he wants to talk to you about?'

'I have a good idea. He's going to offer me a seat if I'll stand as a Liberal.'

Martin thought, that's great news! Tim Hopwood was the leader of the Liberal Party. The party was not large enough to form a government, and it would probably not be by the next election; but by the one after that, and with Dick providing the drive and the brains to make it go fast in the right direction. . . .

He jumped out of his chair. 'Marvellous, Dick!' His excitement wavered. 'But are you a Liberal?'

'Near enough,' Dick said, smiling up at him. 'As I told you, it doesn't matter what colour coat you wear, as long as it does not conceal the true colour of your skin. Unless Hopwood has some strings attached, I'll accept.'

'Make sure it's a safe Liberal seat,' Martin said, his sense of excitement returning. 'You're not old, but you're not young enough to spend twenty years fighting in a constituency that's going to vote Tory or Socialist till the crack of doom.'

'I will,' Dick said. 'I have an idea which seat he has in mind, as a matter of fact. I'll let you know, of course, when I come back tonight. And on Monday I'll probably have to go back to Bude, and sell or lease my house.'

'Don't sell it, for God's sake.'

'I'd like to keep it, if I can. And I've got to find a place in London, close to Parliament. I'll have to know the tube system a lot better than I do . . . and the bus routes . . .'

Martin said, 'You're going to need a driver. A secretary. Someone to see for you.' He felt himself on the edge of a great cliff, seagulls wheeling, the sea a permanent blue far below rippled by waves, the horizon far. He said, 'Take me, Dick. Let me be your eyes. I don't have much money, just my proportionate pension from the Indian Army, and my government pension – but it will help, won't it? I don't know what the *Journal* and ITV are paying you . . .'

He realised that he was gabbling on, while Dick Armstrong sat in his chair, half smiling. 'I was wondering when you'd get round to it,' he said. 'Yes, I'd love to have you. We'll work together.'

Martin leaped forward, hand outstretched. Dick was on his feet. They shook hands and embraced, hugging each other and laughing with delight.

Caroline's voice behind him made Martin jump, though he

realised at once that Dick was not surprised; he had heard her steps on the carpet. 'What *are* you doing, Daddy? Are you and Mr Armstrong. . . . ? It is Dick Armstrong, isn't it? I've seen you on the telly.'

Dick Armstrong laughed, a deep strong laugh, his arm went round Caroline's shoulder and he kissed her on the cheek. Still laughing, he said, 'No, we are not like that. We've just concluded a pact, though.' He told her briefly of their plans.

'That's wonderful!' Caroline exclaimed, and then immediately, 'And I've come down to tell you that Paul and I have made a pact too. We're going to live together and be interpretive journalists. Mr Mullins has promised us he'll give us a trial.'

'What kind of things do you want to do?' Dick asked.

'Oh, publish the truth. Working on Grandpa's Memoirs made me think of it. We'll take some case, some event, some programme, that's important to everyone, and find out what's really happening, not what's supposed to be happening.'

'Muckraking journalism, it's sometimes called,' Dick murmured. 'As necessary as muckraking in a farmyard.'

'I have a lot of contacts,' Caroline said, 'and Paul's good at asking the right questions.'

'And looking in other people's desks,' Martin said sourly.

His daughter said, 'We'll have to do things like that and worse, if we're going to find the truth. I've learned how many liars there are in the world . . . and why.'

'Where are you going to live?'

'In his mother's flat. You know she's gone to America with Mr Bigelow? She phoned Paul from New York last night – twenty-five minutes! He must be rolling in money.'

'There's a good place for you to start,' Martin said. 'The Essex Club – where the money comes from, where it's supposed to go, where it actually goes. But be careful.'

'The Essex Club's an idea,' Caroline said, 'but I doubt whether that sort of gambling club is of importance to many people – only the fringes of the bourgeoisie.'

Dick began to laugh again and said, 'I trust you're not going to do anything so bourgeois as marry this young man?'

'No,' Caroline said. 'I'm not sure we like each other well enough for that, though we have a good sexual adjustment . . . which I didn't honestly expect.'

'Must you talk like this?' Martin said, rather aggrieved that Dick had brought up the subject of marriage. Surely it could have been left unsaid; or perhaps Lois should have talked to the girl about it.

Caroline said firmly, 'Yes, I must, Daddy. Grandpa's taught me.'

'How much is Mullins going to pay you?'

Caroline said, 'Well, nothing actually ... only standard rates when he accepts something.'

'If he ever does.'

'He'll jolly well have to. ... And I'm going to do some modelling for Paul.'

Martin was outraged. 'You're going to pose for those porno pictures he was making when Grandpa gave him the job? I absolutely forbid it. What would happen to me if any of my friends in the Rag or the Cavalry recognised you?'

Dick was laughing again. 'It would mean that your friends in the Rag or the Cavalry had bought some porno pictures,' he said.

Caroline said, 'If I pose for anything that you'd call pornographic it won't be about sex, it will be about love, and how men and women express it. ... But at first at least we're going to do plain nudes and he's going to study fashion photography. There's a lot in that if you can do it for the right people – not for the *Vogue* crowd, but for people like us, young people with not much money. ... Where's Grandpa? I've got to tell him. And Mummy, I suppose.'

'Definitely,' Martin said. 'They're down in the village. They'll be back any minute. I hope you're staying to dinner?'

'I'm staying till Monday,' she said. 'Paul's getting the front room ready for us to work in. And buying the sort of food we're going to eat. Spaghetti. Hamburgers. Hot dogs. Lasagna. Chianti.'

'Ah, love's young digestion,' Dick said dreamily. 'But please don't put on more than five pounds, Caroline. You look very beautiful as you are ... and the nudes won't look so good either, still less the fashions.'

She stared at him a moment and Martin knew she was thinking – but you can't see me, how do you know? Then she understood that he saw her and appreciated her through other senses. She leaned forward and kissed him on the cheek.

The Field-Marshal, from the door, said, 'I knew you'd fall for him as soon as you met him, Caroline. ... But be careful, Dick, she's not really only twenty-one, but ageless.'

Dick said, 'She is older than the rocks among which she

279

sits; like the vampire she has been dead many times, and learned the secrets of the grave; and has been a diver in deep seas, and keeps their fallen day about her; and trafficked for strange webs with Eastern merchants; and, as Leda, was the mother of Helen of Troy . . .'

'What on earth . . . ?'

'Walter Pater; on the Mona Lisa.'

'I've never seen the Mona Lisa,' the Old Man said. 'Drink time, I think. Caroline, get me a whisky, please. . . . I can't say I'm very interested in paintings.' He sank carefully into his usual chair. 'I'm really relieved we've been stymied in the Zvornos matter. I'd still like to know who made that coup possible, but I suppose we never will now.'

Caroline gave him a drink, saying, 'What do you think can have made Mr Bigelow give up . . . go out of the art business, he said in his cable, didn't he?'

'The same that makes all things happen, or stop happening,' the Old Man said. 'Pressure. Like the pressure that made George Cunningham at first refuse to talk about the mutiny of 206 R.A.C., and then the greater pressure, applied by Bigelow, that changed his mind.' He began to laugh. 'I had the devil of a job making Cunningham believe that Bigelow had acted without my knowledge. Do you think he did the same to Langford?'

'Probably didn't have to,' Dick said. 'Langford's in the catering business, in the wider sense of the word. He's vulnerable. . . . Sir, I'm going to run that tape you gave me, on my next TV broadcast – Tuesday night.'

'The thirteenth? It's the tenth today. Good. That'll make them sit up.'

'The Vojja Lovac conference tape?' Martin asked.

'Yes.'

Dick said, 'The U.S. Senate is voting on the nomination of Jordan as Vice-President on the fifteenth. That'll put him out.'

'And take Bartlett out of the New Year's Honours List, where I hear he's at present down for a Life Peerage,' Martin said. 'Incidentally, Charles Gibson is strongly rumoured to be in for a K.'

'Good, good!' the Old Man said. 'It's overdue to him, as a painter, but Charles has never cared enough for the conventions to please the politicians.'

Caroline said seriously, 'Grandpa, don't you realise that

Charles Gibson is not your friend? He's your enemy.'

'What makes you think that?' the Old Man said, sipping, the blue eyes narrowed under the beetling white brows.

'He told Grandma to sell the Picassos . . . and then lied to you about it. He knew all the time they'd been sold. He knew Grandma had spent the money on Madame Olga. Everything he has learned from you, that might harm you, he has passed on to people like Henry Bartlett. Even if it's only gossip, he passes it on as a fact. It was he who sent that photograph to Paul. I'm sure he knew who Belprato was, all the time. He's . . . I never thought I'd use the word, but it's the right one . . . he's wicked.'

The Old Man in the chair swirled the whisky slowly round in the glass. He said, 'You're almost right, Caroline. He's wicked. But he's my friend, and more than a friend, and always will be – because he's me. As soon as I met him, I felt drawn to him. At first I couldn't think why. Then, as I got to know him better I saw that he was a negative of me, like that colour reversal film they make colour prints out of . . . where the blue in the print is yellow in the negative. My curse is responsibility. It is a drug. I crave it, and every moment of every day, since I was six years old, have longed to be able to get rid of it, to kick the habit, you say, don't you? Charles is exactly the opposite. His drug is irresponsibility. If he can do something that will have an effect, especially an interesting one – he does it. He doesn't care a damn what the outcome is, even if it works against him . . . just so long as the thing gets done, the banana peel put down, the opportunity for adultery taken, the tale told, the seduction done. Then he enjoys the results . . . fights with husbands, pregnancies, suicides, abandonments, damage suits, resignations. How often I've prayed that I could do something like that, just once.

'I know what Charles has been to you all——' he looked slowly round, the faded eagle eyes resting on each of them in turn '——but you don't know what he has been to me. My life would have been different without him. Sometimes for the better, sometimes for the worse. It makes no difference which. He's my Siamese twin, the reverse of my medal . . . I wonder what he'll do when I die.'

There was a long silence, then Caroline said, 'But, Grandpa, haven't you been irresponsible, in a way, in writing the Memoirs? I mean, you said at the beginning that you didn't care what comes out, or who it hurts.'

The Old Man nodded. 'It was Charles, remember, who urged me to do it that way. He put the idea into my head. He was saying, in effect – *Come in, try my drug.* I've done my best, but every now and then Charles has had to see that I don't retreat into responsibility – protect my friends, my family, myself. . . . That's why he sent that negative to Paul. He guessed that, without a push, I'd keep quiet about it.'

'Is there anything else you're tempted to keep quiet about, Grandpa?' Caroline asked.

He looked full at her, and said, 'No. Nothing at all.'

After a long while, returning his look as directly, she said, 'If you say so. . . . I've got to fly. Miss Parmentier's invited me to tea and I promised I'd take her autographed copies of your photographs – Grandpa's and Mr Armstrong's. Now she's in love with both of you. I won't be back till after supper.'

Late in the afternoon Martin found his wife at her desk in the old day nursery. He had been looking for her for some time, but searching, he now recognised, in places where he knew she would not be. All the while he had been turning over in his mind what he had to say to her, and trying to find words that would express it well, without begging on one side or bitterness on the other.

He expected to find her bent over her account books and catering schedules; but she was leaning back in her chair, pencil in hand, drawing circles on a piece of paper. He never remembered seeing her doodling. She didn't turn but said over her shoulder, 'Martin?'

He said, 'I've come to tell you . . .'

She said, 'Dick's spoken to me. I think it's the best decision you ever made.'

A load was lifted from his mind. He did not know and could not have explained why he'd thought she would raise objections, but he had; or why he cared, but he did.

He said, 'I'll have to live in London with him.'

'Of course.'

'I don't know how soon we can get set up. He has to go back to Bude.'

'Yes. And before he can bring his furniture up you'll have to have somewhere to go to in London.'

'I'm going to start looking on Monday. . . . And, Lois . . .'

'Yes?'

'I'm sorry I was angry with you over your visiting Charles.'

She turned round then and looked him in the eye. She said, 'He doesn't matter, Martin. I wasn't sorry you were angry. You had a right to be, as long as I mattered to you.'

'You did . . . you do . . . only, Lois, it's no use our trying to go back. Because I've learned that we don't have anything to go back to. It never was right for us.'

'That was my fault.'

'No, no . . . I never really tried to feel with you. . . . Anyway, these few days before I move to London, may I come back to your room?'

'Ours,' she said. She stood up and held out her hand. 'Come on, I'll help you move your clothes.'

To be or not to be, that is the question . . .

Clive spoke the line passionately, holding the skull at arm's length and glaring at it intently, as though inside the white dome, in the vacancy behind the empty sockets, an answer was written on the enclosed air.

'Go on,' Charles Gibson said from the easel.

'I don't know any more. I used to, but I've forgotten.'

'*Whether 'tis nobler in the mind to suffer The slings and arrows of outrageous fortune Or to take arms against a sea of troubles, And by opposing, end them,*' Gibson recited.

Then the lines sprang back complete into Clive's mind. But Gibson had spoken them badly, with no feeling at all. Here was a man facing the crisis of his life, not someone reading his laundry list aloud. Gibson was a great painter, but obviously he could not project himself into another's place.

'*To be or not to be,*' he began again, '*that is the question Whether 'tis nobler in the mind to suffer . . .*' He finished the speech without a break.

'Wonderful! You can stand down now, Clive. I had intended to work on the costume today, but your expression was so good there, that I've been watching that. I think I've got it. Just sit down – have a drink – while I work on it.'

'Don't you want me back there, to see it?'

Charles shook his head, his brush flitting quickly across the canvas. 'No, it's a momentary thing,' he said, his eyes never leaving the painting. 'Not even the greatest actor in the world can hold an expression like that for long – it becomes gelid, congealed, even if it meant to be, and originally was, full of passion. Just for a moment there, while you were crying *take arms against a sea of troubles . . .* you had it.'

283

'I was feeling it,' Clive said moodily. 'I'm faced with a sea of troubles.'

'What's the matter?'

'You know . . . bastard half-brother somewhere, father about to be investigated for murder, sister living with a pimp, grandfather admitting he's a pansy. I wish I could take up arms against all *that*.'

'You did, against me,' Gibson said, standing back momentarily, looking intently at a portion of the painting, then darting forward again.

'It didn't work,' Clive said. 'I only made a fool of myself.'

'That's because I didn't want to be sacrificed on an altar. Some people do. Like the Old Man.'

'What?' Clive said, astounded. 'Grandpa wants to be sacrificed? What do you mean?'

Charles put down his brushes, rinsing them carefully in a bowl of turpentine, and came over to where Clive was standing by the front window. He said. 'He's very old. He's done great things but can do them no more. Of what use is he to himself, or to anyone?'

'But . . . ?'

'I'm not thinking as you would think, or your mother, or any of you, but as *he* would. I know him well . . . as I know you. I've learned more about you since you came here with that pistol in your pocket than in all the years I've been seeing you at Ashwood and the odd visit here, as a child, a schoolboy, a Sandhurst cadet. . . . Do you remember how smitten you were with that red-haired model I had? . . . I don't think you enjoy being a soldier.'

Clive thought, that's right; I don't. It was fun at first, being an ensign of the Guards – public duties; Germany; he'd even enjoyed Ulster in an odd way, because he had liked looking into people's faces and wondering which of them was acting a part. Was this woman really a housewife, or a part-time whore? This man really a respectable clerk, or a secret maker of bombs?

He shook his head. 'I don't. But what else can I do? I'm no good at anything, never was. I'm rotten at maths . . . I'm never going to be one of these business men who organise a firm and make a million pounds. I can't sell anything. Wherever I look, I only see myself.'

'Well spoken,' Gibson said. 'The young man of genius trying to find in just what quarter his genius lies. . . . Do you feel odd in those clothes? Do you feel out of place, in any way? I mean, now.'

Clive looked around, at himself, at Gibson and said, 'No. Why?'

'You're wearing a slashed black velvet doublet and black silk tights, with a heavy gold chain round your neck. In your left hand you're holding a skull. You're standing in the window looking out over the Thames and seeing only yourself, inside. There's a man down there on the pavement, gaping at you. He thinks he's seeing an apparition. But you are unaware of him, and of the oddness of what you are wearing and doing . . . because he's the audience. You are an actor. I thought I was right when I said I would paint you as Hamlet, and by God, now I know I was.'

Clive considered carefully. Charles was right. He was an actor. But first he must be a doer. Surely, no one could play Hamlet really well unless, just once, he himself had taken arms against a sea of troubles?

Gibson said, 'I'd like to spend a little time on the costume now. Then . . .'

'You won't be long, will you?' Clive said. 'I'm going down to Ashwood for the weekend.'

Miss Parmentier sat up straight in the high-backed chair, as always. Her long thin-boned hand went out unerringly for the teapot, though Caroline knew that she could hardly see it. She was a tall woman with a long face, the old eyes a dim blue now, the voice slow speaking but firm. 'Did I tell you I was a second cousin of the previous Lord Stockbridge?'

'You did mention it,' Caroline said. She held out her cup and Miss Parmentier refilled it. The photographs of the Field-Marshal and Dick Armstrong were propped on the mantelpiece behind her, where Miss Parmentier could at least look toward them.

Miss Parmentier said, 'You know, I was his daughter's companion from the middle of the war till she died, in 1945.'

'Daphne Fuller?'

'Yes. We were relatives, of course. Looked rather alike, too, though she was nearly twenty years older . . . and a great deal plainer, I may say.'

'I've heard she wasn't very pretty.'

'What else have you heard about her?' The voice was suddenly sharp.

'Just that she was a great friend of Sir Henry Bartlett and his wife.'

'That's true,' the other said. 'Much too great a friend for her own good. Colonel Bartlett – as he was when they met – was nothing but a social climber. He still is, for all his titles and honours. No family at all!'

'But Miss Daphne liked him, didn't she?'

The old lady said nothing for a while, then said, 'Why are you asking me about General Bartlett? What is he to you?'

Caroline thought, the time has come for plain speaking; it might be the best answer, at that. She said, 'Miss Parmentier, my grandfather the Field-Marshal is trying to find out, in order to be able to defend himself against other charges, where Sir Henry Bartlett got the money he came into just after the last war. The present Lord Stockbridge has been heard to say that you call Sir Henry a thief. What do you mean, exactly?'

The old lady drank some tea, looking thoughtfully at Caroline over the edge of her cup. She said after a time, 'You're a modern young woman. You may not be shocked the way I was when I learned the truth. . . . When Daphne got ill she was in a great deal of pain. She needed to talk. She told me everything . . . Henry Bartlett was Daphne's gigolo. And his wife knew about it.'

'Pheew!' Caroline whistled thoughtfully.

'They met Daphne in 1932 when she was sixty and he was I think forty. She was a spinster – with that face and heavy body not even her money could buy her a husband. Let alone a lover. . . . Colonel Bartlett recognised very quickly what she needed – everything a man could give her. He didn't love her. He didn't even like her, I think. He deliberately set about ingratiating himself with her. His wife aided and abetted. In return, they got invitations to London balls and country house-parties . . . hunting, grouse shooting, salmon fishing . . . they met aristocracy, royalty, and all the important people in politics. Daphne even slipped them money – cash – lots of it – so they could keep up, and not seem to be sponging on her, which they were . . .'

'Pheew!' Caroline whistled again.

'About 1943, Daphne became ill. Cancer. I came to her as a companion. I slaved . . . looked after her day and night . . . the Bartletts visited sometimes, when he was in England, but mostly he pretended he had too much work, no time to spare.' She sniffed angrily, 'Liar! Poor Daphne loved him, like a spaniel. More, Abjectly. . . . She promised she'd leave some of her money to me. But a month before she died I was cashing cheques for her to the tune, eventually, of a hundred and sixty thousand pounds, in one and five pound notes. When she knew she had not long to live, she sent for Henry Bartlett – he was just back from the Balkans – and gave him the money. She died. She didn't give me anything. Not a penny. Nor leave me anything in her will. It all went to the present viscount.'

Caroline thought, Belprato said that Bartlett deposited a hundred and fifty thousand pounds when he started his big account. Perhaps this dear old lady had somehow pocketed the other ten thousand for herself; or perhaps Bartlett had kept it in cash, in his house, for emergencies.

Miss Parmentier said, 'So now you know where Henry Bartlett got his money. Daphne Fuller gave it to him in cash, secretly, so that people wouldn't suspect what their relation- ship had been, the way they would if she left it to him in her will. That money was earned . . . if that's the right word . . . shamefully. A gentleman would never have taken it, or would have given *me* some of it. . . . I've always wanted to tell the truth about Henry Bartlett but Daphne made me promise to keep it secret. Now, for Field-Marshal Durham and Mr Arm- strong, I've broken my promise, and I'm glad.'

'Thank you,' Caroline said, 'I don't know what use my grand- father will make of this information, but I know he'll be very glad to have it.'

Half an hour later, thinking hard, she was in a bus heading up towards central London, and Soho.

The November wind tugged at the window panes and draughts moaned softly through the cracks in the old sashes to shake the heavy curtains. Tomorrow was Armistice Day, Lois thought. Her father would go to the Hawkford War Memorial to lay a wreath, and come back looking suddenly not a day older or an hour, but a whole year, as though of all the year only that one day existed, and only in it were packed the year's growing, the year's dying.

She pulled the bedjacket more closely around her, and sipped the last of the hot lemon and whisky Martin had brought up with them when they came to bed nearly two hours ago. It was cold in the glass now, but she felt better. Martin, sitting up beside her, had long since emptied his glass.

He said, 'Do you think we could live together?'

'Here?' she said, 'I don't see how you . . .'

He interrupted her. 'No, in London. You said just now you were going to give up the catering, and paint. You can do that as well in London as here. Better. And it would be cheaper for all of us.'

She thought, is he trying to get me to housekeep for him and Dick? She'd done that long enough. But in fact she didn't mind housekeeping at all. She just didn't want it to continue to be the centre of her whole life, the axis of her being.

'We could work out something about housekeeping,' she said.

'We could afford a maid, or even a part-time cook,' he said. 'As long as there are only the three of us, it wouldn't be difficult. This seat that Dick's been offered is nearly an hour out of town, and if he's going to nurse the constituency the way he'll want to, we'll be away a lot. I know you don't have big meals when you're alone. We could share making the dinners.'

Why not, she thought? Caroline was leaving home. The army would look after Clive. But what about her father?

Martin said, 'I was wondering . . . I hate to think of it but it does seem the most sensible idea. Why don't you sell this place?'

She nodded. She had often thought of it, over the years, the dead, deadening years, but had always thrust it at once out of her mind. The house had belonged to her mother. In 1945, after her mother's death in the accident, Lois had found to her astonishment that the house had been left to her, not to her father. In a way it had been a curse, for she knew that her father had no home of his own, never had had, in fact, since her mother persuaded him to move into Ashwood House.

She said, 'I've thought of it, but where would Daddy go? He has his roses, his books, everything. I couldn't ask him to move into some pokey flat and that's what it would have to be. A flat near us, in the same building really, where we could look after him. After he . . .'

'After he dies,' Martin finished the phrase for her – 'it might be too late for us then. I don't want us to get settled into our own separate ways. We're not young, and we wouldn't find it easy to change back again to living together.'

She thought, he's right. This house was going to be much too big for them now. If she sold it, they could get good service flats in London, and have a lot of money left over, too. Caroline and Paul were going to need help until they got started.

Even Clive might not be as safely tucked up as they'd thought. When he came down this evening, they'd talked a bit and she'd asked him when his battalion was due to go to Germany again. He'd replied, 'Early next year, but I'm not going with it. I'm leaving the army.' He'd said that before, in moments of boredom, so. . . .

A door banged loudly down the passage. 'Damn!' Martin exclaimed, 'someone's left a door open.'

The door banged again and Martin got out of bed. He opened the bedroom door and switched on the passage light. Lois heard a whimpering noise, hurriedly slipped her feet into mules and went out into the passage. Martin and Dick Armstrong were standing outside Clive's bedroom door. The seeing-eye dog Rachel was there, whining and pointing down the passage.

'I heard something,' Dick Armstrong said. 'Someone went along that way. Is Clive in his room?'

'No.'

'Run to the Field-Marshal's room, quick,' Dick cried.

Martin broke into a run, followed by Lois. She reached her father's bedroom door just as Martin, having opened it, was switching on the light inside.

Her son Clive was stooped over the bed, pressing down on a pillow he was holding over the head of the person in the bed. He looked round with teeth set. Martin seized the pillow and jerked it away, sending his son reeling with a violent shove to the chest.

'What the hell are you doing?' he shouted.

Clive said nothing, standing impassive now at the foot of the bed, where Martin had pushed him. Lois saw that her father's eyes were open. Her heart missed a beat – he was dead! But the eyes moved, then the head and he said, 'Who was it?'

'Clive,' Martin said; and then, 'Good God, sir, you don't think Lois or . . .'

The old man in the bed said, 'All of you have good reason . . . including perhaps a realisation that you would be doing me a good turn.'

'That's what Charles said,' Clive muttered.

'Charles egged you on to this?' Martin said furiously, 'I'll murder that swine! He's . . .'

'He's right,' the Old Man said. He sat up slowly, pulling himself upright in the bed. Lois arranged the pillows higher behind him. He was wearing blue and white striped flannel

289

pyjamas and now said, 'Bring me my dressing gown, please. Hang it over my shoulders. Good.'

Once again, as after Belprato's attempted murder of the Old Man, a realisation of what had so narrowly been prevented swept over the group, but this time it was Martin who erupted in fear and anger. He seized his son by the throat and shook him back and forth, shouting, 'You tried to kill him, your own grandfather! I'll see that you . . .'

The Old Man in the bed interrupted, 'Let him go, Martin. Clive, bring me a strong whisky in a little warm water, please.'

'Yes, sir,' Clive muttered, and hurried out of the room, his head bent. Lois thought, my father not only controls his own emotions, he controls ours. We, who were frightened and angry, are now calm and unafraid. Her heart beat less violently, her hand ceased its involuntary trembling.

The Old Man said, almost to himself, 'You can't blame him. I don't. . . . It would have been a heart attack. No one would have bothered to have an autopsy, at my age. . . . I heard him coming. At this age you usually sleep lightly. But how did you know? Ah, I can guess. Dick heard him.'

'Yes, sir.'

'I closed my eyes and waited. It seemed at that moment that I'd been waiting long enough. . . . Is it past midnight?'

'Yes, sir. It's Armistice Day now.'

'Then it's fifty-six years exactly that I've been waiting for actual death . . . surcease . . . to catch up with the reality. This body has been a husk . . . nothing inside – oh, the brain's worked all right, too well . . . since 1917. It started bleeding to death at Le Cateau, when I saw Ted Crandall dead in the wheat field. Then it . . . not blood, but soul, spirit, humanity, whatever you call it . . . flowed out faster when I counted the bullet wounds in Dick Newby's face by High Wood . . . an artery opened when I tried to put the pieces of Peter Curran together outside Passchendaele. After that it was only a matter of time. I remember the bells ringing a year later, and people shouting Peace, peace. That was the end. . . .'

Clive silently handed him a tumbler and he drank deeply. After a while he swung his legs out of the bed and said, 'There was one time when I lived again. I was a fool to think it could ever come back . . . I've felt warm here—' he touched his belly '—once or twice. Angry even. Not pretend anger to frighten people, but real anger. Love . . . Writing the Memoirs has made me realise that the man who lived that life was not real.

290

... A pity they came too soon, Clive. What made you decide to do it?'

'I was feeling very unhappy, sir.'

'In the Guards? Because of the photo and the rumours?'

'Partly, sir. Yes, sir.'

'Why don't you get out?'

'I want to.'

'What would you do?'

'Charles said I should become an actor.'

'What the hell does Charles ... ?' Martin began.

The Old Man said, 'He's probably right. Only tell by trying. You'll need money. So will Caroline and Paul. And Martin, you will too – Dick won't be able to pay you anything, will you?'

'No, sir.'

'That only leaves you and me, Lois. You should go to London. Sell this place.'

'But ...'

'Forget about me. What more can I want, at eighty? I'm nothing but a weight around your necks.'

'No, Daddy,' Lois cried, sitting down on the bed beside him and taking his hand. It was surprisingly warm in hers, then she realised that he had been cupping the glass of warm whisky in it.

Caroline came in, rubbing her eyes. 'What's going on here?'

'Nothing,' the Old Man said. 'Let's all go to bed.'

CHAPTER TWENTY-FIVE

The Field-Marshal sat at his desk in his upstairs study, the chair swivelled so that he was looking through the window up the rainswept rose garden. The *Observer*, which he had been reading, lay open on his lap, his reading glasses on the desk.

The Field-Marshal felt depressed, and his bones ached. Well, being half smothered wasn't conducive to good condition in the aged. It was the fact that one of his own family had done it that depressed him. It had been Clive, but it might have been any of them – yes, even Caroline, for a different motive. Whoever might have been the one to act, the message would have been the same: we don't want you any more. And he wasn't sure that he wanted himself.

He looked at the pile of typescript at the back of the desk, with the front page titled:

MEMOIRS

* * * *

DURHAM

It was nearly done now. What remained to tidy up, Martin could do, using the notes and tapes Paul and Caroline had left.

Everything seemed peaceful. Friends and enemies alike seemed to be waiting. What would he do now, finally? Choose peace, quiet and his accumulated honours? Or detonate the bomb? Dick Armstrong's broadcast of the Vojja Lovac conference recording on Tuesday would solve that. If only Bigelow had been given time to unlock the secret of those three bank accounts, so Dick could include that information in his broadcast, the explosion could have been even more devastating. Even so, Jordan would not become Vice-President of the United States, and Henry would not become Lord Bartlett ... and he himself would still be Sir John Durham, Field-Marshal, Knight Grand Cross of the Order of the Bath, and all the other noble titles, though he was a murderer and a looter, and had won his greatest fame in a state of total incompetence for the task entrusted to him.

Also, the broadcasting of the tape would make Jordan and

the government here very vindictive. Redoubled efforts would be made to link him with the theft of the Zvornos Collection . . . to the peril of Stefanie.

There was a knock on the door and the Field-Marshal called, 'Come in.'

Clive came in, dressed in a dark suit and Brigade of Guards tie, and wearing a poppy in his buttonhole. His face was composed, and when he spoke, his voice was steady and resonant – 'Grandpa, I know it's no good apologising for what I did, but I do. I must have been temporarily insane. Please forgive me.'

'Of course,' the Field-Marshal said. 'When you get back to London tomorrow, see your lieutenant-colonel at once about resigning your commission.'

'Yes, sir.'

The Field-Marshal nodded in dismissal and the young man went out. He did that well, the Old Man thought. If we'd been in a theatre, half the women in the audience would have had handkerchiefs to their eyes. . . . Where was he? Dangerous for Stefanie. His mere survival was dangerous for Stefanie. Suppose he started going gaga, as he might without warning at his age – say, from a stroke. He could give everything away. He'd been right last night when he said, perhaps a little self-commiseratingly, that no one wanted him, that he was in the way; but it was true. Lois wanted to join Martin in London; if she did and started painting again, their marriage might, like a lizard's tail, regenerate itself. Caroline didn't need him, though she liked, even loved him. Lois didn't need him or his income. If she sold the house she'd get at least a hundred thousand for it, perhaps a lot more.

He got up and paced the study floor. The roses . . . the Red Durham was an established success and bringing in good royalties, as rose royalties went, both here and in America. But who would carry on the search for the Black Durham? If only he could find out, or work out, perhaps by computer, the breeding lines of the 'Night'. 'Night' itself, though he'd crossed it many times with 'Avon', 'Crimson Glory', 'Chrysler Imperial' and many other likely dark reds, had never reproduced in the hybrid its own blackish crimson; but the blackness must be there, back in its ancestry . . . which was unknown. Well, some-one would carry on the work, that was certain; then the rose, when it came, would be the 'Black Johnson' or the 'Black Wallace'; or perhaps the fellow would have the decency to

293

hyphenate his name into it – the 'Black Wallace-Durham'.

Those damned lithographs were a link between Zvornos and the Villa Grimani; and someone might take it into his head to trace it, which would lead to peril for Stefanie. He had tried, when he started writing the Memoirs, to clear away mysteries and secrets, but in the end, there would be more left – why had he ceased his relationship with Wilfred when he did? The answer – that he had met Stefanie – must never be suspected. With whom had Count Zvornos left the collection when he went to New York and was murdered? The answer – with Stefanie – must never be suspected. So what must he do?

There was another knock at the door and the Field-Marshal swore under his breath. He had nearly made up his mind and now . . . 'Come in!' he snapped.

Caroline came in. 'What is it?' he growled, 'I've got work to do before . . .'

She said, 'Miss Parmentier talked, yesterday. I haven't had a chance to tell you till now.'

The Field-Marshal sat down, He felt on edge and nervous. What was going to come out? How would it affect what he wanted – ought – to do?

Caroline said, 'Henry Bartlett was Miss Daphne Fuller's gigolo. His wife knew about it, and helped, so that they could both get taken into the Stockbridge family's circle. Before Miss Fuller died she gave Henry a hundred and fifty thousand pounds in cash.'

The Field-Marshal looked away from the girl's steady, wide eyes. Henry a gigolo. Here was the rottenness so many had suspected in him, but never been able to put their finger on. He would never have got off the ground in politics if this had been known or suspected at the time. And it explained the lying and mystery over his sudden wealth; he'd rather have been accused of theft or bribery than this.

'Now you've got him,' Caroline said softly. Quite right, the Field-Marshal thought, wearily. Let this become known and Henry could say goodbye to that damned peerage he'd been climbing after all his life, like a bloody monkey after a coconut high up the palm tree.

'I could tell Dick Armstrong,' he said, half to himself, 'and he'll find a way to include it in his TV talk, with the tape.'

But this was going in the opposite direction to the way his thoughts had been leading him just before Caroline came in.

She said, 'You realise what this means?'

'What?'

'That Sir Henry probably didn't have anything to do with getting the Zvornos Collection out of Zvornos Castle ... or that if he did he was acting from some other motive than having been bribed. Perhaps he simply believed that the paintings belonged to the Count and that he ought to have them before the Communists got them, but he didn't want the Communists to know that British or American officials had had a hand in it.'

The Field-Marshal nodded. She was right. Henry was cleared on that charge. But the fellow was nothing but a damned gigolo. A disgrace to the army.

Caroline might have been reading his thoughts. She said 'Grandpa, he gave that wretched ugly old woman something she needed. You're a man; you don't know how important it is for a woman to feel that she's wanted, even if she knows perfectly well that it's not genuine. She got what she needed, the Bartletts got what they wanted, so who suffered?'

The Field-Marshal found himself chuckling, a short sardonic laugh. Now that he'd got that old snob Henry by the short hairs, he had no wish to hurt him. They'd been through too much together; and whatever Henry had done, according to the defects of his character, he himself had done as bad, according to the defects of his.

Caroline's firm young voice continued. 'Why don't you write to General Bartlett and tell him you know where his money came from but it's all past, let bygones be bygones ... that you won't hint in the Memoirs that he had anything to do with the disappearance of the Zvornos Collection, because you know he didn't ...'

She was right. This would be going in the right direction, but not far enough. He must. . . . She interrupted his chain of thought, 'Yesterday, when I asked you whether there was anything you were tempted to keep quiet about you said No, nothing at all. But you were looking at me when you said it, and you winked. What did you mean?'

'I don't remember winking,' the Field-Marshal said, bending his fierce brows at her.

She did not flinch. 'Yes, you did, Grandpa. You had your back to all the others and no one saw but me. You were lying, but you wanted me to know you were – not the others. . . . Was it a love affair?'

'Was what a love affair?' he asked, stalling for time. The

large brown eyes on him were like a doe's, big and soft and all-knowing.

She said, 'The thing that you would keep quiet about . . . hide from everyone, the world, us . . . even perhaps yourself?'

He said, the words forced out of him, 'Yes, it was.'

'I thought it must be. And the woman is still alive, and you are afraid of hurting her reputation. It must have been very wonderful. You must have loved each other very much if you will lie to keep this secret, but publish about Wilfred Eden. . . . Was it at Ancona?'

'How on earth did you know that?' he gasped.

'Oh, clues . . . what you were like before, and after. And all these years you've been having your letters sent through France, so no one would know. . . . Don't be afraid, no one else has noticed a thing. And Daddy must have been there at the time.'

'He never noticed,' the Field-Marshal said. 'It was, as you say, Caroline, a great love.' He felt near to tears and realised that he had never cried in his life, that he could remember. He needed to break the last bowl of reticence for this child, that was of his blood and seed.

He said, 'I killed your grandmother for her. It was done as I described, but what I told you about the cancer was not true. Margaret did not have cancer. The mental instability, yes, that was true – but we could have put her in a home, perhaps even looked after her here. But I dreamed that I might, if I survived, live with Stefanie.'

'Stefanie,' Caroline murmured, 'what a beautiful name.'

'I left it to God – Fate. . . . If I were killed in the accident it was not to be. If I survived, it might be. . . . I did survive. Her husband had already been killed by a Communist gang. Yet, even so, it was not to be. Why?' He held out his hands, palms up. 'Because Margaret's blood was on my hands.' He laughed sharply, almost a bark. 'I have seen my hands red since 1914, but when I killed Margaret, I seemed to redden everything I touched . . . *the multitudinous seas incarnadine*, Shakespeare says, doesn't he? Don't tell anyone, ever, Caroline.'

'Of course I won't,' Caroline said. 'Never. . . . You saw her when you went abroad in August, didn't you?'

He nodded.

'You came back so calm, content, different from what I've ever known you. Did she want you to stay?'

He burst out. 'I'm eighty! As I said last night, I'm in the

way. I can only be a burden. No one wants me. No one! Thank you, Caroline, for everything.' He stood up, took her in his arms and kissed her on her warm, soft, parted lips. 'Go along now. . . . *Go, child! Do as I say!*'

She went to the door unwillingly, looking back at him. She said, 'I don't think it's true, Grandpa. The last thing you said.' She went out.

The Field-Marshal sat down, staring again down the garden. The time had come for decision. *To be or not to be.* . . . People would think it was *to do or not to do,* but it wasn't. It was a matter of being – what? The old field-marshal who'd torn down so many veils, for the sake of duty? The silent soldier, who went to his grave with his secrets, for the sake of love?

He made up his mind. The Memoirs must never be published. Stefanie's future mattered more than any piddling revelations he might be able to make about how men sometimes had to behave in war. Those who had been to war knew anyway, those who had not never really would. In the end, where he stood now, all that mattered was personal – as many of his 'enemies' had been trying to tell him all the time, about the Memoirs . . . the Cunninghams trying to protect the reputation of their dead brother, even of Martin; 'Papa' Belprato wanting revenge for the death of a beloved son; Langford and Herrick thinking of their regiments' reputations – so many others, hugging their own prides, their own loves, trying to forget their weaknesses and failures. Was he not the same? He stared one last long minute up the garden, thinking of his roses. Stefanie's face came unbidden before his eyes, not as it had been when they first met and fell in love, but as it had been a few weeks ago.

He took a sheet of notepaper, with his name, titles and address embossed at the head of it, and began to write, carefully but without pause:

Dear Henry,
I have decided not to publish my Memoirs, nor will they be published posthumously. From recently learning the source of your wealth I know that you were in no way connected with the disappearance of the Zvornos Collection from Zvornos Castle. I now agree with you that the whole matter of the Zvornos Collection should now be forgotten, by all parties, and I rely on you to see that this is done, as far as lies in your power. A tape copy of the original wire recording of the conference

after Vojja Lovac, now in safe hands, will not be made public unless my family are harassed.

We are both old men and should not go to our graves in bitterness. Let sleeping dogs lie.

Yours, John.

P.S. I would take it as a personal favour if you would use your best endeavours to get Charles Gibson the K which I think he deserves.

P.P.S. I advise you to make peace with Miss Janet Parmentier. I gather that money would help.

He folded it, put it in an envelope, sealed it, and addressed it to Sir Henry Bartlett, O.M., etc., at Rackleigh Manor, Rackleigh, Surrey and put it on the desk top. Then he took another sheet of paper, and wrote:

Dear Charles,

You may not be surprised to learn that I have decided not to publish my Memoirs after all. I trust you soon get the knighthood I believe you have been hoping for for a good many years. I suggest you mention the matter to Henry Bartlett, whom you will find in a receptive mood.

Thanks for your company and long friendship.

John Durham.

That letter folded into an envelope, he took another sheet of paper, but paused, pen in hand. It was easy enough to exonerate Henry Bartlett from complicity in the Zvornos affair – but who then was responsible? Had Matt Jordan, perhaps with Sovik's agreement and connivance, arranged it? Count Zvornos had been on Jordan's military government staff and could have put the proposition to him. Perhaps Jordan and the Count had done it, on their own. The calling-off of Belprato when he had been so close to finding out something, by his own people in New York, pointed to strong American influence. Or the Count could have done it on his own, if he had had the right contacts, and enough money . . . both of which he had obtained when he enlisted the services of the Orlando gang.

He supposed some people thought he himself had done it. There was, after all, the link of the Picassos. Such people would believe that his story of Soapy Woodham finding them was a lie and that in fact the Count had given them to him as bait to join the 'recovery' conspiracy. And that any talk of Henry or

Jordan or Sovik being responsible was merely to divert attention from himself. Did it matter? He had been trying to learn the truth about the Zvornos affair, but from the opposite point of view the attempts to push it back under the rug could be read as having the highest motivations: a patriotic concern; greater political awareness than he, a plain soldier, had ever pretended to; a desire not to tarnish great reputations without positive proof, and then only in a matter of current importance.... Let sleeping dogs lie. Sovik was still in power and the Yugoslavs would buy the Tridents. Jordan would, after all, be Vice-President, Henry a peer and Charles a knight. Stefanie would live out her life in the comfort she was used to, and doubtless, in her will, would arrange for the remaining paintings to return to their proper home ... wherever that might be.

He began to write:

Dick –

You remember we arranged for you to broadcast the Vojja Lovac conference tape next Tuesday, November 13, on your TV show. I do not now wish this to be done. Please keep the tape secure, in some place where it can not be seized by government agents or anyone else, and use it, or the threat of it, only to protect my family against harassment.

That letter sealed and addressed, he began a fourth:

Martin – Give the letters to Henry Bartlett and Charles Gibson yourself. See that Dick reads his at once. My Memoirs are not to be published. Burn the MS and all notes in the presence of Caroline, who will witness that it has been done. Thank you for all that you have done for me.

From outside the door he heard Martin call, 'It's nearly time to go to the service, sir. We're all ready.'

He called back, 'Go on without me. I'll follow in a few minutes in the Bentley.'

'All right.' Footsteps receded, and he began another letter:

Dearest Lois, and all my family – Don't grieve for me. I know what I am doing, and am content. Sell the property and set about living your own lives. Think of the future, not the past, as I have done, too much. It was not all my fault, only some.

Mullins and Crookenden will have to be paid back the

299

*money they have advanced to me, as the Memoirs are not now
going to be published. Take it from my estate, and from the
sale of the house, if necessary. Please also give Caroline ten
thousand pounds, which she will know what to do with. I am
sorry that this will have to come out of the sale of the property,
but it was your mother's and she is responsible for my having
to find the money now.*

Your loving father.

Now he should write to Stefanie. He stared at the wall. The
clock ticked, louder and louder. *No more, Giovanni, no more.
Remember me.* Time was passing. Time was the road to death.
He was far along the road, where he had sent many others. He
was not afraid.

*It is unfair that you have made me so happy when I have
given you only pain. But it seems that I am fated to cause
misery, so what I am going to do is for the best. I love you.*

He re-read it. The clock ticked steadily. He tore the letter
up, and put the pieces in his pocket. He could not write to her.
Their last meeting had said it all. It was time to act.

He quickly wrote one final note:

*Caroline – Get the ten thousand pounds to Signora Stefanie
Grimani at the Villa Grimani outside Ancona, in cash, somehow. Tell her I love her.*

This last letter he put in a sealed envelope inscribed *For
Caroline – Personal* and took it along the passage and stuck it
in the mirror on the girl's dressing table. Returning to his
study, he laid out the other envelopes in a row; then, opening
a desk drawer, he searched under the pile of papers and pulled
out a long legal envelope. His will was in order: this was a
copy and Forsythe had the original. He put the will on the
desk beside the letters. That was about it ... oh, proof of
identity. Better take the big wallet, that had several cards in
it, besides a note about whom to notify in case of accident.

He went downstairs, put on his Burberry and peaked tweed
cap, and walked round to the garage. Lois's van was there but
Martin's car was gone. The Bentley stood proud in its British
racing green. He found his chamois leather cloth and gave the
car a rub over the bonnet, and touched up the chrome over the
radiator, where the big B shone between the spread wings.
She'd get spotted with rain in a minute, but at least people

would see the polish underneath.

He adjusted the spark and mixture, took the starting handle and with a single powerful swing started the engine. He waited five minutes, readjusted the spark and mixture, and settled down in the driver's seat. He engaged first gear and drove slowly out, the narrow tyres crunching on the gravel, then into the road.

Armistice Day. The fifty-fifth anniversary . . . the fifty-sixth anniversary of Peter Curran's death. He tried to see Peter's face again, as it had been when they were young men together. It would not come. Then he tried again, when they were small boys, bird-nesting, running down the corridors of the prep school. Still no vision came, no memory. Not even when he tried to see the shell hole outside Passchendaele where Peter had died. Nothing.

That was strange. Normally on this drive, and on this day, the whole of that war spread before him without any act of volition on his part, a huge painting so crowded that there would have been chaos only, one by one, images would glitter momentarily with a terrible clarity, before being replaced by others. Today, nothing. Was he purged, the unwilling guilt exorcised? Had writing the Memoirs, though of a later time, facing all that he had been and done, changed the make-up of him, as a human being? He didn't know; but the slate was clean, at last. There were no loose ends. It was time to go.

The church clock of Hawkford began to strike eleven, the chimes first, then the first heavy strokes of the tenor bell. He saw the little knot of people standing by the war memorial, facing the rector in his white surplice. He was too young to have experienced either war. There were a dozen old men, half a dozen middle-aged ones, all with medals pinned to the outside of their overcoats, scarves round their scraggy necks, heads bared and bent. A few women. No children. It was the two minutes silence. Henry Bartlett was there, not looking up. His own wreath was there beside him on the front seat of the Bentley. He slowed, crawling past, looking at all of them as the clock finished striking eleven. Caroline had raised her head. She had recognised the distinctive burble of the Bentley's exhausts. He caught her eye and raised his right hand from the wheel. Goodbye.

He drove on. The big car breasted the top of Hawkford Hill. To the south-east he saw the feathery elms lining the drive of Whitmore Court. The view to his right extended far across

Surrey, the spire of King's Feltham church in the middle distance. The black rain-wet road dropped steeply away below the wheels. There was the curve and the wall, two hundred yards down. He pressed his foot steadily harder down on the accelerator. The wall approached, old Tudor bricks . . . Now, a hard jerk to the left and he'd go straight into it. The needle showed seventy . . .

He swung the wheel to the right, braked momentarily, then accelerated still more. The heavy car's tail swung violently, tyres screaming. For a moment he thought it was over, then it settled back onto all four wheels, and he was round. A little old family saloon chugged up, the driver, an old lady, open-mouthed. He passed her, and slowed the Bentley gently.

He drove on for five minutes, not looking at the signposts, aware of where he was going but not thinking about it.

That settled it. There'd be a boat from Folkestone or Dover some time in the afternoon. It didn't matter where it went . . . Bolougne, Calais, Ostend, Dunkirk; all roads would lead to Ancona. He'd be penniless, relying entirely on Stefanie; soon, even for nursing. He'd be sponging on her, living off her, a helpless child in her care. He'd give no orders, have no responsibility.

Wasn't that what he had dreamed of, longed for?

He swore violently. Now he'd have to go back and get his passport, and they'd ask him questions. Steering with one hand he pulled out his wallet. Ah, he had taken the big one – the one in which he kept his passport. He drew it out and looked at it. He knew it was up to date. But why had he taken this wallet? Normally, he only used it when travelling abroad. So he knew he was going to Ancona before he left the house? He had made up his mind to kill himself and he hadn't. Why? He remembered Caroline's last words. She had looked like Stefanie then, not the features, the expression. She must have persuaded his secret mind that someone did, after all, want him.

He put away the passport and wallet, and at the next signpost, in King's Feltham, headed the car towards Leatherhead. He'd call the family from there and tell them to see that all the letters were delivered, otherwise not to worry. He'd get in touch with them in good time. Meanwhile, where ignorance is bliss . . .

Envoi

Truth is truth and love is love,
Give us grace to taste thereof:
But if truth offend my sweet,
Then I will have none of it.

Alfred Edgar Coppard

All Sphere Books are available at your bookshop or
newsagent, or can be ordered from the following address:
Sphere Books, Cash Sales Department,
P.O. Box 11, Falmouth, Cornwall.

Please send cheque or postal order (no currency), and allow
19p for postage and packing for the first book plus 9p
per copy for each additional book ordered up to a
maximum charge of 73p in U.K.

Customers in Eire and B.F.P.O. please allow 19p for
postage and packing for the first book plus 9p per copy
for the next six books, thereafter 3p per book.

Overseas customers please allow 20p for postage and
packing for the first book and 10p per copy for each
additional book.